last 100 pgs water damaged
12/15/17

DATE DUE

28 DAY

Valentine

Valentine

Jane Feather

Five Star
Unity, Maine

Five Star Romance.
Published in conjunction with Bantam Books, a division of
Bantam Doubleday Dell Publishing Group, Inc.

October 1996
Standard Print Hardcover Edition.

Five Star Standard Print Romance Series.

The text of this edition is unabridged.

Set in 11 pt. News Plantin.

Printed in the United States on permanent paper.

Library of Congress Catalog Card Number: 96-86090
ISBN 0-7862-0860-0 (hc)

Valentine

Prologue

Vimiera, Portugal — August 1808

The great copper ball of the sun hung in the metallic-blue sky where not a cloud offered a veil to the punishing heat torturing the bare plain beneath. Far in the distance, snow-capped mountains shimmered like a mirage, and behind the low hills surrounding the plain, the Atlantic Ocean crashed against the wild, rocky coastline.

But for the fifty men of His Majesty's Third Dragoons, sweltering in their scarlet tunics, gasping on the parched earth, the cold surf-tipped waves of the ocean and the icy white of mountain snow were a dream.

Again and again the thin blue line of Frenchmen came at them over the hills. They fired into the line, saw men fall, saw the line falter, retreat, only to reappear, reinforced. Their own men lay dead and dying, their bodies crushing the wild thyme that scratched a living with spindly olive trees and cactus, releasing its fragrance into the unstirring, burning air.

How many more Frenchmen were there the other side of the hill? How many more times would they pour onto the plain?

The major commanding this little company of dragoons stared into the shimmering distance behind them, across the sluggish gray river to the hills from which his reinforcements would come. His ear strained to catch the triumphant bugle call that would signal relief. It had been promised. It wasn't possible it wouldn't come.

But as the long afternoon in hell dipped toward sunset, he began to believe that there was to be no reinforcement. They were destined to die here in this blazing furnace, watering the parched ground with their blood.

A tiny breeze wafted from the sea as the sun began to sink behind the hills. It stirred the regimental colors, planted in the ground beside the dead body of the young cornet who'd been carrying them.

"Here they come again!" a private shouted from behind the insignificant earthwork that offered their only protection from the enemy guns.

The major looked out over the plain at the inexorable advance of the enemy line. An ensign came up behind him, panting, perspiration dripping from beneath his shako. His eyes were wild with panic, and the unbelievable words that spelled a fearful death tumbled from his lips.

Chapter One

London —
June 1810

"Marry one of *them?* Good God, man, don't be absurd." Sylvester Gilbraith, fifth Earl of Stoneridge, stared incredulously at the nervous little man sitting dwarfed behind the massive desk in the lawyer's office on Threadneedle Street.

Lawyer Crighton cleared his throat. "I believe his lordship was very fond of his granddaughters, my lord."

"What has that to do with me?" demanded the earl.

The lawyer shuffled the papers on his desk. "He wished to ensure they were well provided for, sir. Their mother, Lady Belmont, has her own substantial jointure and requires no additional provision. She will, of course, remove to the dower house as soon as you are ready to take up residence at Stoneridge Manor."

"The mother doesn't concern me," the earl commented curtly. "Be so good as to explain in words of one syllable the precise conditions of my cousin's will. I feel sure I must have misunderstood you."

The lawyer regarded his client unhappily. "I don't believe so, my lord. There are four granddaughters, the children of Viscount Belmont and Lady Elinor. . . ."

"Yes . . . yes . . . and Belmont was killed at the Battle of the Nile twelve years ago, making me, by virtue of the entail, Stoneridge's heir." The earl began to pace the room, his large stride eating up the narrow space from window to door. "Get to it, man."

Lawyer Crighton decided that the new Earl Stoneridge was even more intimidating than his predecessor, the crusty, gouty fourth earl. Sylvester Gilbraith's clear gray eyes were uncomfortably penetrating in his lean face, and the white scar slashing across his forehead lent a menacing cast to his well-bred countenance. His mouth was a taut line of impatience, one characteristic he obviously shared with his late cousin.

"Perhaps it would be best if your lordship were to read the conditions for yourself," he suggested, selecting one of the papers in front of him.

A glint of sardonic amusement enlivened the cool eyes. "Afraid to be the presenter of ill tidings, Crighton?" His lordship extended a slim white hand and twitched the paper from the lawyer's grasp. He flung himself into a chair, crossing one buckskin-clad thigh over the other, and began to read, flicking all the while at his top boots with his whip.

The long case clock in the corner ticked, a fly buzzed indolently at the open window, and the shout of a costermonger rose on the June air from the street below. Lawyer Crighton swallowed nervously, and the sound seemed magnified in the tense stillness of the room.

"Good God!" Stoneridge flung the paper onto the desk as he sprang to his feet again. "It is iniquitous. I inherit the title, Stoneridge Manor, and the London house, but not an acre of land or a penny of the old curmudgeon's fortune unless I marry one of these girls! This couldn't stand up in a court of law, it's the will of a lunatic."

"I assure you, sir, the will is perfectly legal. His lordship was in sound mind, and I witnessed it myself, together with two members of this firm." The lawyer pulled his chin. "Only the title and the two properties are entailed. His lordship had the right to do as he pleased with the rest of his fortune."

"And he's left it to a gaggle of girls!"

"I believe them to be very personable young ladies," Crighton ventured. The earl's expression indicated he found the observation less than reassuring.

The lawyer cleared his throat again. "Lady Emily is twenty-two, my lord, and I understand she is betrothed. Lady Clarissa is twenty-one, and I believe unattached. Then there is Lady Theodora, who is approaching twenty. And Lady Rosalind, who is still a child . . . not quite twelve."

"So I seem to have the choice of two," his lordship said with a grim smile. "If I refuse to make such a choice, my cousin's fortune is divided among his granddaughters, and I am left with an empty title and not a feather to fly with." He swung toward

10

the fireplace, resting an arm on the mantel, gazing down into the empty grate. "The bastard was determined to be revenged for that entail somehow."

The lawyer cracked his knuckles, and the earl raised his head, casting him a look of powerful dislike. Hastily, Crighton rested his hands on the desk. The violent estrangement between the Gilbraith and Belmont branches of the Stoneridge family was as well-known to him as it was to the London ton . . . but its genesis was lost in family memory.

The fourth earl had never been able to reconcile himself to the fact that his distant cousin's family would come into the title. It had added gall and wormwood to his bitter grief at the death of his only child.

"I don't believe it's as simple as that, my lord," the lawyer said diffidently. "There is a codicil."

The earl's clear eyes sharpened. "A codicil?"

"Yes, my lord." Crighton drew out another piece of heavy vellum. "The young ladies and their mother are not to be informed of these conditions of the will until one month after you have been notified."

"*What?*" A sharp crack of disbelieving laughter broke from the earl. "For one month they are to believe they inherit nothing? And you say the old man was fond of them?"

"I believe, my lord, that his lordship wished to be fair . . . to give you a fair chance," Crighton said. "There will be some incentive for one of the young ladies to favor your suit . . . should you, of course, decide to press it."

"And just how am I supposed to pay court immediately after his death to a young lady in deep mourning for her nearest male relative?" The earl's eyebrows disappeared into his scalp. "I'd look an egotistic fool . . . but perhaps that was my cousin's intention."

Lawyer Crighton cleared his throat yet again. "Lord Stoneridge instructed his relatives that there was to be no formal mourning period. They are forbidden to wear mourning or to refrain from their usual pursuits." He scratched his head. "If you knew his lordship, sir, you'd understand that such instructions were quite in character. He was not a conventional man."

11

"And why is he going to such lengths to give me a fair chance, as you put it?" The earl shook his head in disbelief.

Crighton was silent for a minute before saying, "His lordship would not care to see Stoneridge Manor go to rack and ruin for lack of funds to maintain it, and I also believe he wished it to remain in the hands of a member of his son's family."

"Ah." The earl nodded slowly. "One could almost feel sorry for the devious old devil . . . torn between loathing the idea of a Gilbraith in residence and ancestral pride."

He drew on his York tan gloves, smoothing the fine leather over his fingers, a deep frown between his chiseled brows, wrinkling the scar. "A union between a Gilbraith and a Belmont would be something indeed."

"Indeed, my lord."

"I give you good day, Crighton." Abruptly, his lordship strode to the door.

The lawyer bounced up to bow his client from the room and down the narrow flight of stairs to the street door. He waited politely as the earl mounted the glossy black being held at the door by a street urchin and rode off down Threadneedle Street toward Cheapside.

Lawyer Crighton returned to his office. It was to be hoped the young Belmont ladies hadn't heard the scandalous accusations dogging the heels of the Earl of Stoneridge. Such rumors would hardly endear a prospective suitor, particularly one of Gilbraith parentage — surely sufficient a disadvantage.

Sylvester rode back to his lodgings on Jermyn Street. Two years ago he would have gone to one of his clubs and sought companionship, port, and a game of faro. But he could no longer bear that instant of silence as he walked into a crowded room, the averted eyes, the stiff acknowledgments of his onetime friends. Never the cut direct — except from Gerard. He'd been acquitted, after all. But he'd not been exonerated.

Cowardice was a charge that clung like slime.

"It's insufferable! How can we possibly be expected to live five miles from a Gilbraith!" The young lady at the pianoforte slammed her hands onto the keys in a crashing chord. "I don't understand why grandpapa should have insisted on such a thing."

"Your grandfather didn't insist we live in the dower house, Clarissa," Lady Elinor Belmont said mildly, examining her embroidery with a critical frown. "I think a paler shade of green . . ." She selected a silk from the basket on the table beside her. "But while we're hardly in danger of debtors' prison, we need to husband our resources. If I dip into capital to set us up in our own establishment, it'll cut into your dowries."

"I don't give a hoot about a dowry," Lady Clarissa declared. "And neither does Theo. We've no intention of marrying, *ever*."

" 'Ever' is a big word, dear," her mother remarked. "And there's still Emily and Rosie to consider."

Clarissa swung round on the piano stool, her big blue eyes stormy. "It's just so galling," she said. "To have to remove to the dower house, when we've always lived here."

"Don't fuss so, Clarry. We've always known it would happen . . . ever since Papa was killed." A tall young woman looked up from a fashion magazine, a ray of sunlight picking golden glints in her dark brown hair. "And the dower house is very spacious. Besides, once Edward and I are married, you can all come and live with us."

"Poor Edward," murmured Lady Elinor with an amused smile. "I hardly think a young man, even one so accommodating as Edward, would relish starting married life in the company of his mother-in-law and three sisters-in-law."

"Oh, fustian, Mama!" Her eldest daughter leaped to her feet and flung her arms around her mother. "Edward *loves* you."

"Yes, I'm sure he does, Emily, dear, and I'm much obliged to him," Lady Elinor said placidly, returning the hug. "Nevertheless, we shall remove to the dower house and make the best of it."

Her two elder daughters knew the tone. Behind their mother's mild exterior lay a will of iron, rarely exerted but never to be ignored.

"Mama, where's Theo? She promised to help me cut up these worms." A young girl wandered into the room, extending a cupped hand.

"Rosie, that's revolting! Take them away," her sisters com-

13

manded in unison.

The child blinked through large horn-rimmed spectacles. "They're not revolting. Theo doesn't think they are. They're to be part of an experiment . . . a bio . . . biological experiment."

"Theo doesn't know the first thing about biological experiments," Emily said.

"But at least she's interested," Rosie responded with asperity, peering at the contents of her palm. "If you're not interested in things, you never learn anything. That was what Grandpapa said."

"That's very true, Rosie, but the drawing room is not the best place for worms," her mother declared.

"Alive or dissected," Clarissa put in, closing the lid of the pianoforte. "Take them away. Theo's gone fishing . . . heaven only knows when she'll reappear."

Lady Belmont bent over her basket of embroidery silks so that her daughters couldn't see the tears glazing her eyes. While they'd all had a close relationship with the old earl, Theo had been the closest to their grandfather and was struggling with a well of grief that Lady Belmont understood as perhaps the other girls didn't. Theo had needed a father. Kit's death when she was seven had left her with needs that her mother couldn't satisfy. The others had adapted, it seemed, and their grandfather's influence had been important, but not as vital as their mother's. It had been the opposite with Theo.

In the days since the earl's death, she had plunged herself into the affairs of the estate and the solitary pursuits that had always pleased her with a single-minded dedication that would shut out her grief. She paid little or no attention to the household routine these days. Clarissa was right — Theo would return before dark, but there was no knowing exactly when.

That same afternoon Sylvester Gilbraith downed his tankard of ale in the tap room of the village inn and leaned back, resting his elbows on the bar counter behind him. The room was dark and smoky, and he was aware of the surreptitious glances of the inn's customers as they drank and spat into the sawdust at their feet. They didn't know who he was and speculation was

14

rife. Not many gentlemen of quality fetched up at the Hare and Hounds in Lulworth, demanding a room for the night.

But it didn't suit Lord Stoneridge to declare himself just yet. He guessed that the village inhabitants and the estate workers would share the Belmont hostility to a Gilbraith. Such attitudes were passed down from the manor and rapidly became entrenched, even when the reason for them was long forgotten.

He pushed himself away from the bar counter and strolled outside. Summer had come early this year. The village street was bathed in sunshine, the mud hard-ridged, and the groom in the stableyard drowsed against the wall, sucking a straw, the brim of his cap pulled well down over his eyes.

He straightened, rubbing his eyes with his knuckles as his lordship beckoned. A sharp command brought him running across the cobbled yard.

"Saddle my horse."

The lad tugged his forelock and disappeared into the stable, reemerging after five minutes leading the earl's black.

"Is there a cross-country route to Stoneridge Manor?" His lordship swung himself astride his mount, tossing a coin to the lad.

"Aye, sir. Through the village, and take the right fork. Follow the footpath 'cross the fields, and it'll bring you onto Belmont land be'ind the manor."

Lord Stoneridge nodded and turned his horse. He'd never seen his ancestral home, except in paintings, and for a reason he couldn't identify wanted to familiarize himself with the house, its grounds, and its dependencies before he announced himself.

He followed directions and found himself approaching the house from the rear. He broke through a spinney, and the long, low Tudor manor house faced him on a hill, across a swift-running stream, spanned by a narrow stone bridge.

Stoneridge Manor. His home . . . and it would be the home of his children. Gilbraith children. A surge of grim satisfaction rose in his breast. In two hundred years a Gilbraith had not set foot in Stoneridge. Now it would be theirs. The Belmonts' unfortunate tendency to produce female progeny had finally excluded them.

Except . . .

With a muttered oath he turned his horse to ride along the stream. The house and its immediate park were nothing. The wealth lay in the estate — its woods and fields and tenant farmers. Without access to those revenues, the house itself was merely a gentleman's residence, and devilishly expensive to maintain. In fact, he couldn't possibly maintain it with the mere competency he'd inherited from his own father.

But what the hell did four chits and their mother know about running an estate, about managing the affairs of tenants? They might imagine they could rely on a bailiff, but they'd be robbed blind. The land would run itself into the ground in a few years.

The fourth Earl of Stoneridge had been demented . . . whatever that idiot lawyer had said.

He slashed at a gorse bush with a vicious stroke of his riding crop, and his horse whinnied, throwing up its head in alarm.

"Easy." Sylvester patted the animal's neck as they moved through a stand of oak trees. As he emerged into the sunlight again, he saw a prone figure some way along the bank of the stream. There was something about the intent stillness of the figure that intrigued him.

He dismounted, tethering the horse to a sapling, and approached, his footsteps soft and muffled in the damp mossy ground.

He spotted the girl's sandals a few yards from where she lay on her stomach, her bare feet in the air, the hem of her unbleached linen dress lying against her thighs, revealing slim brown calves. Two thick black plaits lay along her back. Her sleeves were rolled up and both hands were in the brown water of the stream.

A gypsy tickling trout was Sylvester's immediate conclusion.

"We thrash poachers where I come from," he observed to her back. The girl's position didn't change, and he realized that his approach hadn't startled her. She must have heard his footsteps, soft as they were.

"Oh, we 'angs 'em in these parts," she said in a soft Dorsetshire drawl, still without looking around. "Less'n we're feelin' kind. Then we transports 'em to the colonies."

He couldn't help smiling at this cool riposte. Clearly this gypsy wasn't easily intimidated. He stood silently, affected by her intense concentration as she engaged in a battle of wits with the fish lying inert in the shadow of a camouflaging flat brown stone. Sunlight danced on the smooth surface of the water, and her hands were utterly still while her prey became accustomed to them. Then she moved. Her hands shot up from the water, flourishing a speckled brown trout.

"Gotcha, master trout!" She chuckled, holding the thrashing fish in the air for a second before tossing him back into the stream. The fish leaped out of the water, an agile flashing curve, sunlit drops of water along its back, and then it was gone, leaving a widening circle of bubbles on the surface.

"Why on earth did you throw it back? It looked big enough for a substantial dinner," Stoneridge asked in surprise.

"I'm not 'ungry," she said in the same cool tone as before. Rolling over, she sat up, squinting at him against the sun. "We shoots trespassers in these parts, too. An' you're on Belmont land . . . boundary's just beyond those trees." She gestured with an outflung arm.

"If I am trespassing, I'll lay odds I'm in good company," he said, his eyes narrowing as he examined her face. A gamine face, brown as a berry, with a pointed chin and small, straight nose. A fringe of black hair wisped on a broad forehead over a pair of large pansy-blue eyes. Quite an appealing little gypsy.

She merely shrugged and scrambled to her feet, shaking down the folds of her coarse linen smock, tossing the heavy black plaits over her shoulders. "Not your business what I do. You're not from these parts, are you?"

She was standing with her bare feet slightly apart, her hands resting on her hips, and there was a distinct challenge to her stance and the tilt of her head. He wondered if it was unconscious — her habitual way of viewing the world. It amused him. And she really was quite an appealing gypsy.

He stepped toward her, smiling, reaching out a hand to catch her chin. "No, I'm not, but I've a mind to become better acquainted with them . . . or rather with their Romanys." His hand tightened and he brought his mouth to hers.

The Earl of Stoneridge never fully understood what happened next. One minute he was standing upright, his lips pressed to

17

hers, the sun-warmed scent of her skin in his nostrils, the firm line of her jaw in his palm, and the next he was lying on his back in the stream. Someone had instructed the gypsy poacher in the martial arts.

"Rat . . . cur . . . ," she yelled at him as she stood on the edge of the bank, dancing on her toes, her eyes almost black with outrage. "That'll teach you, you filthy toad . . . tryin' to take advantage of an honest girl. You come near me again and I'll cut your —"

The rest of the tirade was lost in an indignant screech as he lunged off the bed of the stream, braceleting her bare ankles with finger and thumb. A violent jerk and she thumped onto her backside onto the hard ground. She yelled, grabbing at tufts of mossy grass, trying to save herself as he yanked her off the bank until she was sitting, hissing and spitting, in the thick mud of the shallows.

Sylvester stood up, glaring down at the livid girl. "Sauce for the goose, my girl," he declared. "Whoever taught you to wrestle omitted to teach you not to crow too soon." He dusted off his hands in a gesture that he realized was futile and squelched out of the stream, clambering onto the bank.

The girl picked herself up out of the mud. "Don't you call me 'your girl'!" she yelled, gouging a lump of mud from the bank and hurling it at his retreating back. It caught him full between his shoulders, and he swung round with a bellow of anger.

She had scrambled onto the bank, and there was murder in her eyes. He looked at the sodden, mud-smothered figure all set to do battle in whatever fashion presented itself, and suddenly he burst out laughing as the absurdity of the situation hit him.

He was soaked to the skin, his boots full of water and probably ruined beyond repair, all because that bedraggled bantam took exception to a kiss. How was he to have guessed that a gypsy girl would react with all the outrage of a vestal virgin?

He threw up his hands in a gesture of appeasement. "Let's declare honors even, shall we?"

"Honor?" she spat at him. "What do you know of honor?"

The laughter died in his eyes and his body became rigid, his hands dropping to his sides, curling into fists.

You stand accused of dishonoring the regiment. How do you answer, Major Gilbraith?

He stood again in the crowded courtroom at Horseguards, heard again the dreadful hush from the benches of his fellow officers of His Majesty's Third Dragoons, felt again the gimlet eyes of General, Lord Feringham, presiding over the court-martial. How had he answered? *Not guilty, my lord.* Yes, of course: Not guilty, my lord. But was he? If only he could remember those moments before the bayonet struck. If only Gerard had testified to what Sylvester believed had happened: He'd been holding an impossible position at Vimiera; Gerard was to come up in support; but before he could do so, they'd been overwhelmed and suffered the greatest military disgrace to befall a regiment — they'd lost the colors. Gerard, his boyhood friend, said he'd been on his way in support. He hadn't been aware of a renewed French attack on the isolated outpost . . . but whatever had happened, they'd arrived too late. Major Gilbraith had been taken prisoner, his men left for dead, the colors captured.

Major Gilbraith's head wound had kept him lingering between life and death in a foul French prison for a twelve-month, until he'd been exchanged and brought home to face a court-martial. Had there been a renewed French attack before Captain Gerard could come to his aid? Or had he yielded his colors prematurely?

No one had an answer. Sylvester could remember nothing of the minutes before the bayonet had driven into his skull. Gerard said he'd seen nothing and could have no opinion on the issue of honor. And there the matter lay. There was no concrete evidence to convict . . . but neither was there concrete evidence to exonerate.

And people believed what they chose. It was clear enough what Gerard believed. His shoulder had been the first to be turned.

That ominous feeling crept up the back of Sylvester's neck, the little prickles, the weird surge of unfocused energy in his head, tightening his scalp. His hand went to his forehead, to the slash of the scar, as he tried to relax, to will the promise of pain to disappear. Sometimes he could divert the coming agony if he caught it at the very beginning and was able to be still, close his eyes, change the seething thoughts, defeat the rise of this hideous panic.

But he was standing in hot, bright sunlight, far from the cool darkness he would need. A jagged flash of light appeared in the corner of his vision, and he knew it was too late. He had perhaps twenty minutes before the ghastly, degrading pain took over . . . twenty minutes to reach his room at the inn.

Theo Belmont stared. What was happening to him? He looked as if he were standing in a graveyard alive with spirits. His face was deathly white, his eyes suddenly dulled, his shoulders sagging. It was as if muscle and sinew, his very life-blood, had been leached out of him. Abruptly he turned from her and stumbled over to his horse tethered at the stand of trees. He mounted clumsily and rode off, slouching in the saddle, his head lowered almost to his chest.

Who was he? Not that it mattered. Strangers passed through Lulworth often enough, rarely causing a ripple on the surface of tranquil village life. Generally, though, they kept to the roads, not straying onto other people's property.

She shrugged and bent to wring out the dripping folds of her smock, thrusting her feet into her sandals. Absently, she rubbed her backside . . . it had been a very hard fall. The stranger clearly made no concessions when it came to avenging himself — but then, he'd had a pretty hard fall himself.

She grinned, remembering the neatness of her maneuver. Edward would be proud of her.

Theo made her dripping way along the bank toward the stone bridge. She crossed and hurried up the hill toward the house, shivering as a stiffening sea breeze pressed her wet clothes against her skin.

"Theo, whatever happened to you?" Clarissa appeared on the long stone-flagged terrace outside the drawing room. "I saw you coming up from the stream."

"I fell in, if you must know," Theo said, for some reason reluctant to give a full account of the encounter. She hadn't exactly come out of it bathed in glory, and honesty forced her to admit that she *had* been playing a game that could have given the stranger the wrong impression.

"Fell in?" Clarissa persisted. "How?"

Theo sighed. Her sister never let go until she was satisfied. "I was leaning over, trying to tickle a trout, and I lost my balance." She stepped through the open doors into the drawing room.

"Theo!" Emily squeaked. "You're dripping all over the carpet."

"Oh, sorry." She looked down at the puddle forming at her feet.

"Theo, dear, I'm not going to ask how you come to be in that condition," her mother said, laying down her embroidery. "But I think it would be best if you were to go out again and come in through the side door. This carpet is not ours to ruin."

"Of course . . . it belongs to a Gilbraith now. I was forgetting. Forgive me." Theo turned on her heel and marched out again.

Lady Belmont sighed. There was no point ignoring the facts. They were going to have to get used to it eventually — and the sooner they were reconciled, the happier they would be. But she was under no illusions about Theo, who was going to have the most difficulty. The house and the land were in her blood. A most powerful spiritual legacy from both father and grandfather to the girl child they'd adored.

Chapter Two

"A messenger came from the village, my lady."

"Oh, thank you, Foster." Lady Belmont smiled absently at the butler as she took the envelope from the silver tray. She didn't recognize the hard black script and frowned, having expected a message from one of their neighbors — an invitation to some quiet function, probably. The late earl's dictates on mourning were known to everyone, but the countryside, nevertheless, knew she would accept only discreet invitations.

"Ask Cook to come for the day's menus in half an hour, would you, Foster?" Elinor took the message into the small parlor where she dealt with household matters and her own correspondence. She broke the wafer with a slim paper knife and unfolded the single sheet.

Lord Stoneridge would do himself the honor of calling upon Lady Belmont this afternoon. If it was inconvenient, perhaps her ladyship would suggest an alternative time. His lordship could be reached at the Hare and Hounds.

Well, it had to come sooner or later. Elinor folded the sheet again, unaware of her restless fingers repeatedly pressing the crease. The move to the dower house wouldn't take more than a day or two . . . they would have plenty of help. She would go down to the house this morning and walk through the rooms again. They were furnished pleasantly enough, but she would need to decide where to place her own personal pieces that she'd brought with her to Stoneridge Manor on her wedding day. . . .

Elinor blinked rapidly and stiffened her shoulders. The sense of loss was always with her — the futile anger that she'd had so little married life, that Kit's life had been snatched from him so violently and so early . . . too, too early! That French monster bore the blood of half a generation on his hands.

"Mama, we're walking to the vicarage. Do you have any messages for Mrs. Haversham?" Emily came in, looking fresh and elegant in a walking dress of crisp cambric, a chip-straw bonnet on her glowing brown curls, jean half boots on her narrow feet.

"I asked Cook for the calves'-foot jelly you promised Mrs.

Haversham," Clarissa put in, peeping over her taller sister's shoulders. Her eyes sharpened suddenly as she saw her mother's face.

"What is it, Mama? Has something upset you?"

Elinor smiled and shook her head. Clarissa was the most sensitive of her daughters, quick to feel and respond to her mother's moods.

"Nothing really, but I'm afraid we must be prepared for a difficult interview this afternoon. Lord Stoneridge is to call."

"Oh, why can't he leave us alone!" Clarissa wailed. "Why does he have to come and call? He could just say he wanted to move in and we could move out . . . and we'd never have to see each other."

"Don't talk nonsense, Clarissa," Elinor rebuked sharply. "The proprieties must be observed, as you well know. We shall be neighbors, and we shall be courteous at all times. Is that clear?"

"Yes, Mama." But Clarissa's eyes were mutinous, and her soft mouth hardened.

"I don't suppose he'll be here much, anyway," Emily said with practical reassurance. "He's bound to be in London during the season . . . and I'm sure he'll be at the hunting box and in Scotland a lot of the time. Lulworth's too sleepy a place for an out-and-outer."

"Emily! Such vulgarity," her mother protested, but she was laughing. "How do you know his lordship is an out-and-outer, as you so inelegantly put it?"

"I don't," Emily said. "But I'll lay odds he is." Her lip curled. "Probably a dandy, like that awful cousin Cecil."

"All Gilbraiths are awful like cousin Cecil," piped Rosie's voice, and Elinor realized she hadn't seen the child behind her sisters.

"That will do . . . you're setting Rosie a shocking example. Come here, child."

Rosie appeared from behind Emily's skirts, and her mother scrutinized her appearance with a frown. "Your stockings are wrinkled, and you have jam on your smock. You really are too old to go around looking like a haystack. I don't know what Mrs. Haversham will think."

Rosie rubbed at the sticky smudge, peering through her glasses, her lip caught between her teeth. "I wasn't going to see Mrs. Haversham. Robbie promised to show me his pickled spider. He says it has ten legs, but I know it can't. Spiders only have eight."

"You can't go to the vicarage without greeting Mrs. Haversham," Emily pointed out, bending to straighten the child's stockings.

"Is Theo going with you?" Elinor adjusted the sash at Rosie's diminutive waist.

"No, she's riding the estate with Beaumont. They have to decide which fields to leave fallow for the autumn sowing."

"And do something about Squire Greenham," Clarissa added.

"Oh, yes, the Master's been complaining again about the way we maintain our coverts," Emily said. "He's bellowing that the hunt will never be able to draw the coverts if we don't maintain the rides properly. And the Belmont game-keepers aren't marking the fox earths either . . . and how can the huntsman stop the earths if he doesn't know where they are?"

"That is so *cruel!*" Rosie exclaimed, her cheeks pink, her eyes blazing behind her glasses. "It's horrid of them to stop the earths so the foxes can't get away when they're chasing them. Theo said once when she was hunting, she saw a fox running all over the covert, trying every opening to its earth and they were all blocked . . . and then the hounds caught it and ripped it apart. It's disgusting and it's not fair!"

Her voice quavered, and her mother and sisters knew a bout of noisy, heartfelt tears was imminent.

"It's not hunting season for another four months," Clarissa said swiftly. "And I promise that you and I will go out at dead of night before the hunt and unstop all the earths."

Lord Stoneridge might have a word or two to say on that score, Elinor reflected, since it was now his land. However, there was no point upsetting Rosie further. She said mildly, "You will be sure to be here when Lord Stoneridge calls, won't you?"

Her elder daughters glanced at her, and she saw that the same thought had crossed their minds. But they merely nodded.

"Of course, Mama. Come along, Rosie. We have to hurry, you'll have to come as you are. Robbie and the pickled spider won't notice, and I daresay Mrs. Haversham will turn a blind eye." Emily took the child's hand and hustled her out, Clarissa on their heels.

Elinor passed a hand wearily over her eyes. The next few days were going to be a trial, but once they were settled in the dower house, surely they could maintain a civilized distance from the new earl. The social engagements offered in the neighborhood couldn't possibly appeal to an out-and-outer. Whatever that might mean.

She rang the bell and when Foster appeared said, "When Lady Theo comes in, will you ask her to come to me, please?"

"Certainly, my lady." Foster bowed. "Cook is waiting."

"Send her in . . . oh, and, Foster, Lord Stoneridge will be calling this afternoon. I will receive him in the drawing room. Bring up a bottle of . . . of . . ."

"I believe Lady Theo would suggest the eighty-nine claret, my lady."

Elinor smiled, despite her heavy heart. "She would know, of course. Her grandfather took her round every rack in the cellar until she could lay hands on a particular bottle blindfold."

Foster's eyes grew a little misty, but he said only, "I'll bring up a bottle, ma'am." He turned to the door, then paused, coughed. "Forgive me, my lady, but I imagine Lord Stoneridge's arrival means that you and the young ladies will be removing to the dower house shortly."

"That is so, Foster."

He coughed again. "I trust your ladyship will not wish to dispense with my services."

Elinor shook her head. "Of course not, but I can't help feeling that you would do better to remain at the manor. I'm sure Lord Stoneridge will need your knowledge of the house and the staff."

"I would prefer to come with you, my lady. As would Cook and Mrs. Graves." With a bow he left the room.

Elinor sighed, tapping her fingers on the blotter. Life at the dower house would be so much pleasanter with the butler, the housekeeper, and the cook who'd served her and the old earl for two decades. But was it fair to the new owner to remove the established staff?

Her jaw tightened. The new owner was a Gilbraith. She owed him nothing, and the staff who'd been loyal to Kit and his father owed a Gilbraith no loyalty.

The cook tapped at the door, and Lady Belmont turned her attention to the day's menus, putting aside the thought that she hadn't spoken to Theo yet about Stoneridge's call.

Theo entered the house just before noon. She was ravenous, having been on horseback since seven, but it was clear to her mother and sisters as she entered the paneled dining room that she was in good humor.

"There'd better be baked eggs," she said, sniffing hungrily. "Did you have a good morning . . . Beaumont had a splendid suggestion for Long Meadow . . . he thinks we should marl it as Mr. Coke did at Holkham and plant —"

She stopped, running her eyes around the room. There was tension in every face, except Rosie's. Rosie was dissecting a chicken wing with the tip of her knife with all the care and attention of a surgeon.

"What's happened?"

"Nothing unexpected, Theo," Elinor said, helping herself to a slice of ham, her voice level. "Lord Stoneridge is calling this afternoon."

"I see." Theo lifted the lid on the dish of baked eggs and replaced it again. She sat down in her accustomed place and crumbled a piece of bread between finger and thumb, her eyes fixed, unseeing, on the rich patina of the cherrywood table. "Is he evicting us this afternoon?"

"No, of course not. We must discuss arrangements . . . there's much to organize."

"And a Gilbraith will, of course, be prepared to conduct these matters in a civilized fashion," Theo said acidly. "That wasn't Grandpapa's opinion."

Elinor decided this wasn't a moment for discussion. She said briskly, "I'll expect you to be here, Theo."

Theo pushed back her chair, all appetite vanished. "Would you excuse me, Mama? I promised to visit the Gardners in the village. Joe's injured hand isn't improving, and his wife's close to her time."

"I expect you to be here when Lord Stoneridge calls, Theo," Elinor repeated calmly, her eyes holding her daughter's.

"I understand," Theo said, tossing her napkin onto the table as she rose to her feet. She left the dining room without another word.

She could not . . . *would* not . . . welcome a Gilbraith. He was going to take her house, her land, her tenants . . . everything that she held dear . . . everything that embodied the memory and spirit of her father and her grandfather . . . everything that she had worked to maintain for the last three years, since she'd taken the reins of the estate management into her own hands. The land was fertile, the tenants hardworking and content. It was hers, and he was going to take all that from her. She knew every stick, every plant, every ridge of mud on this land. She knew the tenants, their trials, their triumphs, their grievances. She knew the feckless and the industrious; she knew their children. And they knew her.

Theo realized that she was standing at the foot of the stairs, her knuckles white against the carved newel. The hall was empty, the massive oak front door open, dust motes tossing in the broad path of sunlight. Her eye roamed the room, resting on every familiar object — the bench beside the door, where in distant memory her father would sit to have his muddy boots removed; the long Jacobean table and the burnished copper bowl full of rose petals; the deep inglenook fireplace where, during the winter, the fire was never allowed to die and guests were welcomed with warm spiced wine, where on Christmas Eve the tenants would gather.

She uttered a short, savage execration, grabbed her gloves and whip from the table, and went back outside, striding round to the stable. The Earl of Stoneridge could go hang. She had work to do.

There was an uneasy silence in the dining room. "She'll come back, Mama," Emily said with faltering confidence.

"I trust so," Elinor said, laying down her napkin. "Rosie should be presented. Would one of you ensure she looks respectable?"

She left the room, and Clarissa and Emily sighed. "Theo's going

27

to be difficult," Clarissa stated. "It's not fair on Mama."

"It's not fair on any of us," Emily asserted crossly. "I wish Edward would come back from that horrible Peninsular War and we could get married. Then you could all come and live with us and we could tell this . . . this *Gilbraith* to go to the devil!"

"Emily!" exclaimed Clarissa, torn between shock and sympathy with her sister's fervent wish.

"Come along, Rosie. You need to change your dress," Emily said with a return to elder-sisterly dignity. "See if you can find Theo, Clarry. She listens to you."

"Not always," Clarissa said, but went off in search of her younger sister.

Theo was nowhere to be found. The groom in the stable said she'd taken the new gelding for an airing. Full of tricks, he was, the groom said. Feeling his oats . . . it was to be hoped Lady Theo could hold him.

In a contest between Theo and a raw young gelding, Clarissa would back her sister anytime — particularly in her present mood. She returned to the house to change her gown and prepare herself for the upcoming ordeal.

Sylvester rode up the driveway of Stoneridge Manor, his nostrils flaring at the scents and sights of his ancestral home — his birthright. The lime washed, oak-timbered structure stood foursquare at the head of the crescent sweep of the drive — as it had done for three hundred years; the soft red-tiled roof glowed in the afternoon sun; the intricate diamond cuts of the mullioned windows sparkled. His eye took in the neat, well-weeded driveway, the perfectly clipped box hedges, the soft blue water of Lulworth Cove beyond the rose garden.

His — for a price. But this afternoon he'd get an idea of how stiff the price would be. Two sisters — Lady Clarissa, and Lady Theodora. Etiquette dictated that he consider the elder first, and unless there was something radically at fault with Lady Clarissa, he could see no reason to disobey the dictates of convention. It was to be a marriage of interest, on his side if not on the lady's. But the lady, thanks to her ever-loving grandfather, was not to know that.

He was smiling as he dismounted and handed his mount into the charge of a waiting groom.

"He's here!" Rosie catapulted through the long glass doors of the drawing room, her cheeks pink. "I watched him ride up the drive."

"What does he look like?" her sisters demanded in the same breath that their mother said, "That will do. Rosie, come here and sit quietly."

"He's riding an enormous black horse," Rosie confided, sitting beside her mother. "And he has a beaver hat on and a green coat and brown britches —"

"Lord Stoneridge, my lady," Foster intoned from the doorway, bringing a summary halt to Rosie's recitation.

His lordship bowed as the ladies rose to their feet.

"I bid you welcome to Stoneridge, my lord." With a courteous smile Elinor crossed the faded tapestry carpet, her hand outstretched.

The earl bowed over the hand, privately reflecting that Lady Belmont was a handsome woman with her soft brown hair, blue eyes, and elegant figure.

"May I present my daughters?"

Sylvester noted the diamond sparkle on Lady Emily's ring finger as he took her hand. The betrothed sister . . . but a most attractive young woman, very like her mother. He turned his attention with particular interest to Lady Clarissa.

"My lord." Clarissa twitched her hand from his grasp a moment too soon for courtesy, and Sylvester's lips thinned. Darker than her sister but with the same blue eyes. A shorter, less elegant figure . . . rather thin if the truth be told. But still passably handsome. Although not in the least friendly.

"And this is Rosalind."

He shook hands with a child who regarded him with frank curiosity from behind spectacles that completely dwarfed her face. "Are you interested in biology?"

"Not particularly," he said, taken aback.

"I didn't think you would be," she said as if confirmed in some negative opinion. "Gilbraiths probably aren't interested in that kind of thing."

29

Sylvester shot a startled look at Lady Belmont, who was looking chagrined. "You may return to the schoolroom, Rosie," she said sharply.

Rosie seemed about to protest, but Clarissa, sensing her mother's acute discomfiture, shooed her from the room. Theo's absence was bad enough without Rosie speaking her mind in her usual blunt fashion.

"Won't you be seated, Lord Stoneridge?" Lady Belmont indicated a chair as she resumed her seat on the sofa. "Ah, thank you, Foster. I'm sure Lord Stoneridge will take a glass of claret."

"Thank you." Devoutly hoping that wine would ease the tense atmosphere, Sylvester took an appreciative sip, commenting, "A fine vintage."

"Our cellars are well stocked, sir," the butler said. "The Gentlemen keep us well supplied."

"Oh, I didn't realize there was a smuggling trade on the Dorset coast."

"A very active one," Emily said. "But Theo deals with them. You should ask her if you wish to know how the system works."

"Theo?" He looked puzzled.

"My sister, sir."

"Lady Theodora?" He was still puzzled.

"She had some urgent business to attend to on the estate," Elinor said. "I'm certain she'll return shortly." But she wasn't in the least certain.

Sylvester put down his glass. It was time to come to business. "I wonder if I could have a word or two in private, ma'am."

Elinor rose immediately, relief apparent in her face that this awkward pretense at purely social intercourse was over. "Yes, there's much to discuss. Come into my parlor, Lord Stoneridge." She swept from the room, the earl on her heels.

"Well, what do you think?" Emily demanded as the door closed.

"Satanic," Clarissa said promptly.

Her sister went into a peal of laughter. "You're such a melodramatic goose, Clarry. But I own I can't like him . . . not that I was expecting to. His eyes are so cold, and there's an impatience . . . a haughtiness about him."

"That scar," Clarissa said. "A great slash across his forehead.

30

I wonder how he acquired it."

"In the war, probably. I wish I knew where Theo was."

Emily wasn't the only one wishing that. In the parlor Elinor was listening to the earl's succinct proposal in stunned silence.

"I believe such an arrangement will make the transition easier for everyone," Sylvester said at the end of his explanation. "It will be more comfortable for you in the dower house if one of your daughters lives at Stoneridge Manor. And I will undertake to dower my wife's sisters."

"You are most generous, my lord," Elinor said faintly, although she felt that the dispassionate tone in which he'd laid out his plans was anything but warm. But he could have no motive other than generosity and some kind of family feeling.

That was a novel thought — a Gilbraith having family feeling for a Belmont.

"I take it you agree to my plan, then, ma'am?" Sylvester paced the small room, trying to hide his impatience. Four weeks was a very short time to court and wed, but if the knot wasn't firmly tied at the end of the month, the true conditions of the earl's will would be revealed. He needed the absolute support of Lady Belmont from the beginning.

"I'm not prepared to coerce one of my daughters into marriage, sir," Elinor said with some asperity.

"No, of course not. I wasn't suggesting such a thing," he said brusquely. "But I would like to feel I had your approval. My intentions are, after all, of the most honorable."

And so they were in all essentials, he quieted his conscience.

Elinor was silent for a minute, regarding her visitor gravely. His cool gray eyes returned her scrutiny without flickering. There was a restlessness, a pent-up tension in the man, almost like an aura. And something else . . . some pain, she thought, deep inside him. He had the Gilbraith look — lean features, strong jaw, well-shaped mouth, and the physique of an athlete . . . a man who took care of himself.

Elinor realized as she took inventory that she was responding to Sylvester Gilbraith as a man — a fiercely attractive man, despite the scar. When had she last recognized a man's sexual attraction?

31

It shocked her and she stood up abruptly, turning her back on her visitor as she pretended to search for something in her desk.

What kind of husband would he make? Gentle . . . generous? Not gentle, she decided. Not a husband for Clarissa.

But maybe for Theo. Theo, who'd twisted the gouty, irascible old earl around her little finger. Theo was not intimidated by strong men; indeed, she would not be happy with anyone who always deferred to her own powerful will. She could well become distinctly shrewish, if her challenges went ignored. Elinor couldn't suppress a half smile. A shrewish Theo was not to be contemplated.

And as Lady Stoneridge, she wouldn't lose her beloved house and estate. The earl's proposal was not an outlandish suggestion; such marriages were often arranged in entail situations, and the kinship was so distant there could be no bar there.

But could Theo be brought to accept a hated Gilbraith, even with such powerful inducements?

Elinor turned back to the earl. He'd taken a seat beside the window during her cogitations, and she was pleased to see that he knew when to curb his impatience.

"If you wish to press your suit with my daughter Theo, my lord, you have my approval," she said formally.

Sylvester frowned. "I had thought to address Lady Clarissa, ma'am. She is the elder, it seems only appropriate."

"Maybe so, but you and Clarissa would not suit, sir."

Sylvester absorbed this firm statement in frowning silence before saying, "Forgive me, Lady Belmont, but since I haven't had the honor of meeting Lady Theodora, I don't know how to answer you."

"No, it's most vexing, I agree," Elinor said. "But Theo doesn't bend easily, to my will or anyone else's. However, you'll meet her shortly. You'll find her knowledge of the estate useful to you. She knows more than the bailiff about most matters and has had the management of the estate in her hands since she was seventeen. My father-in-law trusted her judgment implicitly."

"An unusual young woman." Sylvester contented himself with the dry comment.

32

Elinor smiled. "Something of an understatement, Lord Stoneridge."

"Why is she called Theo?" he asked abruptly. "Thea, I would expect. But Theo is a boy's name."

"She was always an intrepid child, much more interested in a boy's pursuits. Her father always called her Theo . . . the son he never had."

A strong-willed, managing, tomboy hoyden! Dear God, what was he getting himself into?

"I can't wait to meet her," he murmured.

"Has he gone?" Theo stuck her head round the corner of the door, keeping the rest of her on the terrace.

"No, he's with Mama," Emily said. "You really are too bad, Theo. Mama is so vexed that you weren't here."

"He's very toplofty," Clarissa said. "He looks as if there's a permanent bad smell under his nose." She offered an imitation of the earl, wrinkling her small nose.

Theo chuckled. "Well, I think I'll go back to the stables until he leaves."

"You will not." Emily moved with surprising speed for such a decorous young woman. She caught her sister's wrist and pulled her into the drawing room. They were engaged in a spirited tussle when the hall door opened to admit their mother and the Earl of Stoneridge.

"Emily . . . Theo!" Lady Belmont exclaimed.

Emily flushed, dropping her sister's wrist. Theo, who was still laughing, turned toward the door, an apology on her lips.

But both laughter and apology died. *"You!"* She formed the word without speaking it as she stared at the tall figure of Sylvester Gilbraith behind her mother.

"Well . . . well . . . ," Sylvester murmured, advancing into the room. "I believe you must be my missing cousin, Lady Theodora." He bowed, mockery glittering in his eyes. "What a surprise. You're quite an actress, cousin."

Theo ignored his outstretched hand. "And you are no gentleman, sir. But I would hardly have expected anything else from a Gilbraith."

33

Sylvester drew a sharp breath, but Elinor spoke before he could respond. "I don't know what you're talking about, Theo, but your rudeness is inexcusable. Lord Stoneridge is our guest —"

"Hardly that, Mama," Theo broke in, her face white with anger, her eyes blue-black. "I believe we are Lord Stoneridge's guests. If you'll excuse me, I have pressing business elsewhere." She spun on her heel, brushing past Sylvester, dusting off her sleeve where it had touched him, an expression of acute distaste on her face.

"Theo!" Elinor took a step forward, but Sylvester held up a hand.

"I think this is mine to deal with, ma'am," he said, tight-lipped, two spots of color burning on his cheekbones.

Elinor hesitated; then she made a tiny gesture of acknowledgment, and Lord Stoneridge strode out of the drawing room in pursuit of his cousin.

"What's going on?" Bewildered, Clarissa looked after his lordship. "Have they already met?"

"It would seem so," Elinor said, calmly taking up her embroidery.

"But . . . but Theo never said." Emily ran to the window, looking anxiously across the lawn as if expecting to see a scene of violent mayhem. "How could you let him go after her, Mama? He looked ready to murder her."

"I could cheerfully wring her neck myself," Elinor responded. "I am strongly of the opinion that your sister and Sylvester Gilbraith will be very good for each other."

"What do you mean?"

Elinor smiled, threading her needle with a crimson thread. "His lordship had a proposition to put to me. . . ."

Theo had reached the first landing when Sylvester caught up with her. She turned at bay, her stance apparently relaxed, but he could read her readiness in every muscle.

"You wish to take inventory of the bedrooms, my lord. Don't let me stand in your way," she said through her teeth.

"You're not in my way in the least," he replied, his anger as high and as visible in eye and mouth as Theo's. He moved toward her.

34

She shifted her stance, her hands hanging loose at her sides, her eyes fixed on his face.

"You won't manage it twice, gypsy," he said quietly. "This time I'm ready for you."

"You take one step closer, my lord, and you'll go down those stairs on your back," she said as softly as he. "And with any luck you'll break your neck in the process."

He shook his head. "I don't deny your skill, but mine is as good, and I have the advantage of size and strength." He saw the acknowledgment leap into her eyes, but her position didn't change.

"Let's have done with this," he said sharply. "I'm prepared to forget that silly business by the stream."

"Oh, are you, my lord? How very generous of you. As I recall, you were not the one insulted."

"As I recall, you, cousin, were making game of me. Now, come downstairs. I wish you to ride around the estate with me."

"You wish me to do *what?*" Theo stared at him, her eyes incredulous.

"I understand from your mother that you've had the management of the estate for the last three years," he said impatiently, as if his request were the most natural imaginable. "You're clearly the obvious person to show me around."

"You have windmills in your head, sir. I wouldn't give you the time of day!" Theo swung on her heel and made to continue up the stairs.

"You rag-mannered hoyden!" Sylvester exclaimed. "We may have started on the wrong foot, but there's no excuse for such incivility." He sprang after her, catching her around the waist.

She spun, one leg flashing in a high kick aimed at his chest, but as he'd warned her, this time he was ready for her. Twisting, he caught her body across his thighs, swinging a leg over hers, clamping them in a scissor grip between his knees.

"Now, yield!" he gritted through his teeth, adjusting his grip against the sinuous working of her muscles as she fought to free herself.

Theo went suddenly still, her body limp against him. Instinctively, he relaxed his grip and the next instant she was free, bounding up the next flight of stairs.

Sylvester went after her, no longer capable of cool reasoning. A primitive battle was raging, and he knew only that he wasn't going to lose it. No matter that it was undignified and totally inappropriate.

Theo raced down the long corridor, hearing his booted feet pounding behind her in time with her thundering heart. She didn't know whether her heart was speeding with fear or exhilaration; she didn't seem capable of rational, coherent thought.

His breath was on the back of her neck as she wrenched open the door of her bedroom and leaped inside, but his foot went in the gap as she tried to slam the door shut. She leaned on the door with all her weight, but Sylvester put his shoulder against the outside and heaved. Theo went reeling into the room and the door swung wide.

Sylvester stepped inside, kicking the door shut behind him. He glanced around. It was a pretty bedroom, redolent of girlhood from the delicate dimity hangings to the china doll on the window seat.

Theo backed away, her heart beating so loudly she was sure he could hear it. For some reason he seemed a lot bigger than before. Perhaps it was because he was towering over the dainty familiarity of her childhood bedroom. With a nasty jolt she recognized that she had been unpardonably rude. Even in the light of his provocation, she'd gone above and beyond what was forgivable.

"Very well," she said breathlessly. "If you wish it, I'll apologize for being uncivil. I shouldn't have said what I did just now."

"For once we're in agreement," he remarked, coming toward her. Theo cast a wild look around the room. In a minute she was going to be backed up against the armoire, and she didn't have too many tricks left in the bag.

Sylvester reached out and seized the long thick rope of hair hanging down her back. He twisted it around his wrist, reeling her in like a fish until her face was on a level with his shoulder.

He examined her countenance as if he were seeing it for the first time. Her eyes had darkened, and he could read the sparkling challenge in their depths; the flush of exertion and emotion lay beneath the golden brown of her complexion, and her lips were slightly parted as if she were about to launch into another of her tirades.

To prevent such a thing, he tightened his grip on her plait, bringing her face hard against his shoulder, and kissed her.

Theo gasped against his mouth, her body stiffening in preparation for a struggle.

He raised his head; a finger of his free hand stroked her eyelids closed, and his mouth returned to hers.

Theo was so startled that she forgot about resistance for a split second and in that second discovered that she was enjoying the sensation. Her lips parted beneath the probing thrust of his tongue, and her own tongue touched his, at first tentatively, then with increasing confidence. She inhaled the scent of his skin, a sun-warmed earthy scent that was new to her, and his mouth tasted of wine. His body was hard-muscled against her own, and when she stirred slightly, she became startlingly aware of a stiffness in his loins. Instinctively, she pressed her lower body against his.

Sylvester drew back abruptly, his eyes hooded as he looked down into her intent face. "I'll be damned," he muttered. "How many men have you kissed, gypsy?"

"None," she said truthfully. She'd kissed Edward several times, but those exploratory embraces bore no relation to what had just happened. Her anger had vanished completely, surprise and curiosity in its place. She wasn't even sure whether she still disliked him.

"I'll be damned," he said again, a slight smile tugging at the corners of his mouth, little glints of amusement sparkling in the gray eyes. "I doubt you'll be a restful wife, cousin, but I'll lay odds you'll be full of surprises."

Theo remembered that she *did* dislike him — intensely. She twitched her plait out of his slackened grip and stepped back. "I fail to see what business that is of yours, Lord Stoneridge."

"Ah, yes, I was forgetting we haven't discussed this as yet," he said, folding his arms, regarding her with deepening amusement. "We're going to be married, you and I."

37

Chapter Three

"Married?" Theo stared at him, convinced he'd taken leave of whatever senses a Gilbraith could possess.

"Yes, I have your mother's permission to address you," he said with a smile that struck Theo as demented.

"My mother?" She shook her head. "My dear sir, you are in need of a physician . . . or Bedlam," she couldn't help adding. She moved to walk past him to the door.

He laid a restraining hand on her arm. "Hear me out, cousin."

"I have no wish to listen to the ramblings of a lunatic," she declared. "I suggest —"

The suggestion was stillborn as she found herself swinging through the air to land with a jarring thump on a chair in the corner of the room. Lord Stoneridge leaned over her, his hands braced on the walls on either side of her head. His face was very close to hers.

"Now do I have your attention, cousin?" he demanded with deceptive mildness. Sensing an almost imperceptible shift of her leg, he continued in the same tone, "If you're thinking of bringing your knee into play, I most earnestly recommend that you reconsider."

Theo, who had been thinking of doing just that, reconsidered.

"Do I have your attention, cousin?"

"I appear to have little choice but to listen to your raving," she said tartly, wishing she could move back, away from a disturbing proximity that confusingly seemed to embody both menace and promise.

Sylvester straightened and ran a hand through his crisp dark hair, disheveling the close-cropped cut. "We're going to have to deal better than this," he said in some frustration. "We can't always be manhandling each other."

Theo closed her eyes, forcing herself into stillness. If she didn't react, he would go away and this crazy nightmare would fade. But he was talking, telling her that the only equitable solution to the entail was for him to marry a Belmont. Her mother would no longer have to worry about finding dowries for all her daugh-

38

ters, since he would provide them from the estate. Lady Belmont would remove to the dower house, but she'd still have close contact with the manor. And Theo herself . . . well, she could judge her advantages for herself.

Advantages! She opened her eyes once his even tones had ceased. "I wouldn't marry a Gilbraith if he was the last man on earth," she stated, standing up now that he'd moved far enough away to allow her to do so.

"That's history," he said. "It has nothing to do with us . . . with any of us, anymore. Can't you see I'm trying to rise above a quarrel that happened in the mists of time?"

"Perhaps." She shrugged and went to the door. "Maybe I should have said I wouldn't marry *you*, cousin, if you were the last man on earth."

She left, leaving Sylvester staring into empty space. His hands were tightly clenched, and slowly he opened them, flexing his fingers. He was not going to be routed by an insolent baggage fifteen years his junior. Not while he had breath in his body.

He followed her downstairs, his step measured, consciously banishing all signs of his white-hot fury from his expression. Theo's voice came from the drawing room, shaking with emotion as she demanded to know why her mother had consented to such a hideous proposal.

Sylvester paused outside the open door, waiting for Lady Belmont's response.

When it came, it was calm and equable. "Theo, dear, no one is forcing you into anything. I consider Lord Stoneridge's suggestion to be both generous and perfectly reasonable. But if you dislike it, then there's nothing more to be said."

"My sentiments exactly, Lady Belmont." Sylvester stepped into the drawing room. "I'm desolated to have caused my cousin such distress. . . . I was perhaps somewhat premature in making my declaration."

"Perhaps you were, Lord Stoneridge." Elinor's look and tone were disapproving. "However, let's agree to bury the issue. I trust you'll join us for dinner, sir."

Ah . . . so he hadn't lost the mother's support. She considered

39

him inept, no doubt, but she didn't know that her daughter was a castle to be taken by storm or not at all. However, the door remained open.

Taking his cue, Sylvester bowed and accepted with appropriate thanks before saying, "I was hoping my cousin would ride around the estate with me, but I daresay I'm too much in her bad graces to ask for such a favor." He smiled at Theo.

The ground had been neatly cut from beneath her feet with that swift and delicate apology. She had no choice but to accede if she were not to appear childishly churlish. The trouble was, her mother didn't know what a shark lay behind that engaging smile.

"If you wish it, cousin," she said stiffly. "But we can't go far this afternoon, it's nearly four and we keep country hours. Unfashionable, I know, but we dine at six." She managed to convey both her contempt for anyone who would find the hour outmoded and her belief that Sylvester Gilbraith was such a fribble.

Sylvester had his temper on a tight rein. "Then perhaps we should postpone it until the morning," he said easily. "If I'm to join you for dinner, ma'am, I should return to the inn and change my dress."

"By all means. Until later, Lord Stoneridge." Elinor held out her hand in farewell.

Sylvester smiled, bowed to the room in general, offering no special attention to his hotheaded soon-to-be betrothed, and left, not completely displeased with the afternoon's events. At least he knew the price of his birthright now. It was certainly high, but he had a feeling it might have its compensations . . . once he'd established supremacy.

"Why must we make a friend of him!" Theo exploded. "Isn't it bad enough that we have to be neighbors without inviting him for dinner?"

"I will not be deficient in courtesy," Elinor said icily. "And neither will you. I suggest you mend your manners, Theo." She swept from the room, leaving her daughters in uncomfortable silence.

"You really have vexed her," Clarissa said after a minute. "I haven't heard her use that tone in ages."

Theo pressed her palms to her flushed cheeks. She was in a turmoil, her chaotic thoughts chasing each other in her head. "I don't understand *how* she could have considered his proposal, Clarry. It . . . it's . . . oh, I don't know what it is."

"You're not being practical," Emily said. "Such arrangements are made all the time. It's the solution to so much —"

"But he's detestable!" Theo broke in. "And he's a Gilbraith."

"Ancient history," Emily said calmly. "It's time to forget that."

"Emily, I'm getting the impression you want me to marry him!" Theo stared incredulously at her eldest sister.

"Not if you don't want to, love," Emily said. "And if you find him detestable, then there's nothing more to be said. But you're not a romantic goose, like Clarry, who's looking for a parfit gentil knight on a white charger —"

"Oh, that's so unfair, Emily," Clarissa declared. "I've no intention of marrying, *ever.*"

"Wait till your knight rides up," Theo teased, forgetting her own troubles for a minute in this familiar discussion.

But Clarissa was frowning. "I wonder why the earl chose you, Theo. Surely it should have been me, as the elder."

"I expect Mama steered him away," Emily said. "She'd know he wouldn't suit you."

Emily was more in her mother's confidence than the others and knew how Elinor regarded Clarissa's romantic leanings and how she worried over her sometimes fragile health. The Earl of Stoneridge didn't strike Emily as the embodiment of a romantic hero, or particularly gentle either.

"Well, I can't imagine why she thought he might suit *me*," Theo said, helping herself from the sherry decanter on the sideboard. "Ratafia, Emily . . . Clarry?" Her sisters found sherry too powerful a brew, but, then, their tastes hadn't been formed by the old earl, who'd educated his favorite granddaughter in all such matters with meticulous care.

She poured the sticky almond cordial for them and sipped her own sherry, frowning. "I suppose, since she knew he wouldn't suit Clarry, and for some reason she thought the idea in general to be worth pursuing, I was the only option. Unless he'd be prepared to wait for Rosie."

The thought of their grubby baby sister peering myopically at the immaculate earl as she instructed him in the anatomy of her dissected worms sent the three sisters into peals of laughter.

"Heavens!" Emily gasped, choking over her ratafia. "Look at the time. We have to change for dinner."

"We aren't supposed to dress formally, are we?" Clarissa went to the door. "Mama didn't say anything."

"No, and I for one shall wear the simplest gown I possess," Theo declared. "And I hope his lordship turns up in satin knee britches and looks like the overweening coxcomb that he is."

"I don't think he's a coxcomb," Emily said seriously, as they went up the stairs.

Theo said nothing. She wasn't yet ready to confide in her sisters what had happened in her bedroom. If that kiss hadn't been the act of a coxcomb, she couldn't imagine what would qualify. The fact that she'd enjoyed it was something she preferred to forget.

Sylvester, even if he'd been inclined to appear at the manor in full evening regalia, couldn't have done so, since he'd left all such clothes with Henry, his servant and former batman, in his lodgings on Jermyn Street.

He rode up to the manor at five-thirty, immaculately but unassumingly dressed in a morning coat of olive superfine and beige pantaloons. And he had his plan of campaign neatly mapped out. Lady Theo would discover that cold incivility had its consequences. He would concentrate his attentions on Lady Belmont and the two elder daughters. If they could be charmed into favoring his suit, it would be more difficult for Theo to defend her position.

Thus it was that Theo, bristling to do battle despite her mother's warning, was not given an opportunity.

The earl was a perfect guest, well informed, an amusing conversationalist, exerting a powerful charm. He was attentive and deferential to Lady Belmont, on whose right he sat, discussed music knowledgeably with Clarissa, and to Emily's shyly hesitant inquiry about London fashions offered an enlightening description of the new gypsy bonnet that was all the rage.

Theo sat neglected. Her hand froze on her fork when he mentioned the word "gypsy," but he cast not so much as a glance in her direction. For once in her life she could think of nothing to contribute to the conversation and felt herself to be a dull clod, toying with her green goose and peas like a child in the nursery while the adults amused themselves.

"We'll leave you to your port, Lord Stoneridge," Lady Belmont said as the covers were removed. She rose from the table, nodding toward her daughters.

"That seems unnecessary, ma'am. It's dull work sitting alone and communing with oneself." Sylvester rose with a small bow. "Perhaps I may join you in the drawing room."

"You'll be forgoing a fine port," Theo said, hearing her voice for the first time in an age. She tried to make the comment sound light, in keeping with the general tone of the evening, but had an uncomfortable feeling that she sounded merely sullen.

"You take port, cousin?" Sylvester raised an eyebrow.

"I was accustomed to doing so with my grandfather," she said, this time knowing she sounded stiff.

"Then, if Lady Belmont has no objection, perhaps you'd join me in a glass."

Caught — hook, line and sinker. Her chagrin was clear on her face as she threw up her hand unconsciously in the gesture of a fencer acknowledging defeat. Sylvester smiled at her for the first time. It was a smile so full of understanding for her predicament and the neatness of his trap that she lowered her eyelids abruptly to hide her own unwitting response.

"You're too kind, my lord. But I find I have no taste for port this evening."

"As you wish." His bow was ironic. "Then I must forgo the pleasure also."

And now he'd cast her in the role of a spiteful spoiler! Theo sat down again and reached for the port decanter. "Allow me, my lord." She filled two glasses and raised her own in a mock toast.

Elinor smiled to herself and ushered Emily and Clarissa out of the dining room.

"So what shall we drink to, cousin?" The earl raised his own

43

glass. "A truce, perhaps."

"I wasn't aware we were at outs," Theo said, sipping her port.

"Gammon!" he said bluntly.

Theo bit her unruly lip and said nothing, helping herself to a sugared almond from a chased silver dragée dish.

"Tell me about the Gentlemen," the earl invited, leaning back in his chair, crossing his legs. "I understand you're something of an expert."

"Most landowners are," she said. "At least along the coast."

"So . . . ?"

"You expect me to educate you in local customs, my lord?" There was a bitter tinge to the question.

"Yes, I do," he said simply. "I expect that . . . just as I expect you to introduce me to the estate people, show me around the land, and tell me whatever I need to know."

Theo inhaled sharply, and her fingers tightened around the stem of her glass. "I am to make it easy for a Gilbraith to take over the Belmont inheritance?"

His hand shot out along the glowing surface of the table, and his fingers closed around her wrist. "Yes," he said softly. "That is exactly what you are going to do, cousin. And shall I tell you why? You're going to do it because you love this house and this land, and you won't be able to endure watching me make mistakes."

He released his grip and sat back again, his cool gray eyes regarding her over the lip of his glass. "So let us begin with the Gentlemen."

How did he know that about her? It was true, she wouldn't be able to sit back and watch while he put up the backs of the tenants because he didn't know some small but vital personal detail, or made the wrong decision about a field or a copse because he didn't know the idiosyncracies of the land. The prospect of watching him make a fool of himself should have pleased her — but not at the expense of her land and her people.

But how had he guessed that?

"I know a lot more about you, cousin, than you might imagine," he said, as if he'd read her thoughts. He sat forward again, stretching a hand across the table to catch her chin. "I suspect we're

44

alarmingly alike."

"*Never!*" she declared with low-voiced ferocity.

"Except that I seem to be able to control my temper rather better," he said carelessly, half standing so that he could lean forward and reach her mouth with his own.

She tried to turn her head aside, but his fingers tightened on her chin, and with a curious sinking sensation Theo yielded to a kiss that was rapidly becoming familiar. Except that this time she was aware of a power behind the pressure of his lips on hers and a responding power in her own body that seemed to leap through her veins.

"There," he said, drawing back with a smile. "Point made, I believe. We'll leave further discussion for a new day, I think. You shall tell me about the Gentlemen when we ride around the estate in the morning. Let's join your mother and sisters."

He pushed back his chair and came round the table, politely drawing her chair out for her. Theo felt as if she'd been picked up by a tornado, hurled into distant space, and dropped again into a disrupted world where everything was upside down.

Elinor looked up from her embroidery as they entered the drawing room. "Tea, Lord Stoneridge?"

"Thank you, ma'am." He took a cup and strolled over to the pianoforte, where Clarissa was sitting at the keyboard. "May I turn the music for you, cousin?"

She gave him a quick smile. "If you can bear to hear my fumblings, sir."

He merely smiled, shaking his head in mock reproof for her modesty, and Theo blinked as her sister flushed delicately. It seemed as if he was beginning to resemble Clarry's parfit knight. How many parts could the damnable man play?

She took her own cup and sat down beside her mother, listening to her sister, who was an accomplished pianist. It was a remarkably domestic scene, she observed acidly to herself, her mother and Emily tranquilly occupied with their embroidery, the soft notes of the piano carrying through the open doors to the terrace, the earl's long fingers turning the sheets of music with perfect timing, his dark head bent close to her sister's brown curls. All it needed was a dog on the hearth and a kitten

45

with a ball of wool.

Clarissa was persuaded by the earl to sing a folk song, a performance as accomplished as her playing, before she laughingly begged to be excused from any further performance.

"Cousin Theo, may we hear you?" Stoneridge asked courteously, gesturing to the vacant piano bench.

Theo shook her head. "You wouldn't enjoy it, my lord. I am an indifferent player at best."

"But, then, you have other talents." He replaced the lid over the keys and strolled across to the sofa.

"Indeed, she does, my lord," Emily said swiftly. "No one is as accomplished a rider, for instance, and she has a head for figures that amazes —"

"Hush, Emily!" Theo jumped up from the sofa, unable to bear another minute of her sister's playing into the hands of this detestable, scheming Gilbraith. "My accomplishments, my lord, are few, and in general have no place in a drawing room." She walked quickly to the open door, stepping onto the terrace to cool her cheeks. Her mother's voice came clearly behind her.

"I was thinking, Lord Stoneridge, that although it will take us a few days to remove to the dower house, it seems unnecessary for you to be staying in the village. I see no reason why you shouldn't move to the manor in the morning. I'm here to chaperon the girls, and our kinship and present circumstances make your presence perfectly proper."

No! It was a silent scream of protest. Theo's fingers curled into her palms as she stood in the doorway, staring out into the star-filled night, the lighted room at her back.

To have him under the same roof . . . at every meal . . . to bump into him at every turn. It was impossible. Her mother didn't know what she was suggesting.

But perhaps she did.

In despairing fury she heard Lord Stoneridge's graceful thanks and equally graceful acceptance.

Chapter Four

The following morning Lady Belmont received a note from Lord Stoneridge: Lady Belmont was to be in no hurry to remove to the dower house. She must remain at Stoneridge Manor until the dower house was furnished and decorated exactly as she wished it to be. He would accept her kind invitation to take up residence at the manor in two days, when his servant and baggage had arrived from London. Until then he was her obedient servant, Stoneridge.

"Reprieve," breathed Theo when her mother had read out the note at the breakfast table. "Surely we can be gone from here in two days, Mama."

"But it'll be wretchedly uncomfortable with the painters and carpenters everywhere," Emily protested. "And Mama is to order new curtains and covers for the drawing room. We'll be living in a goldfish bowl until they're completed."

"It's high summer," Theo said, buttering a piece of toast. "We don't draw the curtains anyway."

"I'll have to move my museum," Rosie said, tapping the shell of a boiled egg. "It's very delicate. The snake skeleton has broken twice already, and I had to stick it together. And there are the birds' eggs. I can't think how to transport it all." She looked up from her egg with a worried frown.

"We'll pack it up very carefully in boxes," Clarissa said soothingly.

"And we'll carry it by hand down the drive," Theo added. "Nothing's going to be broken."

"That's all right, then," Rosie said matter-of-factly, returning to her egg. "I shan't mind moving in that case."

"Neither shall I," Theo declared. "Please, Mama, can't we leave before Stoneridge moves in?"

Elinor refilled her teacup. "There is not the slightest need for us to do so, dear. Lord Stoneridge is being most accommodating."

"Yes, much more than anyone would have expected of a Gilbraith," Clarissa said. "I own I quite like him now. He has a sweet smile in spite of that scar."

47

Yes, Theo thought, a sweet smile with shark's teeth. She looked helplessly round the table.

"I don't see why you should worry now, Theo," Emily said. "Lord Stoneridge has withdrawn his suit. He won't trouble you again."

How to explain that his very presence troubled her to such an extent she couldn't have a clear thought? How to explain that she knew absolutely that the earl had declared open season and she was his quarry, whatever he might say in public? How to describe those kisses and what happened to her when her body was pressed to his?

It couldn't be explained. She pushed back her chair. "Excuse me, Mama. I have to go into the village."

"Any special reason?" Elinor inquired with a smile. "Something I can help with?"

"No, no errand of mercy," Theo said, going to the door. "I have to put in our order with Greg at the Hare and Hounds. The Gentlemen ride tonight."

Elinor folded her napkin carefully. "Don't you think you should perhaps consult Lord Stoneridge now, Theo? He may have his own choices for his cellar."

Theo flushed; then she said, "Lord Stoneridge may do as he pleases. But we have the dower-house cellars to look after. At this point they stand empty."

"Very well, but remember that we have limited funds. You can't order without a thought for money as you used to do with your grandfather," Elinor reminded her gravely.

"I'll remember." Theo left the room, controlling the urge to slam the door. Tears sheened her eyes — tears of anger as well as grief for her grandfather. Why had he left them nothing? Nothing but the dower house. Not a penny for dowries, all of which had to be found from their mother's jointure. It was fairly substantial, but not enough to live as they were accustomed. It was so unlike him. He'd been a crusty old curmudgeon, but never ungenerous. And he'd loathed Gilbraiths. Yet he'd abandoned his son's family and left every sou to a Gilbraith. And he'd abandoned *her*. It was a selfish rider, and yet she couldn't help it. He'd led her to believe she was special to him . . . as precious as his son had been. But he'd abandoned her.

She rode into the village half an hour later, her face taut, and dismounted in the stableyard of the Hare and Hounds. "How's your grandma, Ted?" she asked the groom who took her horse.

"Much better, thanks, Lady Theo," the lad said, touching his forelock. "Them 'ot poultices did wonders for 'er knees. Scrubbin' the kitchen floor she was last even."

"Well, I'm sure she shouldn't be," Theo said, forgetting her own troubles in this village issue. "Not at her age. What's your sister doing?"

"Oh, she jest sits b' the fire and moans," the lad said, grinning. "Belly's big as an 'ouse now. It's as much as she can do t' sit at table. Right lazy cow she is."

Theo, totally in agreement with this description, chose not to respond. "Is Greg in?"

"Aye . . . Gentlemen are ridin' this night."

"So they are, Ted." She winked at him, receiving a conspiratorial wink in return.

She went through the kitchens, greeting the staff, helping herself to an apple tartlet cooling on a rack on the table.

"You always was partial to my apple tartlets, Lady Theo," the cook said with a pleased smile. "So's young Lady Rosie. I'll pack up a few fer ye to take back to the manor when yer done with Greg."

"Thank you, Mrs. Woods." Theo went through to the taproom, deserted at this early hour. Greg was behind the bar, laboriously counting bottles.

"Morning, Greg."

"Mornin,' Lady Theo." He turned with a smile, revealing a few blackened teeth amid large gaps.

The street door was open, and sunlight poured across the uneven stone-flagged floor, scattered with sawdust. The air was heavy with the smell of pipe smoke and stale beer, and dust lay thick on the rough planking tables. Theo flicked at a bench with her gloves and sat down with easy familiarity.

"Come with yer order for the Gentlemen, then," Greg stated, coming round from the bar counter. "I've 'ad a good few this mornin', from Squire Greenham and the vicar . . . powerful fond of a drop of port is Vicar." He grinned, wiping his hands on his baize apron. "So what's the manor goin' to be needin' this run?"

Theo's race darkened. "I'm not ordering for the manor, Greg. It's not for me to do so —"

"On the contrary, cousin."

Startled, she twisted to look over her shoulder. The earl in riding dress stood in the doorway, tapping his whip into the palm of one gloved hand, his expression hard to read against the dazzling background of the sun.

"I thought you'd gone to London," Theo said.

"No . . . but I've sent for my servant and my traps. There's no need for me to accompany the message." He ducked his head to step beneath the low lintel. "Now, what's all this about not ordering for the manor?"

Greg was regarding the inn's guest with astonishment. "Beggin' yer pardon, sir, but you're not 'is lordship, are you?"

"Yes, he is, Greg. I can't imagine why Lord Stoneridge hasn't made himself known to you before this," Theo said coldly.

"Perhaps imagination isn't your strong point," the earl said, carelessly flicking her cheek with a fingertip as he perched on the edge of the table beside her.

Theo brushed at her cheek as if a fly had settled there and said pointedly, "You'll forgive me, my lord, but I have business to transact with Greg for the dower-house cellars."

"I forgive you," he said with a bland smile, not moving from his perch. "And you'll forgive me, I'm sure, if I suggest that you also take care of the manor's needs at this time."

"Those needs are no longer my concern, sir."

"I think you will find that they are," he said, a hint of steel in his voice now, a cold glint in the gray eyes. "Have done with this nonsense, cousin."

Greg abruptly dived behind the bar counter, reemerging with a crusted bottle and three glasses. "A glass of burgundy," he suggested with a hearty chuckle. "Best eighty-nine vintage. It's the last bottle left of that consignment, but I'm hopin' the Gentlemen'll manage a few more this run."

Theo accepted the diversion with relief. She couldn't imagine

50

what the innkeeper must have thought of that terse exchange, but clearly she had to yield the issue. It would be childishly spiteful to refuse her help, but Gilbraith could have asked for it instead of demanding it.

Sylvester played no part in the exchange between Theo and Greg. He listened attentively, sipping his wine. His cousin was both knowledgeable and efficient as she listed the manor's needs. It was highly improper, however, for a young lady of breeding to be so at ease in a local taproom. Had her grandfather encouraged this familiarity? It surprised him that Lady Belmont would allow such behavior. It would have to change once they were married. Just as this racketing around the country like an itinerant gypsy would have to stop.

She glanced at him at the end and said, "I trust that will do for you, my lord."

"I trust so, cousin." He offered a mock bow. "I shall know who's responsible if it doesn't, won't I?"

Was he accusing her of deliberately misordering, just to spite him? Her eyes widened in indignation and the earl laughed.

"I'm truly grateful for your assistance," he said, setting his glass on the table.

Theo closed her lips tight on a retort and turned back to Greg. "Now, I need a separate order for the dower house. . . ."

"That's somewhat modest," the earl observed when she finally nodded her satisfaction and rose from the bench.

"A modest household has modest needs, sir," she said coldly. "Greg, that account should be sent to Lady Belmont at the dower house."

She gathered up her gloves and whip. "I'll send Alfred with the gig to collect the supplies in the morning. . . . Lord Stoneridge, I give you good day." She walked out of the taproom toward the kitchen.

Sylvester blinked, realizing that she was wearing a most unusual riding habit — it seemed to have a divided skirt. Surely she wasn't riding astride?

"Make sure both accounts come to me at the manor, Greg," he commanded. "I have an arrangement with Lady Belmont."

"Ah," Greg said, nodding wisely. "One that Lady Theo doesn't

51

know about, I daresay."

Sylvester agreed. It was an outright lie, but he had it in mind to present Lady Belmont with a housewarming gift — a tactful, graceful gesture, but one he suspected would be lost on his fiery young cousin, who, if he'd confided in her, would probably have contrived to insult him in front of the inn-keeper. He strode out of the inn and round to the stables, where be assumed Theo's horse was waiting for her.

She emerged from the kitchen, slipping the parcel of apple tartlets carefully into the deep pocket of her jacket. She saw the earl leaning against the stable wall, idly chewing a straw, and ignored him.

"Ted, my horse, please."

The lad brought the neat dapple-gray mare, and Theo swung astride her without assistance.

"An unusual choice of saddle," Sylvester commented, crossing the cobbles. "But perhaps not for a gypsy."

"It's convenient," she said shortly, gathering up the reins. "I have always ridden astride round here. No one remarks it. Good day, Lord Stoneridge."

Something else that would have to be discouraged in his countess. Shaking his head, he mounted his own horse and rode out after her. It was just his luck that the only possible Belmont daughter had to be this intransigent romp who clearly detested him. . . . Perhaps he could persuade Lady Belmont to reconsider an offer for Clarissa.

But no . . . the pursuit might be harder with Theo, but winning over such a passionate nature would be worth the effort. Besides, Theo's knowledge and expertise in estate management made her an invaluable resource.

He urged his horse into a gallop, coming up with her as she turned out of the village toward the cliff top above Lulworth Cove.

"A word with you, cousin."

"Why can't you leave me alone!" she exclaimed in a low voice.

His lips tightened. "It would be so much easier for everyone if you'd accept the inevitable with good grace," he said with calculated severity. "We are going to be neighbors whether you like it or not. You are behaving like a spoiled hoyden who should have had some manners whipped into her years ago."

"I *do* accept the inevitable," she said, flushing. "But I don't have to cultivate you. You seem to be deliberately trying to annoy me, following me around, pestering me, making me sound horrible . . . and I'm not."

She sounded so desperately aggrieved that he couldn't help being amused. Leaning over, he placed a hand over hers and said, smilingly persuasive, "I believe you, Theo, and I don't intend to make you sound horrible. But I do wish to get to know you, and you're making it very difficult for me."

Shark! Theo snatched her hand away and nudged Dulcie's flanks, turning her aside onto a ribbon track descending the cliff to the cove. The mare stepped surefooted down the steep path, clearly familiar with the terrain. Sylvester set his black to follow, holding him on a tight rein as he picked his way cautiously through the loose sand and scree.

Theo heard the horse behind her and began to feel as if she were truly hunted quarry. It was time that odious Gilbraith tasted her mettle. It was time to stand and fight.

The mare reached the smooth, flat sand of the beach, and Theo dismounted, knotting the reins on the horse's neck, waiting until the black had touched solid ground.

She tossed her hat aside and unbuttoned her jacket with slow deliberation. "Very well, my lord. Since you won't leave me alone for the asking, then I challenge you to combat. The best of three falls." She slipped out of her jacket and regarded him steadily.

Sylvester's eyes were unreadable as he met her gaze for a long minute. Then in silence he swung off his mount.

Theo placed her jacket on the sand and stood facing him, a lithe, slender figure in her white shirt, her feet braced, her legs unhampered by the divided skirt. She raised her arms and tightened the pins that held her plaits in a knot at the nape of her neck. Her breasts lifted with the movement, their crowns dark for an instant against the fine cambric shirt.

"The best of three falls, my lord. And if I win, you keep your distance from now on. Is it agreed?"

Sylvester shrugged out of his own coat and rolled up his sleeves. "Certainly," he said calmly. "And if *I* win, gypsy, I'll have some courtesies from you that might make you redefine the meaning of the word."

He could mean only one thing. Theo stared at him; her lips tingled abruptly with the memory of his kisses, and there were strange vibrations deep in her belly as her body of its own accord responded to the memory of his hardness pressed against her.

She swallowed, unconsciously absorbing his physique properly for the first time — the wide belt outlining the slender waist, slim hips, powerful thighs straining against the soft buckskin of his riding britches. He was so large! The power in those broad shoulders, the muscles rippling in his bared arms, were downright intimidating. Only a fool would be convinced she could win a combat with such a figure. . . . She might . . . but it was no certainty.

And if she lost . . . ? If she lost, he'd put his hands on her again in the way that set her body on fire; he'd put his mouth to hers. . . . Dear God, how could her body not know what her mind knew — that she loathed the man and everything he represented?

"Damn you to hell, Stoneridge!" She turned and leaped into the mare's saddle.

Sylvester watched as she rode the animal straight into the waves lapping the curving shoreline. He shook his head, half in amusement, half in annoyance. What kind of marriage was he letting himself in for, with a wife who chose unarmed combat to settle a disagreement?

He bent to pick up her jacket and his own coat, shaking the sand off them and laying them on a flat rock. Then he sat down on another rocky outcrop, stretching his legs along the sand, squinting into the sun as he watched his combative young cousin ride her mare in a mad gallop through the waves breaking gently on the shoreline.

When she turned the horse out toward the curious horseshoe-shaped rock formation at the entrance to the cove, he drew breath sharply. Surely she wasn't going to swim the animal out to sea. He half rose from his rock about to yell at her and then saw that she'd reached a sandbar about twenty feet from the shore and was cantering along it in a fine mist of spray from Dulcie's hooves.

Hotheaded gypsy! He sat back on his rock, lifting his face to the sun, closing his eyes, waiting for her to return.

Theo rode until some of her frustration had dissipated, become a part of the sea air and the salt spray. Dulcie moved beneath her with obvious enjoyment, kicking up her heels as the little waves slurped over the hard-packed ridged sand. Waves crashed with monotonous rhythm against the rocks protecting the entrance to the cove, but within their shelter the water was smooth as glass, and the sun was hot on her head and the back of her neck.

She glanced toward the beach. Sylvester Gilbraith was still there, and there was something about his posture that told her he wasn't going anywhere in a hurry. She couldn't stay in the middle of the cove indefinitely.

Turning Dulcie, she rode back to shore. Her habit was soaked to her knees, her boots sodden, her shirt sticking sweatily to her back. Her hairpins had loosened, and the two thick braids now looped on her shoulders.

She rode up the beach to where the Earl of Stoneridge in his shirtsleeves leaned back on his rock, hands linked behind his head.

"You are detestable," she stated. "I loathe you."

"Do you?" He opened his eyes and squinted indolently up at her through narrowed lids.

"Perhaps you'd be good enough to pass me my jacket," she said with icy restraint.

He shook his head. "Come and get it, gypsy."

"Damn you!" she threw at him, swung Dulcie round, and cantered off along the beach.

"This damning is becoming repetitious," Sylvester murmured, mounting his horse and setting off after her. The black ate up the distance between them, even when Theo leaned low over Dulcie's neck, urging her to increase her pace. The dapple stretched her neck in a gallant effort, but she hadn't the chest of her pursuer, and Theo drew back on the reins, allowing her to find her own pace.

The black drew up alongside. Theo cast a sidelong glance at the earl. To her infuriated astonishment she saw that he was laughing. And then she saw the gleam in his eye, the purposeful set of his mouth, and with a desperate kick at her flanks, urged Dulcie to renewed effort.

Sylvester caught his own reins between his teeth, leaned over, and lifted Theo bodily off the mare. Interestingly, it was much easier to do with someone riding astride than sidesaddle, he thought with a flicker of amusement, snatching the mare's reins and hauling her to a halt as he adjusted the rigid figure of his captive on the saddle in front of him.

"Oh, young Lochinvar is come out of the west,
Through all the wide Border his steed was the best,"

he quoted, eyes alight with laughter at her stunned expression. "And don't damn me again, cousin, or I'll be obliged to take reprisals."

Shifting his hold, he drew her tight against his chest, the black coming to a panting halt beneath them as the riderless mare snorted and kicked up sand.

Theo was still so astonished that for the moment she was dumbstruck. His fingers were on her face, tracing the curve of her cheek, the line of her jaw, the shape of her mouth.

"You have such an appealing countenance, gypsy. But I can't appreciate it when you're forever hissing and spitting at me and wanting to throw me all over the beach." Smiling, he cupped her chin and slowly lowered his head.

She tried to resist, to fight off this insidiously sweet assault, but it was a lost cause. Her body was no longer under the sway of her mind. She lay against him, feeling his supporting hand flattened and warm, pressing her damp shirt to her back, his breath on her face, the honeyed mingling of tongues. Her blood flew through her veins, her pulse beating fast in her throat, and the sun was hot and red against her closed eyelids.

His hand slid round her body, feeling for the swell of her breasts beneath the thin shirt. She was wearing nothing beneath

56

the cambric, and her nipples pressed small and hard into his palm. His fingers slid between the buttons, tracing the satin curve, and she shuddered against him with a soft moan, one arm lifting to come round his neck, pulling him closer to her, her mouth opening hungrily beneath his, her tongue now urgently pursuing its own exploration.

He raised his head, leaving her mouth slowly, reluctantly, and looked down into her face, lying against his chest. His hand was still against her right breast, and the sweat-dampened material of her shirt clung translucently to the other, outlining the swelling curve as clearly as if it were uncovered.

Her eyes opened and passion swirled in the midnight depths . . . passion and confusion.

"You really should wear a chemise," he observed, still smiling. "You invite the most scandalous attentions, gypsy." He cupped her breast beneath the shirt, flicking at the nipple with his forefinger in example.

Theo drew a deep breath and struggled to sit up. His hold tightened while the caress continued, and she yielded with a tiny sigh of defeat.

"Now, isn't this pleasanter than threatening me with combat?" he murmured, his voice lightly teasing.

"It was a challenge, not a threat," Theo said, finally roused from her sensual trance by his tone and the frustrating reflection that the damnable Gilbraith had simply taken his so-called courtesies anyway.

It had happened again, and she'd had no more strength to resist it than a baby. She thrust his hand aside and pushed herself up against his chest, blinking in the dazzling sunlight. She felt most peculiar. The black shifted restlessly at the sudden change of weight on his back, and she would have slipped to the ground if Sylvester hadn't grabbed her waist.

He chuckled but said seriously, "I might be willing to accept a friendly challenge, but I'll not settle real problems in that way. Best you remember that, little cousin . . . particularly as we're going to be under the same roof for a time."

"I wouldn't count on that," Theo said, as much for something to say as anything else. With a neat wriggle she slid out of his

57

hold and onto the sand.

"Oh, and why shouldn't I?" One eyebrow lifted in quizzical inquiry as he looked down at her.

Why shouldn't he? Not a reason in the world! Her mother seemed to have fallen for his charm without so much as a whimper.

Why couldn't she learn to keep her mouth shut? Or keep her unruly body under control? She was tingling from top to toe, every inch of her skin sensitized. As if aware of this, the detestable Gilbraith was gazing at her chest with fixed attention, and she could feel her nipples lifting under his eyes.

"A word of advice: Wear a chemise in future," he said coolly. "Or don't take your jacket off . . . unless you're prepared to follow through on the invitation you're issuing."

"You behaved like a cur the first time we met," she said, trembling now with renewed outrage. "Maybe there was the smidgeon of an excuse then . . . you didn't know who I was. But I tell you Stoneridge, you are an unmitigated cad and a coxcomb!"

She sprang onto Dulcie's back and rode off along the beach to the broad path at the far end that led up to the cliff.

Sylvester grimaced ruefully. One step forward, two steps back. There was something about the wretched girl that brought out the worst in him. She was so damned combative, she made him want to shake her into submission half the time, but despite the occasional brattishness, there was something about her spirit that sparked an answer in his own, and he'd lay any odds that she'd prove to be a wonderfully tempestuous partner in lust — with the right education.

He watched her disappearing up the path, and his loins stirred at the memory of her breasts against his hands and the eagerness of her mouth beneath his. Come hell or high water, he intended to have the schooling of his recalcitrant cousin.

He rode back along the beach to where their coats still lay over the rock. It occurred to him that her feelings were as confused as his own. Her responses were always passionate — even when she was damning him up hill and down dale. Indifference would be much harder to overcome, so perhaps the key to victory lay in keeping up the pressure and confusion.

He dismounted and collected their coats. Theo's had something in the pocket — a packet of succulent apple tartlets. Well, she'd abandoned them, he reflected, consuming them with leisurely pleasure before remounting.

As he rode up the manor's driveway, Elinor appeared from the rose garden, a pair of pruning shears in her hand, a basket of yellow and white roses over her arm.

"Lord Stoneridge." She greeted him pleasantly. "How good of you to call."

He doffed his hat and dismounted to walk beside her. "I have Lady Theo's coat and hat to return, ma'am."

Elinor's eyebrows disappeared into her scalp. "I think you'd better explain, sir."

He gave her a disarming smile. "I'm afraid we had a slight . . . a slight altercation on the beach. My cousin rode off in some haste."

"And what was she doing without her coat and hat in the first place?" Lady Belmont's eyes were sharp, although her tone seemed only mildly curious.

"My cousin challenged me to a bout of unarmed combat, ma'am," he said. This time his smile was rueful.

Elinor sighed. "A challenge you refrained from accepting, I trust."

"In a manner of speaking, ma'am," he said. "My cousin was induced to withdraw the challenge. She's not in charity with me, as a result."

"Oh, it's Edward's fault," Elinor said, shaking her head. "He taught Theo all that nonsense when they were little more than children, and whenever he's here, they practice throwing each other all over the long gallery."

"Edward?"

"Emily's betrothed, Edward Fairfax. His family are neighbors, and the children have known each other from the nursery. For a long time I believed he and Theo would make a match of it, but for some reason they all put their heads together, and the next thing I knew, Edward and Emily were betrothed." She smiled slightly. "I'm convinced it's the right match, but I still don't know what led the three of them to come to that conclusion with such amicable suddenness."

"And where is Mr. Fairfax?"

"Lieutenant Fairfax. He's with Wellington in the Peninsula," she said, casting him a sideways glance. "You were also in the war, sir?"

"Yes . . . and a prisoner of the French for a twelve-month," he replied shortly.

She merely nodded. "So you dissuaded Theo from this combat, and she's annoyed with you as a result."

"Actually, ma'am, she holds me in acute dislike." He kicked a loose stone out of Lady Belmont's path. "I'm at a loss to understand exactly what I could have done to cause it."

"Evidently you and Theo had met before you called yesterday."

"Yes . . . an unfortunate encounter," he admitted. A deep frown corrugated his brow.

Elinor glanced up at him as he walked beside her, adapting his natural impatient stride to her own strolling pace. It wasn't easy for him, she reflected, sensing again that pent-up tension in the lean, powerful frame, the depths of pain within him. She couldn't decide whether she liked him or not, but thought that she probably did . . . or at least would, on further acquaintance. She was very aware of his attraction, however, and wondered how Theo was managing to ignore it.

"You should understand something about Theo," she said matter-of-factly. "This house, the estate, the people are a part of her. It was the same for her father, and her grandfather. They mean everything to her, in a way that her sisters . . . and indeed, myself . . . can't begin to identify with. She was her grandfather's favorite. And she feels betrayed by him. You, sir, are an interloper. You're taking from her something as important as the blood that flows in her veins."

Sylvester was silent, listening to the voice of conscience. Supposing he told this woman the truth . . . that none of them had been betrayed by the old earl — at least, not in the way they thought. But why should *he*, at the expense of his own future, put right the old man's memory? He owed him nothing. The devious old man had created this mess . . . he'd set them all up.

"But I'm willing to change that, Lady Belmont," he said after a minute. "I'm offering your daughter the chance to stay here, to see this inheritance pass down to her own children."

"Yes, and it seems the perfect answer," Elinor said, pausing to clip an unruly twig of box hedge with her secateurs. "But Theo may not see that just yet."

And I don't have all the time in the world to persuade her. He suppressed the irritable reflection and adjusted his stock, his long fingers restless in the linen folds as he asked abruptly, "Will you speak for me, ma'am?"

Elinor paused on the path, regarding him steadily from beneath the wide brim of her straw gardening hat. Her voice was level but very definite. "No, Stoneridge. You must speak for yourself."

He made haste to retrieve his error. "I understand. Forgive the impertinence." He bowed, touching his hat, his eyes rueful.

She did like him, Elinor decided. And those crinkly lines around his eyes were most attractive. She smiled and patted his arm. "I don't blame you in the least, sir. When it comes to Theo, a wise man marshals all the battalions he can."

"Then perhaps I should start marshaling," he commented dryly.

Elinor followed his eyes. Theo and Rosie were coming down the path toward them, their eyes on the ground. The child suddenly darted forward, falling to her knees in the flower bed beneath the box hedge. Theo squatted beside her.

"Not more worms," Elinor sighed. "Or is it snails now? I can never keep up with Rosie's obsessions."

Theo stood up, glancing down the path, seeming to see them for the first time. Sylvester wondered if she'd give him the cut direct and walk away, but, perhaps in deference to her mother's presence, she walked toward them.

She'd changed out of her habit into a simple linen gown, less rustic than the unbleached holland smock she'd been wearing for trout tickling, but still very countrified with its plain scoop neck and elbow-length sleeves. She was hatless, and her hair hung in one thick blue-black rope down her back. He watched her approach, the way the gown moved over her hips with the easy swing of her stride.

"Dear me, Lord Stoneridge, this is an unexpected pleasure," she said, reaching them, her eyes the deep velvet blue of pansies in her sun-browned face. "I confess I wasn't expecting to see you again today."

"You left your coat and hat on the beach," he said, handing her the garments. "I thought you might have need of them . . . or at least your coat," he added pointedly. "But I see you've rectified the situation."

He had intended conciliation, but her greeting had been so derisory that he responded with immediate punishment, reminding her of those moments on the back of his horse . . . of her passionate response to the most improper attentions. His eyes skimmed pointedly over her breast, and the slight flush that warmed her cheeks was satisfaction enough. But her recovery was swift.

"I have no particular need of the coat, my lord. But I'm grateful for what's in the pocket." She held up the garment. "Rosie, I have some of Mrs. Woods's apple tartlets for you."

"Oh," Sylvester said in confusion. "I'm afraid I ate them."

"You ate them?" Theo stared at him in surprise. "But they were in my pocket. They were for Rosie."

Sylvester scratched his head, looking so confounded that Elinor was hard-pressed to keep a straight face. "I do beg your pardon," he said. "But they were so tempting . . . and I thought you'd abandoned them." He looked at Rosie, who was gazing up at him from behind her glasses with an expression of puzzled inquiry.

"Forgive me, Lady Rosalind. . . ." That sounded absurd; the child was holding a fistful of snails in one grubby palm. He tried again. "Rosie, I'm very sorry. I didn't realize they were for you."

Rosie said solemnly, "That's all right. It wasn't as if they'd been promised, or anything. They were just going to be a surprise."

Sylvester blinked. "Is that supposed to make me feel better?"

Theo went into a peal of laughter. "Yes . . . in Rosie-talk."

"Oh." He looked so chagrined that Theo took pity on him. "Never mind," she said. "Rosie and I will walk down to the

62

Hare and Hounds this afternoon and beg some more from Mrs. Woods."

"That will be my responsibility," Sylvester said, remounting. "I'll confess my thievery and beg a replacement. It's the least reparation I can make." He raised his hat. "I give you good day, Lady Belmont . . . Cousin Theo . . . Rosie."

" 'Bye," Rosie said unconcernedly, her concentration now on the contents of her palm. "Oh . . . ," she said, suddenly looking up at him. "You aren't in a hurry for us to move, are you? I have to move my museum to the dower house, and it might take a long time . . . because everything has to be packed up *very* carefully and carried by hand down the drive."

"Rosie!" Elinor exclaimed.

It was Sylvester's turn to laugh. "No, little cousin, I am not in the least anxious for you to leave the manor. I'm sure we can all manage to live in harmony for as long as it takes." He shot his other cousin a quick, quirking smile. "Isn't that so, cousin?"

"That remains to be seen, sir," Theo said, but without conviction.

Chapter Five

The door to the earl's bedroom stood open. Theo paused in the corridor outside. She'd been in that room many times, particularly in the weeks leading up to her grandfather's death. She knew the elaborate carving of the bedposts, could trace in her mind's eye the whorls and twists that her hand had played over during the interminable vigils she had kept by the bedside. She knew the rich serpentine designs on the embroidered canopy, matching the patterns in the Chinese carpet. She thought she knew every knot in the paneling, every thin fissure in the plaster ceiling.

The room was empty, and she stepped through the doorway, looking round. The furnishings hadn't changed, and yet the room felt different. Her grandfather's spirit no longer inhabited it, the faint musty smell of sickness and old age was gone. The new earl's possessions were scattered round, his silver-backed hairbrushes on the dresser, his boot jack beside the armoire, unfamiliar books in the bookshelves.

Her eye fell on the portrait of her father in his dress uniform. It hung above the fireplace, opposite the bed, where her grandfather could see it whenever he was awake. He'd had it hung there, he'd told her once, so that it was the first thing he saw in the morning and the last thing at night. And it hung there now for the indifferent eyes of a Gilbraith.

The anger and frustration — inextricable with her grief and never far from the surface these days — rose anew, closing her throat, contracting her scalp, filling her eyes with bitter tears. She stepped farther into the room, drawing close to the portrait. Viscount Belmont smiled out at her, his hand on his sword, his blue eyes as clear as rainwashed pools. She tried to conjure up her own memories of that face, of his voice, of his scent. She could remember his arms round her when he lifted her onto her pony. She thought she could remember his voice, deep and warm, calling her his madcap Theo. . . .

"Can I help you, cousin?"

She spun round at the earl's slightly ironic voice behind her. She had no right to be in this room . . . not anymore . . .

not without an invitation from its present owner. She looked at him blindly, seeing not Sylvester Gilbraith but the embodiment and cause of her grief and the deep rage that accompanied it.

She flung out a hand as if to ward him off and moved to push past him.

"Hey, not so fast!" He caught her arm, turning her sharply to face him. "What are you doing in my room, Theo?"

"What do you think I'm doing, my lord?" she demanded. "Stealing something? Spying on you, perhaps?"

"Don't be foolish," he said brusquely. "Were you looking for me?"

"Why ever would I want to do that?" she demanded, her voice heavy with scorn and the tears she wouldn't shed. "If I never laid eyes on you again, I'd be very happy, Lord Stoneridge."

Sylvester's quick indrawn breath told her she'd gone too far, but she didn't care, blindly wanting to wound the man who was standing where her father should be standing. She pulled her arm free and pushed him aside.

Sylvester seized her plait, preventing further progress. "No, you don't," he said furiously. "I am sick to death of this incivility. What the hell have I done to deserve it?"

"You don't have to do anything . . . you just have to be," she exclaimed in a low voice. "And if you're too insensitive to understand that, sir, let me tell you that that's my father's portrait hanging on *your* wall!"

Startled, he turned to look behind him, dropping her braid. Theo took advantage of her release and left him, almost running in her anxiety to get away before she was overcome by her tears.

Sylvester swore softly, but he made no attempt to go after her. He examined the portrait, wishing he'd noticed it early enough to avert that scene. He hadn't realized who it was. The house was full of family portraits.

He went in search of Foster. "Have the portrait of Viscount Belmont moved into Lady Theo's room, Foster. Unless Lady Belmont would prefer it."

"Lady Belmont has her own pictures of the late viscount, my lord," Foster informed him gravely. "But I'm sure Lady Theo will appreciate the gesture."

"Yes . . . good," the earl muttered.

That done, he turned his thoughts to dealing with Theo. He'd been in the house two days, and whenever Theo couldn't manage to avoid him, she was abominably rude to him. So far, he'd failed to persuade her even to ride round the estate with him. It was hardly a promising courtship. Perhaps that devious old devil had known he'd be on a fool's quest and had relished the thought of making a laughingstock of his unknown but detested heir.

He strode through the open doors of the drawing room onto the long stone terrace. Perhaps that was it, and he'd fallen into the trap through greed . . . through need, he amended, sitting on the low stone wall separating the terrace from the sweep of green lawn.

And it wasn't just the need for money. He needed a purpose, a function, in the world, and managing an estate the size of Stoneridge would take all his skills. He'd joined the army at the beginning of the war — or rather the first Revolutionary war. The present battle against Napoleon was a different matter from those early skirmishes with the untried ragtag French revolutionaries. For fifteen years the army had been his life. There'd been women . . . some passionate affairs . . . but they'd been part of the heady excitement of the war, the deprivations, the terrors, the fierce exultations of victory. He'd felt no urge to marry, to set up his nursery. For the last twelve years, after the death of Kit Belmont, he'd known he would come into the Stoneridge title and inheritance, and he'd been content to wait for that time before committing himself to marriage, children, and new responsibilities.

And then Vimiera had happened — twelve months in a stinking French jail in Toulouse. And then the court-martial.

He stood up abruptly, beginning to pace the length of the terrace. He'd been acquitted of cowardice. But not in the hearts and minds of his peers. He'd resigned his commission, ostensibly because of the lingering effects of his head wound, but everyone knew the real reason. He couldn't endure the turned shoulders. He would have returned to the Peninsula a marked man, the story flying ahead of him. There would be endless humiliations, some small, some large. And he didn't have the courage to face them down.

Not when he didn't know what had happened. How could he defend himself when he didn't know exactly what had happened?

Gerard had said he was on his way with reinforcements . . . that he hadn't delayed. But, goddammit, if there'd been no delay, how the hell had he been cut off so completely? He'd been hanging on for support as his men fell around him. . . . He could remember thinking . . .

Sylvester pressed his fingers into his temples, feeling the ominous tightening in the skin. *Thinking what?* He could remember nothing clearly of that afternoon, and yet something was there, a shadow of knowledge.

"Is something wrong, Lord Stoneridge?"

Elinor's soft voice broke into the spiraling confusion of his thoughts. He looked up, his expression dazed, his fingers still massaging his temples.

"You don't look well," she said, coming swiftly toward him. She reached up to lay a cool hand on his brow. His skin was clammy, and he was as pale as a ghost, his eyes no longer cool and penetrating, but shadowed with that pain she'd sensed in him from the beginning.

He shook his head, trying to calm his rioting thoughts and the desperate struggle for memory. Elinor's concerned expression penetrated the confusion, and her hand was cool on his brow. Mercifully, he felt the tension behind his temples ease, and he knew that this time he was going to be spared the agony.

"I'm quite well, thank you, ma'am," he said, forcing a smile. "A troublesome memory, that's all."

Elinor didn't press it. "Has Theo introduced you to Mr. Beaumont, the bailiff, as yet?"

"Your daughter, ma'am, has not seen fit to address a civil word to me in the last three days," he said caustically. "Let alone offer me any assistance in learning about the estate. I should tell you that I begin to lose patience."

"Well, perhaps that's for the best," Elinor said in a musing tone. "Something needs to shock her out of her present frame of mind." She bent down and pulled an errant weed from between the flagstones.

"I don't think I understand you, Lady Belmont."

Elinor straightened, examining the weed with a frowning concentration that it hardly warranted. "Theo hasn't grieved properly for her grandfather yet, Lord Stoneridge. I suspect she won't be herself again until she's able to do so. Perhaps we've indulged her sufficiently and it's time to provoke that grieving."

"I'm still not sure I understand you." Sylvester knew he was being given some valuable advice but wasn't quite sure what he was to do with it.

Elinor smiled slightly. "Follow your instincts, Lord Stoneridge, and see where they take you."

"Mama, the seamstress is here." Emily appeared round the corner of the terrace. "She has the samples for the new curtains, and there's one I particularly . . . Oh, good morning, Lord Stoneridge. I beg your pardon for interrupting." Her tone lost much of its exuberance as she offered him a small bow. "I didn't realize you were talking with Mama."

"Please don't apologize, cousin," he said, returning her bow. "Your mother and I were simply passing the time of day."

Elinor linked her arm in her daughter's, offering his lordship a half smile and a little nod, as if to say, You know what to do now. "We'll meet at nuncheon, Lord Stoneridge."

Sylvester watched them go off arm in arm. Lady Belmont seemed to think she'd been perfectly clear, but for the life of him, he couldn't interpret her words.

He strolled across the lawn, intending to walk to the cliff top, hoping that the sea air and fresh breeze would bring enlightenment. He hadn't gone more than twenty feet before he tripped over a pair of sturdy stockinged legs sticking out from beneath a bush.

"Ouch! You made me drop it!" An indignant Rosie crawled backward out of the bush and glared up at him, the sun glinting off her lenses. "You made me drop it," she repeated.

"Drop what?"

"A grasshopper. It was sawing its back legs together . . . that's how they make that noise. I most particularly wanted it for my museum. Theo was going to help me mount it."

68

Sylvester frowned at this other member of the Belmont family who held him in scant regard. "Well, I beg your pardon, but your feet were sticking out like a booby trap."

"Well, only a booby wouldn't have been looking where he was going," the child said, diving headlong back beneath the bush.

Sylvester raised his eyes heavenward. How was it that two daughters had tongues like razors and the other two were apparently as sweet-natured and malleable as a man could wish? And why, oh why, couldn't fate have offered him one of the sweet ones?

"There's no call to be uncivil," he said to the stockinged legs.

"I wasn't," came the muffled response. "But booby traps catch boobies, don't they? Otherwise they wouldn't be called that, would they?"

"There is a certain inexorable logic in that," he said with a twitch of his lips. "Nevertheless, child, you could find a more courteous way to make your point."

Shaking his head, Sylvester continued on his way.

Theo didn't appear at nuncheon, but no one seemed troubled by her absence. "I expect she's been offered hospitality with one of the tenant farmers, my lord," Clarissa said in answer to the earl's question. Her voice was a little cool, as if he had no right to question her sister's whereabouts. They had a way of closing ranks, these Belmonts.

"Theo's at home in every kitchen on the estate, sir," Emily said. "She always has been . . . since she was a little girl."

"I see." Frowning, Sylvester turned his attention to the ham in front of him. "May I carve you some ham, Lady Belmont?"

While he was sitting around the table making polite small talk and carving ham like some ancient paterfamilias, his energetic, managing young cousin was dealing with the business that kept the establishment going. It wasn't to be tolerated another day.

Elinor accepted a wafer-thin slice of ham, noticing the tautness of his mouth, the jumping muscle in his drawn cheek. She could guess the direction of his thoughts. Whether Theo agreed to marry the Earl of Stoneridge or not, Stoneridge Manor was no longer hers, and Elinor suspected that its lord was soon going

69

to make that clear to her daughter in no uncertain terms.

Theo hadn't returned when it was time to dress for dinner, and Elinor felt the first stirrings of anxiety. "Did Lady Theo mention where she was going this morning, Foster?" she asked as she crossed the hall on her way upstairs.

"I don't believe so, my lady." Foster lit the branched candelabra on the long table by the front door.

"Are you concerned, ma'am?" Sylvester had overheard the question as he left the library, a ledger under his arm.

"No . . . no, of course not." Elinor spoke with an assurance that didn't convince Sylvester, or the butler. "Theo often goes out all day. It's just that usually . . ." She shook her head. "She does usually send a message if she's going to be particularly late."

Sylvester waited until she was out of earshot on the first landing; then he said, "Is there cause for concern, Foster? Should we send some people in search?"

"I don't believe so, my lord. Everyone knows Lady Theo. If an accident had befallen her, someone would have sent word."

"But she could have had a fall in a field somewhere," he suggested.

"Possibly, my lord, but unlikely." Foster turned toward the baize door leading to the kitchen regions. Sylvester sighed. The message had been clear: The butler didn't share his family concerns with an outsider.

The butler didn't, the bailiff didn't, the housekeeper didn't. And as for the tenants and villagers, he might as well be a fly-by-night visitor for all the attention they paid him.

He stalked upstairs to his own room, where Henry was laying out his clothes for the evening.

Henry cast his lordship a quick glance and decided this was not a good evening for chat. When Major Gilbraith wore that particular look, a wise man kept a low profile. He poured hot water into the basin and busied himself brushing down a dark-blue coat and cream pantaloons while the earl washed the day's dust from face and hands and put on a clean shirt.

"Henry, how do you find the people in these parts?" the earl asked abruptly, stepping into his pantaloons.

"Find 'em . . . not sure what you mean, sir." Henry passed

his lordship a starched square of snowy linen. "Will you be wanting the diamond stud, sir?"

"Thank you." Sylvester fastened the folds of his cravat with the diamond stud and peered critically at his reflection before turning for his coat. "Do you find them friendly?"

"In the taproom of the inn, sir, folks are friendly enough," Henry said, wondering where this was leading.

"And in the house?"

"A bit wary, like," Henry admitted, smoothing the coat over his lordship's shoulders with a pat and a twitch. "Weston has a good cut, m'lord. Better for you than Stultz."

Henry had been a gentleman's gentleman before joining the army and finding himself in a French prison with the sorely wounded, fever-racked Major Gilbraith. He was more than happy now to have resumed his previous profession and, after the long months of nursing the major back to health, was a more than competent nurse when the crippling headaches struck. Indeed, he was the only person Sylvester could bear to have around him, to witness the hideous degradation of that nauseating, intolerable agony.

"Do they say much about the new earl?" Sylvester asked with a wryly quirked eyebrow.

"Not too much . . . leastways not in my hearing, m'lord."

"No, I suppose they wouldn't. What about Lady Theo?"

"Oh, she's everyone's darlin', m'lord," Henry said. "Can't do a thing wrong. The apple of his late lordship's eye."

"Mmm." Sylvester picked up his hairbrushes and tidied his close-cropped curls. "Spoiled, to put it another way."

"As I understand it, sir, she's suffering something powerful over her grandfather's death," Henry said. "Leastways that's what folks say. She's not herself, they say."

"I sincerely hope not," Sylvester murmured, slipping a lacquered snuffbox into his coat pocket before going down to the drawing room, bracing himself for another strained evening with Theo.

Emily and Clarissa were standing at the open window when he entered the drawing room. They were gazing out intently across the lawn where the evening shadows were lengthening.

"I don't imagine she'd come back this way," Clarissa said, turning back to the room with a sigh. "Not from the stables."

"No sign of the truant, then?" Stoneridge asked, trying to sound cheerfully casual. He crossed to the pier table. "Sherry, ma'am? Or would you prefer madeira?"

"Sherry, thank you. No, Theo's not back yet." Elinor's smile was tight as she accepted the glass he brought her.

"Foster seemed convinced that if there'd been some mishap, one of the tenants would have brought news."

"Yes, that's true . . . but . . ." She bent to her embroidery. "The estate is very large and there are many areas that are off the beaten track."

"Perhaps we should send . . ." Emily's soft voice faded as Theo's energetic tones came from the hall.

"They're not already at dinner, are they, Foster? I can't believe how late it is. . . . Oh, Mama, I'm so sorry. . . ." The drawing room door flew open and Theo ran across the room, holding out her hands. "I had no idea how far I'd ridden. Were you dreadfully worried?" She bent to kiss her mother, seizing her hands in a fierce grip.

"I was about to become so," Elinor said calmly, but the relief in her eyes was clear as the tension left her shoulders.

"Well, I'm back, and absolutely starved." Theo threw her hat, gloves, and whip onto a side table. "And I'm truly, truly sorry for frightening you all." She offered her mother and sisters a conciliatory smile. "Am I forgiven?"

"I'd prefer it didn't happen again," Elinor said, sipping her sherry.

"It won't." Theo poured herself a glass of sherry, ignoring the earl, who was standing by the fireplace, resting one arm on the mantel shelf, his own glass in his other hand. "It must be dinnertime," she said hungrily. "The most wonderful smells are coming from the kitchen."

Her boots were mud splattered, the skirts of her riding habit white with dust, the collar of her shirt creased and limp, her hair escaping from its pins in a blue-black cloud around her face. She looked tired, but healthily so, and thoroughly disheveled.

Abruptly, Sylvester realized that he'd reached the end of his patience. He glanced at Lady Elinor, expecting her to say something about her daughter's unceremonious entrance and appearance. Elinor merely sipped her sherry. What had she said earlier that morning about having indulged Theo's unspoken grief long enough . . . that it was time to shock her out of her present frame of mind? Elinor had told him to follow his instincts, and right now his instincts told him it was time to make a stand.

"Forgive me, Cousin Theo," he said crisply, "but I don't consider riding dress to be appropriate at the dinner table."

Theo whirled on him, her eyes dark. "And what business is it of yours, pray?"

"It happens to be *my* dinner table, cousin; therefore, I consider it to be very much my business."

Theo went white beneath the gold of the sun's bronzing. *"Yours?"*

"Mine," he affirmed quietly. "And I don't accept riding dress at my dinner table." Stretching his arm, he pulled the bell rope hanging beside the fireplace.

Foster appeared immediately in the stunned silence. "Would you ask Cook to put dinner back for fifteen minutes?" the earl requested politely.

He turned back to Theo as Foster left. "You have fifteen minutes, cousin . . . unless, of course, you'd prefer to have a tray in your room."

"Mama?" Theo swung round on her mother, her eyes both enraged and appealing.

Elinor didn't look up from her embroidery. "Lord Stoneridge is entitled to set his own rules in his own house, Theo."

How could her mother betray her in this fashion? Stunned, Theo stared at Elinor's bent head.

Lord Stoneridge glanced pointedly at the clock.

Clarissa came swiftly across the room. "Come, Theo, I'll help you change. It won't take a minute."

Theo shook herself free of her numbed daze. Her eyes focused, flitting across the earl's impassive countenance before she turned to her sister. Her voice was distant but even. "No, it's all right, Clarry. I find I'm not in the least hungry." Turning on her heel, she left the drawing room, her skirts swishing with her long, impatient stride.

Hotheaded gypsy! He hadn't intended to deprive her of her dinner, but it damn well *was* his house. Sylvester refilled his glass as Elinor calmly instructed Clarissa to pull the bell for Foster again.

"Foster, you may serve dinner immediately," she said when the butler appeared. "Lady Theo won't be joining us."

"I hope she's not indisposed, my lady." Foster looked concerned.

"I don't believe so," Elinor said, laying down her embroidery. "Shall we go in, Lord Stoneridge?"

Sylvester offered his arm, following her lead.

Chapter Six

Theo's empty seat glared at them throughout a miserably uncomfortable dinner. Elinor did her best to maintain a steady flow of small talk with her daughters and the earl but knew that she fooled none of them, although the earl at least kept up his end of the conversation in the face of his cousins' reproachful eyes. Elinor found herself wondering why he persevered with Theo in the teeth of such violent opposition. The material benefits of this marriage would be all on Theo's side. If she couldn't see that, why didn't the earl simply wash his hands of his generous impulse?

The meal finally wound to a desultory close, and Elinor, clear relief in her eyes, rose with Clarissa and Emily. "We'll leave you to your port, Stoneridge."

He stood up politely as they left the room and then with sudden decision picked up the port decanter in one hand, two glasses between the fingers of his other, and followed them out. He crossed the hall and ascended the stairs two at a time, unaware of Foster's startled observation.

Outside Theo's room he paused, raising his arm to knock with his elbow, and then changed his mind. This was an offensive where surprise was probably his strongest weapon. Using the little finger of the hand that held the glasses, he lifted the latch and nudged the door open with his knee.

The light was dim, but he could see Theo sitting on the window seat, a hunched white figure with her knees drawn up, her chin resting atop them.

"Why are you sitting in the dark?" he asked, stepping into the bedroom.

"Since it's your house, my lord, I imagine you've dispensed with such courtesies as knocking before entering," she commented bitterly.

"Not at all," he returned without rancor, hitching a chair with his foot out from the corner of the room. "But I assumed that if I had knocked, you'd have turned the key in my face."

He sat astride the chair, facing her, his arms resting along

75

the back, supporting his burdened hands. Deftly, he filled the two glasses from the decanter and extended his arm toward her. "Port, cousin?"

Theo uncurled from the window seat and reached for one of the glasses.

"I'm not sure how much good it's going to do you on an empty belly," Sylvester observed, setting the decanter on the floor at his feet.

"And whose fault is that?"

"Yours, and you know it. You didn't have to stomp off in a tantrum."

Theo sipped her port. It slid comfortingly down her tight throat and settled in her stomach with a warming glow.

"You insulted me," she said, adding acidly, "not that that's unusual."

"And you've been insulting me at every opportunity since we met. We can't go on mauling each other in this manner, Theo."

There was silence in the dusk-filled room. Sylvester regarded her over his glass. Her discarded riding habit lay in a crumpled heap in the corner of the room, and she was wearing nothing but her chemise and drawers, her hair tumbling lose down her back. It was the first time he'd seen it unbraided, and he realized it was long enough for her to sit on.

She seemed unaware of her scantily clad appearance, frowning into the gloom, lost in her own thoughts. Then she said abruptly, as if there were no bones of contention between them, "Thank you for the portrait."

It was the first time she'd said anything civil to him, and he blinked in genuine surprise. She'd been staring at her father's picture, now hung on the wall behind him, when he'd entered the room.

"I'm sorry it didn't get moved earlier," he said. "It was an oversight."

"Why? Why did it have to happen?" With shocking suddenness she hurled her empty glass to the floor as she sprang to her feet. The glass shattered but she didn't notice. Tears poured soundlessly down her cheeks, and her face was contorted with anguish. Her voice filled the room in a low torrent of rage at

76

fate's injustice. "It's so unfair! He was so young . . . he meant so much to everyone . . . he was so important . . . and now everything's gone . . . lost . . . wasted. . . ."

She was grieving for her father as well as for her grandfather, and sometimes, through the wild, tumbling storm of words, Sylvester found it hard to distinguish which man at any one moment was the focus of her sorrow. But it didn't matter. Sylvester understood pain and loss and the raging fires of injustice, and he knew that for the moment she wasn't aware of him in the room. The whole fetid seething cauldron of grief poured from her in words and tears, and she stood still in the middle of the room, her hands clenched in tight fists.

Only when she kicked blindly at a piece of broken glass with her bare foot did he move. Swinging himself off the chair, he caught her against him, lifting her clear of the floor.

"Be still," he murmured into her hair. "You'll cut your feet to ribbons."

She struggled in his hold, although he sensed that she was so far gone in her agony that she'd no sense of who or what he was. He held on to her, stepping backward to the window seat, sitting down with her, clamping her against his chest, feeling the heat of her skin beneath the thin chemise, the desperate shifting of her thighs and buttocks in his lap, and despite the circumstances, his body hardened in response to the sinuous wriggles.

Eventually, her struggles ceased as the violent paroxysm of weeping eased a little. She still sobbed but rested against him, her face buried in his chest. He stroked her hair, murmuring soothing nonsense words.

He didn't notice when the door softly opened and then closed just as softly. Elinor stood outside, her hand on the latch, deep in thought. She'd come up to check on Theo, and the sound of her desperate sobbing had reached her through the closed door. She'd not been expecting the sight that greeted her on the other side of that door.

Well, she'd told the earl to follow his instincts when it came to his dealings with Theo. It seemed he was taking the instruction to heart. Probably she should wrest her daughter from his arms. But Elinor didn't think she would. She returned downstairs to await developments.

Slowly, the tempest subsided, reality asserted itself, and when Theo renewed her struggle to free herself from the iron arms holding her, it was no longer a blind reaction to her anguish.

Sylvester, recognizing her return to the world, loosened his grip immediately. Theo raised her head and stared up into the gray eyes that were for once not cool, ironic, or mocking.

"What's happening? What are you doing?" she demanded, sniffing, wiping her running nose with the back of her forearm.

"I'm not doing anything," he said. "You're sitting on my knee looking like the fall of Troy, and all I've got to show for it is a ruined coat." He brushed at his sodden coat with a rueful grimace before pulling a handkerchief out of his breast pocket. "Hold still."

Theo submitted to having her nose wiped because she was too taken aback to protest. She pushed tear-soaked strands of hair from her wet cheeks and drew a shuddering breath through her mouth deep into her aching lungs. Her nose was blocked, her throat was sore and scratchy, and he felt as weak as a kitten.

But she also felt drained and peaceful, as if some poison had been drawn from her. Her head fell against his shoulder, and she lay with her eyes closed, waiting for strength to flow back into her weakened limbs.

With some calculation Sylvester decided he didn't have much option but to stay as he was until she was ready to move.

He traced the curve of her cheek with his finger. She shifted on his lap again with predictable results. Deliberately, he slid his hands beneath her, cupping her backside in his palms as if preparing to tip her immediately off his knee, but for longer than was strictly necessary, his hands stayed where they were.

"Up." At last, with a brisk movement, he propelled her to her feet. "I'm sorry to unsettle you, gypsy, but having you on my lap with nothing but those flimsy undergarments covering your nether regions is more than flesh and blood can bear."

Startled, Theo looked down at herself and realized what he meant, and suddenly she was acutely conscious of the intimate lingering warmth of his hands on her bottom. She flushed but flew to the attack. "I didn't put myself in your lap," she said, but her throat was too scratchy for her usual vehemence. "And I didn't invite you in here, either."

She shivered suddenly as her heated skin cooled in the night air, emphasizing the scantiness of her attire. She took a hasty step backward, instinctively trying to put some distance between them, as if it would lessen the indelicacy of the situation.

She cried out as her foot scrunched heavily on a shard of broken glass.

"For God's sake, that was what I was trying to avoid in the first place." Sylvester leaped up and pushed her sharply so that she fell back onto the bed, her bleeding foot waving in the air. "Stay there until I've picked up this mess."

Theo lost interest in displays of outraged modesty. They seemed pointless and certainly too late. She hitched herself into a cross-legged position on the bed and peered at her cut sole. "Did I break the glass?"

"Yes." He looked up from his knees, shards gathered in his cupped palm. "Don't you remember?"

She shook her head. "I think I must have lost my senses."

"I trust you have them back again," he said with a dry smile, getting to his feet. "I think that's all of it." He put the glass on the dresser and dipped a washcloth into the cold water in the jug. "Let me look at your foot."

Theo stuck it out for his inspection, falling back onto the bed. She wasn't at all sure that she had regained her senses. If she had, why was she lying here in her underwear submitting to the ministrations of a man she loathed? But perhaps she was just too exhausted to care. She closed her swollen eyes.

The next minute she felt cool water on her hot face, the cold washcloth applied to her eyes. "Better?"

She opened her eyes. "Yes . . . thank you." There was a flickering smile in the gray eyes, and for the first time she thought he didn't look in the least like a man one should . . . or could . . . loathe. It was almost as if she'd never seen him clearly before, but always through the veil of her anger and grief.

"You need to eat something," he said, tossing the damp cloth back into the washbasin. "I'll go and organize a tray while you get yourself into bed. Then we're due for a little talk."

Theo pulled herself up against the pillows and took stock. She felt as if she'd been put slowly through a metal wringer and in no fit condition to engage in a "little talk" with Lord Stoneridge, the subject of which she could guess easily enough.

The decanter of port and the earl's intact glass were still on the floor beside the chair. She slid off the bed and gingerly stepped over, filling the glass and taking a sip. Port was supposed to be fortifying. On this occasion it went straight to her knees, and hastily she sat on the bed again, cradling the glass between her hands.

Her eyes went to the portrait that had somehow unlocked the grief. Her father smiled at her through eternity. His inheritance could be hers. If she was prepared to pay the price. She sipped her port.

Elinor emerged from the drawing room as Sylvester came down the stairs. "You've been with Theo, Stoneridge?" It was couched as a question.

Sylvester paused on the bottom step, his hand on the newel. "Yes, ma'am," he said. "I was intending to ask Foster to have a tray prepared for her. She was hungry when she returned."

Elinor regarded him thoughtfully. "Do you intend to take the tray up to her yourself?"

"With your permission, Lady Belmont." Their eyes met.

"It seems you've already dispensed with it, sir," she said dryly. "I trust your coat isn't ruined beyond repair."

Sylvester's gaze followed hers. He plucked at the damp patch on his breast. "If it is, it was for a good cause, ma'am."

Elinor nodded. He really was showing the most remarkable persistence. "Well, I suggest you capitalize on your present advantage," Elinor said, turning to the drawing room. "Theo recovers very quickly from setbacks."

"You do surprise me," the earl muttered in sardonic undertone as Lady Belmont disappeared into the drawing room. He called for Foster, who appeared from the kitchen regions with his usual stately tread.

"Lady Theo needs some supper," Sylvester said. "Prepare a tray and bring it into the library. I'll take it up myself."

Foster's countenance was a mask of disapproval. A lady's bedchamber was no place for a gentleman, particularly one who went up armed with a port decanter.

"Perhaps one of the maids could take it up, my lord."

"I'm sure one of them could," his lordship said impatiently. "But *I* am going to take it up."

"Very well, sir." With a stiff bow Foster returned to the kitchen.

Five minutes later Foster entered the library with a laden cloth-covered tray. "I've placed a glass of claret on the tray, sir. The same that you had at dinner. It's one of Lady Theo's favorites." The butler was still radiating disapproval.

"I'm sure she'll appreciate it."

Sylvester took the tray and strode past the stiff figure and up the stairs.

"For heaven's sake, do you never do as you're told?" he exclaimed as he entered Theo's room. "I told you to get into bed. What are you doing?"

"Drinking port," Theo said in a rather dreamy tone. "It's supposed to be fortifying."

"And is it proving to be so?" he asked with a quizzically raised eyebrow, setting the tray on the dresser. It was almost full dark now, and he lit the candles on either end of the dresser.

"I don't know about fortifying, but it's certainly making me feel a little woozy."

Sylvester sighed. At this rate she was going to be in no fit state to hear him out, and he was mindful of Lady Belmont's caution. In the morning she'd probably be as obdurate and uncivil as ever. "Get into bed," he directed.

"It's too early to go to bed." Theo stood up, assessing her balance with a frown. Then she gave a little satisfied nod. "I have a very strong head, you should understand."

Strong head or no, she was not entirely sober. The sooner the contents of the tray went into her belly, the better. "You'll find it easier to eat your supper in bed," he stated, scooping her back onto the bed, pulling down the covers, and inserting her between them. The ease with which this maneuver was accomplished struck him as sufficient indication of Theo's presently feeble state. He pulled the pillows up against the headboard and sat her firmly against them.

"Now, cousin, you will eat your supper."

Theo blinked, wondered fleetingly if protest for its own sake was sensible, inhaled the rich aroma from the tray he set on her knees, and decided it wasn't.

"I think you'd better forgo the claret, however," Sylvester stated, flicking away the cloth.

"No!" Theo grabbed at his wrist as he reached to remove the glass. "I can't eat without wine . . . besides, isn't this the ninety-eight St. Estèphe?"

"I believe so." Sylvester yielded the issue. He understood it too well for argument.

Theo examined the contents of the tray. A bowl of mushroom soup, a cold roast-chicken breast, a custard tart. "This wasn't what you had for dinner," she stated. "I could smell suckling pig."

"But you chose not to appear at the dinner table," he reminded her evenly. "I should be thankful for small mercies if I were you." He swung the chair to face the bed and sat astride it again, folding his arms along the back.

Theo contemplated an acid retort and then decided that she didn't really have one. She dipped her spoon into the soup.

Port clearly had a mellowing effect, Sylvester reflected, refilling his own glass that Theo had left empty on the floor. He decided to wait until she'd eaten something before beginning the talk he had in mind, so he sipped his port and watched her.

The effects of that violent storm were fading fast and, under the influence of supper, disappeared almost completely. Her eyelids were back to normal again, and her nose was no longer red. In the soft glow from the candles, her hair shone with its usual luster and her complexion had lost its drawn pallor, returned now to rose-tinted gold.

The chemise left her arms and neck bare, and the creamy skin glowed in the candlelight. His eyes drifted to her bosom, to the lace edging that sculpted the soft rise of her breasts, accentuating the deep cleft between them. His own thighs remembered the feel of hers, the unconsciously sensuous wriggling of her buttocks beneath the paper-thin lawn of her drawers.

Such voluptuous reflections were not conducive to the rational attack he was preparing to mount. He put them aside and said briskly, "Would you explain as simply as you can, cousin, exactly what it is about me that you dislike?"

The question took Theo so much by surprise that she choked on a mouthful of chicken. He reached over and slapped her back vigorously before continuing. "Is it my appearance? There's not much I can do about that. My manner . . . conduct toward you? That's been dictated by you, cousin, so if you wish that to change, you'll have to change your own conduct toward me. . . . What else could it be?"

Theo took a considering sip of her wine. Her earlier fuzziness had vanished with her supper, and she was clearheaded again, although still exhausted. The earl was regarding her with a raised eyebrow, waiting for his answer to a question that she found rationally unanswerable.

It wasn't his appearance . . . far from it. If she allowed herself to admit it, he was far and away the most attractive man she'd ever had dealings with — not excluding Edward, whom she'd loved for years. And if she allowed herself to remember the feel of his body, the taste of his tongue, the scent of his skin . . .

No! Best not to permit those memories. They muddled all cool thought.

His manner toward her was certainly objectionable — arrogant, controlling, uncivil. But she stood charged on the same counts, and honesty obliged her to admit her guilt. He was very different with her mother and sisters, which seemed to indicate that she *was* singled out for special treatment.

"Having trouble with your answer, cousin?" Sylvester inquired with that familiar ironic tinge to his voice.

Her cheeks warmed slightly. "Not in the least," she said, pushing the tray off her knees. "You are a Gilbraith."

The earl sighed. "That old chestnut won't do anymore, Theo. I was brought up to have no more love for Belmonts than you have for my branch of the family, but it's childish and stupid."

Theo's lips tightened. "I don't believe it is."

Making a supreme effort at self-control, Sylvester began to count on his fingers: "I am not responsible for the old quarrel;

83

neither can I be held responsible for being a Gilbraith, I didn't choose my parents; I am not responsible for your father's death; and finally, cousin, I am not responsible for the entail."

All of which was perfectly true. But some stubborn demon in her soul wouldn't yield so easily. "Maybe so, but I can't like you," she said with blunt dispassion, ignoring the little voice that asked how she could be so sure, when she hadn't given him a chance.

"I see." The earl's face closed. "Then there's nothing more to be said." He rested his chin on his folded arms, and his eyes were as cold as she'd ever seen them. "Except this. You should understand from now on that you're to have no say in matters of the estate." He ignored her swift indrawn breath, continuing in the same flat, unemotional tone, "I shall instruct Beaumont that he is no longer to consult you. If he has difficulties with this, then he will be replaced."

He stood up, a towering figure in the fragile child's room. "Neither will you continue to interfere in the affairs of my tenants, cousin. They serve one master — the Earl of Stoneridge — and that will be made very clear to them. As of now you have no further influence. If you attempt to circumvent these instructions, I shall forbid you the freedom of the estate. Is that quite clear?"

Theo felt as if she'd been punched in the stomach. She hated him because he had the power to do this, but somehow she hadn't imagined it happening. Even from the dower house she'd believed she would continue to wield the real influence, the earl merely titular head of the estate.

She shook her head, moistening her dry lips. "You can't mean that. . . . You don't know anything about the people, about the land."

"I can learn, cousin. And since you've refused me your help, then I shall learn without it." He walked to the door. "I bid you good night."

She sat stunned in the silent room, hearing the click of the door latch, his footsteps receding down the corridor. The pursuit was over. He would leave her strictly alone now, which was what she wanted . . . what she'd been fighting to achieve.

They'd move to the dower house, and there'd be nothing but

the most superficial contact between the two houses. There'd be no dowries, of course. He wasn't obligated to provide them, not when there was no familial connection. But Emily was already settled, and Clarry would marry only the embodiment of her romantic fantasy — and such an embodiment would surely be prepared to dispense with such a mundane consideration. Rosie was too young for it to be a concern. As for herself . . .

She dashed an angry tear from her eyes. She didn't want a husband, but she *did* want Stoneridge. If she agreed to help him get to know the place and its people, would he rescind the ban? No! She'd be damned if she'd succumb to blackmail.

She flung back the bedclothes and got wearily out of bed, setting the empty tray on the dresser, tidying the room in desultory fashion before changing her underclothes for her nightgown. She lay in bed wide-eyed in the darkness, listening to the familiar creaks and groans of the old house as it settled for the night. She'd known for twelve years that she had no claim on the house, but coming face-to-face with that reality was a different matter.

Despite her fatigue, sleep eluded her. She tossed and turned until the sheets twisted themselves around her hot limbs and the pillow felt like a burning stone. She kicked off the sheets and tried to lie still, hoping the cooler night breezes coming through the open window would help her to relax.

Downstairs in the library, the Earl of Stoneridge stood at the window, looking out at the moon-washed lawn. He'd lost. Defeated by a stubborn, self-willed, spoiled, rag-mannered young gypsy who refused to look beyond blind prejudice and see what was good for her . . . for all of them.

He'd lashed out in fury and disappointment at her flat rejection. He'd seen to it that she'd suffer until the true conditions of the will were made known. But for some reason the thought of her distress gave him less satisfaction than it should.

He'd had his chance and he'd failed. The bitterness rose in his throat. What a perfect revenge the old earl had devised. A wonderful three-part revenge — first the humiliation of a forced courtship to an insolently contemptuous wildcat who would never make a man a decent wife, then the hideous mortification of rejection, and then the wretched existence of an idle, impoverished nobleman with a grand house and no means to maintain it.

What other kind of a life was there for him, a disgraced soldier in the midst of war? Society might ignore the whispers if they concerned a wealthy earl in full possession of a magnificent inheritance. But the spectacle he would now present would be pathetic.

He passed a weary hand over his face, then blinked rapidly and stared out of the window. A figure was flitting across the lawn to the rose arbor. An unmistakable figure in the moonlight, with that cascade of raven's-wing hair falling down her back, and her lithe, swinging stride.

What the hell was she doing at this time of night? He glanced at the clock. It was two in the morning. Flinging the library window wider, he straddled the sill and jumped down into the soft earth of the flower bed beneath. He ran across the lawn, entering the fragrant arbor, his feet loud on the flagged pathway beneath the arch.

Theo heard the steps and spun round, her hair flying round her with the abrupt movement. She had one hand at her throat, her heart pounding with fright.

"What the devil are you doing out here?" Sylvester demanded, reaching her. The terror lingered in her eyes, purple in the darkness, and he put his hands on her shoulders in a gesture that combined both exasperation and reassurance.

"What are *you* doing?" she gasped, twitching out of his grasp. "You frightened me."

"Well, so you should be frightened," he declared. "Running around outside at this hour."

"There's nothing to scare me, except you," she said crossly, her heart slowing. "Everyone knows me around here. No one would harm me."

"Maybe so, but it's still insane." He took her shoulders again. "Where were you going?"

"Why should that matter to you?" she said. "You haven't yet forbidden me to walk around the gardens . . . or did I miss something?"

"You know, I've never before had the slightest urge to offer

86

a woman violence," the earl said in a tone of mild curiosity. "But you, cousin, are in a category all of your own."

Theo stepped backward away from his hands. It seemed a prudent move. She drew the folds of her thin cloak around her and regarded him as steadily as the renewed thumping of her heart permitted. She took a deep breath and said what she'd told herself she wouldn't say.

"I will agree to help you in your work on the estate, sir, if you still wish it."

"Such concession, cousin." He stepped forward. Theo took another step backward. "But I'm not sure that I do still wish it." There was an openness in her face, a vulnerability about her eyes . . . the result of explosive emotions and the shocks and surprises of the evening. *Take advantage of her disadvantage.* There was still, he thought, one last possible tactic.

With a swift movement he caught her arm and swung her into his body, twisting the folds of the cloak securely round her, imprisoning her limbs before she could employ them to devastating effect. "This is what I wish."

Theo was engulfed in a kiss of savage force, a kiss that bore as little resemblance to lovemaking as a pistol shot, and yet, perversely, she was responding with the same passion, whether it be anger or desire, she neither knew nor cared. Her body was clamped so tightly to his that she could feel the buttons of his coat pressing through the flimsy cloak and nightgown into her flesh. Again she was aware of the hard shaft rising against her belly, and again she pressed herself into him, moving her body against his with a soft moan of need.

His hands moved down to her buttocks, clamping her against him, and she arched her back, her breasts aching for the touch she remembered from the beach, her head falling back as his mouth devoured hers.

Silver moonlight sliced through the night-closed rosebuds wreathed over the arch above them, throwing her face into relief as he raised his head, his breathing ragged, his loins heavy.

Her eyes opened, sensual currents racing in the dark depths of her gaze as she met his own eyes and read the same message there.

"I don't want your help, cousin," he said slowly. "I want your partnership." He bent to take her mouth again, and his hands moved now inside her cloak, lifting her nightgown, baring her legs, her thighs, his hands smoothing over her skin, sending shivers from her scalp to her toes. He stroked upward, over her bottom, and she jumped at the shocking intimacy of the touch, then lost all sense of shock as his flat palm slipped between her thighs, and the most secret parts of herself were invaded in a deep caress that opened gates of pleasure she could never have imagined.

"Partnership," he murmured against her mouth. "In this and in everything, Theo. Join with me, and I promise I'll show you a landscape you wouldn't believe existed." His fingers parted her, opened her, moved within her, and Theo heard her own ecstatic cry shivering in the moonlight.

He held her against him until strength returned to her limbs and her breathing slowed. He ran his flat palm over her mouth, and her own scent and taste was on his skin. Then, smiling, he tilted her chin. "Are you willing to renegotiate, cousin?"

Theo nodded slowly. In this strange half world of rose-scented moonlight, when she no longer seemed to know exactly who she was, when all the tumbling confusion and distress of the last days receded into the mists of fatigue, it was a decision that seemed to make itself . . . a decision that now seemed inevitable.

"Partnership?" His voice was low and intense, his thumb caressing her mouth, his eyes smoky with passion.

She could partner this man. They were alike in so many ways. Perhaps that was what she'd been resisting, what had frightened her with its power. "Partnership," she agreed in a low voice.

Triumph and a sweet wave of relief surged through him. He'd snatched victory from the jaws of defeat. "Good," he murmured with quiet satisfaction.

He gathered her to him again and kissed her, this time with a gentleness that startled and delighted her as much as the earlier fierceness.

And then he released her, putting her away from him, wrapping her cloak around her. "You must go to bed now, Theo. We'll talk to your mother in the morning."

88

She allowed him to escort her back to the house and up to her room, to remove her cloak, to tuck her into bed as if she were an exhausted Rosie.

"Sleep," he said softly, kissing her brow.

And she did.

Chapter Seven

"Theo . . . Theo, love, are you awake? It's gone nine." Clarissa's voice from the doorway brought her sister swimming up from the depths of a black and dreamless sleep.

She opened her eyes, stretched, and yawned. "Is it really that late?"

"Yes, and you went to bed so early." Clarissa came into the room, an anxious frown between her eyes. "Emily and I wanted to come to you last evening, but Mama wouldn't permit it." She sat on the edge of the bed, regarding her sister with the same anxious frown. "Are you feeling quite well?"

"Yes, of course." Theo sat up, blinking the sleep from her eyes. "I feel a bit as if someone hit me over the head with an ax, but . . . Oh, God . . ." She stared at her sister as memory flooded back. No wonder she'd slept so late; it had been almost three before she'd gone to bed . . . been put to bed.

"What is it?"

Theo combed her hands through her hair, tugging at the tangles. "I believe I said I'd marry Stoneridge," she announced slowly. "Clarry, I must have been mad."

"Oh, Theo, are you all right?" Emily spoke from the door before Clarissa could respond to Theo's startling statement.

"I don't think I can be," Theo said. "I'm heading for Bedlam. Oh, God!" She fell back on the bed and pulled the covers over her face. "Tell me it didn't happen."

"What didn't happen?"

"She agreed to marry Stoneridge," Clarissa informed her elder sister with a grin.

"Oh, I am glad," Emily said with heartfelt warmth. "He's such a nice man, Theo. I'm sure you'll suit . . . and you won't have to leave the manor now."

Theo flicked the covers from her face and said vigorously, "Stoneridge is *not* a nice man. . . . He's many things, but nice is not one of them."

Clarissa nodded. "Yes, I agree. It's too . . . too sloppy a word to describe him."

"Well, forgive me," Emily said with some asperity. "I don't have your linguistic precision, clearly. Anyway, *I* like him, and so does Mama."

"But *I* don't," Theo wailed. "I detest him."

"But you can't," Clarissa said practically. "You wouldn't agree to marry a man you detested."

"Oh, you don't know how persuasive he can be," Theo said bitterly. Those moments in the rose arbor were embarrassingly vivid, his hands on her, *inside* her. Dear God, how had she ever let it happen? But she hadn't let it. It had just happened.

"Well, it's understandable that you'd have cold feet," Emily said with the brisk wisdom of one who'd been there before. "When Edward and I agreed to marry, I felt sick with nerves for days . . . worrying whether I was doing the right thing."

"Edward is not Stoneridge," Theo pointed out. "Edward *is* a nice man." She pushed aside the covers and got to her feet. "I'll have to tell him I made a mistake."

"Theo, you can't possibly do that!" Emily was genuinely shocked. "That's just like a common jilt . . . a flirt . . . Mama would never permit it."

"Mama wouldn't expect me to marry a man I loathed just because of an indiscreet moment," Theo stated.

"An indiscreet moment?" Clarissa inquired, her eyes alight with curiosity. "What happened?"

Theo felt herself blushing. "Nothing . . . it was nothing."

"Oh, come on, Theo. What happened? I'd dearly love to have an indiscreet moment."

Clarissa on the track of truth was like a terrier with a rat.

"I expect Theo means that the earl kissed her," Emily said with the same knowledgeable air as before. "It's perfectly proper between engaged couples. . . . It's not at all indiscreet."

"But perhaps Theo means the earl kissed her before they became engaged," Clarissa said with a gleam in her eye. "Now, that would be indiscreet, wouldn't it?"

"Oh, be quiet, both of you!" Theo pulled off her nightgown and went to the dresser, bending to splash cold water on her face.

"Well, did he?" persisted Clarissa.

"If you must know, he did a great deal more than that," she said, her voice muffled by the towel as she dried her face.

"Theo!" exclaimed Emily.

"*What* did he do?" demanded Clarissa, regarding her sister's naked body with a new interest.

"I'm not saying." Hastily, Theo grabbed her chemise and pulled it over her head.

"Well, of course the earl is quite old," Emily observed judiciously. "A lot older than you, and much more worldly, I'm sure."

"Well, he would be — he was a soldier," put in Clarissa.

"But so is Edward."

"And I'll lay odds Edward's a lot more worldly now than he used to be," Theo said, glad to turn the spotlight away from herself. She rummaged through the armoire for a dress . . . something as plain as she could find. When she told Stoneridge she'd made a mistake, she didn't want him to remember what had led to the mistake.

"Have you told Mama yet?"

"No . . . It only happened a few hours ago. Everyone was asleep."

"You had an assignation in the middle of the night?"

"Not exactly. . . . It wasn't an assignation . . . it was an accident." She pulled a hairbrush through her hair before deftly plaiting it. "In fact, this whole damn business has been one mistake after another."

"That's a bad word, Theo."

The three sisters whirled to the door. "Rosie, you really must learn not to creep up on people," Clarissa scolded.

"I wasn't. What's a jilt?"

"How long have you been hiding there?" Theo demanded, her mind racing backward, trying to remember what they'd been saying. It definitely hadn't been suitable for the child's ears.

"I wasn't hiding. I was just standing here," Rosie protested. "Is anyone going to come and catch butterflies with me?" She flourished the white net she held.

"No, not at the moment," Emily responded distractedly. Like Theo, she was trying to remember exactly what they'd said.

92

Rosie came into the room, hitching herself onto the bed. "So what's a jilt? Is Theo going to marry the earl?"

"One of these days those big ears of yours are going to get you into deep trouble," Theo threatened, scowling fiercely at her little sister.

"Is this a private party, or can anyone join in?" Elinor appeared smiling in the open doorway. "I was wondering why I was breakfasting alone. How are you feeling, Theo, dear?"

"I haven't been ill, Mama," Theo said.

"No, she's going to be a jilt," Rosie said. "But they won't tell me what that is. . . . Oh, and she's going to marry the earl."

Her elder sisters sighed; their mother frowned. "Theo isn't marrying anyone, child, without my permission. And since there's been no discussion in my hearing on the subject, you may assume you misheard. Is that understood?"

"Yes, Mama." Chastened, Rosie slipped off the bed. "I just wanted someone to catch butterflies with me."

"Off with you." Her mother shooed her out the door before turning to the others. "Clarissa, Emily, I'd like to talk to Theo in private." The two exchanged a quick look with Theo and made themselves scarce, closing the door behind them.

Elinor sat on the window seat, regarding Theo gravely. "Now, perhaps you'd like to tell me what's going on."

Theo sighed and flopped onto the bed. "It's a mess, Mama. . . ."

Elinor received a greatly edited version of the previous night's events, but if she guessed at the missing pieces, she gave no indication.

"So in the cold light of day you've changed your mind?"

"Yes," Theo said baldly.

"Then you'd best explain that to the earl with all dispatch," Elinor said, rising to her feet. "It's a most unpleasant thing to do to anyone under any circumstances, and you owe it to Stoneridge not to leave him in ignorance of the true state of your regard another instant."

"You're vexed," Theo stated.

Her mother turned at the door. "I simply wish that you had

managed things with more principle, Theo. To agree to marry a man in one breath and withdraw it in the next smacks of an indelicacy that I find hard to accept in one of my daughters. I'm not going to imagine what went on between you and the earl last night, but if it gave him permission to believe you held certain feelings for him, I trust you will find it very uncomfortable to disabuse him."

She went out, leaving Theo ready to weep with frustration. Her mother had put her finger on the problem with disturbing accuracy. . . . And why was Elinor so set on this match? Theo was in no doubt that her mother was on the earl's side and had been from the first minute.

So it was going to be uncomfortable telling him. But better to endure even excruciating embarrassment for a few minutes than a lifetime of misery. Her face set, she went downstairs in search of Stoneridge.

Foster hadn't seen his lordship. He didn't believe he'd breakfasted as yet, although it was nearly ten o'clock, and his lordship was known to be an early riser.

Puzzled, Theo went back upstairs, pausing outside the closed door to the earl's bedroom. It opened as she stood there in frowning indecision, her hand half-lifted to knock.

Henry came out, closing it softly behind him. "Can I be of assistance, Lady Theo?"

"His lordship . . . ," she said. "I need to speak with him urgently. Could you ask him to spare me a moment?"

"His lordship is indisposed, Lady Theo," Henry said. He'd known the worst the moment he'd entered the earl's bedchamber at sunrise. As he'd moved to open the curtains in his customary fashion, a thread of voice had spoken from the darkness of the bed curtains: "No light, Henry." It would be many hours before the Earl of Stoneridge was fit to talk with anyone.

"Indisposed?" Theo blinked in surprise. Men didn't become indisposed . . . at least not strong, powerful men like Stoneridge. Indisposition was for gouty old men like her grandfather.

"That is so, Lady Theo," Henry reiterated, politely but firmly indicating that he wasn't about to expand on the statement. "If you'll excuse me." He bowed and slid past her toward the stairs.

Theo stared at the closed door. What abominable timing! Why couldn't he have become indisposed . . . or whatever it was . . . an hour or two later?

She went downstairs to the breakfast parlor to discuss the earl's puzzling condition with her mother and sisters.

Stoneridge lay in the merciful dimness, fighting the nausea that increased with each knife of pain slicing through the right side of his head. Retching exacerbated the pain to an intolerable level, so that if he had the strength, he would scream, would bang his head against the bedpost — anything to divert the agony. But already the insidious weakness was in his limbs, even though they could find no rest, and the debilitation would get worse until uncontrollable tears would squeeze between his eyelids.

The door opened and Henry padded softly to the bed. "Will you take some laudanum, my lord?"

"I'll never keep it down," Sylvester said. It worked only if he could take it the minute the warning signs appeared, but this morning he'd awakened, as so often happened, when the attack was well established, and there was nothing now that he could do except endure.

"Lady Theo wished to speak with you, sir," Henry said, laying a cloth soaked in lavender water over his temples. "She said it was urgent."

Sylvester lay still; for a second the throbbing eased. He knew it merely heralded renewed violence but was pathetically grateful for the tiny respite. Why would Theo need to speak to him urgently? Second thoughts?

The pain overwhelmed him in a throbbing wave, and he moaned, grabbing for the bowl beside the bed, retching in desperate agony as the pain pierced his skull as if nails were being driven through the bone with a hammer.

Henry held the bowl, it was all he could do. And when it was over, he wiped his lordship's gray face, offering a sip of water. Sylvester lay still, trying to concentrate.

"Henry, I want you to ride to London immediately."

"To London, my lord?" The man's surprise was clear in his voice.

"Deliver an announcement to the *Gazette*. It must be there

95

tonight so that it can appear tomorrow."

He held the pain down, ignored it, his hand reaching to grip Henry's with convulsive pressure. "Go immediately."

"But I can't leave you, sir."

"Yes, you can. . . . Just tell Foster no one . . . *no one* . . . is to come into this room unless I ring. Now fetch paper and pencil, I'll tell you what to say."

"Very well, my lord." Henry fetched the required items. Arguing would only make matters worse.

Sylvester endured through a fresh wave of agony, and then, his voice a mere thread, dictated: "The Earl of Stoneridge is honored to announce his engagement to Lady Theodora Belmont of Stoneridge Manor, daughter of the late Viscount Belmont and Elinor, Lady Belmont." He waved a hand in weak dismissal. "That will have to do. See to it, Henry. And bring a copy of the *Gazette* back with you in the morning."

"You'll be all right, my lord?" The valet still hesitated.

"No, man, of course I won't. But I'll live. Just do it!"

"Aye, sir." Henry left without further protest, delivering his lordship's orders to Foster. Ten minutes later he was riding toward the London road, the announcement of the earl's engagement to his distant cousin safely tucked into his breast pocket.

Theo spent the rest of the day close to the house, waiting for the earl to reappear. Her mother refused to discuss the issue, and her elder sisters wanted to talk about it ad infinitum, and she found both attitudes a sore trial, since they merely highlighted her own confusion. She paced the corridor outside the earl's closed door, questioned Foster twice as to Henry's exact instructions, and tried to imagine what could have felled a man like Sylvester Gilbraith so suddenly and so completely.

It didn't occur to her to wonder where Henry had gone. The man was not yet part of the household, and his comings and goings were of little concern.

By evening she was feeling desperate. With each hour that passed, the engagement seemed to become more of a fact and less of a floating proposition. Every hour that Sylvester continued to believe they were to be married made disabusing him more and more difficult — not to mention unprincipled and hurtful.

She contemplated writing him a note and slipping it under the door but dismissed that idea as the act of a coward. She owed him a face-to-face explanation.

But what was the explanation? She didn't like him? She didn't want to marry anyone? At least not yet? She couldn't contemplate living her life with a Gilbraith? She was afraid of him?

There was some truth in all of that, but most important, she *was* afraid of him . . . of what happened to her when she was with him. She was afraid of losing power, of losing control over herself and her world. And if she lost it, Sylvester Gilbraith would take it. He would immerse her in that turbulent whirlpool of emotions and sensations into which so far she'd only dipped her toes. Part of her clamored for that immersion, and part of her was terrified of its consequences.

She went to bed with nothing resolved, to spend the night tossing and turning in a ferment of indecision — one minute clear and determined, her speech prepared, firm, rational, kind, and sympathetic — and the next minute the words lost themselves in confusion as she thought of what marriage to Sylvester Gilbraith *could* bring her. Stoneridge Manor and the estate, certainly, but more than that, much more than that. He'd awakened passion, shown her a side of herself she hadn't known, taken her to the brink of a sensual landscape she was impatient to explore.

If Theo had seen the object of her fear and confusion during the long, dreadful hours of the night, she might have felt less fearful.

The man was a husk, immersed in pain, blind to anything but the dehumanizing agony. He was swallowing laudanum now in great gulps, no longer rational enough to know it would do no good until the hideous nausea left him. Perhaps a little would stay down, enough to take the edge off, even for a few minutes. He knew he was crying, that ugly animal moans emerged without volition from his lips, but he was too debilitated to keep silent, thankful only that there was no one to witness his shameful weakness. He gave no thought now to his marriage, to Henry's errand, to Theo, or to what action she might be considering. He begged only for surcease.

And mercifully it came, after the sun rose and the household

97

began its day's business. The last dose of laudanum stayed in his stomach, spread through his veins, and brought unconsciousness.

It was midday when Elinor decided she could no longer respect the earl's orders as relayed to Foster. He hadn't been seen for thirty-six hours. No one had entered his bedchamber since Henry's departure, and all kinds of sinister explanations ran rampant in her imagination. Was he a drunkard? Or addicted to some unnatural practices that kept him secluded for days at a time? If this man was to marry her daughter, there could be no such mysteries.

She knocked softly, and when there was no answer, quietly lifted the latch, slipping into the room, closing the door behind her, feeling she must respect the earl's privacy this far at least.

The reek of suffering hung heavy in the darkened room, and heavy, stertorous breathing came from behind the drawn bed curtains.

On tiptoe she approached the bed, drawing aside the hangings by the carved headboard. It was so dark, it was hard to make out more than the white smudge of the earl's face on the pillow, but as her eyes grew accustomed, she saw the lines of endurance etched deep around his mouth and eyes, the dark stubble along his jaw. She recognized from her father-in-law's illness the drugged quality of his breathing, and her eye fell on the empty bottle of laudanum on the side table beside the bowl he'd been using for the last harrowing hours.

What was this mysterious sickness? A legacy of the war, perhaps? There were many men across the continent crippled by such legacies.

She picked up the fetid bowl, covered it with a cloth from the washstand, and carried it away, leaving the room as quietly as she'd entered it.

Theo was coming up the stairs as her mother descended them. "Has Stoneridge come out of his room yet, Mama?"

"No, and I don't believe he will do so for some time," Elinor said. "He's sleeping at the moment."

"But what's the matter with him?" Theo exclaimed in frustration. "How could he just disappear like that for two days?"

98

"I expect it's something to do with his war injury," Elinor replied matter-of-factly. "Nothing to do with any of us." She continued past her daughter, taking the bowl into the kitchens.

Theo chewed her lip. Then she ran up the stairs to the earl's door. Her hand lifted to knock, but something held her back. Some overpowering sense of intrusion.

Her hand fell and she turned away. He couldn't stay there forever, but neither could she spend another day pacing the house, checkmated.

There was always work to do and she'd bury her frustration in fresh air, exercise, and useful business.

Thus she wasn't in the house when Henry returned in the late afternoon. He was tired, having ridden since early morning, changing horses frequently to maintain his pace. But the roads were good, and he'd made excellent time. Tucked in his pocket was a copy of the *Gazette*, snatched at dawn from a vendor with the ink barely dry.

He left his horse in the stable and hastened into the house, wondering if the earl was still abed, or whether the attack had been a short one. They were very rarely short, but they'd never lasted more than two days.

Foster greeted him with the lofty condescension of an old retainer not yet prepared to accept a newcomer. "His lordship remains in his bedchamber, Henry."

"I see. Then he'll be wanting some tea, no doubt," Henry said briskly, not in the least put out by Foster's attitude. "Do us a favor and ask them in the kitchen to brew a pot. And hot water for his lordship's bath. I'll be down to fetch it when I've seen how he's doing."

Without waiting to see how his request was received, he hurried up the stairs, entering his lordship's chamber without ceremony.

The curtains were still drawn at the windows but had been pulled back around the bed.

"Ah, Henry, good man. You succeeded?"

The earl's voice was strong, and Henry stepped over to the bed, knowing what he would see. Stoneridge smiled at him, his eyes clear, his complexion, despite the stubble, pale but healthy.

He exuded an aura of peace, as if some hideous demon had been exorcised.

"Aye, my lord, I have it here." He handed the paper to his employer. "I'll fetch you up some tea and toast, if you'd like."

"Mmmm, thanks," Sylvester said absently, his eyes scanning the announcements. "I'm hungry as a hunter." He nodded with satisfaction at the brief notice of his engagement. It would require a lot more than vague reluctance or simple indecision on his fiancée's part to undo that announcement. He never thought he'd be thankful for an attack, but that one might well have proved timely.

"You'll be wanting a bath, too, sir."

"God, yes, I'm rank," the earl declared, folding the newspaper, running his hand over his chin with a grimace of distaste. "I must reek to high heaven."

Henry grinned with relief. "Not that you'd notice, sir. But I'll see to it right away."

Two hours later the earl examined his reflection in the cheval glass with a nod of satisfaction. His tasseled Hessians glimmered in the fading sunlight, olive pantaloons molded his calves and thighs, and his coat of dark-brown superfine outlined the muscles of his shoulders as if it had been made on him.

His close-cropped hair had a luster to it, his skin bore the glow of health and well-being, and he was filled with the euphoria that always followed the hell. His young cousin wasn't going to be able to present him with any insuperable difficulties. He picked up the *Gazette*, tapping it against the palm of his hand. No, that hotheaded gypsy was going to come sweetly to heel.

He left his bedroom, strolling toward the stairs. He heard Theo's voice in the hall, talking to Foster with that breathless catch that meant she knew she was late. He glanced at his fob watch. It was almost six o'clock, and he'd lay any odds she'd only just come in from the fields.

He stepped into a deep window embrasure as he heard her booted feet racing up the magnificent wooden staircase.

"Late again, cousin." He stepped out of the shadows just as she came abreast of him. His eyes teased her, his smile told her that his scolding tone wasn't in earnest.

"Oh, you startled me!" She stopped dead. "You're always doing that, Stoneridge."

"I beg your pardon, gypsy." He caught her wrist, pulling her into the embrasure with him. "I've missed you." His hand cupped her chin.

"Where've you been? What's been the matter with you?" she demanded in bewildered frustration, trying to pull back from his hold.

"Just an old war wound," he said with a dismissive head shake, his fingers closing over her chin.

"I have to talk —" The rest was lost under his mouth, and the familiar tingling began as her blood heated. His hand ran down her back, curved over her bottom in a lingering caress. Warning bells jangled, but she could barely hear them through the pounding blood in her ears. She reached against him, her own hands lifting to encircle his neck, flattening against his nape, holding him much more strongly than he was holding her. The taste and the smell of him sent all her senses reeling, and the whirlpool beckoned like the sirens' song. . . .

Until he reached behind him to untwine her hands from his neck and the bells crashed their warning with renewed force. But he gave her no chance to speak. His thumb flattened on her reddened lips, his eyes smiled, but his voice was cool and collected.

"Make haste and change, Theo. We don't want any more unpleasantness over the dinner table." As if in reinforcement, the long case clock in the hall chimed six.

"But I —"

"Hurry," he said, increasing the pressure of his thumb. "You can't keep everyone waiting while dinner spoils."

Her eyes darkened with frustration, but he read acceptance in them also. Removing his thumb, he bent and kissed her eyelids, then, chuckling, pinched the tip of her nose and strode off toward the stairs.

"Hell and the devil," Theo muttered, wringing her hands, not knowing whether she wanted to strangle him or hold him so tightly he would never break free.

She stood in the embrasure wasting precious minutes until Clarissa came running up the staircase. "Theo . . . oh, there you are. What are you doing? Lord Stoneridge asked me to help you dress. He said you were going to be very late otherwise."

Theo glanced at her hands. She wanted to strangle him . . . that was all. He'd outmaneuvered her, and the damn man was *still* giving the orders.

Clarissa was urging her down the corridor, and with a sigh, she yielded. There was nothing to be done at the moment. After dinner she'd have her discussion. He'd have to understand that his indisposition . . . or whatever it was . . . was responsible for the delay.

"Which gown?" Clarissa demanded, flinging open the armoire. "The sprig muslin with the green ribbon knots is pretty."

"I'm not interested in pretty, Clarry. Just clean and tidy," Theo stated repressively, flinging off her riding habit. "Pass me the green linen."

"But that's so plain!" Clarissa bemoaned.

"It's clean and tidy," Theo articulated carefully, lifting the ewer to pour water into the basin.

"But you're dining with your fiancé. . . ."

"I am not!" She splashed water vigorously over her face. "In the name of goodness, Clarry, stop this romantic twaddle. I am *not* marrying Stoneridge. It's as simple as that."

Clarissa knew that mulish turn to her sister's mouth and knew better than to persevere. She handed her the despised green linen dress and brushed out Theo's hair. The blue-black waves sprang out from each brush stroke. Only Theo had their father's dramatic coloring; the others took after Elinor, with their soft brown hair and gentle blue eyes.

"Shall I put it up in a knot on your neck?" she asked tentatively. "You know how it suits you."

"Plait it," her sister said shortly.

Clarissa sighed and did as she was asked.

"Good . . . thank you." Theo thrust her feet into a pair of openwork sandals, more suited to an afternoon's wandering through the garden than the dinner table. She glanced up at the pretty marquetry clock on the mantelshelf. It was barely six-twenty.

102

"Come, let's go downstairs." She smiled at her sister, hugging her briefly. "You're an angel, Clarry. I'm sorry if I was snappish."

"You were," Clarissa responded with a resigned sigh. Her volatile sister could always dispel lingering resentments with her smile.

They went downstairs and entered the drawing room arm in arm.

It was immediately apparent to both of them that something was afoot. Foster was delicately edging the cork out of a bottle of the late earl's supply of vintage champagne.

Theo instantly froze. Who had had the gall to instruct Foster to broach such a precious bottle? Not her mother, surely? Her mother didn't know the first thing about what was in the cellars. Theo's eyes flickered to the Earl of Stoneridge, who was in his customary position by the empty fireplace, resting his elbow along the mantelshelf. Of course, she thought bitterly, the Earl of Stoneridge had the right to drink any bottle he chose, even though he'd put no effort, knowledge, or funds into its acquisition.

"Come," he said, extending his hand toward her. "We were waiting for you."

She looked round the room. Her mother was sitting on the sofa, her embroidery in her lap. Emily held a copy of the *Gazette* in her hand, and it was she who spoke.

"Oh, Theo, love, it's so exciting. See, here's the notice of your engagement."

"*What?*" The blood drained from her face and then flooded back in an angry tide. "Show me that." She almost snatched the paper from Emily.

The simple statement set the fact in stone, rendered indecision merely ashes in the wind.

Clarissa read the announcement over her shoulder. Her sister was quivering, and she laid a steadying hand on Theo's shoulder. She didn't know why Theo was having such difficulties, but since she was, she'd offer what silent support she could. Theo would do the same for her, whether she agreed with her or not.

"Pray accept my heartfelt congratulations, Lady Theo," Foster said. The cork slid out between his finger and thumb with barely a pop, and he poured the straw-colored bubbles without losing a drop.

"Stoneridge, could we —"

"After dinner," he said smoothly. "If you'd like to walk a little, I'm sure your mama would permit it."

Manipulative devil! After what had passed between them, what had her mother's permission to do with anything? Theo felt like a drowning man clinging to a weed-encrusted rock. Everytime she grasped a tendril, the slimy fronds slithered through her fingers.

Elinor took a glass from the tray Foster presented. "Theo, dear, you and Lord Stoneridge will discuss whatever you feel necessary after dinner. He will listen to you as you will listen to him."

Theo waited angrily for her mother to offer a toast to the happy couple, but Elinor didn't abandon her quite so completely. She raised her glass, took a considered sip, and said, "A happy thought, Stoneridge."

He inclined his head in acknowledgment and sipped his own wine. The girls exchanged comprehending looks and followed suit.

No point wasting vintage champagne, Theo thought, regarding her for-the-present established betrothed over the lip of her glass. He looked remarkably well for a man who'd been indisposed for two days. Had it been a trick? Had he anticipated her morning-after change of mind? Surely not? Not even a Gilbraith could be that devious . . . or could he?

Chapter Eight

The Black Dog in Spitalfields was an unwholesome establishment, generally frequented by cutpurses and villains of various trades. It was well-known to the Bow Street Runners, who, more often than not, were indistinguishable in appearance from their quarry on the other side of the law.

On the evening of the day the *Gazette* carried the news of Sylvester Gilbraith's engagement to Theodora Belmont, a man stepped out of a hackney carriage outside the tavern and stood on the mired cobbles, his aquiline nose twitching at the stench of rotten garbage and human waste flowing in the open kennels running alongside the filthy lane.

A ragged urchin seemed to stumble against him, but before he could regain his footing, Captain Neil Gerard of His Majesty's Third Dragoans had collared him. The lad, no more than seven or eight, stared in wild-eyed terror at his captor, who pried open the boy's clenched fist with fingers of steel.

"Thief!" the captain declared with cold dispassion as he retrieved his watch from the grimy palm. He raised his silver-handled cane as the child screamed. No one took any notice of the scene or the child's cries as he fell to his knees beneath the relentless blows. Such violence was relatively mild by the standards of this part of London, and even the urchin knew, as he lay sniveling in the gutter, that he'd escaped lightly. If the gent had handed him over the beadles, he'd have faced the hangman's noose in Newgate Yard or the transportation hulks lying in the Thames estuary.

Captain Gerard kicked at the skinny huddled body by way of parting and strode into the inn, ducking his head beneath the low lintel.

His eyes streamed from the thick smoke rising from a dozen clay pipes and the noxious stench of the sea coal burning in the great hearth, despite the warm summer evening. Men glanced up from their tankards or their dice and then looked down again. Jud's tavern was a flash house — a place where a man could do business of a certain kind without drawing attention to himself.

A man could find a prizefighter, a murderer, an arsonist, a lock breaker, a highwayman, if he knew who and how to ask and had the right currency.

The man behind the bar counter had the brutally disfigured countenance of one who lived by violence. A scarlet cicatrix slashed his cheek where a French sword had cut to the bone, his nose had been broken in so many fights that he could no longer breathe through it, and his mouth was permanently open, revealing one black front tooth. A stained patch covered the empty socket of his left eye.

"Well, well, if it ain't the cap'n." He greeted the newcomer with what might have been a smile but was more of a sneer. "It's that day agin, is it? Amazin' 'ow the time passes." He drew a tankard of ale and drank deeply, wiping the froth off his mouth with the back of a filthy hand.

"What can I offer ye, then, sir?" His sneer broadened. He knew the captain wouldn't touch anything in this house.

Captain Gerard didn't deign to reply. This weekly ordeal of humiliation grew harder each occasion, but he had no choice. And most particularly not now. He drew a heavy leather pouch from his pocket and dropped it onto the counter with a clunk.

"Oh, what 'ave we 'ere, then?" Jud opened the pouch and shook the golden guineas onto the counter, where they gleamed dully against the stained planking.

"Only four, sir?" His voice took on a mocking whine. "An' there was I thinkin' we'd agreed on a bit extra . . . now just 'cause me memory's gettin' better by the day. . . . Unusual that, innit?" He wiped the counter with his sleeve, his one eye glittering with malice. "Most people forgets things as they get on . . . but not me . . . not Jud O'Flannery."

Neil Gerard felt the familiar fury mingling with the humiliation of his helplessness. This man had him. He held in the palm of one massive filthy hand the captain's reputation, his social standing, possibly even his life — a firing squad was the penalty for cowardice in the face of the enemy.

"That Major Gilbraith, now, 'e was a good sort," Jud mused. "A brave man . . . everyone says as 'ow 'e was one o' the best officers they 'ad in the Peninsula. Even old Nosey thought so."

106

The Duke of Wellington, so familiarly referred to, had indeed thought highly of Sylvester Gilbraith. It was that opinion that had saved the major from the conviction for cowardice that as easily as acquittal could have resulted from the hazy facts. But the duke had insisted that his old favorite be given the benefit of the doubt.

And that left Neil Gerard with an insoluble problem that would stay with him for as long as both Sylvester Gilbraith and Jud O'Flannery existed together on earth.

But Jud didn't know that his old captain's problem had suddenly worsened. Sylvester was now the Earl of Stoneridge, about to make an excellent marriage. He would be bound to reenter Society. The old story would be resurrected, there would be whispers — but Society forgave quickly, particularly when it was only a rumor and the subject had such impeccable entrées to the secluded world of privilege inhabited by the ton.

Reopening the story was the last thing Captain Gerard wanted. People would ask questions, maybe increasingly searching questions, and what if Sylvester began to probe? What if his own memory of those moments before the bayonet thrust began to clear? What if he decided to defend himself vigorously in the clubs of St. James's? Defense of Sylvester Gilbraith would inevitably lead to fingers pointing at Neil Gerard, who should have come up in support of the beleaguered outpost . . . and unaccountably failed to do so.

Neil reached into his pocket and dropped another guinea on the counter. He stared at his nemesis with loathing, and Jud laughed, sweeping the coins into the palm of one hand.

Sergeant O'Flannery had witnessed the moment when his captain decided to abandon Major Gilbraith's small force to the enemy. Sergeant O'Flannery had received the order to withdraw the men, while his captain had galloped back behind the safety of the picket line.

Only Sergeant O'Flannery had known what lay behind the order to withdraw, and Sergeant O'Flannery's grasp grew ever greedier and tighter.

Neil glanced around the taproom, peering through the stinging smoke beneath the blackened beams. Among the drinkers there would be a man who would rid him of Sylvester Gilbraith, for a price. But if word got back to Jud of such a scheme to rob him of his golden goose, then Captain Gerard's own life wouldn't be worth a day's purchase. Jud O'Flannery was the unquestioned king of London's underworld; there wasn't a purse fat enough to tempt a thief or a murderer to cross swords with him. And he had his spies in every malodorous hole in the city.

He swung on his heel and strode out of the fetid room without another word. The sergeant spat contemptuously in the sawdust at his feet as the elegant figure stepped out into the street.

Gerard climbed back into the waiting hackney. The removal of the now Earl of Stoneridge would mean he'd never again have to make these mortifying visits to Spitalfields — visits that Jud insisted he make in person. So Gerard had to crawl into that den of thieves to pay his blackmail, and that humiliation seemed to afford the vile Sergeant O'Flannery even greater satisfaction than the money itself.

There were flash houses other than Jud's tavern where a man could find a hired assassin. Not one who'd be willing to take on Jud O'Flannery, of course, but one who'd see no harm in doing away with some unknown gentleman. One who'd ask no questions if the price was right.

Neil frowned in the dim light of the hackney, hanging on to the strap as the iron-wheeled vehicle rattled over the cobbles, swerving to avoid a mangy mongrel. If he could get rid of Stoneridge while he was still in the country . . . an accident of some kind . . . then all his troubles would be over. There was no reason why he'd have to identify himself to a potential murderer, and if he chose his man from a neighborhood away from Jud's immediate vicinity, it was unlikely Jud would hear of it. It was a risk worth taking.

But if that failed, if Sylvester did reenter Society, what then? They'd been friends before Vimiera. True, he'd been the first to ostracize Gilbraith. Everyone had been watching to see what attitude he would take, and he'd known they would follow his lead. Once he'd cut Gilbraith, it was assumed he'd known the truth but had been unwilling for the sake of old friendship to tell a tale that would condemn the major. Society had turned its shoulder against Sylvester Gilbraith, and he'd slipped out of sight, taking his shame with him. It would take a lot to bring him back to face that mortification again.

Society didn't know of Jud O'Flannery, who had been required, as the only noncommissioned officer present at the events in question, to attend the court-martial. Jud had threatened to produce his own version of those events if his captain condemned Gilbraith out of hand. And the sergeant had thus ensured for himself a tidy little income that he could increase at will.

But supposing, if Sylvester did return to London, Gerard was the first to welcome him back into Society's fold? Supposing he extended the hand of friendship, generously prepared to put suspicion behind him? Society would surely follow his lead, and the old scandal would die. Sylvester would be a fool to reopen it.

But Sylvester was a fiercely proud man, capable of acts of desperate courage if his loyalties or principles were involved. If he believed there was reason to clear his name, he'd do it at whatever personal cost. He'd certainly face Society's censure to prove his point.

No, the best plan was to arrange by proxy a neat accident in Dorset. Somewhere in this grim world of murder and thievery, he'd be able to go incognito and recruit a man willing and able to arrange such an accident.

The thoughts and plans of a desperate man swirled in the captain's head as the hackney bore him back through the mean streets of London's East End to the broad, elegant thoroughfares of the few square miles occupied by his own kind.

While his erstwhile friend was thus occupied, Sylvester Gilbraith was coming to the end of an awkward dinner in the company of his betrothed and her family. Theo's silence cast a pall over any attempt at conversation. If it had been a sullen silence, it would have been easier to ignore, but her preoccupation was so clearly painful that all conversational sallies sounded irrelevant and trivial.

Finally, Sylvester could endure it no longer. He tossed his napkin onto the table and rose to his feet. "Forgive me, Lady Belmont, but I'm afraid we're all going to suffer from indigestion if Theo doesn't unburden herself soon." He strode round the table to where Theo sat, staring at a strawberry on her plate as if she'd never seen such a thing before.

"Come along, cousin." He pulled back her chair. "Let's get this over with."

"Get what over with?" She looked up at him over her shoulder, startled out of her absorption.

"I'm hoping you're going to tell me," he said dryly, taking her elbow and drawing her to her feet. "Excuse us, ma'am."

"Certainly," Elinor said with relief.

A footman jumped to open the door for them, and Sylvester hustled Theo out into the hall.

"Now, shall we have this discussion in the library, or would you prefer to go for a walk?"

"There's nothing to discuss." The words tumbled free. "I can't marry you, Stoneridge, that's all."

"It seems to me we have a great deal to discuss," he said coolly. "Or do you consider it sufficient simply to make such a statement out of the blue? A woman's prerogative to change her mind . . . is that it?"

Theo flushed. She'd expected him to put her in the wrong, and God knows, he was entitled to, but it was horrible to see herself in such a light. "You don't understand —"

"No, I don't," he said curtly. "But you're going to explain it to me. Now, do you wish to go into the library, or shall we go for a walk?" If the stakes hadn't been so high, he would have felt compassion for her. Her eyes were stricken, and she pushed a hand distractedly through the wispy fringe on her forehead. But he couldn't afford sympathy. She was at a disadvantage, and he was going to exploit that to its limit.

"Which is it to be?"

Theo felt stifled. His eyes were devoid of understanding, his mouth a taut line, and she felt as if a great stone was pressing down on her.

"Outside," she said, turning on her heel and almost running out the front door.

Sylvester followed in more leisurely fashion as she made off down the lawn toward the stone bridge at the bottom of the hill. She stopped on the bridge and leaned against the low parapet, gazing down into the clear brown stream flowing sluggishly beneath. Two swallows dived among the clouds of midges hovering over the surface of the water.

Sylvester stepped onto the bridge, his feet loud in the stillness. He leaned against the stonework beside her. Theo said nothing, but he felt the little tremor run through her as his arm brushed hers.

"I trust you're not being missish, gypsy," he commented.

"Of course I'm not!" She turned angrily toward him. No one had ever accused her of such a thing before.

"Then what the hell's the matter with you?"

"I'm frightened!" she cried with the same anger. She hadn't meant to tell him, but the words had spoken themselves.

Whatever he'd been expecting, it hadn't been that. "Frightened? My dear girl, of what?"

"*You!*" The admission was a ferocious whisper.

"*Me?*" Sylvester was astounded. "What have I done to warrant your fear?"

Theo picked at a piece of loose stone on the parapet and tossed it into the stream.

"It's not so much what you've done, as what I'm afraid you'll do," she said in a low voice.

Sylvester frowned. "What do you think I'm going to do to you, you silly goose?"

"I am not a silly goose," she said, recovering some of her sangfroid. "I'm afraid you'll swallow me up . . . take over."

"I still don't understand." He searched now for patience. This was obviously a much more complex issue than he'd thought.

"I'm afraid I'll lose myself if I marry you," she said. "You'll take control and I'll be swept up." She stared straight ahead of her across the river, aware that her cheeks were hot, knowing that she was failing lamentably to express herself, but it was so damnably embarrassing to explain.

"Let's move out of sight of the house," Sylvester said abruptly, conscious of the manor's sparkling windows like so many shining eyes looking down at them from the top of the hill. Taking her arm, he chivied her across the bridge and a few yards along the bank toward the stand of oak trees from where he'd first laid eyes on his cousin.

"Now . . . I'll see what I can do to calm your fears." He was smiling as he stood her against an oak tree, his eyes somewhat amused. He thought he understood. "Perhaps this will help. . . ."

It was no good. The minute his lips touched hers, Theo was lost. There was nothing her mind could do to control her responses. Her hands slid inside his coat, on their own voyage of exploration, feeling the warmth of his skin beneath his shirt, the ripple of muscle down his back, and then the hard, muscled tautness of his buttocks.

Her teeth nipped at his lower lip as their tongues plunged and warred, and her legs twined and twisted around his, her loins pressing urgently against his. She moved a hand round his body to mold the hard shaft of flesh straining against the skintight knit of his pantaloons, and as she felt the flesh jumping against her caressing hand, she was filled with a wild exultation, knowing that he was as lost in lust as she was.

She went down to the grass beneath the urgent pressure of his hand on her shoulder and fell back, the grass beneath her damp with early-evening dew. Lifting her against him for a brief moment, he unfastened the hooks at the back of her dress, then let her fall back onto the grass. She twisted and lifted her body to help him as he pulled the dress away from her. He unbuttoned her chemise, baring her breasts to the cool air, and his tongue flickered over the rosy crowns, one finger delicately stroking the satin swell.

Theo felt herself to be a burning brand of desire. She had no modesty, no ability to restrain her movements as her thighs opened, exposing the aching cleft of her body to the hand that moved downward, slipped into the waist of her drawers, and flattened over her belly. Fretfully, she scrabbled at her undergarments, pushing them away from her body, kicking them off her feet.

Her hips arched as she reached for him to pull him down to her, her own hands trying to find a way to touch his skin, to reach the turgid flesh that her body knew in its every crevice would bring her ultimate joy.

And then suddenly, with a harsh exclamation, Sylvester pulled back from her. He looked down at the half-naked girl, lying open and expectant, her eyes wild with passion, her arms still raised as if waiting for him to return to their embrace.

"God in heaven!" he whispered, running a hand through his hair, fighting for control. He took a deep, shuddering breath and reached for her discarded drawers. "Put these back on."

It was taking Theo longer to return to sanity. "Why?" she drawled, her eyes narrowing. "Come back."

Sylvester bent, caught her inviting hands, and hauled her to her feet. Lust was well under control now, and he was torn between laughter and exasperation as he held up her undergarment. "Lift up your foot."

"But why?"

"Because, my passionate baggage, I have no intention of siring an heir before my wedding night. Now, lift up." He slapped her calf in emphatic punctuation.

Theo obeyed, but her heated blood was taking a long time to cool. She fumbled with the buttons of her chemise as he pulled up her drawers with a businesslike efficiency. Then she said in a low voice, "Now do you understand what I'm frightened of? You swallow me up . . . I lose myself. I don't know what I'm doing."

He stroked her disheveled hair away from her face. "Tell me the truth, now. Are you frightened or disappointed at the moment?"

Theo thought. "Disappointed," she said finally, a rueful smile hovering on her own lips.

Sylvester laughed. "So am I." Then he spoke gravely. "There's nothing to be afraid of. I feel what you feel. If you lose yourself in me, so will I lose myself in you. Lovemaking is the ultimate partnership. It's not a weakness, little gypsy. Not something to be taken advantage of. I promise you that never, never will I take advantage of your passion. Do you understand that?"

Never again, he amended silently, squashing a surge of self-disgust.

Slowly, Theo nodded. But she was still frightened by the power of those feelings, by the wild surgings of her body. It would be the most potent weapon if anyone chose to use it. She bent to pick up her dress, slipping it over her head.

Sylvester leaned back against a tree, arms folded, watching her with a half smile. "So am I going to be obliged to send another notice to the *Gazette*, or does our engagement still stand?"

"I suppose so," she said, accepting defeat. "*You* want my knowledge of the estate. I want the estate. We both get something that we want out of it."

"That's certainly one way of putting it," he said wryly, pushing himself off the tree. "Come, let's go back to the house and put everyone's mind at rest."

Elinor went to bed that night a peaceful woman for the first time since her father-in-law's death. Her daughters were now provided for; even Rosie would be assured of a respectable dowry when the time came; and her most troubled and troublesome child was consigned to the care of a man Elinor was willing to wager would make Theo the only kind of husband who would suit her. She wasn't entirely sure she could describe the kind of a man that was, but some maternal instinct told her that Theo would discover it soon enough.

Sylvester rode into Dorchester the following day on an important errand, unaware that his betrothed was also out and about on a matrimonial errand of her own.

Theo rode through Lulworth village and turned off toward Castle Corfe. Just before the castle ruins, she stopped at a small cottage, more an outhouse than a proper dwelling. Dulcie had been here before and grazed contentedly on the grass verge at the end of her tether as Theo disappeared into the gloom of the low thatched-roof cottage.

"I give you good day, Dame Merriweather." She set a cloth-wrapped parcel on the table without comment.

"Aye, good day to ye, girlie." An old woman — so old it seemed hard to imagine that life spurted beneath the wrinkled skin hanging on her like an overlarge cloak — sat on a three-legged stool by the hearth. But the old eyes were sharp as they

114

noted the parcel that she knew contained meat and cheese from the manor kitchens, and there'd be a few coins too. Enough to eke out the livelihood she made as herbalist to the village folk in the Dorsetshire countryside.

She turned her gaze on her visitor, whom she'd known from Theo's childhood, when on one of her country rambles the ten-year-old girl had stumbled upon the cottage, weeping with fury, carrying a rabbit, its foot severed by a trap, her own knee bleeding from a deep gash where she'd knelt on a razor sharp stone as she'd struggled to free the wounded animal.

The old dame had bound up the gash, given the child a drink of rose-hip syrup and a piece of lardy cake, and sent her on her way, promising to care for the rabbit.

The rabbit had gone in the pot that night, and the dame had lived off it for a week, but when the child returned, she told her that it had hopped off on its three legs, perfectly able to survive in the wild.

Since then Theo had visited regularly, always bringing something with her, even if it was only half a loaf from the breakfast table. Once she'd grown into adulthood, the gifts had been more substantial and always carefully chosen. Meat and cheese were in short supply on the old herbalist's table.

"So what can us do for ye, girlie?" The dame knew this was no purely social visit. There was a tension in the slender frame that told its own story.

"You've ways of preventing a woman conceiving a child," Theo said directly, leaning against the rickery table.

"Aye, and ways of stopping a birth, if that's what ye need." The dame heaved herself to her feet. "A sup of elderberry wine, m'dear?" She took a bottle from a shelf beside the hearth, unstoppered it, and poured a generous measure into a tin cup.

"My thanks, dame." Theo took the welcoming cup and drank, handing it back to her hostess, who refilled it and drank for herself.

"So which is it ye want, girlie?" The old herbalist turned back to her shelves.

"I've no desire to conceive as yet," Theo said.

"That's easily seen to." A wrinkled claw scrabbled among the bottles and pouches on the shelf. "This'll do it for ye."

She pulled out the stopper and sniffed at the contents, her nose wrinkling like a pig's searching out truffles.

"A lover, 'ave ye, girlie?"

"No," Theo said. "Not precisely. But a husband in a few weeks."

"Ah." The dame nodded. "Best to look after the lovin' before ye starts breedin', m'dear. If ye don't get it right afore, it'll never come right after, mark my words."

"That's rather what I thought," Theo said. "How should I take this?"

She received precise instructions and was on her way five minutes later. When the time came to give the Gilbraith an heir, it would be of her own choosing.

Sylvester entered the drawing room before dinner that evening with a smile in his eyes. He was feeling immensely pleased with himself, and his smile broadened when he saw that Theo had made an effort with her appearance and was wearing a relatively fashionable gown of dark-blue silk that matched her eyes, and her hair, instead of hanging down her back in its uncompromising rope, was looped in two braids over her ears, the fringe a soft wisp on her broad forehead.

"Ma'am." He bowed to Lady Belmont. "Cousins. I trust you spent a pleasant day."

"Not really," Rosie said. "I lost a dragonfly that I was trying to catch and tore my net on a tree branch."

"I'm sorry to hear it, Rosie," he said. The child was not usually in evidence in the evening, but since she was dressed in a crisp muslin gown with a broad sash, her hair demurely confined in a velvet ribbon, and her hands and face seemed unusually clean, he assumed she was to join them at the dinner table.

"It's very exasperating," Rosie said, sipping lemonade. "What did you do today?"

"Ah, well, I did some interesting shopping." He drew from his pocket a small square box.

"Cousin." He approached Theo, taking her left hand in his. "Permit me."

Theo stared at her finger, at the delicate circle of diamonds and seed pearls slipping over it. It was exquisitely simple. The man who had chosen it for her must know more about her tastes than she'd given him credit for.

Her eyes lifted to meet his. There was a question in the earl's, a touch of hesitancy. He wanted her to be pleased with his choice.

"It's lovely," she said, and his smile crinkled the skin around his eyes.

Raising her hand, he kissed her fingers, and then, when she looked completely astonished at such a reverent salute, he kissed the tip of her nose.

"The banns will be read for the next three Sundays, gypsy; and we'll be married the following Monday."

Chapter Nine

The Spanish sun was a brass-taloned eagle clawing at the baked earth of the Zaragoza desert. Edward Fairfax wiped his brow with a grimy handkerchief as he ducked into the welcome dimness of the stone house that served as battalion headquarters.

"It's hot as Hades out there," he observed redundantly to the men sprawling, scarlet tunics and collars open, on the various chairs and benches furnishing the building's single room. "The pickets are liable to get heat stroke, poor buggers."

"Change 'em every two hours, lieutenant," a gravelly voice spoke from the darkest corner of the room.

"Yes, sir." Edward nodded in the direction of his colonel as he loosened his tunic and unfastened his collar before lifting a copper jug to his lips. The clear, cold stream of water coated his parched throat, washing away the desert dust on his tongue.

"Mail cart came in earlier," a bearded man said, indolently gesturing toward the table where a pile of letters and newspapers lay. His hand dropped again into his lap as if the simple movement in the heat had exhausted him.

Edward riffled through the pile, extracting a letter from his mother. He'd been hoping for one from Emily, or better still, one from Theo. It wasn't that he didn't enjoy his betrothed's letters — they were warm and sweet and loving; but Theo's were full of the kind of information that he hungered for, about the land and the people they both knew, and they were always funny. She seemed to know that humor was in short supply in Wellington's Army of the Peninsular, sweltering through yet another Spanish summer.

His mother's letter, however, contained startling information. "Good God," he said.

"Not bad news, I trust?"

"I don't know what you'd call it." He frowned, rereading the relevant paragraph. "My fiancée's younger sister has just become betrothed to the new Earl of Stoneridge. Somewhat suddenly, as far as I can gather."

"Stoneridge?" A burly captain stood up, buttoning his tunic.

"Didn't Gilbraith come into that title?" He tightened his belt buckle.

"Sylvester Gilbraith . . . wasn't he the center of that scandal at Vimiera?" the colonel inquired.

"What was that, sir?" Edward looked attentively toward his superior.

The colonel frowned. "Damn murky business. Gilbraith lost the colors. He was badly wounded and apparently surrendered. Spent a year in a Froggie jail until he was exchanged. Court-martial acquitted him of cowardice, but it was damn murky, nevertheless. He resigned his commission. They say if the Peer hadn't stood up for him, he'd have faced a firing squad. But Wellington would have it that he knew the man and he was no coward, however it looked."

"And how did it look, sir?" asked Edward.

The colonel stretched an arm for the water jug, taking a gulp. "Murky . . . damn murky. Reinforcements were on the way, and he knew it, but they say he surrendered without a whimper."

Edward frowned. "But if he was wounded . . . ?"

The colonel shook his head. "Seems he yielded the colors and surrendered before he was wounded. Some bloody Froggie bayoneted him for the fun of it. By the time the reinforcements came up, it was all over."

"What about the men of his company?"

"Those who survived said the French were advancing for the umpteenth time, and he ordered them to surrender without firing a shot. Shocking business."

"Yes," agreed Edward. He wandered outside into the inferno of the summer afternoon. Theo couldn't marry a coward — it was unthinkable. Presumably she didn't know the story, and probably it was best if she never heard it. She'd be as miserable as sin with a man she couldn't respect. And why was she marrying Stoneridge, anyway? A hated Gilbraith. But he thought he could guess the answer to that. It would be the only way she could remain in control of her beloved home. Theo, despite her volatile nature, was ever pragmatic when it came to the estate.

But she wouldn't have agreed to marry the earl if she hadn't liked him. Theo was not that pragmatic. And did the man know what a pearl he was getting? It would be so easy to misunderstand Theo if one didn't take the time and trouble to look below the swift, efficient surface, to listen to what she was saying beneath the impatient, blunt words.

Edward had known the Belmont girls since childhood, and he knew how easily Theo could be hurt and how hard she would fight back. Life with her could be wonderful . . . or it could be sheer hell.

He smiled slightly to himself as he strolled through the heat. The few men not huddled in what little shade the village offered stared curiously at the absorbed lieutenant. His loosened tunic indicated that he was not on duty . . . only a madman would wander voluntarily in the midday sun.

Edward was thinking of how close he and Theo had come to making a match of it themselves, until Theo had decided it would be a bad idea. She'd said she wanted him as a friend, and she was afraid that having him as a husband would spoil their friendship.

If the truth be told, he'd been relieved. He'd been growing closer to Emily, appreciating her sweet-natured softness. He guessed that Theo had seen this, just as she'd been aware of her sister's affection for him. In typical fashion she'd come to a quick decision and implemented it without fuss.

Edward was so absorbed in these thoughts that he didn't realize he'd walked through the village and was approaching the farthest picket line. The sniper in the sparse olive grove beyond the pickets caught the sun-sparked glitter of the lieutenant's silver buttons on his tunic.

The sniper had only just taken up his position. He knew that he'd be able to get one victim before the English were wise to him. This bare-headed arrogant young officer, strolling with such apparent disregard for his safety, seemed the perfect choice.

He raised his rifle and sighted. Gently he squeezed the trigger.

Edward's life was saved by a kestrel. The hawk swooped down on a shrew scurrying along the roadside. Edward turned sideways to watch it, and the bullet that was destined for his heart went into his shoulder in an agonizing, fiery stab.

He yelled in surprise, his hand pressed to the spot where blood pumped in great gobbets; then he flung himself to the ground beside the shimmering white ribbon of the road, rolling beneath a cactus bush, terrifyingly conscious of how skimpy a shelter it was. But the sniper would have to fire again directly into the blinding light of the midday sun, a handicap that was Edward's only hope of seeing another dawn.

"You look harried, Lady Belmont," Sylvester observed two days before his wedding.

Elinor paused on the staircase, giving him a distracted smile. "I'm not harried exactly," she said. "Just somewhat exasperated. The seamstress has been trying to do the last fitting for Theo's wedding dress for two days, but she's never in the house. I finally managed to collar her this morning, but she's hardly being cooperative."

"Perhaps I can be of service," Sylvester suggested, raising an eyebrow.

The earl had proved to be rather good at managing his betrothed, Elinor reflected. "If you're not afraid of a quarrel just before your wedding day."

"Ma'am, I'm not in the least afraid of Theo," he replied. "And if she wishes to quarrel, then I won't stand in her way. Indeed, I believe it might do her some good . . . release some of her tension."

"You may be right, Stoneridge," Elinor said with a smile. "I'll leave you to your errand of mercy. You'll find the battlefield in the sewing room in the east wing."

Sylvester strolled up the stairs, humming to himself. It was true that Theo was as jumpy as a scalded cat as the wedding day grew closer, but he sensed it was as much excitement and anticipation as apprehension.

The sewing-room door stood open, and he could hear Theo's voice from halfway along the corridor.

"Oh, for heaven's sake, Biddy, do be quick. What does it matter if the hem's a bit crooked? No one's going to notice."

"Of course they'll notice, Theo," Clarissa stated. "You can't walk up the aisle with half your skirt above your ankles and the other half dragging on the ground."

"Don't exaggerate, Clarry."

"Now hold still, do, Lady Theo. . . ."

"Your mother says you're being tiresome, my love." Sylvester lounged against the doorjamb, regarding the scene with an amused eye. Theo, her eyes mutinous, her mouth set, stood on a low stool, billowing white gauze clouding around her. A woman knelt in front of her, her fingers darting through the material like silverfish as she pinned and tucked.

"You're not supposed to see the wedding dress before the wedding, my lord," Clarissa squeaked in horror, holding a pincushion from which she was supplying the seamstress.

"Oh, I think we can forgo convention," Sylvester said, stepping into the room.

"This is just stupid," Theo announced. "I have a dozen perfectly good gowns that I could have worn. It's hardly some grand-Society occasion."

It was true that it was going to be a very small family ceremony in deference to the recent death of Theo's grandfather, but Lady Belmont was insisting that some traditions had to be observed.

His lordship came over to the stool, taking his bride-to-be around her slender waist. "Now, stand still. The more cooperative you are, the sooner it will be over."

His hands spanned her waist, and he felt the tension surge through her at his touch. She quivered like a fawn about to take flight before the hunter. Standing on the stool, her eyes were almost on a level with his, and the deep pansy-blue darkened almost to black, the mutinous glare fading.

His lips curved in a comprehending smile, and he tightened his grip on her waist. A smile trembled on her own mouth.

"That's better," he said. "Most young women take an interest in their wedding preparations . . . instead of fighting them at every turn."

"Most young women don't have as much to do," she responded a shade tartly, although she continued to keep still under his hands. "The farrier is due at the home farm this afternoon, and I have a bone to pick with him over his last account. He billed us for shoeing both shire horses, but Big Jack had a sprained tendon and has been out at grass for two months."

Sylvester frowned and the warm light died in his eyes. "Why didn't you tell me about this? I am quite capable of conducting such business with the farrier."

"Oh, I can't remember to tell you every last detail," she said. "It's a relatively trivial matter . . . and anyway, you haven't met the farrier yet."

"And I assume you were going to rectify that this afternoon?" His eyebrows lifted in an ironic question mark.

Theo's flush was answer enough. "You're not yet familiar with the ledgers," she said stiffly.

"That is no excuse. Stand still," he snapped as she moved to jump off the stool despite his hold. He took a step closer to her, and his riding boot crushed a white lace flounce. The seamstress gave a little cry of distress, and he glanced down impatiently. With exaggerated caution he moved his boot, glaring at Theo.

Clarissa flinched unconsciously, her eyes fixed on the earl's large hands at her sister's waist. He seemed to fill the sewing room with his anger and his physical presence. She cleared her throat and said awkwardly, "I'm sure it just slipped Theo's mind, sir. But you'll be able to accompany her and meet Mr. Row this afternoon."

"I fully intend to meet Mr. Row this afternoon," the earl stated. "And I shall dispense with an introduction. My absentminded cousin will be far too busy making wedding preparations with her mother to perform it."

Clarissa could think of no more oil to pour on these troubled waters. The seamstress, apparently oblivious of the stinging atmosphere, knelt back with a sigh of satisfaction.

"There, Lady Theo. That's all pinned. If you'd like to slip out of the gown now, I'll have the stitching done in a trice."

The earl released Theo's waist. "I'll tell you the results of my discussion with the farrier later this afternoon, cousin." He turned to the door.

"No, wait!" Theo jumped off the stool, tripping over the yards of train in her haste. She seized his arm. "He's such a tricky son of a bitch that —"

"What did you say?" The earl interrupted this impassioned

123

beginning in genuine shock.

"I don't know. What did I say?" She looked startled.

With astonishment he realized his blunt and unconventional fiancée genuinely didn't know what he was objecting to. " 'Son of a bitch,' my dear girl, is not appropriate language for the granddaughter of the Earl of Stoneridge, let alone for his wife."

Theo dismissed this objection with an impatient gesture. "Yes, but you don't understand. You're a newcomer and Johnny will think he can fool you. You don't know what a tricky bastard —"

"*Theo!*"

"Your pardon, sir." She tried to look contrite, but her eyes were now alight with mischief. "It keeps slipping out."

There was something wonderfully absurd about the contrast between the impish grin on Theo's brown face, the energy coursing through the slender frame, and the demure white lace and flounces of a gown that looked as if it had found its way onto the wrong back.

Sylvester tried and failed to look stern. "Try to put a curb on your tongue in future."

Theo merely shrugged and said, "Just give me a minute, and I'll be ready to come with you." Immediately, she began to pull her wedding dress over her head.

"Theo!" Clarissa squawked, staring at the earl, who still stood in the room. The seamstress, whose priorities were very straightforward, ignored the earl's presence and rushed to help before Theo's rough treatment tore the flimsy silk.

Sylvester chuckled. It was so typical of Theo. "I'll give you five minutes to join me in the stables," he said through his laughter, striding out of the sewing room before Clarissa's sense of the proprieties could be further outraged.

"Damnation!" Theo muttered through the yards of filmy gauze train as it was edged over her head. "Be quick, Biddy."

At last she was free of the confining material. She scrambled back into her riding habit, grabbed her whip, hat, and gloves from the table, and ran from the room.

"Always in a hurry, Lady Theo is," the seamstress observed

comfortably, gathering up the gown and carrying it to the long sewing table.

Sylvester had his fob watch in his hand as Theo reached the stables, panting, cramming her hat on her head. Dulcie had been saddled and stood placidly beside the earl's black. The massive gelding was shifting on the cobbles, tossing his head and snorting. It was unusual behavior for the well-behaved Zeus, she thought, before her eye was caught by something much more important.

"Seven minutes," Sylvester observed. "Not too bad, considering."

Theo ignored this. She was staring at the sidesaddle on Dulcie's back. "What's that?" she demanded. "Where's my proper saddle?"

"Ah," Sylvester said. "Cousin, it's time you started riding like a lady. The Countess of Stoneridge can't go racketing around the countryside like an itinerant gypsy."

Theo glanced around the stableyard. Two grooms were busy soaping saddles in the shade of an oak tree. "You have no right to make such a decision for me," she said in a fierce undertone.

"If you won't make it for yourself, Theo, then I do have the right," he said as softly. "In two days you'll be my wife, and it doesn't suit my pride to wed a hoydenish romp."

"*Your* pride!" she exclaimed in a whisper. "If it didn't trouble my grandfather, and it doesn't bother my mother, what the *hell* right have you to complain? I don't give a fig for your pride." Even as she said it, she knew it was a silly challenge, and it was one that Sylvester ignored.

He simply caught her round the waist and lifted her into the saddle. "Let your left knee rest on the —"

"I know how to do it," she broke in crossly.

"That's something, I suppose." He smiled, perfectly happy to conciliate now that he had her where he wanted her. He still held her on the saddle, however, but Theo had no intention of making a spectacle of herself by jumping down again. She had the uncomfortable conviction that Stoneridge would simply put her back in the saddle, and such a jack-in-the-box display in front of the grooms was not to be considered.

125

"Let go of me, Stoneridge!" She snatched up the reins, glowering at him.

He held her for a second longer, then nodded and released her, turning to mount the restlessly pawing black.

"Easy, now." He stroked the animal's neck as he gathered up the reins and prepared to spring into the saddle. "Easy, fellow. What's the matter with you?"

"I expect he's objecting to his rider," Theo said, wishing she could have come up with a wittier retort.

Sylvester merely chuckled, and his eyes narrowed as he looked up at her. "Shall you object, gypsy? Somehow I doubt it."

Theo's jaw dropped as a host of unbidden emotions rushed through her at this wickedly suggestive comment. Her eyes darkened in the telltale manner he'd become accustomed to, and Sylvester laughed aloud, swinging himself into the saddle.

He was barely seated before the black raised his head and snorted, his eyes rolling wildly. Before Sylvester had time to grasp the reins securely and get his other foot into the stirrup, Zeus took off at a headlong gallop, crashing over the cobbles, his head up, nostrils flaring.

Sylvester pulled back on the reins, struggling to find his other stirrup as he fought to keep his seat. The horse jumped the railed fence separating the stable from the pasture, his rider clinging on for dear life, and bolted toward the cornfield on the far side.

Theo was so taken aback that she didn't immediately move; then she kicked at Dulcie's flanks and the mare set off in pursuit. Even galloping flat out, there was no way Dulcie could catch the bolting gelding. The black's speed was terrifying as he sailed over the hedge separating the fields. Theo could see that Sylvester had both feet in the stirrups now and was lying low on the animal's neck, gripping the mane as well as the reins, trying to keep his seat.

If he fell from that height at that speed, he'd be lucky not to break his neck, she thought in horror. What could have happened to cause the well-schooled black to bolt? It was all she could do to keep the horse in sight as he careened toward a copse, every now and again rearing up on his hind legs, snorting and bucking violently. Somehow Sylvester stayed on his back.

126

"Dear God," she cried silently, knowing the danger that now threatened when the horse crashed into the copse. A low branch, catching his rider across the head or the throat at that speed would fling him from the horse with a broken neck or a fractured skull.

But Sylvester was aware of the danger. He knew Zeus was not simply bolting; he was also trying to unseat him as he bucked and reared. The horse was an intelligent animal and was as aware as his rider of the dangers of the copse. He charged sideways, intending to smash his rider's leg against a tree trunk. Sylvester saw it coming and yanked his leg upward as the horse veered to the right. It made his seat even more precarious, and he saw the low branches ahead almost too late to fling himself along the animal's neck.

His feet were out of the stirrups now, and he couldn't get them back in. It was all he could do to hang on to the mane. There was only one thing he could do. As Zeus catapulted down the narrow ride, Sylvester reached up, grabbing a branch overhead, hauling himself out of the saddle as the horse charged ahead.

He dropped to the ground, badly shaken but miraculously unhurt. Dulcie came galloping down the ride toward him, Theo white with shock and dread.

"Are you all right?" She drew back on the reins and the mare hung her head, blowing vigorously after the strenuous ride.

"Just about," he said. "I couldn't knot the reins, so I hope to God he doesn't trip over them and break a leg."

"What could have happened to him?" Theo dismounted. "I've never seen a horse do that before."

"Certainly not Zeus," Sylvester agreed. "Is Dulcie up to both our weights?"

"We can't both ride with a sidesaddle," she pointed out, not without a hint of satisfaction, despite the grim circumstances.

"We'll ride bareback," he said brusquely, moving to unstrap the girths. "Zeus will have run himself out soon, and I have to catch him before he does himself some damage."

He lifted the saddle from the mare's back and offered Theo his cupped palms as a mounting block before swinging up behind her, reaching for the reins.

127

The mare walked wearily through the copse and out into the sunlight of a stretch of gorse-strewn common land. Zeus stood on a small hill, pawing the ground and snorting. His neck and flanks were in a lather, and green foam bubbled around the bit. The reins dangled to the ground, and he had one hoof inside them.

"If he takes off again, he'll catch his foot," Theo said, even in her anxiety aware of the powerful body at her back, the earthy scent of his skin, the strength in the arms encircling her.

Stoneridge, however, seemed unaware of her proximity. He dismounted rapidly when they were about ten yards from Zeus. "Stay here, I've a better chance of not spooking him if I approach on foot."

Theo stayed where she was, watching, her heart in her mouth. Zeus lifted his head as the man drew near. He snorted, pawing the earth, his eyes still rolling wildly.

Sylvester spoke softly to him, extending his hand, stepping purposefully toward him. The familiar voice seemed to pierce the animal's terror and weariness, and although he tossed his head and blew through his flared nostrils, he didn't take off.

Sylvester lunged for the reins, grabbing them, and Theo heaved a sigh of relief, trotting over to them.

"Now, let's have a look at you," Sylvester said, looping the reins around his wrist, stroking the sweat-lathered neck. The animal whimpered and showed the whites of his eyes.

Theo dismounted and tethered Dulcie to a gorse bush. "There's blood on his flank," she said as Sylvester bent to run his hands down the horse's fetlocks and under his belly, beneath the girth. "It looks as if it's coming from the saddle."

Sylvester unstrapped the girths and lifted the saddle away. Zeus snorted and stamped, tossing his head as the leather left his back.

"Dear God!" Sylvester breathed, and Theo gasped in horror. The animal's back was pouring blood.

Sylvester tossed the saddle to the ground, turning it over. He bent over it and then swore savagely. "Bastards! Vile bastards!"

Theo dropped to her knees beside him, running her hand over the bloody saddle. A line of sharp tacks had been hammered into the leather, so that the minute Sylvester's weight had dropped

128

onto the saddle, they'd buried themselves agonizingly into the animal's hide.

"Who could have done such a thing?" Theo stared, horror-struck.

"Some vicious piece of scum in the stables," he declared. "And, by God, when I find him, I'll thrash him to within an inch of his life."

"Of course it's not someone from our stables," Theo said, her eyes flashing at this insult to Belmont people. "No one would do such a thing."

"Someone did," he stated flatly, twisting out the tacks. "Some rat with a grudge."

"No!" Theo jumped up. "It's impossible that one of my people would do such a thing."

"*Your* people!" he said. "Exactly so. People who resent a Gilbraith —"

"No!" she cried again. "It's impossible for one of the Belmont people to have done such a thing. I've known them all since I was a child."

"My dear girl, you don't know the first thing about human nature," he declared. "Your faith is touching, but this was done by someone in the stables; where else could it have been done?"

"I don't know," Theo said. "But I *do* know that no one there is that vicious. They wouldn't hurt a horse in that fashion, even if they did have some kind of a grudge against you. And, anyway, they don't."

"I'm well aware of how Belmont people regard a Gilbraith," he said, his mouth a taut line. "And this is the work of some twisted cur. I will get to the bottom of it if I have to confront every member of the estate."

"If you accuse someone of doing this ghastly thing, you'll never be accepted by them," Theo said, her eyes flaring with the passion of her conviction.

"I'm not interested in acceptance," he told her. "I'm interested in respect and obedience. And I intend to have both. Someone is going to pay dearly for this. And if I can't find the culprit, then they'll all pay."

He strode back to the horse, now standing quietly on the grass.

"Come on, old fellow, let's get you home."

Theo bounded after him. "Just you listen to me, Stoneridge. These people are tenants, hardworking farmers, not feudal bondsmen, and they'll respect you if you respect them. You don't know them and you have no right . . . no right at all . . . to accuse any one of them of such a dastardly act. You have no justification and no right!"

"Get on your horse," he said, paying no attention to this tirade. "We'll lead Zeus and send someone back for both saddles."

"Are you listening to me?"

"No," he said, lifting her willy-nilly onto Dulcie and swinging up behind her, taking Zeus's reins in his free hand. "I quite understand why you would wish to defend these people, it's perfectly natural. But you're ignoring reality. I've already had several confrontations with people who don't wish to change their ways, and some spiteful brute clearly thought he would get his own back."

Theo looked over her shoulder at him with withering contempt. "Obviously, my lord, you don't have the first idea of how to establish good relations with your tenants. You'll find, as a result, that you'll never know any of the important things going on around the estate. If they don't trust you, they won't talk to you."

"I have no particular desire to be talked to," he stated, tight-lipped. "And trust does not depend on overfamiliarity with villagers and laborers."

"That just goes to show how little you know," she said scornfully. "My grandfather knew every one of his tenants and all their families —"

"I am not your grandfather," he interrupted. "Trust comes from respect and the knowledge that the lord of the manor has their best interests at heart, even if they don't always agree with his methods. It's not necessary to joke and gossip with every milkmaid and stable hand in the district. And I tell you, now, Theo, you are going to have to curb your free and easy ways once we're married. It's not appropriate for the Countess of Stoneridge to behave as you do."

"How would you know what's appropriate?" she demanded

130

with icy scorn. "If my grandfather didn't consider it inappropriate, what makes you think you might know better? You've no experience of running an estate. My grandfather always said the Gilbraith estate was another Lilliput. You can't learn to manage tenants if you don't have them, my lord. I suggest you leave well alone what you don't understand."

She was only vaguely aware that her tongue had run away with her. Criticism of her grandfather on top of the insults to loyal Belmont people were not to be borne, and she'd jumped to the defense with blind passion.

But her angry, contemptuous words fell into a dreadful silence. The earl's fingers tightened around the reins, his knuckles whitening, but he said not a word until they reached the stable-yard, Zeus now wearied and docile, his injured back bleeding sluggishly.

Stoneridge sprang to the ground and bellowed for the head groom. The man ran across, quailing at the earl's naked fury. His expression, when he saw the damage to Zeus, was so outraged that no one could believe he bore any responsibility for the wounds. The earl issued rapid-fire orders for the treatment of his horse and the retrieval of the saddles; then he swung back to Theo.

She had not yet dismounted and was still foolishly considering that she'd had the last word, when he came to the mare's head, his hand on the bridle.

"Dismount," he commanded in a low voice.

Theo looked down into his face and realized with a shock that she had never seen such a blazingly angry countenance. The scar on his forehead stood out, a white ridged line; a muscle twitched in his cheek, and there was a white shade around the chiseled mouth. He looked quite capable of murder. Her insulting words and the derisory tone now replayed with dismaying accuracy in her head.

"I will tell you just once more," he said as softly. "Dismount *now*. Or this stableyard is going to witness a spectacle that will live in memory for years to come."

Theo swallowed and swung herself off Dulcie. Her feet had no sooner touched the cobbles than the cold silver knob of the earl's riding crop jabbed into the small of her back, and she was thrust toward the exit of the yard. She had no choice but to obey the pressure if she was not to draw unwelcome attention to this forced march toward the house.

She tried to believe that she'd been justified in her attack, but she knew she'd chosen the most insolent and unforgivable words. Her cursed tongue had taken the high road again, she recognized dismally, and Sylvester Gilbraith was not a man to turn the other cheek to an insufferable insult.

They turned onto the gravel sweep before the house. A post chaise was drawn up before the front steps, and suddenly the cold jab of the riding crop left her back. Sylvester stopped on the driveway and took a deep breath.

Without volition Theo looked inquiringly over her shoulder, sensing the current of tension in him, something that had nothing to do with his anger with her.

"I'll have to see to you later," he said almost absently. "It looks as if my mother and sister have arrived."

Theo felt a surge of relief at the reprieve. With any luck so much would be happening in the next few hours that his anger would at least be blunted.

Sylvester walked swiftly toward the chaise, leaving Theo to follow. He'd been dreading this arrival. His mother was a difficult woman at best, an overbearing witch at worst; his sister, a middle-aged and embittered spinster, bullied unmercifully by Lady Gilbraith. What either of them would make of his bride-to-be, he couldn't imagine. He sensed that Lady Belmont had a vein of steel in her that would make her more than a match for his mother, but the next few days were going to be uncomfortable if not downright hideous.

Lady Gilbraith was descending from the chaise as her son arrived. "Ah, Sylvester, there you are." She took his proffered hand as she stepped onto the gravel. "I could wish you'd had the courtesy to come for us. The roads are lawless."

"You have six outriders, ma'am," he said, raising her hand to his lips. "Much more useful than one son."

"Oh, Mama, don't forget your sal volatile," a high voice exclaimed as a bonneted head appeared in the door of the chaise.

"And your reticule."

"Mary, I bid you welcome." He extended a hand to help a round lady in an alpaca cloak. "I trust the journey wasn't too arduous."

"Oh, the inn where we stayed last night was dreadful," Mary said. "The sheets were damp, and I'm sure Mama will have the ague."

"I was under the impression that Mama always travels with her own sheets," her brother said.

"That's true, of course, but it was most dreadfully draughty. The windows didn't fit properly, and I'm certain the mattress was damp." She dabbed at a reddened nose with her handkerchief.

Since Sylvester knew that his sister was afflicted with a permanently red and dripping nose, he made no comment, turning instead to look for Theo, who was standing at a little distance, hands clasped in front of her, a tentative smile on her face.

A picture of conciliation, he thought, half-amused despite his very real anger.

"Theo, let me make you known to my mother," he said, beckoning her forward, keeping his voice deliberately cool, his mouth unsmiling.

Not promising, Theo thought, coming forward. Maybe if she charmed his mother and sister, he'd be inclined to forget her earlier offense.

"Lady Gilbraith." She bowed, and extended her hand, smiling. "I'm delighted to make your acquaintance."

Lady Gilbraith ignored the hand, raised her lorgnette, and examined her. "Goodness me, what a brown creature you are," she declared. "It's most unfashionable. I'm surprised your mother should allow you to run around in the sun and ruin your complexion in that fashion."

She was not going to like her mother-in-law! And that, Theo reflected, was the understatement of the year. But she would demonstrate to Sylvester that she could behave with impeccable courtesy, despite provocation.

"I have a dark complexion, ma'am," she said. "I take after my father. My sisters are much fairer."

She glanced up at Sylvester and saw a glimmer of relief in

133

his eyes. "Theo, this is my sister, Mary."

Mary sniffed and shook hands. "Theo? What a strange name. You must mean Thea, surely."

"No," Theo said. "I have always been called Theo. It was my father's name for me."

"How very strange." Another sniff accompanied the comment. "Mama, we should go inside. The air feels very damp."

Lady Gilbraith surveyed the gracious Elizabethan facade with a critically proprietorial air that sorely tested Theo's resolution. "Quite a handsome house, I suppose. But these half-timbered buildings can be abysmally cramped inside."

"I don't believe you will find Stoneridge Manor cramped, ma'am," Theo said stiffly. "It's generally considered to be a most spacious example of Elizabethan architecture."

"We shall see," her future mother-in-law stated in a tone that indicated she didn't believe a word of it. "Gilbraith House is a most elegant gentleman's residence. I trust my son will not find his inheritance lacking in any of the amenities." She sailed toward the steps, her daughter at her heels.

Theo stared in disbelief at Sylvester, who met her gaze with a rueful smile. "All right, gypsy," he said. "You've earned yourself a suspended sentence dependent on continued good behavior."

Theo ignored this. "Why didn't you warn me?" she demanded.

"Warn you that my mother is a witch?" His eyebrows lifted in ironic question mark. "Be realistic, Theo." He drew her hand through his arm. "Come, let us go in and do what we can to support your mother. It's not for long. You can curb your tongue for two days."

There was a distinct "or else" lurking behind the last statement, but threats or not, Theo decided she owed him the effort to endure his mother's incivilities with a good grace. She certainly owed it to her own mother.

However, she could strike a bargain as well as the next man. "I can curb my tongue if you can curb yours, sir."

She looked up at him, her head on one side, a challenging spark in her eyes. "Promise me you won't accuse anyone in the stables until I've had a chance to talk with them."

134

Sylvester's lips tightened, but he remembered the revulsion on the head groom's face. The standards and conditions in the stables would be set by him. Maybe Theo had a point. She certainly knew these people as he didn't.

"Very well. But if you let your tongue run away with you in my mother's company, Theo, you will pay in full measure for that outrageous display of incivility. Is it understood?"

Theo grimaced at this uncompromising tone but then reflected she'd won both a reprieve and a vital victory. She shrugged. "Crystal clear, my lord."

Chapter Ten

"*Sylvester, you must change the furnishings in this salon without delay; they're positively shabby.*" Theo lifted an imaginary lorgnette and frowned, her mouth pursing, as she delivered this uncannily accurate mimicry of Lady Gilbraith amid delighted whoops of laughter from her sisters.

"Theo, you mustn't," Emily protested halfheartedly when she'd stopped laughing.

"But you sound just like her," Clarissa said. "And you have that exact manner with the nose." She tried an imitation, and Theo flung herself onto a cheerful chintz sofa, clapping vigorously.

"Would someone help me wrap these rabbit skeletons?" Rosie asked from the schoolroom table, where she was hard at work packing up her museum, listening with half an ear to her sisters' irreverent conversation. They were frequent visitors to the schoolroom, particularly when they wished to be undisturbed by other members of the household.

"Here, I'll help you." Clarissa came readily to the table. "Although I really don't care for skeletons."

"But they're beautiful," Rosie said, carefully aligning a spine.

"It's Mama I feel sorry for," Emily said. "Lady Gilbraith's done nothing but complain since she arrived. The bedchamber was too drafty, the bathwater wasn't hot enough, the servants are too slow."

"She's insufferable," Theo stated, fierceness replacing the laughter in her eyes. "She behaves as if she owns the place. Anyone would think *we* were the usurpers. I don't know how much longer I can continue to hold my tongue."

"You are being remarkably forbearing," Clarissa observed, delicately wrapping a thighbone in tissue paper. "Even when she told you that you don't make the best of yourself and you need the guiding hand of a fashionable woman."

"At least she didn't say that in front of Mama," Emily said, joining the two at the table. "But I really expected you to fly off the handle, Theo."

136

"Unfortunately, I can't. There's a sword of Damocles hanging over my head," Theo said crossly.

"Whatever do you mean?"

"Damocles had a sword suspended over his head by a hair at a banquet so he didn't dare eat anything in case he disturbed it," Rosie explained earnestly.

"Yes, I know the story. I want to know what Theo particularly means by it," Clarissa said, looking inquiringly across at Theo, who had jumped off the sofa and was pacing restlessly around the sunny schoolroom. "Who's holding it over your head?"

Theo sighed. She should have known better than to have started this. "Stoneridge, if you must know. But there has to be a statute of limitations, and when it's up, that old bat isn't going to know what's hit her!"

"Theo!" Emily protested, but with a chuckle.

"A statute of limitations on what?" Clarissa persisted.

Theo sighed. "We were at outs, and I said something he didn't like, so I'm paying for it by being impeccably polite to his mother in the face of unbearable provocation."

"Oh." Clarissa looked as if she'd like more details, but to Theo's relief Emily diverted the subject.

"Perhaps you won't see too much of her after you're married."

"My only comfort is that Stoneridge thinks she's a witch too," Theo said.

"He gave his sister such a set-down yesterday," Clarissa remarked. "Did you notice . . . when she was moaning about ringing and ringing for morning chocolate? He said it wasn't fair on the staff to be expected to provide chocolate ten minutes before nuncheon, and if she woke up at a decent hour and bestirred herself a little, she'd be a lot less invalidish."

Theo grinned. "Yes, I enjoyed that. But he doesn't give his mother set-downs, and I'd dearly like to oblige."

"I could put one of my white mice in her bed," Rosie offered. "She was horrid to me yesterday. She said I was too young to be in the drawing room, particularly with dirty nails. I didn't think they were dirty . . . but they might have been," she added. "I'd been digging for worms."

"I think the white mouse is more likely to suffer than the

Witch Gilbraith," Theo said. "She'd probably squash it. Actually, it'd probably die of fright if she so much as looks at it."

"Oh, then I won't," Rosie said matter-of-factly, bringing a sheet of pinned butterflies close to her bespectacled eyes for examination.

"We'd better go downstairs," Emily said reluctantly. "We can't leave Mama holding the fort for too long."

"This time tomorrow they'll be gone." Clarissa rose to her feet.

"And we'll be installed in the dower house."

"And Theo will be a married lady," Rosie finished for her sisters. "I wonder what that'll be like."

"Are you nervous?" Emily asked, linking her arm in Theo's as they left the schoolroom.

Theo shook her head. "About the future, perhaps, but not about tomorrow."

"Or tomorrow night?" Clarissa gave her a sharp glance as they turned out of the west wing into the central hallway.

Theo grinned. "No, most definitely not about that."

"But has Mama told you what happens?"

"Yes, but I already knew, only I couldn't really tell her that."

"How did you know?"

"Stoneridge has been very informative," she said mischievously.

"Theo, you haven't already —"

"Not quite, because Stoneridge wouldn't," she explained. "But I'm not expecting any surprises."

"Surprises about what, cousin?"

The three gasped at the earl's cool voice coming from the corridor behind them. How much had he heard?

Theo spun round. Sylvester was laughing, his eyes bright, and she knew he'd heard a great deal more than he should. "Were you eavesdropping, my lord?"

"Not at all. I just happened to come up behind you," he said, raising his hands in a gesture of disclaimer. "But I'll tell you something, my love, if you're not expecting any surprises, you might be in for a shock."

He let his eyes rest on their flushed faces as they absorbed this. They were all three distinctly unnerved by his sudden appearance, and he enjoyed the sensation of having the upper hand for once in the massed company of Belmont females. Deliberately, he cupped Theo's chin in the palm of his hand and kissed her mouth.

"Life is full of surprises, cousins." Releasing Theo's chin, he offered a bow of mock formality and turned aside into the long gallery.

"I'm glad Mama wouldn't let him choose me," Clarissa said thoughtfully, examining her younger sister's countenance. "He's very worldly and . . . and, well . . ." She searched for the right word. "*Mature.*" She settled for that, although it wasn't quite what she meant. "Not that I don't like him," she added hastily. "I do . . . but he's a little intimidating."

"An understatement," Emily declared. "But he seems to understand Theo." She knew this was what her mother believed, although Elinor had confided to her eldest daughter that she expected the marriage to be punctuated by fireworks.

"I believe that disposes of my marriage quite satisfactorily," Theo said dryly. "I'm going to my room. There are things I have to do."

Her sisters watched her retrace her steps, then exchanged a speaking look and went downstairs to support their mother in her continuing ordeal with her guests.

Theo closed her bedroom door with a sigh of relief. Tonight would be her last night in this room. Since her grandmother's death, the apartment traditionally occupied by the Countess of Stoneridge had stood empty, the furniture under holland covers, but now, after twenty years, it had been prepared for the new countess.

Apart from new curtains and bed hangings, the furnishings were the same as they'd been for three hundred years. The feather mattress had been refilled, the paneling and cherrywood furniture polished and waxed, the tapestry carpet new stitched where it had frayed, the heavy silver candlesticks polished until the old silver seemed almost translucent. And yesterday she'd seen Dan, the handyman, oiling the hinges on the connecting door between the conjugal bedchambers.

Her lips still felt warmed by that light kiss, and she crossed her arms over her breasts as familiar tingles of excitement lifted the fine hairs on her spine. Tomorrow night the mysteries would be revealed, and she would fully understand these strange surges of desire.

Her private smile was unconsciously smug as she picked up the china doll on the window seat, thoughtfully examining its round placid face and bright-blue glass eyes. She'd keep this room just as it was for her own daughter.

But there must be a son too. A son who would eventually become the sixth Earl of Stoneridge. Her father's blood would run in his grandson's veins, and the child would return Stoneridge to the Belmonts.

Theo sat on the window seat, no longer aware that she was cradling the doll just as she had done as a little girl. She closed her eyes, conjuring up her grandfather's face, clear and strong still in her memory. Her father's face was lost to her, except in the portrait on her wall. Opening her eyes again, she gazed at the picture, looking for the distinctive resemblances between father and son. They were there in the high-bridged nose, the full upper lip, the set of the chin. When the time came, she would make her son in their image.

But there would be no children yet awhile. The little bottle that would ensure that lay hidden at the bottom of one of the drawers in the dresser.

At noon the following day she walked up the aisle on the arm of Sir Charles Fairfax, who had once thought to see her married to his own son.

Sylvester watched her approach, smiling slightly at the demure traditional appearance she presented, the raggle-taggle gypsy he'd first encountered invisible beneath the floating veil, the lithe figure, so quick and so efficient in combat, disguised by the yards of virginal white silk and the gauzy train clouding behind her, borne by her elder sisters.

Rosie, in pink muslin, walked solemnly in their wake, bearing a bouquet of white roses. She seemed to be concentrating on her steps, Sylvester thought, noting how her eyes were riveted to the ground. On second thought, she was probably on the lookout for some interesting example of insect life in the cracks in the paving stones.

Theo stepped up beside Sylvester as Sir Charles covered her hand briefly with his own in affectionate reassurance. He was a dear, sweet man who'd known her since she was a baby, but he wasn't her grandfather . . . he wasn't her father. And she knew Elinor would be feeling the same. Tears filled her eyes and she blinked rapidly, grateful for the concealment of her veil. She would not break down; she must be strong for her mother as Elinor would be strong for her.

Then her sisters stepped aside, and Reverend Haversham began the ceremony.

It was over very quickly, Theo reflected, as her husband lifted her veil and the organ burst into renewed life. Too quickly for such a momentous change in one's life. She was now a Gilbraith.

But only in name.

She'd exchanged her name for the right to call Stoneridge her own. For the right to see her children inherit their grandfather's birthright.

His lips were on hers in the ritual kiss, and their open eyes met. For a puzzling second she thought she saw something almost like triumph in the gray gaze. Then it disappeared, and she saw instead a sensual invitation that she knew was mirrored in her own gaze.

She walked out of the church on her husband's arm, her veil thrown back, hearing the shouted congratulations of the estate and village folk, knowing them to be genuine. They were happy to have a Belmont in the manor . . . even a Belmont now called Gilbraith.

They walked back to the manor through the village as tradition dictated, the villagers following them, children throwing wild-flowers in their path. Theo responded to the shouts of congratulations with laughing comments, calling people by their names, asking after family members who weren't in evidence.

Sylvester was content to smile and wave, presenting a genial, friendly appearance, leaving the personal touch to his wife. Satisfaction bubbled in his chest. He'd done it. In four weeks he'd courted and wed his passport to a complete inheritance. Against all the odds, he'd persuaded this temperamental hoyden to abandon her prejudices and take his name. Of course, fate had given him one ace in his pack — Theo's innate passion. Up to now he'd used it to his own advantage, but from now on it would be an instrument of pure pleasure for them both.

Almost as if she'd read his mind, her hand crept into his, her fingers scribbling over his palm in a gesture that somehow contrived to be wickedly suggestive. He closed his fingers tightly over hers, stilling their motion, and bent his head close to her ear.

"Patience, gypsy. All in good time."

She gave a choke of laughter and a little skip, and Sylvester grinned. For the first time since Vimiera, he felt a lightening of the spirit, a sense of pleasure in the prospect of the future.

The stranger, clad in the rough homespuns of an itinerant peddler, kept to the rear of the cheerful throng of visitors accompanying the bride and groom to the manor. His eyes and ears were everywhere as he assessed the reactions of the locals to their new lord of the manor. The cloaked and masked man who'd employed him in the Fisherman's Rest on Dock Street had given him precise instructions: He was to find an opportunity to create a little mischief for the earl — fatal mischief, if at all possible. The man had been a rum sort, swathed in his cloak and speaking through a muffler so his voice had been distorted, but his gold was good.

The stranger took a coin from his pocket and bit it to reassure himself of that fact. He glanced with a Londoner's contempt for country folk at the smiling, jovial men and women around him. Fawning fools, the lot of 'em — dependent on the goodwill of the manor for their livelihood; falling over themselves to make a traveler welcome. He'd strolled into the taproom of the Hare and Hounds, announced himself as a peddler, and no one had questioned him, even in the absence of a pack. Amazing how gullible country bumpkins could be. They'd give him all the information he wanted and not even know they were doing it.

Tampering with the earl's saddle had been as easy as taking cake from a baby: a little chat with the stable lads, a stroll round the tack room, identifying the fine-tooled leather saddle with its embossed design around the pommel. And then five minutes with a hammer and a handful of tacks in the early hours of the morning in the unguarded stable block. It was a damn shame such a neat plan hadn't had the desired results. But there were all kinds of accidents that could befall a man interested in the sporting pursuits favored by the gentry.

He followed the crowd up the driveway to the gravel sweep in front of the house. The bride and groom turned on the step to wave at the cheering peasantry before disappearing through the garlanded oak door. The throng immediately surged toward the back of the house, the soi-disant peddler in their midst. In the kitchen courtyard tables groaned under the weight of pies and puddings, hams and barons of beef, and kegs of ale were ranged against the orchard wall. The manor clearly knew what its tenants expected on these occasions, the stranger reflected, holding a tankard beneath the foaming tap of the keg. Such bounty would be hard to come by in the city.

He drank deeply and looked around. No one was questioning his right to partake of this bounty. Fools. He could work the crowd and pick every pocket, and they'd never suspect. But he was being paid too well to do something else for it to be sensible to muddle things up. He strolled casually out of the yard. This would be a good opportunity to explore further. No one would take any notice of an inebriated wedding guest wandering the grounds.

In the long gallery the small group of friends and family were gathered with more restrained exuberance than the villagers in the kitchen courtyard. Lady Gilbraith, her daughter in tow, made the rounds of the guests with all the assurance of a hostess dispensing the hospitality of her own house. The Gilbraiths had come into their rightful inheritance, and everyone should know it. Elinor's old friends regarded this assumption of authority with puzzled disgust, but Elinor herself struggled to appear untroubled by it. Her daughters, however, all noticed the tautness to their mother's mouth, the unusual stiffness of her posture as she moved around, discreetly seeing to the comfort of her guests as they reeled from the onslaught of Lady Gilbraith.

Theo left Sylvester's side at the door when it seemed that everyone had arrived from the church, and went to join her mother. Elinor turned smiling as her daughter's hand slipped beneath her arm. She opened her mouth to say something, but the words were stillborn as Lady Gilbraith's voice rasped from a group standing beside one of the long windows.

"Stoneridge is a most generous man. Such a delicate gesture to marry one of those poor girls . . . no fortune among them. A sacrifice, of course. He could expect no dowry, but it's so like him to think only of doing the right thing."

"Indeed, Lady Gilbraith." Elinor's cold tones broke into the stunned silence. "I don't consider marrying one of my daughters to be a sacrifice for anyone . . . not even Lord Stoneridge."

Theo felt the blood drain from her cheeks and flood back again in a scarlet tide of rage. Her eyes searched out the earl. He was deep in conversation with Edward's father and Squire Greenham, his head courteously bent toward the shorter men. He took a glass of champagne from a tray passed by a footman, and the muscles in his back rippled beneath the gray silk of his coat. But for once Theo was unaware of his physique as she made her way across the room, pushing past people with too much haste for strict courtesy.

"Stoneridge?" She plucked at his sleeve.

He looked down at her, a smile on his lips that died as he took in her expression. The blue eyes flared like bonfires against a midnight sky, and he could feel her anger as an almost palpable current flowing from her.

With a word of excuse to his companions, he moved aside, ushering Theo into a secluded corner.

"What's happened to put you in such a temper, gypsy?"

Theo shook her head impatiently. "You have not given me a wedding present."

"Not yet," he agreed, clear puzzlement in his voice and eyes.

"Then I am claiming it now," she said in a fierce undertone. "I wish to speak my mind to your mother. But I thought I would tell you first, since we have some sort of a contract on the subject."

"Is that what you call it?" Sylvester said with a dry smile, not yet appreciating the seriousness of the issue. He glanced across the room toward his mother. "So what's all this about?"

144

Theo told him what Lady Gilbraith had said. "I don't mind, for myself," she said in the same fierce tone. "But she embarrassed Mama and forced *her* to be rude to a guest, which she hates to do, so I am going to tell her ladyship exactly what I think of her."

Sylvester closed his eyes on a surge of anger that was directed as much at himself as at his mother. Only he knew how hideously far from the truth she was. If anyone had been generous in this marriage, albeit unwittingly, it was Theo.

He turned from her, saying curtly, "This is for me to deal with, not you."

Theo looked up at him and saw that he was as angry now as he had been with her in the stableyard. She almost began to feel quite sorry for Lady Gilbraith. The old bat didn't know what was coming her way.

"May I come too?" She took a skipping step to follow him.

"No, you may not!"

It was such a ferocious negative that she fell back to observe the scene from a discreet distance.

"Ma'am, a word with you." Sylvester's voice was frigid as he reached his mother. He turned to his mother-in-law and said, "Permit me to make my mother's apologies, Lady Belmont, for an inexcusable insult. I can only imagine she's suffering from an excess of excitement."

Lady Gilbraith's face seemed to fall in on itself. She gasped, two spots of color burning on her cheekbones, but was rendered speechless.

"You will wish to make your farewells, ma'am," Sylvester said. "And I'll escort you to your carriage. I know you wish to reach Stokehampton before nightfall. Mary . . ." He jerked his head imperatively at his equally dumbfounded sister, took his mother's elbow, and escorted her unprotesting from the gallery.

"Good heavens," Elinor murmured. Sylvester Gilbraith was not a man to tangle with. But he'd come to the defense of his bride, and that could only endear him to his mother-in-law. She returned to her duties as hostess with a sigh of relief that the competition had been removed.

Theo, although she couldn't hear any of the exchange, saw

145

her mother-in-law's discomfiture and her swift disappearance and decided that she'd been suitably avenged.

On his way back to the long gallery twenty minutes later, Sylvester stumbled upon Rosie sitting on the floor in the corridor staring intently at the palm of her hand. An empty champagne glass was beside her.

"Is this one ant or two?" she asked, without looking up. "Sometimes I think it's one, and then it seems to be two."

He squatted beside her, taking her upturned palm. "How much champagne have you had?"

"I'm not sure," Rosie said vaguely. "Is it one?"

"It could have been two, but at this point it's just a dead insect smudge," he declared, folding her fingers over her palm. "And don't let me see you with another glass of champagne, little sister, unless you want some trouble." He rose to his feet, reaching down to pull her upright.

"Is that a sword of Damocles?" Rosie inquired, brushing at her dusty pink skirt.

"A what?"

"That thing that Theo said was hanging over her," she replied absently. "I think I'll walk down to the dower house and see if my museum has arrived safely. Will you tell Mama?"

"Yes, I'll tell her." He shook his head, half smiling as Rosie weaved her way down the corridor, on the lookout for any interesting specimens. He thought he was beginning to get the hang of this new family he'd acquired. There was certainly something rather appealing about them . . . particularly when compared to his own.

Refusing to think any further about his mother, he returned to the gallery, where the reception was beginning to break up.

"Have you had news of Edward, Sir Charles?" Emily linked arms with her future father-in-law as they went downstairs. "I keep reading the *Gazette* for news of his regiment, but by the time we get the paper, it's hopelessly out-of-date."

"The news is old news before it goes into print, my dear," Sir Charles said with a sigh. "But we believe that no news is good news."

"I wrote to Edward about Theo's betrothal several weeks ago."

146

Lady Fairfax took Emily's other arm. "I expect a reply is already on its way from Spain."

"Yes," Emily agreed. "Theo and I wrote too."

"Perhaps he'll have a leave in the next few months," Sir Charles said, patting her cheek. "It's hard for you, my dear. It's always hard for women in wartime. Waiting and worrying."

"Women and fathers," his wife said gently. Edward was their only child.

"Lord Stoneridge was in the Peninsula, I believe," Emily said. "But before Edward was sent to serve there."

"I gather Stoneridge served in Portugal," Sir Charles replied. His host had not cared to expand upon the subject beyond the succinct information that he'd been wounded, captured, and exchanged.

"Are you leaving already?" Theo came over to them. "Thank you for giving me away, Sir Charles."

"My pleasure, my dear." He kissed her cheek. "I hope Stoneridge will be doing the same for Emily before too long."

Emily blushed, but Theo laughed and hugged her sister. "Of course he will. I have a feeling Edward will be home very soon."

"Now, what makes you think that, Theo?" Lady Fairfax asked, drawing her cloak around her.

Theo frowned. Why had she said that? It had just slipped out, and yet she knew it to be true. Her scalp lifted as an odd sense of apprehension darkened her mind.

A hand came to rest on her shoulder, and she looked up at her husband, who had come to stand behind her. Her apprehension vanished. There was quiet intent in his gaze, and it was for her alone.

"Do you wish to walk down to the dower house with your mother and sisters?"

"Oh, yes, of course," she said, a moment too late for real enthusiasm, and laughter sprang into his eyes. His bride had other things on her mind.

"Come, then. Your mother and Clarissa are waiting for you and Emily. Sir Charles, Lady Belmont was hoping that you and Lady Fairfax would take tea with her in the dower house."

"We should be delighted," Lady Fairfax said briskly. "The

aftermath of weddings and suchlike can leave one most dreadfully blue-deviled."

She went off energetically in search of Elinor, and the others followed. The party walked slowly to the dower house, everyone aware of what the walk meant. Elinor was losing her home, but she was as assuredly leaving her daughter in possession of everything that would have been hers if her husband had lived. And in that, there was a sense of rightness.

At the door to the dower house, she kissed Theo on both cheeks and said matter-of-factly, "I shan't visit you, my dear. When you and Stoneridge are ready for visitors, send Billy with a message. You have Foster and Mrs. Graves and Cook to help you if you need advice as to the household." It had been readily agreed by all parties that Theo, as she took the domestic reins of Stoneridge Manor into her own hands, would need the services of the old retainers more than her mother in the much smaller dower house.

Elinor extended her hand to her son-in-law. "I wish you joy, Stoneridge."

"Thank you, ma'am." He kissed her hand.

Her eyes held his for a moment; then she said softly, "Theo isn't always easy to understand, sir, but she's worth the effort."

The earl's eyes flicked to his bride, who was bidding her sisters farewell. He smiled. "I know it, ma'am."

The girls were whispering, their heads close together; then Theo broke away, and three laughing countenances were revealed. There was an air of mischief about them all that both amused and intrigued Sylvester, and he guessed they'd been having a similar exchange to the one he'd overheard in the corridor the previous day. Then Theo stepped away from her family, moving beside him.

Putting an arm around her shoulders, he turned her back toward the driveway. They were both aware of the eyes following them to the curve in the driveway until they were out of sight of the dower house.

Theo gathered up the gauzy train of her wedding dress, throwing it over one arm, and began to run back to the manor, her veil streaming out behind her.

After a surprised moment Sylvester broke into a run, catching her up easily. "Gypsy!" He seized her around the waist and swung her into his arms. "What's the hurry?"

"I was hoping you were going to demonstrate the answer to that," she said, resting her head against his shoulder, fluttering her eyelashes at him in a wonderful parody of a demurely flirtatious miss.

"Oh, I intend to," he declared, and with a swift adjustment tossed her over his shoulder. "It will be a great deal quicker in this fashion, I believe."

Ignoring her vociferous protests at this undignified method of transport, he strode up the steps and into the house.

Theo reared up against his shoulder as they entered the hall. The house felt very strange. "Where is everyone?"

"Out," he said. "Celebrating our wedding. Either in the courtyard or in the Hare and Hounds. And they'll be doing so for many hours."

"You mean the house is empty?" she exclaimed.

"In a manner of speaking," he agreed, a chuckle in his voice, as he took the stairs two at a time, despite his burden.

He kicked open the door of his bedchamber and unceremoniously tossed his bride onto the bed in a swirl of silk and guaze.

"Now, Lady Stoneridge, let us put this marriage beyond all possibility of annulment."

Chapter Eleven

"So what happens now?" Theo lay back on her elbows, regarding her husband with a quizzical smile. The clock on the mantelpiece struck four o'clock. Her wedding night was beginning rather early.

"For a start, you stay where you are and do nothing," Sylvester said. His eyes were narrowed, his mouth a firm, straight line, as he stood by the bed looking down at her as she lay in a cloud of virginal white.

"Shouldn't I at least take my shoes off?" She wriggled her feet, clad in ivory satin slippers, by way of demonstration.

"No, I don't wish you to remove a single garment." He eased the snug-fitting silk coat off his shoulders without taking his eyes from her.

There was such intensity of purpose in the hooded gray gaze that Theo shivered, and all desire to joke vanished. It had only been a way of lessening her own tension, she realized.

She watched as he unfastened his cravat and tossed it to join his coat on the chaise longue. The white waistcoat followed it. With slow deliberation he unfastened the tiny pearl buttons hidden in the ruffled sleeves of his shirt before shrugging out of the garment. It joined the others.

Theo had felt the warmth of his skin, the power in his chest and shoulders, but she'd never seen his naked torso. The muscles in his back moved beneath the taut skin as he turned to throw his shirt onto the chaise. There was not an ounce of spare flesh, and when he turned back, she saw a thin white scar running down his rib cage, curving around the narrow waist, following the thin line of black hair down beneath the waistband of his satin knee britches.

In leisurely fashion he pulled off his shoes and his striped stockings. Theo found that she was holding her breath as the buttons of his britches flew undone. He pushed them off his hips, stepped out of them, and turned to throw them onto the chaise.

Theo's eyes stretched wide as they slid down his back, over the firm buttocks, the long, muscular thighs, the hard calves.

He turned slowly to the bed. The scar was etched into the flat belly, finishing just above one slim hip. Theo stared at his aroused flesh and felt the first faint stirring of alarm, imagining that jutting shaft entering her, becoming a vital part of her own soft body, invading her.

But she couldn't take her eyes from him. He was beautiful in his nakedness . . . beautiful and terrifying.

Sylvester leaned over her, cupping her chin in the palm of his hand, bringing his mouth gently to hers. "There's nothing to fear," he said as if he understood the wild complexity of her emotions. "There may be a little pain at first, but it will soon pass."

Theo only nodded, for once in her life unable to find words. Tentatively, she placed a hand on his shoulder, feeling the smooth round bone fitting her palm before sliding her hand down his arm, over the hard swordsman's biceps, her fingers rustling through the thick dark hair on his forearm. After the barest hesitation, she laid her hand flat on his chest, feeling the steady beat of his heart beneath the skin. Boldly, she touched one nipple with the tip of her finger, and he smiled, holding himself still, leaning over her as she continued her exploration.

She traced the scar with a fingertip, running over the clear outline of his ribs and down to his hip, feeling the sharp jutting bone of his pelvis. She wanted to go further but suddenly found she couldn't. She looked up and saw he was still smiling.

"All in good time," he said softly as if he perfectly understood this sudden shyness. "Let's divest you of some of these bridal trappings."

Bringing one knee onto the bed, he deftly removed the pearl fillet that held her veil in place and lifted the filmy white cloud from her head. Her hair beneath was braided into a coronet around her small head. It was a style that gave a neatness and maturity to her face that was a far cry from her usual gypsy dishevelment or the uncompromising plainness of the one long plait.

He let his hand roam over her body as she lay back on the bed, over the swell of her breasts against the laced bodice of her gown, over her belly, pressing the white silk against her

151

skin into the concave hollow, and down over her thighs, molding them with the rich material. His fingers braceleted her ankles, remembering of their own accord that very first time when he'd clasped the slender bony ankles in the same way and dragged her into the mud.

His smile broadened and he looked up her body. "Any memories, gypsy?"

For answer she kicked in mock petulance against his grip, and he laughed, sliding the slippers off her feet, before running his flat hand up her silk-stockinged leg, beneath her skirt.

His fingers found her lace-trimmed garters. Deciding that he would like to see what he was doing, he took the hem of her gown and slowly drew it up over her thighs.

Theo quivered as she felt the air through the thin silk of her stockings. He slid the garters down her leg and then rolled her stockings down, easing them off her feet. Now the air fell directly onto her bared skin, and a wash of vulnerability swept through her. Her hands fluttered to push down her raised skirt, to cover her exposed limbs, and then fell to her sides as the string of her drawers was loosened.

"Lift your bottom, love," he commanded quietly, peeling the undergarment over her hips.

Theo bit her lip hard and did as she was told. Suddenly she was lost and fearful in a strange landscape, and she forgot how she'd been dreaming about this moment, forgot about the strange surges of longing, about the moments of passion they'd already experienced. She wanted to cover herself, push down her skirt, and flee from the room. The man whose hands were on her with such devastating intimacy was a stranger who now had absolute rights to her body. Whenever and wherever he chose to exercise those rights.

Sylvester felt the change in her when the muscles of her thighs suddenly clenched and she was rigid beneath his hand. A puzzled frown crossed his face. He was doing no more to her now than he'd done that evening by the stream, and she'd been wild with passion then.

He took his hands from her and immediately she relaxed. "What is it?" He looked into her face and read the bewildered apprehension in her eyes. "What do you fear, Theo?"

She moved her head against the coverlet in inarticulate denial, closing her eyes tightly as she pushed her skirt down over the top of her thighs.

"Come," he said with a hint of firmness in his voice. "Stand up and let me take off your gown." Taking her by the waist, he lifted her into a sitting position and then drew her to her feet.

He towered above her, and his nakedness was now a threat. Theo wondered how she had ever longed for this moment. How could she long to be possessed, taken, invaded? And yet what she had feared the most was that very longing that swept all rational thought from her mind. But now she was more coldly rational than she could ever remember being, and she didn't want this. Her body belonged only to her.

But his fingers were deftly unlacing the bodice of her gown, pushing it away from her shoulders so it fell in a puddle around her bare feet. Now only her thin chemise stood between her own nakedness and her husband's, and it was removed with the same efficiency.

He drew her body against his and kissed her eyelids and then her mouth, before saying quietly, "We're going to get the hard part out of the way quickly, Theo. I will do my best not to hurt you, but it will be easier if you try to relax."

She wanted to scream at him that she wouldn't let him do this, but the words wouldn't form themselves. She'd agreed to this by agreeing to marry him . . . she'd agreed to marry him because of this. She was married to Sylvester Gilbraith, and this was what that meant.

She lay back on the bed, closing her eyes tightly. It wasn't pain she feared; it was possession.

Sylvester's mouth took a grim turn as he realized she wasn't going to help either of them. He parted her thighs and stroked softly upwards, opening her tight petaled center, brushing his fingers across the sensitive bud. There was no reaction. His fingers slid into her body, feeling how tight and unprepared she was.

Kneeling between her thighs, he stroked her eyelids until she opened her eyes. His flat thumb ran over her mouth. "Sweetheart,

I'm going to hurt you if you can't relax."

"I'm not afraid of being hurt," she said, staring up into his eyes, reading the concern behind the intent.

"Then what is it?"

"I'm afraid of you . . . of losing my body to you," she whispered.

The candid response, so open and so very like Theo, brought Sylvester a surge of relief. If he knew what he was facing, he could overcome it. He continued to stroke her cheek before saying, "You will lose your body to mine, and mine will be lost in yours. It's a partnership, Theo. This act more than any other."

"I'm not stopping you," she said. "Please, just finish it."

He nodded, reached above her head for the bolster, and slipped it beneath her bottom, angling her body to facilitate his entry. His flesh drove into hers in one determined thrust that breached her maidenhead.

Theo gasped with the tearing pain, but she didn't cry out, simply lay as still as she could beneath him as he began to move within her and her body opened and moistened of its own accord, so that the rhythmic movements ceased to hurt and began to set up a strange response deep in the pit of her belly. But before the response could be more than an intimation of pleasure, Sylvester allowed his climactic explosion to burst upon them both, filling her body with his seed, his flesh throbbing deep within her. And Theo found a curious sense of physical release and no sense of invasion, more of fusion, as she felt the pulsing of his body in hers.

Sylvester fell forward and his heart thudded against her breast. Theo laid a hand on his sweat-slick back; it felt like an acknowledgment she was supposed to make.

Sylvester disengaged slowly and looked down at her with a rueful expression. "I'm sorry, Theo. I thought you'd prefer me to finish it quickly."

"But I think I missed something," she said, sounding slightly aggrieved. "I did, didn't I?"

Sylvester fell on the bed, laughing with relief. "Yes, my dear gypsy. You missed a great deal. But you won't the next time."

"Can we do it again now?"

"There are a few things you need to understand about male

anatomy," he said, still laughing as he sat up. "It takes a while to recover its strength."

"Am I bleeding?" Neither the personal question nor the delicate examination it invited troubled her now.

"A little," Sylvester said. "It's only to be expected. Lie still, and when it's stopped, we'll try this again."

He lay back, drawing her head onto his shoulder, and idly began to take out the pins securing the braided coronet. Theo found his fingers in her hair both soothing and arousing in their intimacy. It was a proprietorial intimacy, she realized vaguely, the very thing a few moments before she had feared.

Her hair was the most amazing color, Sylvester thought as he drew his fingers through the long tresses, arranging them over her breasts with deliberate artistry so that the glossy blue-black offered a startling contrast with the milk-white skin visible between the strands. She was as physically different from her sisters as she was temperamentally, although Rosie had some Theo-like quirks in both areas.

Smiling, he moved a strand aside to reveal the rosy crown of one breast. His finger circled slowly around the nipple feeling it grow small and hard. Theo stirred, a little sigh escaping her. Her leg moved against his with an urgent pressure.

"Are you rested yet?" she murmured into his shoulder.

"Why don't you discover that for yourself?" he suggested, running a hand down her side, into the indentation of her waist and over the flare of her hip.

"Oh . . . like this, you mean?" Her own hand slid down his belly, her fingers reaching through the crisp tangle of hair at the apex of his thighs.

"Exactly like that," he agreed softly, inhaling with pleasure as he rose against the palm of her hand.

Theo eased onto her side to extend her reach, a little frown of concentration between her brows, as she learned the feel of him.

Sylvester stroked over her bottom, slipping his hand between her thighs on his own voluptuous exploration, and Theo began to imitate his caresses, on the theory that what pleased her might also please him.

155

When he entered her this time, her body was open and ready, her eyes gazing intently into his as if, determined not to miss one iota of sensation, she was watching his expression for guidance.

Smiling, he bent and kissed her eyes as he eased deeper within the silken sheath, feeling the little ripples of her body tightening around him.

"I'm not hurting you now?"

She shook her head, her eyes bright. "The opposite. It's wonderful."

He laughed softly and began to move with more purpose, watching her eyes as she picked up his rhythm, her body lifting to meet each thrust. Her fingers scrabbled down his spine, and abruptly she gripped his buttocks, pulling him against the cleft of her body, her feet twisting around his calves. Her eyes were wide and filled with a surprised wonder as the pleasure built, deep and inexorable.

Sylvester held himself in check this time, using his body to orchestrate her pleasure as she climbed to her own pinnacle. There came the moment when her eyes sparked fire, her lips parted on a round O of astonishment, her hips arced off the bed. Sliding his hands beneath her, he held her on the shelf of his palms as he drove to her core. She cried out against his mouth, riding the crest of the climactic tidal wave until it tossed her to shore and she fell back onto the bed, sinking into the deep feather mattress, her limbs in an abandoned sprawl, her eyes closing for the first time.

Sylvester remained within her, enjoying his own leisurely climax, stroking her cheek with a forefinger until her eyes opened and she smiled, lifting a hand to stroke his back as she came out of her own trance to recognize her partner in pleasure.

"Fears laid to rest, little gypsy?" he asked softly, gathering her against him as he fell, heavy with fulfillment, to the bed beside her.

"What fears?" she murmured with a weak chuckle. "I seem to be very sleepy."

"Then sleep." He closed his eyes, stroking her hair as he felt her slip into a light doze.

Theo stirred and awoke. Her sleep had been so light, it didn't seem as if she'd ever lost awareness of the sun-filled bedchamber and the deep mattress. The scent of their lovemaking was still in her nostrils, his skin still clung to hers, his breath was still warm and even on her cheek, his hand heavy on her back, holding her against him. And her memory of that glorious surge of pleasure was as clear as if it had just happened.

She stretched against him. "I'm famished."

"You didn't eat anything at the reception," he murmured lazily. "Too busy preparing to attack my mother, as I recall."

"I don't wish to discuss that," she said, her lofty tone spoiled by a massive yawn. "We might quarrel."

"Might we?" He sat up and looked down on her with a quizzical smile. "I thought it was settled."

"For this time," Theo responded, wrinkling her nose. "But you can't promise me I'll never have dealings with your mother in the future, can you?"

"No," he agreed. "I can't promise you that."

"And will you always take my side?"

"I can't promise you that, either, I'm afraid."

It was intended at least in part as banter, but Theo frowned, hitching herself onto one elbow. "How old were you when your father died?"

"Three. Why?" He had only the vaguest memory of Sir Joshua Gilbraith, so vague that he thought it was probably based on the portrait hanging on the stairs of Gilbraith House.

"So you lived alone with your mother and elder sister all your life?"

He shook his head. "No. When I was five, I was sent away to school. I spent hardly any time at home after that. At ten I went to Westminster School and spent most of the year there."

"Why would they send you away so early?" Theo was horrified at such a grim picture. A five-year-old child was far too young to be sent out into a frequently brutal world on his own.

Sylvester shrugged. He'd never given his childhood much thought. It was a world he'd shared with his school friends; none of them questioned either its harshness or its rightness. Except

Neil Gerard, who'd spent those years in a state of permanent terror. An English public school was no place for the physically timid — let alone the coward. Again some shadow of memory pushed insistently against the dark periphery of his mind. For a second he struggled with it, and then it was gone. Theo was looking at him in some puzzlement, waiting for an answer to her question.

"My trustees believed it wouldn't be good for a boy to grow up without a man in the house," he said. "An all-male environment is considered preferable for the upbringing of boys." Smiling, he brushed a lock of hair from her forehead. "Don't look so worried, gypsy. I suffered in good company."

"But you still suffered?"

"I suppose so." He shrugged again. "But we didn't look at it that way at the time. It was, after all, a highly privileged existence."

"But didn't they beat you?"

"All the time," he said with a chuckle.

"And they never kissed you or cuddled you?"

"Good God, no!" He sounded genuinely shocked at such an idea.

Theo frowned down at the coverlet. No wonder he was such a reserved man. And yet behind that intimidating, controlling exterior she knew there was humor and warmth and sensitivity. One just had to know how to tap into it.

"Well, it sounds dreadful to me," she declared, and dropped the subject, returning to the original topic. "Shall we have a picnic? There must be plenty of food in the kitchen. I know there was a dish of dressed crab, and a salmon mousse, and I believe there was a rabbit pie." She swung her legs energetically off the bed. "I'll bring up a tray."

"Theo, I detest eating in bed," Sylvester protested, half laughing at this enthusiasm.

"Oh, do you? I like it."

"Crumbs," he said succinctly. "In the sheets, sticking to your skin."

"Oh, pah! We'll shake the sheets out afterward." Theo headed toward the connecting door between their bedchambers in search of a wrapper on her own side of the door. "We can have a bottle of the ninety-nine burgundy. You can bring it up. It's in the fourth rack on the left-hand side of the first cellar, three rows in."

Sylvester raised his eyebrows. "One of these days you must draw me a map of the cellars."

"Oh, you don't need a map. If I'm not here to help you, Foster will be. He knows them as well as I do."

She disappeared into her own room and didn't see Sylvester's frown. He did not intend to be dependent on the knowledge of his wife and his butler. But his wedding night was not the moment to tackle the issue. He shrugged into a dressing gown.

In the courtyard his lordship's servant was leaning on a rapidly emptying keg of ale, deep in discussion with the itinerant peddler, a fellow Londoner who had been as pleased as Henry to meet one of his own kind among the country bumpkins.

"So he's been doin' a bit o' cradle snatchin', this bloke of your'n," the peddler observed, peering at the level in his tankard.

Henry squinted up at the sun. "Not what I'd call it. That Lady Theo seems to know what's what. Bright as a button, she is. Knows her way around this estate like the back of her hand."

"But still she's a babby compared with 'er husband."

"What's it to you, any road?" Henry demanded, his sense of privacy and personal loyalty violated by these observations from a stranger.

The peddler shrugged. "Nothin' really. Just interested. Folks in the village 'ave been talkin'."

"Loose-tongued gossips, the lot of 'em," Henry declared.

"There's talk about 'ow the lass is a Belmont and his lordship's some other family and 'ow there's bad blood between the two of 'em," the peddler persisted, bending to refill his tankard at the tap of the keg. The flow was sluggish, and he swore softly, putting his shoulder against the keg to tip it up farther.

Henry grunted. "Don't know about that. Seems to me everyone's well satisfied with the arrangement. His lordship's got himself a wife, the wife's family stay put on the family estate. Suits everyone, stands to reason."

"Mebbe so." The peddler nodded gravely. " 'Is lordship much of a hunter, is 'e?"

Henry shrugged. "Much as most gentry, I reckon. Takes his gun out on a good morning."

"There's good duck huntin' on that Webster's Pond, I've been told," the peddler mused. "Village folks like to keep it to theirselves, so I've been told, so I reckon as 'ow yer bloke don't know that. Pass it along, I should." He pushed himself away from his leaning post. "Well, I'll be on me way. Nice talkin' to ye."

"Aye." Henry raised a hand in farewell, not too sure that he cared for the stranger, fellow Londoner or not. There was something unpleasant about a man who listened to gossip. But his lordship might be interested to hear about the duck hunting on Webster's Pond . . . once he'd become sufficiently accustomed to the marital bed to leave it early in the morning.

Grinning slightly, Henry strolled across the yard to where a group of dairymaids were giggling among themselves. He'd had his eye on that Betsy for several weeks — a rosy-cheeked girl with a nice buxom figure that a man could really get his arm around.

"He's comin' over." One of the girls nudged Betsy in the ribs, whispering vigorously. "I told ye he'd got 'is eye on you, Betsy."

"Get away wi' you, Nellie." Betsy jabbed her elbow into her sister's ribs, but her cheeks were redder than ever.

"Fancy a walk, then, little maid?" Henry winked, noting her blush with satisfaction. "I'll buy you a glass of porter down at the inn."

"Oh, me dad would kill me," Betsy exclaimed in genuine shock. "I can't go into no inn. It's not decent fer a maid to be seen in a public taproom."

Country folk, thought Henry with a derisory head shake. "Well, how about just a walk, then?"

"Go on, our Betsy." Nellie pushed her friend forward. "Our dad won't mind. Mr. Henry's a fine gentleman with a good position."

Betsy looked doubtful, and Henry began to wonder if he was getting in too deep. A simple walk didn't commit a man to any-

160

thing, and he certainly wasn't interested in following his lordship to the altar. Not yet awhile, at least.

"Oh, well, all right then." Betsy spoke before he had time to withdraw the offer. "Jest a stroll to the village . . . but on the main road, mind." She took his arm with a confidence that caused Henry to doubt the earlier maidenly blushes. Perhaps these country folk were less simpleminded than they appeared.

While Henry was strolling down to the village with Betsy, the peddler was walking around Webster's Pond. The ducks were settling down for the evening, sitting on the water or hiding in the tall marsh grasses. It was, indeed, a likely hunting spot.

From which direction would a man appear from the manor? The stranger walked the circumference of the pond, decided the most natural approach would be from the south, and pushed through the undergrowth looking for likely positions for his man traps.

A man picking his way through the wet undergrowth on a misty early dawn, a gun over his shoulder, a game bag at his belt, wouldn't be looking for the evil teeth of a trap, particularly on his own land.

Chapter Twelve

"Theo . . . Theo! Theo, where are you?" Emily burst through the front door two days later, her urgent cry ascending the stairs to the long gallery where Theo was waiting for Sylvester to join her. He'd agreed to a friendly bout of unarmed combat, but with some reluctance, and she was beginning to suspect he was looking for a way to postpone the engagement.

At Emily's cry, however, she ran from the room, her heart thumping with sudden premonition. It was the first visit by any of her family since the wedding, and as her mother had said the duration of the honeymoon was hers to dictate, she knew that only something desperate would have brought Emily in this unceremonious fashion.

Her sister's face confirmed her fears. Tears poured down Emily's distraught countenance, and her appearance was a far cry from her usual crisp elegance. It had rained heavily in the night, and she was hatless, her hair disheveled, her linen gown splattered, her shoes muddied from where she'd splashed through puddles on the drive.

"What is it?" Theo hurtled down the stairs.

"Edward!" Emily gasped. "It's Edward —"

"Killed?" Theo felt the blood drain from her cheeks, and a sick, leaden dread settled in her belly.

Emily shook her head, but she was crying so hard now that she couldn't speak.

Theo seized her by the shoulders and shook her with desperate urgency. "What happened to him, Emily? For God's sake, tell me!"

"Easy now." Sylvester strode across the hall from the front door. He'd been talking to the head gardener in the shrubbery when his sister-in-law had pelted past them up the driveway, her distress so obvious that he'd followed immediately.

"Easy, Theo," he repeated, taking her waist and moving her to one side. "What's happened?"

"It's Edward," Theo said, now almost as distraught as her sister. "Something's happened to him, but Emily won't tell me."

162

"Well, screaming isn't going to do anyone any good," he declared, taking Emily's arm and ushering the sobbing girl into the library, leaving Theo to follow.

His firm authority for the moment had a calming effect, and Emily struggled to control her sobs, accepting the large handkerchief he pressed into her hand.

Theo was hopping from foot to foot in despairing impatience as her sister finally controlled herself sufficiently to be coherent.

"Edward's been wounded," Emily at last managed to blurt out.

"Seriously?" Theo was white beneath the sun's bronzing, and the scattering of freckles across the bridge of her nose stood out in sharp relief. Her eyes were so large with distress, they dwarfed her other features.

"His arm . . . they amputated his arm," Emily gasped before collapsing onto the sofa in a renewed burst of uncontrollable sobs.

"Oh, no." Theo stood in shock, trying to imagine Edward crippled — a man who loved all physical sports; the friend who'd taught her unarmed combat and how to fence; the friend with whom she'd swum in the cove as a child, scrambled over the cliffs, climbed trees in search of birds' nests, ridden to hounds.

Sylvester moved to the weeping girl on the sofa. Her sobs were beginning to catch in her throat in an alarming fashion, and he was afraid she was about to go into strong hysterics.

"Emily!" He took her shoulders, forcing her to look at him. But her eyes were wild and unseeing. She opened her mouth on a soundless scream.

Sylvester slapped her cheek with calculated force, and the wildness in her eyes was replaced with shock and then recognition. "I do beg your pardon, Emily," he said. "But you were about to go into hysterics."

"Mama always does that," Theo said, her own voice shaky as she struggled with her own distress. "Emily's of a nervous disposition, she can't help it." She sat beside her sister, wrapping her arms around her. Her sister needed her support at the moment more than she herself needed time to come to terms with this news. "Poor sweet, what a terrible shock for you. How

163

did you hear about this?"

"Lady Fairfax." Emily's voice still trembled, but it was clear she was in control of herself again and obviously didn't resent Sylvester's swift intervention. "She came to the dower house. They'd received a letter from Edward's colonel."

"How did it happen?" Sylvester asked calmly, going to the sideboard and filling a glass with ratafia. It wasn't what he would have chosen for shock, but he knew his sister-in-law's tastes.

"A sniper," Emily said, accepting the glass with a tearfully polite smile. "He was shot in the shoulder. But why would they have to amputate his whole arm?"

"To prevent mortification," Sylvester explained, pouring sherry for himself and Theo. "Instant amputation may seem an extreme move, Emily, but it saves life." He saw the blood-soaked tables in the hospital tents, the bins overflowing with amputated limbs, the flickering candlelight, the exhausted, blood-reeking surgeons with their great smoking knives; the anguished screams filled his head.

He kept his voice matter-of-fact. "The French do much better than we do with their wounded, because they discovered early that the sooner an injured limb is removed, the better the chance of survival. Before any battle, or even skirmish, they have hospital tents set up and an army of carts and limbers to remove the wounded from the field the instant a truce is declared. We're learning from them slowly, getting our wounded off the field faster, but still not fast enough. Our butcher's bills in the hospital tents still exceed theirs."

Edward Fairfax, although he probably wouldn't acknowledge it at the moment, was a lucky man if an enlightened surgeon had taken drastic action in time.

"What else did the letter say?" Theo took a gulp of her sherry, fighting to keep the horrifying images from overrunning her mind. Edward in agony, biting a bullet as they sawed through bone and sinew . . .

She glanced at Emily and realized that her sister's imagination hadn't stretched to those horrors. She told herself that that agony was over for Edward now, so there was no point in morbid imaginings, but the dreadful pictures still played behind her eyes.

"He's coming home," Emily said. "Obviously he'll never be able to fight again."

There were small mercies, Theo thought resolutely, even in tragedy. A crippled Edward was not a body lying inert on a battlefield. "He'll manage," she said. "You know how strong-minded he is. He won't let something like this ruin his life."

Sylvester perched on the edge of the table, regarding the sisters, hearing Theo's struggle to comfort Emily, understanding her struggle to believe in her own reassurances. He knew better than they the devastating effects of amputation. A young man learning to accept that he was no longer whole. How would this Edward Fairfax handle the card that fate had dealt him? Most men were embittered and filled with self-disgust, seeing in the words and gestures of love and support the patronizing charity of people who pitied them. If Emily was expecting her fiancé to run into her arms as if nothing had happened, she was in for a rude awakening when the wounded man returned.

Returned to the neighborhood and the close contact he'd always had with the Belmonts. The thought obtruded violently into his musings. "What regiment is he in?"

"Seventh Hussars," Theo replied.

"When did he buy his colors?"

"A year ago."

The Seventh Hussars would probably know nothing of the affairs of the Third Dragoons. A young man in the Seventh Hussars would know nothing of Vimiera. His regiment hadn't been part of that expeditionary force, and Fairfax hadn't been in the army then, anyway. Unless he'd heard something . . . but why would he have? He'd know nothing of the past of the present Earl of Stoneridge. Even if he'd heard rumors of the scandal of Vimiera, he'd not associate them with Theo's husband. And it was such an old story now, superseded by so many other scandals.

He glanced at Theo, still sitting with her arm around her sister. Her face was set, that firm jaw unwavering. How would such a straightforward, bold creature view a husband tainted with the charge of cowardice? It wasn't difficult to imagine the answer, and it chilled him to the marrow. He told himself again that there was no reason why the dishonorable past should ever rear its head, but he wished Edward Fairfax to the devil.

"How long will it take him to journey from Spain, sir?" Emily asked, her voice much stronger now, although she was twisting his handkerchief convulsively between her hands.

A man weakened by pain and loss of blood would make slow progress unless he had comrades who would look out for him and ensure he found transport in carts and wagons across country until they reached the coast and a naval ship.

"It's hard to say, Emily. Anywhere from a week to a month."

"That's an eternity," Theo muttered, her mind uncannily following Sylvester's along the route of a severely wounded soldier making shift through war-torn Spain. "Come, Emily, we'll walk back to the dower house and talk to Mama. Does she know about this?"

Emily shook her head. "She was out when Lady Fairfax called. Lady Fairfax didn't want to tell me the news without Mama, but she was so upset, she couldn't keep it to herself."

"I can imagine." Theo rose briskly. "I don't know how long I'll be, Stoneridge." Without a backward glance she hustled Emily into the hall.

Sylvester raised an eyebrow at her departing back. Since their wedding she'd been using his first name quite naturally, but it seemed that with the intrusion of the outside world, old habits reasserted themselves. He would have liked to go with them to the dower house, but Theo obviously felt the Belmont women were sufficient unto themselves.

The reflection left him feeling strangely empty and lacking in some way after the hours of intimacy they'd shared in the last two days.

"What's it like?" Emily asked abruptly, half running to keep up with Theo's hasty stride. Her own future, until this morning so certain and secure, had been abruptly threatened, and the question arose naturally from her own turmoil. "Marriage, I mean. Was it . . . I mean . . . is it . . ."

"It's lovely," Theo said, rescuing her sister from the morass, well aware of what aspect of marriage was concerning her. "But I imagine it helps if one of you knows what's what." She linked her arm through her sister's, saying intently, "You'll find out

166

soon enough, love."

"Oh, but poor Edward!" Tears thickened Emily's voice again. "To have only one arm —"

"Edward will do very well," Theo interrupted, refusing to allow her sister to pity Edward. The one thing he would hate would be pity. "And when it comes to lovemaking, I can assure you one doesn't need two arms. Think of Lord Nelson . . . one eye and one arm didn't put Lady Hamilton off."

"Oh, you can't think it would matter to *me!*"

"No, I don't. And Edward will make the best of it, you know he will. And you'll help him to do so."

She spoke with brisk reassurance to forestall another bout of weeping, and in her heart she believed that her old friend wouldn't allow his disability to ruin his life, but she ached to be with him as she thought of how he must be feeling at the moment, so far from the people who would rally round him and give him the strength to come to terms with his injury.

Elinor was waiting for them as they entered the house. Clarissa had told her of Lady Fairfax's visit and Emily's headlong rush to the manor to find her sister. It was a pity that Theo's honeymoon had been disrupted, and with such wretched news, but Elinor knew that Theo couldn't have been kept in the dark about her best friend's tragedy.

As she'd expected, Theo was pale but dry-eyed, supporting her sister, who looked ready to collapse and did so as soon as she saw her mother. Elinor took her into the drawing room, ensconced her on the sofa with smelling salts and a tisane, then firmly ushered Theo out of the house.

"Go back to your husband, now, dear. You'll come to terms with this in your own way, and there's nothing more you can do for Emily that I can't do equally well."

"No, I know." Theo ran a hand through her hair, pushing her fringe off her forehead. Her eyes were clouded, and there was a tremor to the usually firm set of her mouth.

Elinor took her in her arms. "Oh, Mama," Theo said, her grief and anger at the injustice of it all ringing in the simple word. Her mother simply held her, stroking her hair, until Theo pulled back and offered a small, tremulous smile. "I'll manage now," she said, and Elinor knew she would.

"You should talk to Stoneridge about it," she suggested. "He was in the army; he'll know how people manage to cope with these injuries."

Theo frowned. "But he doesn't know Edward. He couldn't possibly know anything about how Edward will be feeling."

"But he will wish to know what *you* are feeling," Elinor said gravely.

Theo's frown deepened. Sylvester was very good at taking charge of things, and very good at making things happen, witness the fact that she was now Lady Stoneridge. But somehow she couldn't imagine weeping on his shoulder, sharing her innermost feelings with him. She could laugh with him and make love with him, but she didn't think she could cry with him.

Theo walked slowly back to the manor. Perhaps she shouldn't assume that Sylvester could not understand the Belmont grief. She'd married him so that they could all stay together, and in her heart of hearts she knew she expected him to make the effort to become a Belmont. After all, she could never become a Gilbraith. He had taken over the Belmont inheritance, and it was his duty to make himself one of them. But how could he if she didn't include him in the family concerns?

Edward wouldn't have to become an honorary Belmont when he married Emily. Fairfaxes and Belmonts had existed side by side in the Dorsetshire countryside for three generations. There was no competition, no rivalry, no bad blood.

Ah, Edward. Tears welled abruptly, and this time she let them flow. She turned off the driveway, pushing her way through the shrubbery, heading for the rear of the house. She ran down the hill toward the stone bridge over the stream. Her plait thumped against her back, the divided skirt she'd worn for the friendly challenge in the long gallery fluttering around her ankles.

Sylvester saw her from the library window. His instinct was to follow her, and he had one leg over the windowsill before he thought better of it. If she'd wanted his comfort, she could have come to him.

He turned back to the ledgers detailing last year's estate affairs, but he couldn't concentrate. Theo's pale face with the dark

168

smudges of her freckles and her distressed eyes wouldn't leave his internal vision. What kind of man was this Edward Fairfax to inspire such love and friendship from a woman who, Sylvester knew, didn't give lightly of herself?

He was a man coming home with a hero's wound.

He threw down his pen and pushed back his chair with a soft execration, forcing himself to refuse the bitter comparison as it rose ugly in his mind. That had nothing to do with anything. Theo loved Edward Fairfax as one would love a close relative. He was to be her brother-in-law. There was nothing in such a relationship to cause a husband a moment of unease. No sexual passion.

But the power of lust did not last forever. Passion would eventually die without a deep and abiding friendship to water its soil.

But he hadn't married a Belmont because he wanted a deep and abiding friendship in his marriage. He'd married her because he needed what she would bring him . . . because that tricky old bastard had willed it. That he had ended up with a lively, passionate partner in his bed was merely a wonderful bonus.

Resolutely, he picked up his pen and turned his attention to the column of figures detailing expenditure on tenant housing. The old earl hadn't stinted in this regard, and presumably the new one would be expected to follow in his footsteps. Theo would certainly expect it, but there were extravagances here. . . .

It was an hour before Theo walked back up the hill. Sylvester glanced out the window and saw her as she approached the house. On impulse he leaned out and called to her, and she changed direction, coming up to the window.

Her face was still pale, but she was dry-eyed and calm, although her smile was somewhat distracted.

"Coming in?" he asked cheerfully, leaning over to catch her under the arms, lifting her bodily through the window. Setting her on her feet, he tilted her chin and lightly kissed her mouth. She didn't resist the caress, but her usual response was conspicuously absent.

"How did your mother take the news?" he asked, releasing her.

169

"As you'd expect," Theo said with a shrug. "She's had her share of tragedy, and I've never seen her give way."

He nodded and tried to find some way of penetrating her distraction. "How about that friendly match you wanted?"

She looked surprised. "But I rather had the impression that you didn't want to do it."

"Well, I don't believe it's appropriate for a husband to wrestle with his wife, if you want the truth. However, just this once . . ." He smiled, but the invitation fell on stony ground.

Theo shook her head. She didn't feel like playing, and it seemed insensitive of him to suggest it.

"In that case you'll be relieved to know that I've lost interest in the idea myself," she said with a feigned briskness. "I'm going to ride down to the village and see how Granny Moreton's doing. She's been sick for weeks, but she's such a crusty old dame that the villagers aren't as attentive to her as they might be. I'll take her some spearmint tea from the still room and a bottle of rum. She's much better-tempered when she's had a drop or two."

So much for overtures! Sylvester returned to his ledgers as the door closed behind her. He'd tried, and if Theo wouldn't respond, then there was nothing more he could do.

Theo rode into Lulworth, stopping frequently to acknowledge the greetings of the village folk. It struck her that she was treated with an unusual degree of deference since she'd become the Countess of Stoneridge, the women curtsying, the men doffing their hats with meticulous respect. Since these were village folk who for the most part had seen her in and out of scrapes throughout her childhood, had bandaged her scraped knees on occasion, fed her gingerbread and cider on winter afternoons, told her family stories, teased and scolded her as a child, it felt very peculiar and rather uncomfortable.

Her eye fell on a man sitting on the ale bench outside the tavern. She'd not seen him in the village before. He had the pasty, pale skin of a townsman and was staring at her with a rude interest that she'd never before experienced.

"Who's the stranger, Greg?" she asked the innkeeper, who was chatting in the afternoon lull with one of his cronies under the spreading branches of a massive beech tree.

Greg glanced back the way she'd come and spat in the dust. "Peddler, my lady. Says he's passing through, but he's been 'ere a powerful long time for a man on the road, if you asks me."

"Is he staying at the inn?"

"Aye . . . and pays 'is shot every morning, so I've no complaints."

Theo frowned. Folk passed through Lulworth often enough, but they didn't remain aimlessly in the village. Abruptly, she remembered the mystery of Zeus's saddle. Even Sylvester was now convinced that no one in his own stables had been responsible. "Is he doing business among the farms?"

"Not that I know of, Lady Theo. Haven't even seen 'is pack. But 'e's generous enough in the taproom of an evening and can tell a good story."

"Odd," Theo murmured, nudging Dulcie into a walk again. "Good day to you, Greg."

It was silly to allow her imagination to run away with her. But someone had set out to injure the Earl of Stoneridge. Why? What kind of dreadful grudge could someone bear him to warrant such a vicious revenge? Her husband had spent thirty-five years in the world before he'd crossed her life. How could she ever expect to know everything about him? She thought of Edward . . . she thought how well she knew him, well enough to be a part of his agony now, even at such a distance. She couldn't imagine ever reaching such an emotional closeness with her husband. He was a stranger in so many ways. The thought chilled her and she pushed it away. Things could change.

The peddler, well aware that he'd been the subject of the conversation, decided he was close to outstaying his welcome in Lulworth. He'd planted his mantraps in the undergrowth on the manor approach to Webster's Pond, and perhaps it was time to move on to the next village, staking out the traps at dawn until they caught what they were intended to catch.

Of course, it was always possible they'd snap up another victim by accident, but poachers got what they deserved. An accidental victim, however, would be spared the bullet in the head . . . or perhaps "spared" wasn't the correct word. The bullet would put a man out of his misery when the vicious teeth bit into bone and sinew. Gamekeepers had been known to leave men screaming in those traps for days sometimes before loss of blood brought an end to their suffering.

The peddler grinned, picking his teeth. He'd enjoyed a succulent rabbit stew for his midday meal. That Mrs. Woods was a cook to steal a man's heart away. He'd be sorry to move on.

Theo completed her afternoon's business and rode home, still unable to come to terms with the image of a disabled Edward. He was such a sportsman, so agile and swift, a superb marksman, a bruising rider to hounds, such a physical being. . . .

Tears blinded her again, and she hurried across the hall and upstairs, heading straight for her old room, feeling the need to touch childhood memories that would bring Edward alive for her.

Foster, who knew everything that occurred under the roof of Stoneridge Manor, informed his lordship, when asked, that he would find Lady Theo in her old bedroom. The butler's face was impassive, his tone as politely distant as always, but Sylvester could read his unease beneath the tranquil tones.

"Thank you, Foster. You've heard the news about Lieutenant Fairfax?"

"Yes, my lord. A great tragedy. Mr. Fairfax is a fine gentleman . . . one of the finest, if I might be so bold." Foster straightened a stack of papers on the library desk. "He'll make Lady Emily a fine husband."

"I'm sure," Sylvester said, going to the door. He strode up the stairs. Outside Theo's door he hesitated, wondering why he was pursuing her when she'd made it so clear that she wanted to be left alone. But something wouldn't let him walk away. She was his wife when all was said and done, and she was in pain.

Quietly, he lifted the latch and eased the door open. Theo was sitting on the window seat, her forehead resting against the panes, her body very still.

He was about to close the door again, when she said without turning her head, "Sylvester?"

"May I come in?"

"If you wish."

There was no welcome in the flat statement, it was much more "If you must."

Regretting his impulse, he left her without another word, closing the door quietly. He was an intrusion on her grief, an irrelevancy when it came to her beloved friend's agonies. Well, he'd know better another time.

He went back to the library and the ledgers, telling himself that if comforting his wife was one marital obligation he didn't have, he should be grateful. Somehow, though, he couldn't be convinced. He kept thinking of Edward Fairfax. Theo wouldn't have rejected solace from that quarter.

Alone, Theo rocked herself on the window seat, hugging her breasts with crossed arms. Why had she sent him away so coldly? She didn't know, except that she couldn't imagine opening her soul to him. It wasn't that kind of marriage.

A great wave of sorrow engulfed her, and her head drooped against the window again, the glass cool against her hot forehead as she wept, no longer sure whether she wept for Edward or for herself.

Chapter Thirteen

Lawyer Crighton was not comfortable. His neighbor on the London-to-Dorchester stagecoach was a particularly fat lady festooned with boxes, parcels, and hampers. She was on her way to her daughter's confinement and clearly transporting all her worldly goods. She was also an inveterate talker and rattled on continuously with a minute description of every member of her large family and their own extended circles, until he wished every one of them a peaceful but speedy demise.

The man opposite did nothing to alleviate Mr. Crighton's discomforts. He slept throughout the journey, snoring loudly, his open mouth exuding a fetid aroma of stale beer and onions. His farmer's boots were caked with manure and his legs stretched across the narrow space between the two benches, his feet firmly planted between the lawyer's own.

A nervous lady with a canary in a cage and an obstreperous little boy completed the stage's way bill, and after the child had kicked the lawyer's shins for the umpteenth time and the fat lady had offered him a greasy bacon sandwich that turned his stomach, Mr. Crighton was ready to abandon his seat inside for the seat on the box next to the coachman. But he had on his best coat and new Hessians, and the roads were thick with white dust in the still sweltering summer heat.

It was late morning when the stage drew up in the courtyard of the Dorchester Arms, and the lawyer climbed stiffly down, bidding a heartfelt farewell to his fellow travelers. He stood pressing his hands into the small of his back to relieve the ache, squinting up at the bright sunshine.

"Well, good day to ye, Lawyer Crighton." The landlord bustled across the cobbled yard, wiping his hands on his baize apron. "It's that time again, is it?" He snapped his fingers at a liveried inn servant. "Take the gentleman's bag to his usual room, Fred. Yes, sir," he went on to Crighton, his good-natured face wreathed in smiles. "Can't think where the time goes. It'll be Christmas before we blink."

Lawyer Crighton nodded his agreement to this and followed

the landlord into the cool, oak-beamed tap room.

"Ye'll take a bumper of porter, sir," the landlord said, rhetorically. The lawyer paid quarterly visits to the Dorchester Arms when he came to do routine business with his landowning clients in the county, and his tastes and habits were well-known to the innkeeper. He set a pewter tankard on the shiny mahogany surface of the bar counter. "The missus is preparin' a nice saddle of mutton for dinner, and I'll fetch ye up a bottle of best burgundy."

Mr. Crighton took a deep, revivifying swallow of porter, wiped his mouth on his handkerchief, and declared, "I'll be going to Stoneridge Manor directly, Mr. Grimsby. If you'd be so good as to have the pony put to the gig."

The innkeeper nodded, understanding that the lawyer expected an invitation to dine at Stoneridge, as had been standard practice in the days of the old earl. Of course, things might be different now, no one had yet formed a definite opinion on the new Lord Stoneridge, but with Lady Theo still at the helm things couldn't change too drastically.

"I'll be doing business with Squire Greenham tomorrow," the lawyer said deliberately. Again Mr. Grimsby nodded. The squire was not known for his hospitality, and a saddle of mutton at the Dorchester Arms would not come amiss on that occasion.

"I'll tell the ostler to see to the gig, then," he said comfortably. "But maybe ye'd like a nice meat pie as a spot of nuncheon before you go."

Lawyer Crighton acceded to this and settled down in a window alcove looking out on the busy main street of the county town. He enjoyed these quarterly visits to his country-based clients. It was more like a holiday than business, he reflected with a little nod of satisfaction, and a real pleasure to leave the dust and grime and noise of London for a couple of days.

Theo was walking down to the dower house in the early afternoon with an armful of roses for her mother's drawing room. It was very hot, and halfway down the drive she stopped and perched on a fallen log in the shade of an ancient oak, closing her eyes, inhaling the fragrance of the roses, listening to the drowsy bumbling of a bee in the clover-strewn grass at her feet.

"Theo? What are you doing?"

Rosie's curious tones brought her out of her reverie, and she turned with a smile. "I might ask the same of you. Aren't you supposed to be doing lessons at this hour of the day?"

The child took off her spectacles and wiped them on a corner of her apron. Her blue eyes were weak and vulnerable as she peered myopically at her sister. "Reverend Haversham had to go to see the bishop, so he gave us a holiday this afternoon. I'm foraging."

"For what?"

Rosie shrugged. "Anything that takes my fancy. Nothing's wasted."

Theo laughed. "So what's happening at the dower house?" She patted the log beside her.

Rosie sat down. "Emily's still weeping about Edward, and Mama's starting to become a bit exasperated, and Clarry cut her finger on the carving knife yesterday. She almost sliced off the whole top, there was blood everywhere, and she had to have the sal volatile."

This matter-of-fact recital filled Theo with nostalgia and an uprush of emotion that she had to fight to control.

"I wish you hadn't married Stoneridge," Rosie stated, tuning uncannily into her thoughts. "It's not the same without you."

"Don't be silly," Theo said bracingly. "If I hadn't married Stoneridge, we'd have lost the manor. Anyway, you can always come up and see me whenever you like."

"Mama said I wasn't to bother you for three weeks," Rosie informed her. "I wanted to come up yesterday and the day before, but she wouldn't let me, and I most particularly wanted to ask your advice about my white mice. Mr. Graybeard is getting very fat, and I'm wondering if perhaps it's not a boy after all. He could be pregnant. Do you think he could?"

"Only if he's a she," Theo said absently, her ears catching the sound of wheels on the gravel from around the corner. "I wonder who that is." She stood up as the gig from the Dorchester Arms bowled around the corner, Lawyer Crighton on the driver's seat. He drew rein as he saw them.

"Good day to you, Lady Theo," he said with clear pleasure.

"And Lady Rosalind. I trust you're both well."

"Very well, I thank you," Theo said, wondering how she could have forgotten the lawyer's invariable practice of visiting his Dorset clients on the fifteenth of every quarter. He'd be hurt and embarrassed if he realized he was unexpected, so she smiled warmly and said, "It's a pleasure to see you, Mr. Crighton. I'll come up with you to the house." Turning to her sister, she gave her the armful of roses. "Take these to Mama, there's a dear."

Rosie nodded agreeably, burying her nose in the blooms. "Are you coming to visit Mama, too, Mr. Crighton?"

"I shall certainly do myself the honor of calling to pay my respects to Lady Belmont," the lawyer declared ponderously.

"I'll warn Mama, then," Rosie said, as always saying exactly what she meant. Theo stifled her grin, hoping that Crighton hadn't noticed. Her mother found the lawyer a dead bore, not that she'd ever show it.

She swung herself up into the gig, dispensing with the lawyer's helping hand, and settled herself on the seat beside him, waving good-bye to Rosie as the pony set off up the drive again.

"Allow me to tender my congratulations, Lady Theo," the lawyer said with a little half bow. "A most satisfactory arrangement, if I might be so bold."

"Yes, I suppose it is," Theo said, thinking it was a somewhat lukewarm way of describing a marriage.

"There are a few outstanding matters to deal with," Crighton continued, taking out his handkerchief and pushing up the brim of his hat to mop his perspiring forehead. "But the details can be seen to after we've had our usual little discussion on the matter of the investments and the trusts, and the rent rolls."

"What outstanding matters?" Theo inquired with interest.

She sensed the sudden stiffness in the lawyer as he cleared his throat awkwardly. "Oh, just a few details," he said vaguely.

"Details?" Theo frowned. "My grandfather's will struck me as crystal clear."

The lawyer succumbed to a coughing fit, his face reddening under the paroxysm. When he'd recovered, he said, "Oh, dowries, Lady Stoneridge . . . that's it . . . the matter of your sisters' dowries. And your own jointure. It needs to be made all right and tight."

"I see." Theo's curiosity was well and truly roused. She didn't think Lawyer Crighton was telling the truth, or at least not the whole truth.

But they'd accomplished the short drive to the front door before she could decide on a fresh tack.

When they drove up, Sylvester was in his book room reading a pamphlet by Coke of Norfolk on the rotation of crops. It was a subject about which Theo and Beaumont were enthusiastically knowledgeable, and one about which he knew nothing. In fact, the mysteries of agriculture were a closed book, which wasn't that surprising, he supposed, considering that he'd been a soldier for the best part of the last fifteen years. But he was also aware that Theo's taunt about the Gilbraith estate being like Lilliput compared with the Stoneridge lands was not that far off the mark. The Gilbraiths were definitely the poor relations, and even if he'd been interested, he'd have had no opportunity to master the knowledge that Theo had acquired.

God, how it must have galled the old man to think of his great landed wealth falling into the hands of a man not educated for it. Someone who wouldn't know how to appreciate the complexities of estate management, the techniques of farming.

He shook his head with a rueful grimace. He'd probably have felt the same in the same circumstances. Maybe there was more than simple malice behind the old devil's trickery.

He glanced casually toward the open window behind him at the sound of wheels on the gravel sweep outside and then pushed back his chair to get a better view. What he saw brought a cold sweat to his forehead and sent the blood pounding through his veins.

Theo in the company of Lawyer Crighton.

What the hell was the man doing here? Without a word of warning? And dear God, what had he been saying to Theo?

He drew a deep breath, waiting for his pulse to steady. Stupid to panic. It wouldn't make a blind bit of difference now if Theo discovered the truth about her grandfather's will. He had his inheritance, and no one could take it from him.

But he knew he was fooling himself. The thought of that deception coming into the open filled him with a dreadful revulsion. It was a despicable secret that he must live with to his dying day . . . so long as Crighton had let nothing slip, nothing to provoke Theo's needle wit.

His expression schooled to a calm neutrality, he walked into the hall just as Theo and the lawyer came in from the bright sunshine.

"Oh, Sylvester," Theo greeted him, blinking and bedazzled in what seemed like darkness after the brilliance outside. "Lawyer Crighton has come from London for his quarterly business visit. I forgot to mention to you this morning that he always comes on the fifteenth." Sylvester might be affronted at her negligence, but at least the fib spared the lawyer's feelings.

"Just so, my lord," the lawyer said, advancing, hand outstretched. "I have several other prominent landowners in the area whose affairs I'm honored to be entrusted with, so I do the rounds." He gave a hearty laugh at this, but there was a touch of uncertainty to it. He was remembering that the fifth Earl of Stoneridge was inclined to be even more irascible and impatient than his predecessor.

"Indeed," Sylvester said coolly, taking the offered hand in a brief clasp. "Then pray come into my book room, and we'll get on with it." He glanced at Theo, standing in the shadows. He could detect nothing untoward in her manner or her posture. It would seem that the lawyer had let nothing slip to arouse her curiosity, and a smile of relief softened the harshness of his features.

"Theo, perhaps you'd ask Foster to bring some refreshment to the book room," he suggested, turning aside to usher the lawyer in the required direction.

"He'll do so of his own accord," Theo said cheerfully, following them.

He realized abruptly and with a sinking heart that she expected to take part in this business discussion. Presumably she'd always done so in her grandfather's day and couldn't see why anything should be different now.

At the door he let the lawyer walk past him into the room; then he drew the door half-closed and said quietly, "I don't know

179

how long this will take, Theo, but perhaps later we could go duck hunting on Webster's Pond."

Theo blinked, frowning, for a moment not understanding what he was saying; but then he opened the door farther and stepped backward.

"Just a minute," Theo said as he began to pull the door closed. "I'm coming in too."

He sighed and said as quietly as before, "No, Theo, I'm afraid you're not. I prefer to conduct my business affairs alone. I always have done, and I see no reason to change the habits of a lifetime."

"Well, neither do I," she said in a fierce undertone. "For the last three years I have always taken part in Crighton's discussions with my grandfather — that's *my* habit and I'm not changing it."

Her pointed chin jutted at him, the wide, generous mouth set in a taut line, every inch of her slender frame bristling with anger and determination.

"In this instance I'm afraid you must," he said, curtly now, anxious not to prolong this any further. The lawyer must be wondering about the whispered colloquy. Firmly, he stepped back and closed the door in her face.

Theo stared in disbelief at the heavy oak timbers. Her hand lifted of its own accord to raise the latch, but some voice of caution stopped her in time. She couldn't cause a scene in front of the lawyer, and she knew that if she barged into the room, there would be one. Sylvester wouldn't yield simply because she put him in an embarrassing situation.

Seething, she swung on her heel just as Foster appeared with a tray of decanters and glasses. Three glasses — it wouldn't occur to him that Lady Theo would be banned from the book room.

Flushing with anger and mortification, she stalked outside into the sunlight. What was going on? What outstanding matters did the lawyer have to discuss with the earl? Was there something she wasn't to know about?

Theo was not suspicious by nature, but she had a logical mind, and she could see no logical reason for Sylvester to ban her from the discussions. She took part when they talked with the bailiff

180

and the estate agent; why should the lawyer's affairs be any different?

Without making a conscious decision she went back into the house, her steps taking her into the library.

The earl's book room was a small corner office adjoining the library at the side of the house. Sometime long ago in the history of the manor, presumably during one of the many religious and political persecutions that had raged across the country, a Belmont had blocked the inglenook in the library fireplace, creating a small but adequate hiding place that abutted the book-room fireplace.

Theo had discovered it as a child when playing hide-and-seek with her sisters and Edward one Christmas Eve. She'd never expected to put it to such good use.

She pressed the catch in the granite slab inside the vast empty fireplace, and the stone swung creakily inward. It was dark and musty, the air smelling thickly of soot and wood smoke. It was an insane thing for the Countess of Stoneridge to be doing, she thought, but it didn't prevent her from slipping into the cramped cavity. She was going to come out black as a sweep.

She left the slab a little ajar, seeing no reason to enclose herself in blackness. It was her house and she wasn't doing anything illegal — merely somewhat disreputable.

Lawyer Crighton's voice came clearly through the stone, pedantic and ponderous, joined by Sylvester's deep tones full of impatience at the lawyerly long-winded precision.

They were talking about the will.

"Now that you've satisfied the late earl's conditions, my lord, I have pleasure in handing over to you the documents relating to the estate," Crighton said.

Conditions? What the devil was he talking about?

"I now have title, free and clear, to the entire estate?"

"As of your wedding day, my lord."

Cold crept up Theo's spine. A graveyard coldness. She pressed closer to the stone.

"The late Lord Stoneridge's private fortune passes into your hands since you've complied with his condition, but under the terms of the will, you must set up trust funds for the three remaining Belmont girls."

"It's understood."

"I have the papers here, my lord. If you'd sign each one . . . on the line at the bottom. Thank you . . . and I'll witness your signature."

"The estate is to provide them each with a dowry of twenty thousand pounds." Stoneridge's voice was reflective, as if he was reading the fine print. "A generous dowry."

"Indeed, my lord, but one easily afforded by an estate as wealthy as Stoneridge." The lawyer sounded a little bristly.

"Quite so," the earl responded in his level tones. "With such a dowry Clarissa should have no difficulty finding a husband. And I daresay Edward Fairfax will welcome Emily with even more enthusiasm. They're personable girls. . . . Even young Rosie behind those spectacles hides a certain charm." There was a hint of laughter in his voice as he said this.

Theo was feeling sick, her hands tightly clenched, the nails biting into her palms. She wasn't sure she understood what she was hearing, and yet she knew she did.

"Now, for Lady Stoneridge's jointure," the lawyer was continuing. He cleared his throat in his irritating fashion, and Theo could imagine his glancing around the room in search of inspiration. "Perhaps her ladyship should be a party to this aspect of the discussion, my lord?" It was a diffident suggestion.

"There's not the slightest need for her ladyship's participation," Stoneridge declared curtly. "Anything she needs to know, I will explain to her myself."

Theo was submerged in a deadly rage. Still, she couldn't put words to what she suspected — it seemed impossible.

As of your wedding day. Free and clear title to the estate, *as of your wedding day.*

She continued to listen as the lawyer enumerated the statistics of her jointure. It was generous in the extreme. If she outlived her husband, she would be a wealthy woman in her own right. And when she had children, they would be the beneficiaries of that wealth. But Stoneridge wasn't laying down these terms out of his own generosity; Mr. Crighton was dictating the terms to him.

182

This was her grandfather's doing.

She was the currency for Stoneridge to inherit the estate, but by doing so he had to accept obligations that her grandfather had laid upon him.

Her grandfather hadn't abandoned them.

But what had he done to her? What had he done to his favorite granddaughter? He'd tied her body and soul to a man she now loathed with a repugnance beyond description. A man who'd deceived and manipulated her. A man who'd trapped her into a marriage that ended her independence, that destroyed all possibility of other choices for the future. With his smooth serpent's tongue, the Gilbraith had persuaded her mother that he was a generous and honorable man who would fulfill obligations to his wife's family for family and duty's sake.

But he didn't have an honorable bone in his body. He was a liar. A greedy liar.

Numbed but fascinated like the rabbit circled by the fox, Theo listened to the end of the discussion, although nothing more illuminating was said. But she had the picture, and she was convulsed with rage that blinded her to anything but the need to bring this repulsive sham of a marriage to an end, to tell that loathsome, deceiving manipulator what she thought of him.

And through her rage she heard his voice from days past promising that he would never take advantage of her passion. That she could trust him to share her passion and lose himself in lust as she lost herself. And he'd been lying through his teeth. She'd given herself to him in all honesty and trust, and he'd possessed her with cold-blooded greed . . . using her, using her passion.

It was all she could do to slide quietly from her hiding place, close the slab, and go to her room to wash the traces of soot from her hands. Her face was deathly pale in the looking glass, her eyes blank with a pain so deep, it was like a knife in her vitals. For the first time in twenty years her sense of who and what she was, of her own worth in her own world, was destroyed. All her life she'd been indulged and praised. She knew herself to be useful; she knew her talents. But now it was gone, trampled into the dust by a stranger who'd walked into her life and taken everything meaningful from her.

Chapter Fourteen

"When you have business with me in the future, Mr. Crighton, we will conduct it in town," Stoneridge said, rising from his desk to indicate the interview was over. "A letter to me requesting a meeting will be sufficient. I anticipate being in London quite frequently, so there will be no difficulty in dealing with these matters in your own offices."

Lawyer Crighton looked uncomfortable. "I trust I haven't intruded, my lord. But it's always been my custom to make these quarterly visits in person . . . to pay my respects . . ."

"No . . . no." Sylvester waved him impatiently into silence. "I appreciate the courtesy, but it will not be necessary to repeat it, you understand."

"Yes, my lord . . . of course, my lord," the lawyer muttered unhappily as the earl pulled the bell rope.

"Have Mr. Crighton's gig brought around, Foster," the earl instructed when the butler appeared.

So there was to be no invitation to dinner, and he'd been offered only a glass of claret — a glass, moreover, that had not been refilled. Circumstances had certainly changed at Stoneridge Manor, and not for the better, the disgruntled lawyer decided, picking up his hat and gloves from the table in the hall.

The earl accompanied him to the front door, where he shook hands briskly, and then turned back to his book room without waiting to see Lawyer Crighton into his gig. He was aware he'd dealt somewhat brusquely with the man, but he was too anxious to get him out of the house before Theo reappeared.

He paced the small room for a few minutes, considering his next move. Theo was bound to be annoyed at her unceremonious exclusion from the interview, but now the danger was past, and Crighton wouldn't drop in unexpectedly another time; he could afford to be as conciliatory as necessary to smooth her ruffled feathers.

He'd suggested duck hunting earlier. Henry had reported that the sport at Webster's Pond was held to be excellent. Apart from a few poachers, it was rarely hunted, since it was on private Stoneridge land.

Maybe the idea of a competition would appeal to her. He'd never known Theo to refuse a challenge of any kind. The thought made him smile, and as he realized how relieved he was, he understood just how desperately anxious he'd been since Crighton had driven up to the door . . . was it only an hour ago? A lifetime of living with his despicable secret seemed impossible, but he couldn't imagine how he could ever tell her.

He moved to the door just as it opened. Theo came into the room, closing the door quietly behind her.

His words of friendly greeting died on his lips. Her face was paler than he'd ever seen it, and her eyes were depthless caverns.

"So, my lord, your business with Mr. Crighton is concluded?" Her voice was strangely flat.

"Cry peace, Theo," he said, coming toward her, smiling, one hand outstretched. "I know you've been accustomed to participating in these discussions, but —"

"But on this occasion things not for my ears were being discussed," she interrupted in the same expressionless voice. Before he could respond, she continued. "Did you ever consider that I might be too high a price to pay for the estate, my lord? But I imagine no price would be too high."

"You were listening?" His own face now bloodless, Sylvester stared at her, too stunned for the moment to grasp the full horror of this disclosure.

"Yes," Theo said. "I was eavesdropping. Nasty habit, isn't it? But not as nasty as deceit and manipulation, my lord. Did my grandfather know you, I wonder? Did he know what a greedy, dishonorable man he was tempting with his granddaughter's body?"

"Theo, that's enough." He had to take hold of the situation, to stop this dreadful, destructive monologue before something catastrophic was said or done. "You must listen to me."

"Listen to you? Oh, I've listened to you enough, Stoneridge. If I hadn't listened to you, I wouldn't be tied to a despicable, treacherous deceiver."

"Theo, you will stop this instant!" Guilt yielded to anger as her bitter words flew like poison darts across the small room.

185

"We will talk about this like reasonable people. I understand how you feel —"

"You understand!" she exclaimed, and her eyes were now bright with fury. "You've taken everything from me, and you tell me you *understand* how I feel." With a sudden inarticulate sound of desperate rage and confusion, she turned and ran from the room.

Sylvester remained where he was, his body immobile, his ears ringing with her accusations. There was a dreadful truth to them, but it was a black-and-white truth, one that ignored the complexities of the decision that he'd made. Theo, headstrong, forthright, free-spirited gypsy that she was, drew her world with the firm strokes of a charcoal pencil, no shading, no wavy lines.

Somehow she had to be persuaded to accept her grandfather's part in all this. Her grandfather had laid out the board, and he himself was as much a goddamned pawn in the old devil's game as Theo.

With a muttered execration he spun on his heel and began to pace the room, the hateful words pounding with his blood in his veins. *Dishonorable; treacherous; deceitful.* The accusations went round and round in his head until his brain was spinning with them. A dishonorable, treacherous man would give in to the enemy without a fight. Would see his men slaughtered, would surrender the colors, would condemn the survivors of his company to languish in an enemy jail . . .

He closed his eyes as if he could block out the dreadful images; he covered his ears as if he could erase the voice of General, Lord Feringham at the court-martial, a voice that made no attempt to disguise the general's contempt for the man on trial. What price an acquittal when not even the presiding general had believed in his innocence? They'd turned their backs on him in the court when the verdict had been announced. . . .

And now his wife was hurling the same accusations at his head! Her eyes glittered with the same contempt. And it was not to be borne!

He strode out of the room, hardly knowing what he was doing. "Where's Lady Theo?"

Foster, crossing the hall, paused, looking startled at the violent edge to the abrupt question. What he saw on the earl's face had him stumbling over his words in his haste to answer. "Abovestairs, I believe, my lord. Is something wrong?"

The earl didn't reply, merely stalked past him and took the stairs two at a time. Foster stroked his chin, frowning. The slamming of a door resounded through the late-afternoon stillness of the house. The butler knew immediately it was the door to the countess's apartments. Something was badly wrong, and for once he was at a loss. Should he interfere? Send Lady Theo's maid up on some pretext, perhaps? Go himself? He waited, but stillness had settled over the house again. Uneasily, he returned to the butler's pantry and the silver he was cleaning.

Theo gazed, white-faced, at her husband as the door crashed shut behind him. "Am I to be granted not even the privacy of my own room?" she demanded with icy contempt. "I realize the entire house belongs to you, Lord Stoneridge. I suppose it's too much to expect —"

"Theo, stop!" he ordered, his eyes on the bed where an open portmanteau lay. "What the hell do you think you're doing?"

"What does it look like?" She pulled a nightgown from a drawer and tossed it into the bag. "I'm going to the dower house. The one part of the estate you didn't manage to get your thieving hands on!" Her voice was thick, and angrily she dashed tears from her eyes with her forearm before hurling her ivory-backed hairbrushes and combs on top of the nightgown.

She didn't look at him and didn't see his expression as she continued, blind in her rage and hurt. "The dower house was left free and clear to my mother, and not even a deceitful, treacherous liar would be cowardly enough to storm into the house of an unprotected woman."

The repeated insults finally unloosed the crimson tide of rage, and Sylvester fought to hold on to his anger even as he determined to compel her retreat. "By God, you're going to take that back," he stated. "That and every other insult you've thrown at me in the last hour."

"Never!" she retorted, shifting her stance imperceptibly, her eyes sharply focused, calculating his next move.

Sylvester came toward her, his eyes blazing in his drawn countenance. Theo snatched her hairbrush from the portmanteau and hurled it at him. It caught him a glancing blow on the shoulder. He swore and ducked as a shoe followed the brush and he found himself in the midst of a veritable tempest of flying objects as Theo grabbed whatever was to hand — cushions, books, shoes, ornaments — and flung them at his head.

"You goddamned termagant!" he bellowed as a glass figurine flew past his ear and crashed in a shiver of crystal against the wall. He lunged for her, coming in low, catching her around the waist, lifting her off her feet before she could counterattack.

Theo cursed him with the vigor and fluency of a stable hand, and he realized that until now he'd only heard the tip of the iceberg when it came to his wife's vocabulary. In other circumstances the realization might have amused him.

Theo found herself in the corner of the room, her face pressed to the wall, her hands gripped at the wrists and pushed up her back, not far enough to hurt, but coercive, nevertheless. Sylvester's body was against hers, holding her into the corner so she had no space, no possibility of independent movement.

"Now," he said, breathing heavily in the aftermath of that struggle, his voice hard with determination. "Take it back, Theo. Every damn word."

She threw another savage oath at him. Tensing her muscles, she tested her strength against the physical wall at her back. She could feel the rigidity of his body, a barrier as hard and invincible as a wall of steel. At her movement he brought one knee up and pushed it into her backside, pressing her even more securely into the corner.

"Take it back, Theo," he repeated, softly now, but his intention still as hard as agate. "We aren't moving from here until you do so."

He could feel her resistance as pulsing waves emanating from the taut body, and he concentrated every fiber of his being on winning this battle of wills. He knew on the most primitive level that he could not tolerate his wife's contempt. He'd endured a lifetime's worth of scorn and opprobrium from men whose opinion he valued, men he'd counted as friends and colleagues, and he didn't think those wounds would ever close.

"Listen to me," he said into the silence. "You have the right to be angry . . . you have the right to an explanation —"

"You talk of rights, of explanations, when you've taken —"

"Give me a chance!" he interrupted. "You have only half the story, Theo."

"Let me go." She twisted against him, but she knew it was futile.

"When you take back those insults. I'll not tolerate being called a coward by you or anyone."

The intensity in his voice pierced her fury and bewilderment. Vaguely she remembered tossing "cowardly" into the seething cauldron of accusations, but it had been one epithet among many. His hands were warm on her wrists, and she could feel the blood in his thumbs beating against her own pulse. His breath rustled over the top of her head, and the power of his frame seemed to enclose her, to swallow her as it did when they made love, and her confusion grew as her body's memory sprang alive with the knowledge of the hours of pleasure they'd shared.

Sylvester felt the change in her, the confusion tangling now with her anger, the smudging of her hard edges. "Let's be done with this," he said. His thumb moved against her wrist.

His closeness was suddenly more than she could bear. It muddled the clarity of her anger, the absolute knowledge of her betrayal. He'd used her body to betray her, and now it was happening again.

"All right," she said, desperate for release. "All right, I take it back. I've no *evidence* you're a coward."

Sylvester exhaled slowly and moved them both out of the corner. Theo glanced up at him and saw no satisfaction at this small capitulation. His face was drawn, his eyes strained. He looked like a man on his way to the gallows.

"Let's talk about this now," he said.

Theo shook herself free of his slackened grip. "There's nothing to talk about. I don't even want to be in the same room with you." Pushing past him, she made for the door.

She had her hand on the latch, but Sylvester was on her heels. "No, you don't!" He banged the door closed as she pulled it open. He stood with his shoulders against it and regarded her with near desperate frustration. "Damn it, woman, you're going to listen to me." He closed his eyes wearily for a second, rubbing his temples with his thumb and forefinger. "It's not going to do any good to run away from it."

"Why should I listen to you?" she demanded. "You're a liar and a hypocrite! Why should I ever believe a word you say?"

"Because I've never told you a lie," he said quietly.

"*What?* You have the unmitigated gall to deny . . ." She turned from him with an exclamation of disgust. "I loathe you."

A muscle twitched in his drawn cheek, and there was a white shade around the taut mouth, but he fought to keep his voice moderate. "Just consider for a minute. My actions were dictated by your grandfather. It was your grandfather who concocted the terms of the will. I can only guess at his reasons." He explained the details of the codicil.

Theo stared at him as if he were a piece of primeval slime. "You would blame my grandfather for *your* greed. You agreed to such a despicable trick. You deprived me of my freedom and my sisters of their share in the estate, just so you could have everything. And you set yourself up as a benevolent benefactor, willing to do the right thing. . . . Oh, I can't bear it another minute. Let me out of here." This last was an impassioned demand, and she pushed at his chest as he still stood in front of the door.

It happened with hideous lack of warning. Jagged flashes of white light tore across his vision, and that dreadful creeping sensation crawled up the back of his neck. *Why now?* he thought on a silent moan of anguish.

"Move out of the way!" Theo shoved at him again, but even through his dread and frustration, he sensed that she'd lost some of her blind certainty.

Why now? The jagged whiteness exploded across his eyes again, and his heart began to beat fast with the panic that he had to hold down. It only made the coming agony even more intolerable.

Theo was staring at him. She'd seen him look like this once before, but she couldn't remember when. He was shrinking before her eyes, becoming a husk emptied of muscle and sinew.

"All right, go," he said, stumbling away from the door.

"What is it?"

"Get out!"

Just like that? One minute be was insisting they resolve this mess, and the next he was throwing her out of the room without so much as an explanation. And now, perversely, she wasn't sure whether she still wanted to walk away from this confrontation. Perhaps there were aspects that she didn't yet understand. Perhaps there *was* some kind of an explanation, a reason that might make sense. Her grandfather must have had a reason.

"But I —"

She got no further. He said nothing, but his expression silenced her; his eyes were ghastly as they rested on her face, his mouth a rictus of dread. She wrenched open the door as Sylvester turned and stumbled across the room, disappearing through the connecting door into his own apartment.

Outside her own room, Theo stopped and drew a deep breath. She remembered now when she'd seen him look like that. It was that first meeting, that afternoon by the trout stream. What happened to him? Was it the same indisposition that had kept him in his room for nearly two days?

She heard the sound of his bell ringing urgently, and a minute later Henry came pounding up the stairs. He brushed past Lady Stoneridge with barely a word of apology and disappeared into the earl's bedchamber.

Drained and bewildered, Theo went downstairs. She felt forlorn, as if Sylvester had led her into a dark forest and abandoned her. Her anger had somehow dissipated, and without its prop she was left defenseless against her hurt and confusion.

She went outside, into the soft air of early evening, unsure what to do now. Part of her wanted to run to her mother, but something held her back. It would be the impulse of a hurt child, but there was more to her reluctance than that recognition. At this moment she couldn't face revealing even to her mother that the man who'd pursued and courted her so assiduously would have married her if she'd been a ditch drab. It didn't matter who or what she was, she was merely currency, the price he had had to pay for his inheritance.

191

Tears burned behind her eyes, and she blinked them away angrily. She would not cry; neither would she ask for comfort. Maybe later she could tell the story without this searing sense of humiliation, but until then she would find her own strengths.

She wandered toward the rose garden, intending to take the shortcut to the cliff top above the cove. As she reached the springy turf, strewn with bright-blue scabius, she saw a rider coming toward her across the cliff. There was something familiar about him, and she squinted against the setting sun, shading her eyes. Then she was running.

"Edward! Edward!"

The rider urged his horse to a canter and covered the distance between them in a few seconds.

"Theo!" He drew rein. "I was so hoping you'd be in. I was coming to find you."

"Edward." She said his name again, smiling up at him, and for a minute there was silence, but it was filled with so much unspoken emotion, so many thoughts, that the quiet seemed a rush of noise.

He still sat on his horse, the empty left-hand sleeve of his coat pinned across his breast, his right hand holding the reins. Then, with an awkward movement that was so unlike Edward's grace and agility, he swung himself to the ground.

"I still can't get the hang of that," he said. "My whole body's unbalanced, Theo. It makes me mad as fire to be so clumsy and unsteady."

"You'll get used to it," she said, coming into his embrace as he put his arm around her. She hugged him with fierce affection. "Oh, my dear, I have been anguished for you."

"It was my own damn fault," he declared, almost squeezing the life out of her. "Of all the goddamned arrogant, stupid things to have done. I should be dead, Theo!"

"Oh, don't say that!" She stood back and examined his face. He had aged, lines of suffering etched indelibly around his mouth and eyes, but the humorous light still glimmered in those green eyes, and his mouth retained its wry quirk.

"Have you seen Emily yet?"

Edward shook his head. "I only arrived home last night. I

192

was on my way to the dower house, but I wanted to see you first." He ran his hand over his chin, his eyes suddenly stark. "I wanted you to come with me."

Theo understood immediately. He knew Emily's sensitive soul, and he was afraid to spring himself upon her as he now was.

"Emily was distraught," she said quietly. "But she'll be overjoyed to see you."

"Will she?" Then he dismissed the self-pitying question with typical briskness. "So will you come with me? Shall we fetch Dulcie, or shall we walk?"

"Oh, let's walk," Theo said, realizing that she was unwilling to go back to Stoneridge, to spoil this reunion with a return to the dismal tangle at home.

Edward paused, examining her, and she swore silently. They'd always had an uncanny ability to sense each other's innermost feelings.

"Shouldn't I pay my respects to your husband?" Edward asked.

"Not now," she said. "He's busy."

"Oh?" Edward continued to regard her. "I was surprised to hear your news. It seems very sudden."

"It was," she said, unable to hide the bitterness in her tone. "Four weeks from start to finish. Stoneridge doesn't dawdle when his mind is set."

Edward frowned. "What is it, Theo?"

No, she couldn't even tell Edward . . . Edward, from whom she'd never had any secrets, before whom she couldn't imagine feeling embarrassed or ashamed. She couldn't tell him, not yet, at least. Besides, he had troubles and insecurities of his own, and she would not lay her burdens on him now, even if they were tellable.

"Nothing serious, Edward. We're just a trifle at outs." *The understatement of the year.* "Shall I lead Robin? Then you can hold my hand." She smiled at him, and there was no further indication of her own turmoil.

Edward allowed himself to be diverted. Apprehension about his upcoming meeting with Emily had preoccupied him for too long to be put aside until it was over.

"Tell me how it happened." Theo demanded as they walked

193

hand in hand across the cliff and to the drive that led to the dower house.

She listened. She heard the bitter, self-directed anger beneath the light description of his foolhardy stroll to the picket line; she heard the hideous agony behind his brief description of the amputation and the journey across Spain to the coast. But she made no more of it than her friend did. Emily would do the fussing, and Edward would expect it from her. He wouldn't expect it from his childhood comrade.

When they reached the dower house, Edward's firm step faltered. "I don't wish to startle her," he muttered. "Will you go in and warn her?"

"Warn her of what?" Theo inquired with a raised eyebrow. "Her fiancé's return? For heaven's sake, Edward, you used to love to surprise her. Emily loves surprises. She'll burst into tears, of course, but tears of joy. She loves to cry with happiness."

"Oh, Theo," he said. "You know what I'm talking about."

"Yes, of course I do. And I'm telling you not to be such an idiot. Come on."

She tethered Robin to the gatepost of the dower house, then took Edward's hand, running him along the path. "Emily . . . Mama . . . Clarry . . . see who's here."

Elinor was in her boudoir when she heard Theo's exuberant tones quickly followed by Emily's cry. "Edward! Oh, Edward." And the sound from the hall became a confused turmoil of voices and tears.

Elinor went quietly downstairs, prepared to deal with the inevitable surge of emotions attendant on Edward's arrival.

Edward separated himself from his betrothed as Elinor descended the stairs. He came forward, holding out his hand. "Lady Belmont."

"Edward, dearest." Ignoring his hand, she embraced him. "How wonderful to see you."

Edward was flushed, and a determined look crossed his face. "Lady Belmont . . . Emily . . . I came to say that of course I am ready to release Emily from our engagement immediately."

There was a stunned silence; then Theo said, "Edward, you great gaby. How could you possibly say something so idiotish?"

Before Edward could respond, Emily had flung herself against his chest. "How could you possibly imagine it could make the slightest difference? Theo's right, you're a gaby, Edward!" She was weeping against his shirtfront, and he held her tightly, his eyes meeting Lady Belmont's. She shook her head at him in mock reproof and smiled.

"Can I see it, Edward?" Rosie's high voice broke into the tender scene.

"See what?" He released Emily and bent to embrace the girl.

"Where your arm ought to be," Rosie said matter-of-factly. "Is there a stump? Or does it stop right at the shoulder?"

"Oh, Rosie!" It was a universal groan.

"But I'm interested," the child persisted. "It's good to be interested. If you're not interested in things, you don't learn anything, Grandpapa said."

"Very true," Theo agreed. "But that doesn't permit such personal questions, you obnoxious brat."

"I'm not an obnoxious brat," Rosie declared, not at all offended. "Won't you show me, Edward?"

"One day," he said, laughing with the rest of them. Rosie had managed to turn his nightmare into an ordinary, interesting fact of life. She'd somehow managed to puncture his dread that his mutilation would disgust those he loved, would turn love into pity.

"Is it all healed?"

"Yes, but it's not very pretty." He glanced at Emily over the child's head. "It's very red and raw looking."

"Does it pain you?" The soft question was Emily's.

"When the wind's in the wrong direction," he said. "Come and walk with me, love."

Emily nodded, taking his outstretched hand.

"You will dine with us, I hope, Edward?" Elinor said.

"Yes, if I may," he responded.

"In that case I hope the invitation extends to me," Theo declared.

"What of Stoneridge?" Edward raised an eyebrow.

"He has a previous engagement," she said firmly.

For an instant the temptation to pour out her heart to her

195

mother, weep her anger and mortification away, receive the comfort Elinor always had to offer, almost got the better of her. And then she smiled briefly and said, "He went into Dorchester on business. He'll be dining there."

Elinor nodded. Her daughter was lying. The strain in the dark eyes, the jangled chords of her unhappiness, couldn't be hidden from her mother. But Theo always dealt with problems in her own way, and if, as Elinor suspected, this was something to do with her marriage, then it was best that Theo and Stoneridge came to their own resolution. Elinor had no intention of playing either interfering mother-in-law or overprotective mother. It would do far more harm than good where two such strong personalities were concerned.

Chapter Fifteen

Sylvester fell into a laudanum-induced sleep toward midnight and awoke just before dawn filled with the sense of well-being approaching euphoria that always followed the agony.

It didn't take long for the euphoria to dissipate as he lay in the semidarkness remembering what had triggered the attack — a mercifully short attack for once, but it couldn't have come at a more inopportune moment.

He threw aside the bedclothes and stood up, stretching before going to the window, flinging it wide, inhaling the salt-sea fragrances on the light breeze blowing from the cliff top. He stared into the misty, pale light and heard in his head Theo's voice, despairing in its confusion and rage, hurling those dreadful accusations at him.

He glanced toward the connecting door to his wife's bedchamber. Presumably she was still asleep. In other circumstances he would have been tempted to go in and wake her in the way he knew she loved, with the long, slow strokes of passion that would bring the sleepy whimpers of delight to her lips, and her eyes would eventually open, deep, limpid pools brimming with sensuality, her mouth curving with amused pleasure.

But not this morning.

Deciding he'd take advantage of the dawn peace to gather his thoughts and marshal his arguments, he dressed rapidly and went downstairs, where he took a shotgun and a game bag from the gun room and let himself out of the house.

Webster's Pond lay beyond the orchard, through a band of thick undergrowth and massed blackberry bushes. The air smelled of sea and the damp grass beneath the tangled undergrowth. Spiky tendrils from the bushes caught at his buff coat and slashed across his buckskin britches. The sun was veiled in the dawn mist, a suffused reddish glow on the horizon, and the morning was alive with the exuberant calls of the dawn chorus and the indignant chatter of squirrels as he penetrated the undergrowth, disturbing their preserve.

He was following a narrow ribbon where the undergrowth was

trampled into something resembling a path, but it clearly hadn't been used that recently, and the whole feel of the place was of somewhere rarely visited by man. The sport certainly should be excellent.

He caught a glimmer of the pond through the bushes as he pushed aside a tangle of thorny branches with the butt of his gun. It was a large body of water, more of a lake than a pond, thick reeds massed at the edge, lily pads floating serenely across the flat brown surface.

Sylvester took a step forward onto the narrow bank, and something hit him in the middle of the back, sending him crashing to the ground.

"What the *hell!*" Winded, he stared up at his assailant, more angry than alarmed. A young man stood over him . . a young man with the empty sleeve of his jacket pinned across his chest, and a gun on his other shoulder.

"I beg your pardon," Edward said. "But you were about to put your foot into this vile thing." He gestured to the oval jagged-toothed trap concealed in the underbrush. "I saw it a second before you took that step."

"Sweet Jesus!" Sylvester got to his feet, staring at the vicious iron, nausea rising in his gorge as he imagined the bite of those teeth rending his calf, breaking the bone.

"They've never used man traps on Belmont land before," Edward was saying, frowning. He glanced at his companion. "You must be Lord Stoneridge, sir."

There was a crackle of breaking twigs from the bushes, and they both spun round, with a soldier's instinct bringing their guns to the ready, Edward with a neat twist, swinging his weapon under his arm.

"There's a goddamned man trap back there!" Theo exclaimed, her eyes blazing, her mouth a taut line.

"And another one here," Edward said, gesturing, lowering his gun.

Theo bent and picked up a thick chunk of wood. She drove it into the trap, and the teeth sprang forward with well-oiled speed, sinking into their prey.

"I sprung the other one, too," she said. She looked up at Syl-

198

vester, the anger still burning in her eyes. "Was this your doing, Stoneridge? We have never tolerated man traps on Belmont land."

She glared at him, her chin lifted, hostility and challenge in every line of her body. Clearly the night had brought no softening. Sylvester replied calmly, "No, of course it was not my doing. I nearly stepped into the damned thing myself. If it hadn't been for the speedy action of . . ." He turned to Edward. "Lieutenant Fairfax, I presume."

"Yes, sir." Edward extended his hand. "I hope you don't think I'm trespassing, but Theo and I were to meet here for some shooting."

"My dear fellow, I stand in your debt," Sylvester said with a grimace. He glanced at Theo and saw that she too had a shotgun over her shoulder. "Three minds with but a single thought, clearly."

Theo's brow wore a preoccupied frown, and she seemed to have simmered down. She said slowly, "I don't think someone likes you very much, Stoneridge."

"What?" For a minute he thought she was referring to herself.

"This, on top of Zeus's saddle," she said. "Does it strike you as pure coincidence?"

"Don't be fanciful," he responded. "A man trap could catch anyone."

"But hardly anybody comes here. Who told you about the pond? I'm sure I didn't."

Sylvester frowned. "I can't remember. . . . Oh, yes, it was Henry. He said someone in the village had mentioned it."

"Who in the village?"

He shook his head. "I don't know."

"Well, somebody set these traps, and it sure as hell wasn't any Belmont man."

Sylvester glanced at Edward. The young man appeared not to notice Theo's free and easy tongue. But, then, neither did anyone else . . . only her husband, it seemed.

"I think we'd better beat the undergrowth and see if there are any more of these filthy things." Edward picked up a thick stick and swished it through the brambles.

They separated, taking the tangled brush in sections, and found two more.

"Do you notice how they're all along the same route?" Theo said, slamming another dead branch into the last trap. "All placed along the path someone from the manor would take."

"We didn't find a single one anywhere else," Edward agreed. He glanced at the earl, who was staring into the middle distance, deep in thought. "It does seem, sir, as if someone was out to do a mischief to someone from the manor. And no one in these parts would hurt Theo."

"But it isn't anyone from these parts," Theo said definitely. "You know these people as well as I do, Edward . . . even if Stoneridge doesn't," she added belligerently.

Edward cleared his throat a little awkwardly. "Perhaps it's someone from the past, Lord Stoneridge. Someone who bears you a grudge, maybe?"

Sylvester considered this. Someone was creating mischief, and he did seem its object. He looked down at the disarmed trap at Theo's feet, and that sick feeling rose in his gorge again. Who could possibly wish him that degree of harm — lethal harm? He'd not led a blameless existence, far from it, but nothing he'd ever done warranted such a ghastly vengeance.

He glanced sideways at Theo. His wife had more reason to bear him a grudge than anyone, and he knew damn well she was not responsible.

"I'm sure we're letting our imaginations run away with us," he said finally. "I don't know about you, but I've rather lost the urge to shoot this morning."

"Me, too," Edward agreed.

"Then the least I can do is offer you breakfast," Sylvester said cheerfully, putting aside his unease. He clapped Edward on his good shoulder as he turned back toward the house. "I'll send someone to get rid of these things. Come along, Theo."

"I'm still interested in doing some shooting," she said.

"Not on your own, you're not," he retorted, stung out of patience by such obstinacy.

"Why not?" She looked genuinely surprised. "I've hunted here on my own many times."

"That was before some bright spark started planting a mine-field," he pointed out.

"But they weren't supposed to catch *me*."

"Maybe not, but something's not right around here. Don't be obtuse, Theo."

And whose fault is it that nothing's right at Stoneridge anymore? Edward's presence forced her to bite back the bitter accusation. What should have belonged to her had been snatched from her. The familiar places had changed, become hazardous and unpleasant. Would she next begin to see threat in the faces of the people who'd been a part of her life since she could remember?

Edward stepped back toward her. He could sense her distress, just as he could sense the jangled emotions flowing between Theo and her husband.

"Come on, Theo, I'm famished," he said. "And if you insist on staying here, I'll have to stay with you."

She managed a smile of disclaimer and joined him on the path.

Sylvester hesitated, then walked on ahead of them, an outsider to this long-standing friendship. It wasn't lost on him that where he dictated, her friend cajoled.

He walked on, deep in frowning thought, hearing their voices on the path behind him. A leisurely breakfast would give him the opportunity to get to know Lieutenant Fairfax. Did he know anything at all of Vimiera?

At that moment Edward was remembering his colonel's description of the military scandal attached to Sylvester Gilbraith. In his own agonies of the last weeks he'd forgotten all about it, but now it came back to him. Theo had her arm in his as they walked back to the house, but she was distracted, thinking of the peddler without a pack, and responded only briefly to Edward's occasional observations.

Theo probably didn't know of Vimiera, Edward reflected. Such a history bore no relation to sleepy Lulworth life and was so much in the past that there'd be no reason for her husband to have revealed such a humiliating personal fact. He couldn't imagine doing so himself except in the most compelling of circumstances. But something was causing the hostility he could feel in her whenever she addressed her husband.

He looked at the broad back of the Earl of Stoneridge, preceding them on the narrow path. He had taken to the man immediately, as one sometimes does on a first meeting. There was an ease to him, a comradely acceptance. Not once had he referred to Edward's amputation, but neither had he deliberately ignored it. His eyes had encompassed the empty sleeve in the same way they'd taken note of his eye color and his physique.

If he'd ever reflected on the kind of man who would appeal to Theo, Edward realized that he would have come up with a description of someone like Sylvester Gilbraith. Some young sprig would never do. Theo needed a man of substance, someone who would appreciate her straightforward nature, who would not be threatened by her unusual competencies and her fiery spirit. She needed a husband experienced in the ways of the world, who could match her and, when necessary, curb her wilder flights. Someone, in short, like the earl. And yet he knew he had not imagined the antagonism that morning — at least on Theo's part.

The man securely concealed in the crotch of a massive oak tree on the far side of the pond clambered down as the wildlife on the pond settled back into its customary pattern once the three noisy, trampling humans had departed. Of all the cursed ill luck. His daily dawn vigil had been on the verge of being rewarded, and then that damn cripple had interfered. He'd been ready to stroll around the pond and administer the coup de grâce as his victim struggled in the trap. He would have used the earl's own gun, and it would have appeared that in his violent struggles he'd accidentally shot himself . . . or maybe intentionally ended his sufferings in this deserted spot. No one would look too hard for a motive in such a case.

And then he would have returned to London to collect the final payment that would enable him to buy that little tavern on Cheapside.

Now, he'd have to return and report failure. He'd hung around the area too long already. Accidents took too damn long to arrange.

In the breakfast room the earl was all affability and proved himself an entertaining and sympathetic conversationalist. Edward warmed to him even more. It was only toward the end of the meal that he realized they'd talked only of his own experiences of the Peninsular campaign. Stoneridge made political and military observations aplenty, but he offered no reminiscences of his own, although he had been in this war and its two preceding ones, and Edward had little more than a year under his belt.

The man couldn't be a coward. It seemed impossible. Edward had an image of a man who'd do what Major Gilbraith was said to have done, and this man before him, filling his tankard with ale, tactfully encouraging him to talk of his wound, of how he felt about being crippled in this way, didn't fit that image.

Theo said little throughout the meal. She could see how Edward was responding to Sylvester, how he needed to talk to someone who would really understand what it was like out there. His parents would want him to talk, but he'd have to edit the tale. His father would want to hear only of successes, of valor and glory; his mother only of the comfortable billets and the kindness of the villagers and the brave support of the partisans. Neither of them could endure to imagine the reality of battle, the terror and the noise, the heat and the thirst and the screams of the wounded.

They seemed to have forgotten her presence, but she was glad to be forgotten. Unlike Edward, she didn't notice how little Sylvester said of his own experiences. All she could think was how little she knew of the man who was her husband and how little he was prepared to reveal. He'd given her only the skeleton of a barren childhood that she assumed was responsible for the barriers he'd erected around himself. Was the packless peddler the accomplice of someone who wished to hurt him, someone the earl had wronged in the past? He'd wronged her, after all; why shouldn't he have harmed someone else?

Theo put down her coffee cup and suddenly pushed back her chair. "If you'll excuse me, I have some things to do. Edward, will you and your parents dine with us tomorrow? I'll ask Mama and the girls, and we can have a family dinner just like the old days."

"Rosie's bound to insist I reveal my fascinating scars," Edward said with a mock groan.

"Just box her ears," Theo responded with a grin. "You always used to."

"She's rather less of a scrubby brat now," he observed, chuckling. "I'll check with my mother, but I'm certain she'll be delighted."

"I'll see you tomorrow, then." She moved to the door as both men rose politely.

"Theo?"

"Stoneridge?" She paused, her hand on the latch.

"There are a few matters I'd like to discuss. Would you join me in the library in half an hour?"

She hesitated, wanting to say that she had another appointment. But what good would that do? "If you wish it, sir."

"I do." He resumed his seat as the door closed on her departure.

"Forgive me, my lord, but . . ." Edward stopped, flushing slightly.

"No, please continue," Sylvester said, taking a deep draft of ale, leaning back in his chair, his eyes sharp as they rested on his visitor's face, his body as taut as a bowstring as he waited.

"It's none of my affair," Edward said awkwardly. "Forget I spoke."

"So far you haven't," Sylvester pointed out. "Spit it out, man."

"Theo seems unhappy," Edward said in a rush. "I know her very well."

"Better than I do, I'm sure," his host agreed evenly, no sign of his relief showing on his face. He could deflect questions about Theo, but he had nothing to say about Vimiera.

"No . . . no, I'm sure not," Edward stammered, his face on fire.

"Not in the same way, perhaps," Sylvester said in the same tone.

Edward's color deepened, and he buried his nose in his tankard. "Forgive me. As I said, it's none of my affair."

"No, it's not," Sylvester agreed. "However, you're right, she is unhappy at the moment. But content you, my friend, I don't intend that state of affairs to last. May I carve you another slice of sirloin?"

"Thank you, no. I should be going." Edward pushed back

his chair, feeling as if he'd been gently but firmly rebuked by a senior officer for a minor faux pas.

Sylvester accompanied him to the front door. "I trust we'll meet tomorrow evening," he said, smiling with no trace of the hauteur of a minute before. "My compliments to Sir Charles and Lady Fairfax."

Chapter Sixteen

Sylvester watched his guest out of sight, then turned back to the house, a slight frown between his brows. Edward Fairfax had shown no sign of having heard of the scandal of Vimiera. But sooner or later he might hear of it from some friend at Horseguards.

The scandal would dog him to his dying day. The bleak recognition seemed harder to accept now than ever before. He went into the library and stood staring into the empty grate. Was he going to live in terror that his wife would hear of it? Hiding out in the sleepy Dorsetshire countryside, shaking and shivering every time some visitor from London crossed his path?

The sound of the door opening brought his head up. Theo stood in the doorway.

"What happened to you yesterday?" she asked without preamble.

"It's an old wound, that's all. It acts up occasionally."

"How?"

He dismissed the question with a brief gesture. "I get a headache, Theo. There's no need to discuss it further, there are more important matters to address."

She was not satisfied, but it seemed it was all she was going to get. Again she reflected that there was so much about his life he refused to discuss.

But what did it matter? Why should she care what happened to him? Or what had happened to him in the past? Her face was set, the expression in her eyes that of someone who didn't know whether she was hunter or hunted.

"Lock the door," Sylvester instructed.

"Lock it? Why?"

"Because I don't wish to be disturbed. You may leave the key in the lock, however. I don't intend to keep you in here against your will."

"That makes a change," she said with heavy sarcasm, turning the key and stepping away from the door.

Stoneridge was leaning against the big mahogany table in the center of the room, his legs crossed at the ankles, his hands resting on the edge of the table. His eyes were quiet and assessing as they rested on her tense face.

Poor little girl, he caught himself thinking. The compassionate reflection startled him, he was so used to feeling he had to meet her as a combatant, never giving an inch, even when they were in charity with one another. But she was so very young and vulnerable in her uncertainty and her hurt. Somehow he must lead them through this thorny thicket, ignoring her barbs, treating them as the desperate defenses they were.

"Come here, Theo," he said, holding out his hands.

She made no move, merely stood in the middle of the room, her arms crossed over her breast. She had on one of the holland smocks she wore when she went racketing around the estate on her gypsy pursuits, her bare feet thrust into open sandals, her hair in two thick plaits hanging over her shoulders.

He pushed himself away from the table and seized her hands, pulling them away from her breast as he drew her toward him.

He cupped her chin, turning up her face, and a quiver ran through the slender frame, an instinctive response to a gesture that always preceded his lips on hers. He ran his flat thumb over her lips in another familiar gesture, and he saw the light change in her eyes.

"No!" she exclaimed, trying to turn her head aside. "I won't let you confuse things."

He ignored her protest, bending his head to take her mouth with his, his free hand running down her back, lingering on the curve of her hips. He pressed her against the rising heat in his loins and felt her breath quicken against his mouth.

"Don't do this. . . . I don't want this." It was a low-voiced plea as she tried to pull away from him.

He held her steady, saying with soft assertion, "I know that you do."

And she did. Despite everything, she did want this. She told herself she loathed him, and yet it was as it always was. She was reveling in his strength holding her, in the heat and the power of his body, the scent of his skin, a mixture of earth

207

and sun overlaying the lingering tang of soap from his morning's shave.

And deep down inside a part of her cried out for him to make her understand, to show her how to make sense of this misery and her dreadful confusion. She didn't want to loathe him, she wanted to feel warm and loving and to open herself to the warmth and love she had sensed in him. She wanted to believe again in that warmth and sensitivity, believe again that there was something essential in her self that he responded to.

But her hurt was still powerful, and she ignored the tiny voice, trying to withstand the insidious creeping arousal that would sweep all protest, all outrage, all rational thought from her mind and her soul. "You promised," she said. "You promised you wouldn't take advantage of this."

"I promised you a partnership," he said, drawing up her skirt so that his hands were on the bare skin of her thighs. His eyes held hers, piercing the midnight-blue depths as if they would see the secrets of her soul. "I want you as you want me, Theo."

She was about to sink into the warm liquid world of desire, to acknowledge the truth of what he said, to throw caution to the four winds and yield to this pulsing excitement; and then it hit her anew — what he'd done to her, what he'd taken from her.

"No!" She swung one leg sideways, catching him behind the knees as she brought both hands up and pushed against his chest. Sylvester felt himself toppling backward, but he had a fistful of her skirt in one hand and he yanked hard as he fell. The skirt tore, but he managed to hook the back of her calf with the crook of his elbow, and she overbalanced, landing on top of him on the carpet.

"Goddamned gypsy!" he exclaimed, but his eyes were smoky with passion.

He wrapped both arms around her, securing her arms at her back as he rolled over until she was pinned beneath him, lying on her hands. He scissored her legs with his own, and then, satisfied that she was immobilized, kissed her, driving deep into the sweet moistness of her mouth. For a second she resisted, her body tensing as if she thought she could throw him off, and then she yielded, her mouth opening beneath his plunging tongue, as her soul ceased to be a battlefield and desire reigned supreme.

Her ripped skirt was caught up beneath her, and her bare legs moved urgently against his. He slipped his hands between their bodies, raising himself slightly so he could grasp the waistband of her drawers. The flimsy material tore as he yanked downward, and Theo gasped against his mouth and bit his lip. He tasted blood and for a second raised his head. Her eyes were open, wild now with passion, and she was in a world far from this one. Her tongue ran over her own lips, licking away a bead of his blood.

"What a savage little animal you are," he said roughly, his eyes glittering with satisfaction, his swift fingers deft on the fastening of his britches. Her hands were still pinned beneath her, her legs still caught between his so that only her head was free to move, but he could read only an ungovernable excitement in her eyes and the set of her mouth as he pushed a hand beneath her buttocks. A fingernail rasped against the rich damask-soft curve as he lifted her on his palm to meet the thrust of his turgid flesh.

And when he was deep within her and she was watching his face, losing herself in his eyes as he was buried in her body, he began to speak softly.

"I'm not going to apologize, Theo. I'm not responsible for your grandfather's plots, but he knew perfectly well that Stoneridge and the title are nothing without the estate. And he wanted his son's blood to inherit his estate. If it had been divided among the four of you, it would have been almost impossible to administer. An estate can't have four owners and still prosper. This was his way of resolving all those conflicts. I'm no better and no worse than the next man, Theo, and I promise you that no man worth his salt would have turned his back on such an opportunity."

He ran his flat palm over her face in an all-encompassing caress that was also an assertion of possession. "Particularly when the prize was a wonderful, passionate gypsy."

His words punctured Theo's world of self-absorbed arousal as they'd been intended to, but she was too far up her mountain,

209

too close to the peak, for them to send her all the way back to the bottom and the cold, clear lake of reality.

He watched her expression, the faint protest forming in her eyes, and he began to move, stroking gently within her, stoking the fires of passion again, feeling her tighten around him, the deep translucent glow appearing on her skin as her pleasure built.

"This is what's important," he said. "It's been like this between us, Theo, from the first moment. I felt it even before I knew who you were. Even when you were resisting me, you felt this, didn't you?"

She closed her eyes as if to hide her responses from him, and he chuckled softly. "False pride, gypsy. There's nothing wrong with admitting it. Tell me, Theo. You felt this, didn't you?"

Her tongue touched her lips, and her head moved in slight but definite affirmative.

"Open your eyes, love," he insisted, withdrawing to the edge of her body, holding himself there, watching the mobile features beneath him. Her eyes shot open and were filled with the surprised wonder that always flooded her, as if every time the sensations were unique.

Slowly, very slowly, he sheathed himself within her again. Her loins leaped against his thighs and her internal muscles rippled around his flesh. He stopped her mouth with his own, stifling the cry of joy that had no place emerging from the sunny library on a Wednesday morning.

He fell heavily upon her under the surging torrent of his own climax, forgetting that her arms were still pinned beneath their bodies, and for a moment, still lost in sensate bliss, Theo wasn't aware of the discomfort.

Finally he rolled sideways, gathering her to him, holding her head against his chest, stroking her hair, as the violent pounding of his heart slowed.

Theo lay still against him, her numbed arms and hands prickling as the blood flowed into them again. Her body was deeply at peace, brimming with fulfillment, but her thoughts were as torn and disheveled as her clothes.

His words replayed in her head. He wouldn't apologize for manipulating and deceiving her, because according to his view he'd had no choice. He was telling her that Stoneridge couldn't have survived with four owners. The estate manager in her acknowledged that truth, but she would have kept the management of all their inheritances in her own hands . . . wouldn't she? If it was up to her sisters, of course, she would have. But they would have husbands . . . strangers who might have different ideas.

She had a sudden image of herself, a crabbed spinster, squabbling with her sisters' husbands, sowing family dissension over a meadow.

She stirred in his arms, a restless movement of acute mental discomfort, and Sylvester traced the line of her turned cheek on his chest. "Let's hear it, my love."

"You've taken so much from me," she said in a low voice, pushing up against his chest so she was sitting sideways beside him. "By trickery. How can you expect me to pretend that didn't happen?"

"You've lost your independence," he said consideringly, "but marriage has taken that from you, Theo, not I — and you agreed to this marriage of your own accord."

"I believed I would be benefiting my sisters by marrying you, and that wasn't the case."

Sylvester sat up. "No, it wasn't," he agreed evenly. Her hands were making impossible knots in her lap, and he took them between both of his. "Listen to me. When I first came here, I intended to marry one of you. I assumed it would be Clarissa because she was the elder. Your mother said very firmly that Clarissa and I would not suit." A slight smile touched his lips, and his grip tightened on her hands. "I certainly wouldn't dispute that. But you and I, Theo, *do* suit."

"When did you decide that?"

"From the very first," he said, releasing her hands and taking her chin. "From the first curse you threw at my head, gypsy." He laughed softly, running his thumb over her mouth. "Such a tempestuous, fiery, combative creature you are. And I wouldn't have you any other way."

211

She wanted to believe that. Oh, how she wanted to believe it.

"If you'd wanted me for myself, why didn't you simply tell me the truth and court me for myself?"

Sylvester shook his head, and a flash of exasperation appeared in the gray eyes. "My dear girl, be realistic. A Gilbraith taking over your beloved manor! You'd have laughed in my face and sent me about my business without a backward glance."

He stood up and refastened his britches, looking down at her as she continued to sit amid her ruined garments.

"You may have lost your independence, Theo, but so, to a large extent, have I."

Theo looked doubtful. "I don't see how that works. It seems women give up everything and men simply gain everything." She rose to her feet, gathering her tatters around her.

Sylvester ran a hand through his crisp curls and over the back of his neck. "One day I hope that you'll feel you've gained much more than you've lost," he said finally.

Theo, her hand on the key in the lock, paused as if she would say something; then quietly she unlocked the door and left.

A heavy silence fell like a pall at her departure. Sylvester poured himself a glass of madeira and sat in a chair beside the hearth, where a copper jug of golden chrysanthemums blazed in the place of a fire. He'd won a victory, but it was hardly conclusive, and he'd used a weapon he'd promised himself he wouldn't use against Theo again. He'd sworn he would use her passion only for their shared pleasure. But surely there was a greater good to be served here. . . .

"Lady Belmont, my lord." Foster spoke from the library door, and Elinor entered, her face shaded by the wide brim of her straw hat.

"This is an unexpected pleasure, ma'am." Stoneridge moved forward, hand outstretched in welcome, wondering what would have happened if his mother-in-law had arrived half an hour earlier to find her daughter behind a locked door in the throes of passion on the library floor. Knowing Elinor, she'd have slipped quietly away, and they'd have been none the wiser. The thought brought a flicker of amusement, lightening his somber mood.

"I trust I'm not intruding," Elinor said pleasantly, taking his hand.

"Not at all," he said. "Theo is upstairs, I believe. Foster will let her know you're here. May I offer you a glass of madeira?"

"Thank you." Elinor turned to the butler. "I'll go up and see Lady Theo in a minute, Foster. There's no need to disturb her. I wish to have a word with Lord Stoneridge first."

Sylvester raised an eyebrow as he turned to the decanter, wondering what could be behind this tête-à-tête. "Ma'am." He placed a glass on the small table beside the chair where Elinor had seated herself.

"Thank you." She drew off her gloves in a businesslike fashion. "I'll come straight to the point. I have it in mind to go to London for the coming Season. Thanks to your generosity . . ." She inclined her head as she sipped her madeira. "Thanks to your generosity over the girls' dowries, I am well able to afford a come-out for Emily and Clarissa. Emily should have been presented two years ago, but with her grandfather's illness it wasn't possible."

"No, of course not," Sylvester murmured, taking a seat opposite her, wincing at this reference to his generosity. At least Theo wasn't around to hear it. "Would you wish to open Belmont House? I should be delighted to put it at your disposal, of course. . . ."

"Good heavens, no," Elinor said. "I wouldn't dream of expecting to be a charge on you, Stoneridge. I shall hire a suitable house for myself and the girls. Lawyer Crighton shall see to it for me. But it's Theo I wish to discuss with you."

He frowned. "You wish her to accompany you?"

Elinor replaced her glass on the table. "I was hoping to persuade you to take her yourself. She should be presented at court, and while, of course, I'll sponsor her, it would be more appropriate if she were under her husband's roof." She sat back, watching his reaction, her expression hidden by her hat brim.

Sylvester's mind whirled. To go to London. To face the turned shoulders, the raised eyebrows, the whispers.

To face them and face them down. Either that or he must hide out in this backwater for the rest of his life, waiting in dread for his dishonor to catch up with him. Waiting in dread for his dishonor to be revealed to his wife. Without a wife . . . without such a wife as Theo . . . he could have lived with his private shame, as he had done for the last year. But now it was different.

Neil Gerard's face, as it had been at the court-martial, rose in his mind's eye. Neil had averted his gaze, and Sylvester had assumed it was his friend's embarrassment. Gerard couldn't in honesty clear his old friend's name, so he was evasive. And Sylvester had read his own guilt in that evasion and had turned his own head aside to spare Neil further discomfort.

He'd avoided Neil after the court-martial. The one occasion they'd met, his erstwhile friend had given him the cut direct in public, and he hadn't been prepared to court a repetition of that mortification. Like the coward he'd been labeled, he'd fled the scene of his shame. But how long was he to go on in this fashion?

"Lord Stoneridge?" Elinor's soft voice broke into his reverie. She was looking puzzled, and he realized he'd been silent for a long time.

He rose to his feet, crossing to the sideboard to refill his glass. "It wouldn't hurt that ramshackle hoyden to acquire a little town bronze, ma'am," he said with a smile.

Elinor laughed. "My thinking exactly. So you'll open Belmont House for the Season."

"I bow to your judgment, Lady Belmont. But I think I'll leave you to persuade Theo. I don't see her embracing the idea with enthusiasm — she's too wedded to Stoneridge and its affairs."

"Very true," Elinor said briskly. "But her sisters will be most persuasive, and as long as we have your support . . ." She stood up, drawing on her gloves again.

"You have it for what it's worth," he said wryly.

"Then I'll go and tackle her at once."

Sylvester bowed his mother-in-law from the library and then stood in frowning thought, wondering what he'd let himself in for. Theo would wonder why her husband was a social pariah. She would hear the rumors. . . .

If only he could remember what had happened that day at

214

Vimiera, if only he could prove the rumors false once and for all. There had to be another explanation for what had happened. And there had to be a way to discover the truth.

Chapter Seventeen

"Launching three gals in one Season is quite an undertaking," Countess Lieven observed as the barouche drew up before a tall house on Brook Street.

"But only one of them requires a husband," Sally Jersey pointed out, gathering her parasol and reticule together.

"Well, it's to be hoped they're not farouche," the countess declared with a lift of her narrow nose as she stepped out onto the pavement. "Living in the country all these years."

"I can't imagine any daughter of Elinor's being in the least objectionable," Lady Jersey said with her usual good nature. "I'd be quite happy to supply vouchers for Almack's without meeting them."

"Yes, well you do have an unfortunate tendency to take things on trust," her companion said sharply. "We have standards to maintain, must I remind you?" She ascended the short flight of steps to the house behind her footman, who ran up from the barouche to knock on the door. "And what do we know about this young Fairfax?"

"Perfectly unexceptionable Dorsetshire family," Sally told her. "It's not a great match but an eminently respectable one . . . a love match, as I understand it."

"I don't know what gets into gals' heads these days," Countess Lieven sniffed. "Marrying for love, indeed. At least the younger one did the sensible thing, marrying Stoneridge."

The door opened, and Lady Belmont's butler bowed deeply at the august visitors. The footman returned to the barouche as the ladies were admitted.

Countess Lieven looked around the square hall with a critical eye before pronouncing, "Remarkably tasteful for a hired house."

She moved in stately fashion to the wide, shallow staircase, her companion bustling somewhat less elegantly on her heels. "Why do I have a feeling there was some scandal attached to Stoneridge?"

"Oh, it was nothing," Sally said. "Some military matter . . . no one gives such things a thought."

"I feel sure Lieven said something," the countess muttered.

"Yes, men are much more concerned with such matters," Sally declared. "Quite unnecessarily so, I would have said."

"I've never cared for Lavinia Gilbraith . . . an overbearing woman," the countess pronounced. Sally privately reflected that when it came to overbearing, her fellow patroness of Almack's had few rivals; however, she merely said pacifically, "I don't think that should affect our view of the Belmont girls."

"Yes, well, we shall see." The countess wafted through the double doors of an elegant salon as the butler threw them open, announcing the newcomers in discreet accents.

There were quite a few visitors in Lady Belmont's salon, a gratifying number, considering that London was still thin of company at the start of the Season. Elinor put such flattering attention down to the novelty of her daughters. It would certainly explain the cluster of admiring young men at her first "At Home." But it didn't fully explain the group of men of her own generation, gathered beside the fireplace. She was too levelheaded to consider her own charms might have something to do with the attention. If she remembered being one of society's beauties during her own debutante season, leaving many a languishing suitor when she'd married Kit Belmont, it was a fond and passing reflection, swiftly dismissed in favor of more pertinent matters.

Emily and Clarissa were sitting with their mother on a sofa, Edward perched in proprietary fashion on the arm next to his betrothed. Elinor rose and hurried forward to greet her visitors, followed by Emily and Clarissa, their eyes demurely downcast in anticipation of this vital introduction.

"Elinor, my dear, how wonderful it is to see you," Lady Jersey said with genuine warmth, embracing her old friend. "How could you have hidden yourself away all these years? You've been sadly missed, you know? Isn't that so, Countess?" She turned for corroboration to Countess Lieven, who bowed and gave her habitual frosty smile.

"Indeed," she said, extending her hand. "Sadly missed."

Elinor shook hands briskly, not in the least awed by the intimidating countess. "Allow me to present my daughters." She drew Emily and Clarissa forward and glanced surreptitiously at the clock, wondering where Theo was. She'd promised to be here to meet the patronesses, and she was not one to break promises, however little she might relish the occasion.

Even as she wondered, the door opened and Theo came into the room with her swift stride, bringing the freshness of the September afternoon in her wind-pinkened cheeks and bright eyes, wisps of raven hair escaping from her beribboned chip-straw hat and drifting over her forehead.

"Mama, forgive me for being late." She crossed the room, taking her mother's hands in both hers and kissing her. "We went to Richmond to ride this morning, and it seemed to take a very long time to get back."

"Allow me to introduce my daughter, Lady Stoneridge," Elinor said. "Theo, dear, Countess Lieven and Lady Jersey."

"How do you do?" Theo said, extending her hand to each in turn, smiling with her usual frank and easy informality. "I do hope you're going to approve of me."

Lady Jersey smiled, but the countess looked distinctly put out. "Do come and have some tea," Elinor said hastily, moving her guests farther into the salon. "Theo, is Stoneridge not with you?"

"Yes, he's just coming. He took the curricle to the mews himself," Theo explained. A slight frown touched her eyes. In the week since they'd arrived in London, Sylvester had been remarkably reluctant to participate in the Season's social functions, although he'd insisted that Theo accompany her mother and sisters everywhere. She wasn't sure what he did while she was out and hadn't felt able to ask. Their conversations these days tended to be those of polite acquaintances, except when they were making love, and words played little part in those still glorious exchanges. Ironically, Theo found she missed the challenging edge to their relationship; it was as if a spring had been broken somewhere.

On the drive here from Curzon Street, Sylvester had been distracted, even irritable, and had set her down at her mother's door, saying curtly that he would take the curricle to the mews himself, though he had a perfectly competent tiger for such tasks.

Putting the puzzle from her mind, she went to greet Edward while Emily poured tea for Countess Lieven and Lady Jersey, and Clarissa hovered attentively.

"You're supposed to be doing the pretty with your sisters," Edward said in an undertone as Theo came up to him.

She grinned and murmured, "Emily and Clarry can do very well without me. I couldn't give a tinker's damn if the dragon ladies don't approve of me."

"You are wicked," he said, unable to restrain his answering grin. His eyes went with fond pride to his betrothed, who was looking particularly charming in pale sprigged muslin, her soft brown hair threaded with apple-green ribbon.

"You know something," Theo said thoughtfully. "I believe the Earl of Wetherby has a *tendre* for Mama. Have you noticed how he's always at her side?"

"He and Bellamy," Edward said, watching the gentlemen in question as they bent solicitously toward Lady Belmont.

"Yes . . . oh, here's Stoneridge." She turned to the door as her husband entered. He really was a very imposing figure, she thought, surprised by a flash of pride. His coat of dark-blue superfine and pale-blue pantaloons showed off the power of his shoulders and the muscular strength of his thighs; his cravat was simply but gracefully tied, and he wore only a single fob at his cream waistcoat. The restrained elegance of his appearance was in marked contrast to the younger men in the room, sporting wasp waists and impossibly high starched cravats. Even Edward had succumbed to the elaborate cravat, although he'd never be seen dead in a wasp waist or a violently striped waistcoat.

Sylvester stood for a moment on the threshold of the salon, steeling himself for whatever reception he was about to receive.

Despite his resolution to face up to his first social occasion, in the week since they'd arrived, he'd managed to avoid events like this. He'd escorted his wife to the theater, he'd ridden with her in Hyde Park at the fashionable hour, but he'd not visited any of his clubs, and he'd not accompanied Theo on any of the visits she'd made with her mother as Lady Belmont picked up the threads of her old life, or to the rout party they'd all attended at Carlton House. But he hadn't been able to avoid this afternoon's informal "At Home," designed to introduce the Belmont girls to the most important members of the ton, without offending his mother-in-law and puzzling his wife.

His eyes were hard, his mouth taut, as he looked around the salon, recognizing faces among the older contingent, although most of the young sprigs were unknown to him.

"Stoneridge." Elinor came to greet him, smiling warmly. "I'd almost given you up. You're acquainted with Countess Lieven and Lady Jersey, of course."

"Of course." He bowed to the ladies, receiving a frosty nod from the countess and a smile from Sally Jersey. The chill of the countess's reception didn't trouble him, since it was her customary greeting to all but her intimates.

"And I'm sure you know Lord Wetherby and Sir Robert Bellamy. And I expect Viscount Franklin is an old army colleague." Elinor smilingly indicated the group by the fire, her gesture encompassing the five men she hadn't mentioned by name.

There was a silence. An almost palpable touch of ice in the warm room. Theo stared at the men, who as one swept her husband with a disdainful stare as he bowed, his features carved in granite. He made no attempt to cross toward the group, and not a hand was extended in greeting.

Theo saw the telltale muscle jump in Sylvester's cheek; then he turned and strolled over to the window, where he stood alone, his arms folded, the gray eyes hard as iron, a peculiar twist to his mouth. In astonishment she glanced up at Edward. His expression was stricken. Lord Wetherby suddenly broke the silence, addressing a careless observation to the viscount. A teacup clattered in a saucer.

Without conscious decision Theo marched across the room to the window, the skirt of her cambric driving dress swishing around her ankles. "I don't believe I've made the acquaintance of Viscount Franklin, Stoneridge. Won't you introduce me?" She slipped her hand in his arm, smiling up at him, her eyes brilliant with fiery purpose. She almost pulled him around toward the fire, turning her blazing countenance on the men who'd insulted her husband.

"Do you care for tea, Stoneridge?" Emily's clear tones rang across the room. "Unless you'd prefer claret. I know how you enjoy a glass at this time of day."

220

"I'll ring for Dennis," Elinor said calmly, reaching for the bell-pull. "Gentlemen, do you share my son-in-law's tastes? Or are you content with tea?" Her smile as she addressed them could have frozen hell's fires.

"Try one of these macaroons." Clarissa snatched up a plate from beneath the wandering hand of Countess Lieven and brought it over to her brother-in-law. "They're your favorites."

He was suddenly surrounded by Belmont women, the center of their attentions, ministering to his needs and his wishes as if he were the sun to their earth. It reminded him of a pride of lionesses protecting an injured cub. Mortification that they should witness his humiliation warred with gratitude. They didn't know what was behind the insulting reception he'd been given, but it seemed they didn't care.

"Viscount Franklin, were you also in the Peninsula?" Theo addressed the viscount, her arm securely linked in Sylvester's. The viscount, an upstanding gentleman of some thirty-eight summers, resplendent in his regimentals, quailed before the rage in the young countess's purple eyes. Her little white teeth flashed in her sun-dappled face, but it was the smile of a shark closing in on her prey.

Viscount Franklin had fought all his military battles in the political corridors of Horseguards and had never faced an enemy on a battlefield. He cleared his throat, and his booted feet shifted on the carpet. "As it happens, I haven't had the good fortune to serve overseas, countess."

"Oh, really." Theo raised an eyebrow. "Good fortune seems an odd choice of words, sir. I'm sure my husband and Lieutenant Fairfax would describe it differently." Her predator's smile swept the rest of the group. Edward, who'd moved from his perch to stand beside Stoneridge in his own gesture of solidarity, looked embarrassed and muttered something about the honor of his country.

Not a flicker crossed Stoneridge's impassive expression, but the irony of the situation struck him with full force. Theo had no idea what lay behind this ostracism, yet in her eagerness to defend him, she'd hit the target full square.

The viscount seemed at a loss as to how to respond to the

221

countess's dripping sarcasm. His eyes drifted involuntarily to Edward's empty sleeve, the slashing scar across Lord Stoneridge's forehead.

Lord Wetherby broke the uncomfortable pause. "I understand you've acquired Melton's breakdowns, Stoneridge," he said stiffly.

Sylvester didn't bat an eyelid. "Yes, for a steal." He took a glass of claret from the tray that had miraculously appeared at his elbow. "But I'm also looking for a well-mannered pair for Lady Stoneridge to drive." He glanced down at Theo, who, having achieved what she'd set out to achieve, was looking pensive. Her hand was still firmly tucked into his arm, however, and he had the conviction she wasn't about to abandon him to the wolves again. Just in case he couldn't defend himself.

"Are you going to drive yourself about town, Theo?" Edward said, moving the conversation along general lines.

"Stoneridge has agreed to acquire a curricle for me," Theo responded. Her gaze swept the circle with a distinct challenge. "I trust that doesn't shock you, gentlemen?"

"You're to be commended for your skill, ma'am." Sir Robert bowed.

"Well, I trust I shan't overturn it," she returned, her smile now mischievous, bearing no relation to the fire and ice of a minute ago.

"If there was the slightest danger of that, my love, you wouldn't be driving it," Sylvester said blandly. "But I have complete faith in your ability . . . to do anything you set your mind to," he added, and a glint of humor touched his hard expression.

Before Theo could respond, a piercing voice behind them announced, "Stoneridge, there's something I most particularly wish to remind you about."

"Rosie, whatever are you doing here?" Startled, Theo turned to her little sister, who was regarding the earl intently from behind her glasses. A hair ribbon had come undone, her muslin dress had grass stains on it, and she was holding a jam jar, the palm of one hand carefully over the opening, presumably to prevent whatever it contained from escaping.

"I've just come back from the square garden with Flossie. We were gathering specimens, and Dennis told me you and Stoneridge were here," Rosie explained earnestly. "And I thought I'd take the opportunity to remind him that he'd promised to take me to Astley's at the earliest possible chance. I was wondering when that would be." Her round eyes remained fixed unwaveringly on her brother-in-law.

Sylvester laughed, and a ripple of amusement ran around the circle by the fire.

"Rosie!" Elinor had just noticed her youngest child's unconventional arrival and came hurrying across the room. "You're not supposed to be in the drawing room this afternoon. Look at you." She gestured in some chagrin to the child's appearance. "And whatever have you got in that jar?"

"Don't ask, ma'am," Sylvester said, still chuckling. "But I beg you to excuse her — she had a most urgent question for me."

"Oh, dear." Elinor sighed. "What was it?"

"About Astley's," Rosie told her, spreading her fingers slightly over the top of the jar and peering between them. "I hope it hasn't escaped. It's a stick insect, and it's very difficult to see if it's still there or not."

"Out, you horrible little girl!" Swallowing her grin, Theo swept Rosie toward the door, relieving her mother of further embarrassment.

"But when . . ."

"The day after tomorrow," Sylvester said to Rosie's anxious inquiry as she was borne inexorably from the room.

"We must be on time . . . I wouldn't want to miss the grand procession," Rosie declared as Theo thrust her into the corridor.

"We won't miss anything," Theo assured, and closed the door firmly.

Rosie's diversion had broken the intensity of the circle by the fire. Sylvester moved away to pay his respects to the patronesses, exchanging a few words with the young men hovering around Emily and Clarissa. His mortification burned deep, but he was bland and polite, doing what was required. He felt Theo's pensive eyes on his back and guessed at the swirling cauldron of questions she was just waiting to fire at him. Questions he couldn't

223

bring himself to answer.

But in this respect he'd misjudged her. When they'd left Lady Belmont's salon and were once again in the relative privacy of his curricle, Theo made a few casual observations on the company and said not a word about what had happened. But her silence merely masked the tumbling turmoil of her thoughts.

Why had people reacted to Sylvester like that? What could he have done? It must be something that people considered shameful, but she couldn't force him to tell her if he chose not to. And he obviously chose not to. There was a chilly touch-me-not quality to his present silence, much stronger than the distance there'd been between them since they'd arrived in London.

She couldn't believe he'd done something dishonorable. Of course he'd tricked her into marrying him. But if she absolved her grandfather of dishonor in the business, then she had no choice but to absolve her husband. In one light they'd both sacrificed her for the estate, but in another light she could hardly be sacrificed for something she wanted more than anything herself.

No, the worst she knew of her husband was that he was arrogant and controlling and reserved to a fault. And those weren't good enough reasons for Society's ostracism.

The carriage turned onto Curzon Street, and Sylvester broke into her absorption, his voice politely neutral.

"You'll forgive me if I leave you to go in alone. I have some business to attend to with Hoare's bank." He drew rein outside the house.

"Of course," Theo said, springing down without waiting for his assistance. "I'll see you at dinner, I expect."

"Certainly. And we should discuss how we're to arrange this excursion to Astley's. Will Emily and Clarissa wish to accompany us?"

"Oh, yes, and Edward," Theo agreed. "It'll be a family party." She paused, her hand on the curricle door, her velvet eyes grave. "We tend to stick together."

He nodded. "So I gather." Raising a hand in farewell, he gave his horses the office to start.

* * * * *

Theo was in the drawing room, dressed for dinner, when Sylvester returned.

"I'm late, I'm sorry," he said as he came into the room. "I'll pour myself a sherry and then I'll go and change."

Theo was sitting on a chaise longue, her legs curled beneath her in a position that ignored the constraints of her delicate evening gown of pale-blue silk.

She put down her book and smiled at him. "Why bother to change? It's only us."

"I'd hate to show discourtesy to my wife," he said lightly, turning away to pick up the sherry decanter.

Theo could hear the strain beneath the light tone, she could see the tension in his broad back as he filled his glass. Slowly, she uncurled herself and stood up.

"I don't believe your wife would consider it such," she said, coming over to him. She slipped her arms around his waist, resting her cheek between his shoulder blades. "In fact, your wife doesn't give a damn what you wear when you're with her. The less the better, really."

Sylvester put down his glass and reached behind him with both arms to encircle her body as she leaned against his back. He could feel her intensity, the currents flowing from her spirit to his. She was trying to reassure him about a great deal more than his wardrobe.

Such fierce and unquestioning loyalty was as astonishing as it was moving. He drew her around in front of him, and she put her arms around his waist again, looking up at him with a little questioning smile that belied the gravity in her eyes.

Abruptly, hunger for the warmth and comfort she was offering swept through him. He crushed her against him, his mouth finding hers with rough need. She came up on her toes, pressing herself into his body, her lips parting beneath the onslaught of his kiss.

Foster opened the door in his customary discreet fashion to announce dinner and as discreetly closed it again.

225

Chapter Eighteen

The girl in the center of the ring wore a scarlet blouse with billowing sleeves and a ruffled neck, leather britches, and Cossack boots. The gaily caparisoned horse beneath her caracoled, seeming to be prancing on the very tips of his iron-shod hooves, and the girl's balance didn't falter as she pirouetted on the bare back. Then she jumped, flipped in the air, and landed again on the horse, her two feet firmly planted.

Emily squeaked and seized Edward's hand. Clarissa gazed round-eyed, and Rosie leaned forward, her hands on her knees, as if she couldn't get close enough to see. Theo shook her head in admiration.

"How wonderful to do that," she said enviously. "What an amazingly exciting life it must be."

"To be a performer in Astley's amphitheater?" Sylvester asked, raising his eyebrows. "My dear girl, you can't see from here how shabby those costumes are. Just imagine living in a freezing caravan, with no privacy, racketing around from place to place half the year."

"Sheer bliss," Theo declared, her eyes on the ring, where a troupe of jugglers were performing with fire sticks.

"Oh, he's going to swallow it!" Clarissa exclaimed, turning pale as one of the performers tipped back his head and the blazing stick inched into his mouth.

"How does he do that?" Rosie demanded. "It must be a cheat."

"Oh, you have no magic in your soul," Clarissa told her, her hands gripped tightly in her lap.

"I only want to understand," her little sister protested in her customary refrain.

Sylvester leaned back slightly, his eyes resting on his wife's profile as she gazed raptly at the ring, where six horses now circled, their white plumes waving in the air. Each carried a standing rider, all dressed alike, but it was clear that three were male and three female. They began an elaborate dance, a kind of quadrille involving both horses and riders, the latter exchanging horses as if they were exchanging partners.

"Why bliss?" he asked softly.

Without taking her eyes off the ring, Theo said, "It's exciting. It's doing something . . . something risky that you must do perfectly if you're not to hurt yourself. It's a real life . . . not this . . . this . . ." She stopped, but Sylvester knew what she'd been about to say. London bored her, and she despised the inane social round, although she struggled to hide her tedium from her mother and sisters, who seemed to be enjoying themselves.

His gaze shifted from his wife's countenance to Edward Fairfax. Emily still clutched his hand. Edward had taken lodgings in Albermarle Street, although he spent all his time in Brook Street and went to his lodgings only to lay his head on his pillow. Sylvester was still uncertain whether he knew anything about Vimiera, but if he did, he clearly wasn't saying. And he hadn't hesitated to join the Belmont women in their support of Stoneridge.

He closed his eyes as his temples tightened. Theo had still said nothing openly about his humiliation of the other afternoon, and today her sisters and Edward were behaving just as always. Perhaps it was the distraction of the performance.

But perhaps, he thought, it was another way in which they were showing him their support. A kind of blind loyalty simply because he was now one of them. They were the most extraordinary family. But dear God, if only he could prove that their loyalty wasn't misplaced.

The familiar frustration washed through him. If he could just remember, or find someone who remembered, what had happened before the bayonet had slashed across his head. There had to be an explanation for that surrender. An explanation other than abject cowardice. He'd searched the records at Horseguards, forcing himself to meet the eye of men who passed him in the corridors, but the transcript of the court-martial yielded nothing that he didn't already know. It was time to start asking some questions.

Again Neil Gerard's face popped into his vision. Gerard had not yet put in an appearance in town, but it was very early in the Season. When he turned up, Sylvester would tackle him. If he cut him socially, then he would track him down in his lodgings. Somehow he would force the man to talk about Vimiera. Maybe now, now that Sylvester was distanced from the agony of his imprisonment and the immediacy of his shame, he might latch on to some infinitesimal fact or impression that would unlock his memory.

Unless he already knew the truth. Unless he knew everything there was to know: He'd yielded the colors, surrendered, condemned his own men. Perhaps the truth had been too terrible to remember.

Theo took her eyes from the ring for a minute and glanced at her husband. A shiver ran through her as she saw his expression. His eyes were blank, his face drawn, that muscle twitching in his cheek. *What was it?*

She glanced at her sisters, intent on the scene in the ring. With the natural delicacy of Elinor Belmont's children, no one had mentioned the other afternoon. If Theo didn't bring it up, then they wouldn't. They would have discussed it among themselves and with Elinor, but it would go no further than that unless they were given permission.

But for some reason she couldn't bring herself to speculate about some obscure dishonor in Sylvester's past, not even with her sisters or her mother, from whom she rarely held secrets. Just as something had held her back from revealing the true conditions of the old earl's will. Her motives for keeping quiet about it confused her, but for whatever reason, she kept silent.

"I wish I could ride," she declared with sudden fierceness, and was instantly rewarded as Sylvester's eyes focused and he came back to the world of Astley's amphitheater.

"But you do," Clarissa pointed out. "You rode only this morning in Hyde Park."

"You call that riding?" her sister retorted scornfully. "A decorous trot along the tan under the eyes of every old cat in town?"

Sylvester raised his eyebrows and caught Edward's eye. The younger man gave him a sympathetic smile.

"Look at that man swallowing a sword now!" Rosie cried. "That *has* to be a cheat. It must fold up or something as he pushes it down."

"A magician's nightmare audience," Sylvester murmured.

228

Theo's deep chuckle answered him.

"She has an inquiring mind."

"So I've noticed."

The grand finale brought the performance to a rousing close. Sylvester could see that the unsophisticated treat had been a success. Emily and Clarissa had been delighted, Rosie fascinated if less than credulous, and Theo diverted for a few hours.

"Supper," he announced cheerfully, placing Theo's cloak over her shoulders. Her hair was braided around her head, and the slim white column of her bared neck was irresistible. He forgot where they were for a minute and bent and kissed her nape.

Startled, she looked over her shoulder, her eyes glowing with sensual response to the caress. He kissed the corner of her mouth and the tip of her nose.

"Where are we going for supper?" Rosie asked, clearly unimpressed by this delay in the proceedings and quite unaware that her sisters and Edward were tactfully looking in the opposite direction.

"I thought you might enjoy the Pantheon, Rosie," Sylvester said easily.

"Will they have scalloped oysters and ices?" the child inquired, removing her glasses to wipe the lenses on her skirt. "I most particularly enjoy scalloped oysters and pink ices."

"Then you shall have them," Sylvester assured her. "Let's get out of this crush."

He shepherded his small flock ahead of him through the rowdy departing audience, a crowd of townspeople, raucous costermongers, fleet-footed urchins. Astley's was an entertainment that appealed to anyone who could afford the penny entrance fee in the pits.

There was an autumnal nip to the evening air as they emerged into a crowd as noisy and shrill as the one inside. Fruit and flower sellers called their wares, competing with the bellows of pie sellers, and the jangle of an organ grinder with his scrawny monkey dancing frantically.

"I'm just going to look at that monkey." Rosie dived into the crowd in the direction of the organ grinder.

"Rosie!" Theo plunged after her, but Sylvester was quicker.

He grabbed the child's pelisse and hauled her back.

"This is not Lulworth," he said. "You do not run off like that on your own, do you hear, Rosie?"

"I merely wished to see what kind of monkey it was," she said with an injured air. "There are many different kinds of monkeys, you should know, Stoneridge. I have a book about them, and I wanted to identify it."

"It's a little black monkey," Edward said. "Now, come along. Emily's getting cold." He took Rosie's hand and marched off with her, Emily and Clarissa arm in arm beside him, toward the corner where the chaise and Sylvester's curricle waited with coachman, groom, and tiger.

Sylvester and Theo followed, pushing their way through the crowd that seemed suddenly to grow thicker. It wasn't so much that, Theo realized suddenly, as that they were being pressed on either side by three men in the leather aprons of workmen. Three very large men. She glanced up at Sylvester and saw that he was now behind her; the men had somehow separated them just as they drew ahead of the crowd.

She saw the realization of danger flash in his eyes the minute she understood it herself.

"Theo, go to the carriage," he ordered, his voice low and intense as he stepped sideways, his eyes assessing the three men. They wore caps low on their foreheads. A hobnailed boot swung, kicking him on the shin, and his breath whistled through his teeth. He was surrounded now, no room for maneuver, the indifferent crowd behind them as they left the immediate vicinity of the amphitheater.

Sylvester was unarmed. A man on a family outing in the company of women and children didn't carry weapons. His driving whip was with the curricle. One of the men raised his arm, a heavy oak cudgel in his fist, and Sylvester wanted to scream as the memory of the bayonet slicing down at his unprotected head filled him with a momentarily paralyzing terror. He flung up his arms to protect his head at the same moment that Theo kicked the cudgel wielder in the kidneys.

The man bellowed, spinning toward her, giving Sylvester breathing space. Theo kicked again, her leg a perfectly straight

230

weapon, her aim wickedly accurate, slamming into his groin. He doubled over with a scream.

The other two were on Sylvester now, and a knife glinted. He drove his fist upward under the jaw of one of his assailants, a massive bear of a man who simply shook his head and prepared to renew the attack. As he did so, Theo went for him, two fingers jabbing for the eyes. Blinded, he fell back with a panicked cry and her leg flashed upward, her heel driving against his heart just below his ribs.

"Bastards," she said, dusting off her hands. "That was exciting, wasn't it?"

Sylvester had dealt as efficiently with the third assailant, who lay gasping in a fetal curl on the ground, the knife at some distance from his body. The earl, momentarily at a loss for words, turned to his wife. She was breathing rapidly; her eyes shone, her cheeks were flushed, her hair wisped from its braided coronet, and she looked perfectly ready to take on another half a dozen footpads.

Her hat lay on the ground and he picked it up, dusting it off against his thigh, handing it to her silently. She stuck it on her head and grinned at him.

"That'll teach them."

"Yes," he said, "I'm sure it will. Where the *hell* did you learn to fight like that?"

"Edward taught me. You knew I could do it."

"I knew you could wrestle," he said slowly. "I did not know you knew how to fight like a damned street Arab."

"I'm sorry if it vexes you," she said, a shade tartly. "But it seems to me you should be grateful. Those footpads meant business. If you ask me, they were after more than your purse and your watch."

"What on earth —" Edward's horrified tones came from behind her as he took in the scene. "We wondered where you were."

"Oh, just dealing with a minor matter," Sylvester said.

"Footpads," Theo said with another grin at Edward's expression. "You should have seen me, Edward. I remembered all those kicks you taught me, and that business with the fingers." She gestured to prove her point.

"Dear God," Edward muttered, glancing uneasily at the earl.

"I only showed her the technique, sir. I didn't train her in it or anything."

"My wife is clearly an apt pupil," Sylvester said with a sharp exhalation. "And the devil of it is that if she weren't, I'd probably be lying there with my throat cut — which rather inhibits my legitimate outrage."

"So I should hope," Theo declared indignantly. "What shall we do with them?"

"Leave them," Sylvester said, turning away. "Are the girls all right, Fairfax?"

"Yes, they're in the chaise," Edward replied. His expression was strained, his voice low. "I was so busy seeing them safely installed, I didn't see what was happening. Not that it would have made any difference. A cripple isn't good for anything but seeing to the comfort of women."

"Don't be a damned fool," Sylvester said roughly, but he touched his arm in a fleeting gesture of understanding. "Come along, let's get out of here." He indicated they should go ahead of him and then turned back to his assailants. One of them was struggling to his knees.

Sylvester planted a foot in his chest and sent him sprawling. "You will inform whoever employed you that he will discover I don't take kindly to unprovoked attacks. That is a most solemn promise." He lifted his foot again, and the man on the ground cowered, covering his head.

"All right, guv, all right. We was only doin' what we'd been told."

"By whom?" The gray eyes were like the arctic wastelands as he stared down at the man, his foot still menacingly raised.

" 'E was all wrapped up, guv. 'Ad 'is face 'idden in a muffler. I swears it," the man babbled, burying his head. "In the Fisherman's Rest on Dock Street. 'E comes and says 'e wants a little job done. 'E 'ad an 'usky voice, raspy like. Brings us 'ere and points out yer 'onor to us and says get on wi' it. There'll be a guinea apiece. We was only doin' what we was told to do."

"Yes, I'm sure you were." Sylvester believed the man. Whoever was behind this wouldn't be foolish enough to reveal himself

232

to his tools. But the Fisherman's Rest was a clue.

"We wasn't expectin' no woman from 'ell," one of the others muttered, groaning as pain stabbed in his kidneys.

"Something of a surprise for all of us," Sylvester agreed blandly. "Now, don't forget my message." Turning on his heel, he strolled to the waiting vehicles, where an argument seemed to be in full flood between Edward and Theo.

"You cannot possibly drive in an open carriage looking like that," Edward stated.

"Don't be absurd. Who's going to see?"

"Oh, Theo, come into the chaise with us and let Edward drive with Lord Stoneridge," Emily said, her head at the window of the chaise. "We want to know what's happened."

"Now, what's the matter?" Sylvester inquired somewhat wearily.

"Edward's being so silly," Theo said. "He says I shouldn't drive in the curricle, just because my gown's a bit torn."

"A *bit!*" Edward said, pointing at Theo's gown of pale-yellow muslin. "It's ripped all the way up to your waist."

"Well, how could I do a high kick without tearing it? I could have pulled it up to my waist first, I suppose, and regaled the entire neighborhood with the sight of my drawers."

"*Theo!*" protested Emily.

"Of course, they're very pretty drawers," Theo continued, ignoring the flapping ears of tiger and coachman. "They have lace frills and pink ribbon knots, and I believe —"

"That'll do!" Sylvester interrupted this devastating description before it drew an even larger crowd. He scooped her up and bundled her into the chaise. "You may satisfy your sisters' curiosity on the way back to Curzon Street, where you will change your dress."

His tone was scolding, but his eyes were alight with laughter, and something else. Something akin to admiration.

He instructed the coachman to return to Curzon Street and climbed into the curricle beside Edward.

"Was it footpads, sir?" Edward asked directly as the pair of chestnuts sprang forward and the tiger clambered hastily onto his perch at the rear.

233

"Up to a point," Sylvester said. "I'm sure they'd have happily robbed me of my last sou."

"But there was more to it, you believe?"

He nodded. "Another one of those 'accidents' that seem to be occurring with dismaying frequency."

"Who?"

"God alone knows. I'd rather hoped it was some disaffected tenant. But clearly it's not that simple. But don't say anything to Theo. I have enough of a problem second-guessing her as it is, without giving her a cause to get her teeth into."

Edward smiled. "She needs to be occupied."

Sylvester groaned. "Why can't she occupy herself like other young women? Emily and Clarissa enjoy doing the usual things. Shopping and exhibitions and balls and suchlike."

"Theo's not like them."

"No," Sylvester agreed glumly. "She's not like any woman I've ever met. If I don't watch her every minute, she'll be riding *ventre à terre* in the park at the fashionable hour, or attending a prizefight, or presenting herself at Manton's Gallery for some target practice. I can't think what her mother and grandfather were thinking when they encouraged her to be so damnably independent."

Edward bristled. "I believe they both understood they'd have had to break her spirit if she was to be molded in any conventional form," he said stiffly. "And she's a very special person."

Sylvester glanced sideways at the young man's rigid countenance. He smiled and said pacifically, "Yes, she is."

Edward visibly relaxed. "Do you intend to discover who's behind these attacks, sir?"

"If I'm to stay healthy — not to mention alive — for much longer, I think I'd better." Sylvester passed a brougham with barely an inch to spare.

"If I can be of service," Edward suggested tentatively. "I know a one-armed —"

"Oh, for God's sake, you young fool, a one-armed man can ride, shoot, drive, fence, fish, and make love as well as a man with two arms," Sylvester declared. "If I need your help, I'll call upon you, fair enough."

234

The impatient tone was much more reassuring than sympathy or an anxious disclaimer. "Fair enough, sir."

They reached Curzon Street before the chaise and were drinking claret in companionable silence when the girls arrived.

"Is that the ninety-six?" Theo said, lifting the decanter, inhaling the bouquet. "Some bottles in that delivery were corked."

"This one's fine," Sylvester said. "Go and change your dress. We're all famished."

"I'm also very thirsty," Theo responded with a twinkling smile, filling a glass. "All that exercise, you understand."

She was radiating mischief and energy. Sylvester had rarely seen her like this, and he realized with a shock that she was happy, and in the few weeks since he'd known her, he hadn't often seen her truly happy. At least not outside the bedchamber.

And she was happy because that encounter had exhilarated her, had enabled her to do something she was good at, something that pleased and satisfied her and made her feel useful.

She was never going to settle for the life of a society matron. Maybe motherhood would use up some of her surplus energies. Thinking of their passion-filled nights, he couldn't imagine it would be long acoming.

"Take it with you," he said. "You may have ten minutes to change."

"You wouldn't go without me?"

"I wouldn't put it to the test."

"What! After I saved your life?"

"Don't exaggerate. Nine minutes."

There was a distinct glimmer of laughter in the gray eyes, a complicit quiver to his mouth, and Theo felt the warmth of her own response leaping to meet him. These moments of private understanding in public places had been rare occurrences since their arrival in London, and she'd missed them.

Smiling to herself, she went upstairs to change.

The Pantheon on Oxford Street was big and busy, a ballroom and concert hall, with a supper room frequented not by the haut ton but by respectable, wealthy burghers and their ladies. Sylvester had judged that Rosie would feel more comfortable in its relative informality than in the fashionable Piazza, where disagreeable matrons and haughty young bucks would regard such a family party with disdain.

The Countess of Stoneridge also seemed more at home in the Pantheon than at Almack's, he noticed ruefully, as she kept the table in gales of laughter with a series of wickedly accurate comments on their fellow diners.

It was Theo who noticed Clarissa's abstraction first. "What are you looking at, Clarry?" She twisted in her chair to gaze over her shoulder.

"Don't stare, Theo," Clarissa exclaimed, blushing.

"But who . . . ? Oh," she said with complete comprehension. "I see."

"Oh, do turn around, Theo," Clarissa said.

"He is very beautiful," Theo said. "Take a look, Emily. A veritable parfit gentil knight."

Emily turned around and, like her sister, had no difficulty identifying the cause of Clarissa's abstraction. "Oh, yes," she said.

"Who? What?" Rosie demanded, standing up to peer myopically around the supper room. "I don't see a knight. Is he in armor?"

"No, you goose. It's an expression. Sit down." Theo jerked her skirt, pulling her back into her seat. "How do we find out who he is, I wonder?"

"What are you talking about?" Sylvester asked, just as Edward turned from his own examination and chuckled merrily.

"Clarissa's found her knight," Theo said. "Don't blush, love." She patted her sister's hand. "Shall I go and introduce myself?"

"No!" exclaimed both Emily and Clarissa.

"Then Stoneridge shall introduce himself and invite him to come and take a glass of wine with us," Theo said firmly. "Do you see him, Stoneridge? That beautitul young man with the long fair hair, sitting with the elderly woman by the window. An elderly woman, that's a good sign, Clarry. It can't be his lover; it must be his mother."

"Theo!"

Theo ignored her sister's protest. "Go over and introduce yourself, Stoneridge, and invite him and his mother to join us. Pretend you know them, that you've met them somewhere before. And then you can just laugh and say you made a mistake, but invite them anyway."

"I will do no such thing," Sylvester declared. "You managing hussy."

"Then *I* will go." Theo pushed back her chair. "How can you expect anything to happen in this world if you don't make it so?"

Before anyone could stop her, she was weaving her way among the tables, a smile of greeting on her face.

"Oh, how could she?" Clarissa murmured, cooling her burning cheeks with her water glass.

Edward and Emily were convulsed with laughter, as if sharing an old joke. Sylvester felt as if he'd strayed into someone else's life and no one was behaving in a manner he understood. It was a familiar sensation in Belmont company. He took a resigned sip of wine and waited to be enlightened.

Rosie scraped the last morsel of pink ice from her bowl. "Theo never minds talking to strangers," she informed him, as if the confidence would enable him to make sense of the hilarity. Even Clarissa was half laughing, despite her blushes. "She's not in the least shy."

No, "shy" was not an adjective he'd ever have applied to his wife. He watched her. She was talking to the people at the window table, her head bent confidentially toward them. Then she turned, and her eyes flew across the room, brimful of laughter. She raised one hand and made a circle of her finger and thumb in a gesture of accomplishment, and then came back to the table.

"Well, it is his mother, and his name's Jonathan Lacey. And they're going to call in Curzon Street," she announced, resuming her seat. "They seem very respectable, not at all like mushrooms, and he has liquid eyes, Clarry. Huge, and the color of the tawniest port. Utterly beautiful. And you should see his hands. So long and slender."

Sylvester caught himself looking at his own hands. They weren't exactly short and fat, but he knew for a fact that he did not have liquid eyes.

"I'm sure he's an artist of some kind," Theo was continuing, sipping her wine. "Anyway, I could tell his mother liked the idea of calling upon the Countess of Stoneridge, so I'm sure we'll see them in a day or so."

"What did you say, Theo?" Edward asked, wiping his eyes with his napkin.

"Oh, I said I thought we'd met before, then realized my mistake, apologized, and introduced myself. The rest was easy."

"Would someone explain what the devil is going on here?" Sylvester inquired. "I realize I am singularly obtuse, but —"

"Oh, that's because you're not a Belmont," Theo said blithely.

There was a second's awkward silence; then Edward said, "Well, neither am I, but I have the advantage of you, sir. I've known this motley crew since I was in short coats."

"Then you do indeed have the advantage," Sylvester said evenly, pushing back his chair. "It's time Rosie was at home."

"But it's true," Theo said, refusing to allow the evening to end on this fractured note. "You are not a Belmont, so of course you don't understand our jokes. That doesn't mean you can't, if you wish to."

"And you are now a Gilbraith, madam wife," he stated.

"Maybe so," Theo declared. Now they'd started on this road, she couldn't see a way to get off it. She continued with her usual bluntness. "But your mother and sister lack a sense of humor, so I can hardly try to understand their jokes."

"That's out of order, Theo!" Edward exclaimed, unable to help himself.

"No," Theo said. "No, it's not." Her eyes were on her husband. "It's the truth. Isn't it, Stoneridge?"

"Unfortunately," he said quietly. "But we'll continue this discussion when it won't embarrass anyone else."

Only Theo and Sylvester understood what had happened. The others were puzzled and uncomfortable, but nothing further was said beyond the merest commonplace until the three Belmonts, escorted by Edward, were ensconced in the Stoneridge town carriage en route to Lady Belmont's house.

Sylvester handed Theo into a hackney and climbed in after her. She huddled into her cloak, wishing it hadn't happened. Everything had been going so well. She'd been telling the truth as she saw it, but it hadn't come out right. She'd sounded bitter and angry. And it was all because he'd reminded her she was a Gilbraith. The old sense of entrapment had washed over her in an acid tide that all the sweet reasoning she'd done with herself in the last weeks couldn't deflect.

"You shouldn't have reminded me," she said in the darkness of the hackney.

"That you're a Gilbraith? It's the truth."

"Yes, just as it's the truth that you own everything that ever belonged to a Belmont!" Oh, why couldn't she bite her tongue?

Sylvester said nothing, merely rested his head against the cracked leather squabs.

"I can't help it," she said, twisting her gloved fingers into a knot, not sure whether she was apologizing or explaining. "I try to forget it, Stoneridge. And then it comes back to me and I become all twisted and angry again. And I want to hurt you as you've hurt me."

"Have I really hurt you, Theo?" he asked softly. The hackney slowed at a crossroads, and a gas jet outside flickered over his face, showing her the harsh set of his mouth, the strain around his eyes. "Be honest," he said. "How have I hurt you?"

He watched through narrowed eyes as light and shadow played over the gamine features. Theo shook her head in inarticulate confusion and gazed fixedly out the window.

When the hackney drew up at Belmont House, Theo still had said nothing. Sylvester handed her down and escorted her into the house.

"I trust you spent a pleasant evening, my lord . . . Lady Theo." Foster bowed, taking his lordship's gloves and curly brimmed beaver.

"Very pleasant, thank you," Sylvester said.

"And Lady Rosie enjoyed herself?"

"I believe so."

"She consumed enough pink ices for an army," Theo said with an easy smile. Concealing her true emotions from the staff was never difficult, although she found it impossible with her family.

"Good night, Foster." She ran up the stairs.

"Cognac in the library, please, Foster." Sylvester turned aside. The butler nodded to himself. More fireworks, it seemed.

Sylvester was staring into the fire when Foster brought in the decanter of cognac. "Thank you," he said absently. "Just leave it on the table. I'll help myself."

He poured a glass and sipped in morose reflection. Someone was trying to kill him, and he couldn't concentrate on that when Theo's tense little face kept obtruding into his thoughts. Her unhappiness tore at him.

With sudden determination he opened a drawer in the desk and took out a pistol. He checked that it was primed, then dropped it into the deep pocket of his coat.

He went into the hall. "Foster . . . my hat and my cane. . . . Thank you." He ran a hand down the cane, touched the little knob in the handle that released the sword blade. It responded with oiled efficiency.

The butler tried not to stare at the sword stick, but he could also see the unmistakable bulge in his lordship's coat. The night streets were not particularly safe, it was true, but these precautions seemed rather extreme for a late-evening stroll to St. James's or some such gentlemanly destination.

Drawing on his gloves, the Earl of Stoneridge left the house. He was going to the Fisherman's Rest on Dock Street.

Theo was standing at her bedroom window as he went down the front steps. She'd expected him to come up to her . . . to drive away her confusion and dismay with his body as he drew from her the deep, ecstatic responses that made her forget all but shared passion. Instead he was going out. Had he finally wearied of her storms?

The thought stunned her. She saw life without Sylvester, and what she saw was a wasteland.

How *had* he hurt her?

Suddenly she turned back to the room. "My cloak, Dora. I'm going out."

Her abigail blinked in astonishment. She'd just hung the cloak in the armoire. "But it's eleven o'clock, my lady."

"So?" Theo said impatiently, drawing on her gloves. "Quickly." If she delayed much longer, Stoneridge would have disappeared from the street, and she'd never catch him up.

She wrapped the velvet cloak around her, drawing the hood

over her hair as she ran down the stairs.

"Did his lordship say where he was going, Foster?"

"No, Lady Theo." The butler shot the last bolt on the front door.

"Well, I have to find him," she said. "Unlock the door quickly. He can't be far away."

Foster hesitated for a fraction. But the earl had only just left, and Lady Theo couldn't come to any harm on Curzon Street. He unbolted the door again, and she ran past him and down the steps, turning to the right, as Sylvester had done.

Chapter Nineteen

Theo reached the corner of Curzon Street and Audley Street just in time to see Sylvester hail a hackney carriage. There was a second one immediately behind, and without pausing to think, she flagged it down.

"I'm going where they're going," she said, gesturing to the other vehicle before scrambling into the dark, shabby interior.

"Right you are, lady." The jarvey cracked his whip, hoping this would be a long fare.

It was only as the hackney swung round a corner, bouncing over the cobbles, that Theo realized she'd brought no money with her. Never mind. Sylvester would pay her fare as well as his own, and if she lost him, she'd take the hackney back to Curzon Street, where there was money aplenty.

Where could he be going? She pushed aside the grimy leather curtain over the window aperture and stared out in the dark streets. The area they were going through had a very unfamiliar feel, but, then, she was only just learning the topography of the few square miles of London inhabited by the ton. Presumably Sylvester wasn't going to the clubs on St. James's. He'd surely have walked that short distance.

After what seemed a very long time they turned alongside the wide, dark body of the Thames and drove along the embankment. The air smelled different. Dirty and smoky, fetid with a midden stench and the ancient river slime clinging to the sloping cobbles of the embankment.

Theo pushed her head out the window and craned toward the box. "Are they still in sight?"

"Aye," he called down. "Turnin' on Dock Street. This ain't a good place fer Quality, if I might be so bold."

"No, I can see that," Theo said, withdrawing her head. What business could Sylvester have in these parts?

What area of his privacy was she intruding on? A ripple of unease lifted the fine hairs on the back of her neck, and she almost told the jarvey to return to Curzon Street. Then she thought of what she wanted to say to Sylvester. And she wanted to say it now. When he heard it, he'd understand that she wasn't sticking her nose into his private affairs.

Although if she did discover a clue or two on the way, she wouldn't close her eyes to it. The still small voice of ruthless honesty spoke through her private protestations.

The hackney drew up in a dark, narrow cobbled street where the stench of river and sewage was so strong, Theo could barely breathe as she stepped out of the carriage. The other hackney was waiting across the street, presumably on Sylvester's instructions. Public traffic in these parts wouldn't be that frequent, and he would need transport home.

A rusty iron sign creaked over the narrow door of a tumbledown wooden structure. Gusts of noxious smoke drifted through tiny unglazed windows, where dim, flickering lights showed and strident voices bellowed. Something crashed heavily to the floor, an angry voice yelled; there was a burst of raucous laughter, and the door flew open abruptly, a man sailing through the air to land on his backside in the filth of the kennel.

With a roar he clambered to his feet and charged back through the door, head down, fists flailing.

Theo stepped back just in time as he came flying out again, this time followed by a furious red-faced woman wielding a rolling pin.

"Get outta my tavern, you great ox!" the woman bellowed, adding a few choice epithets that were new to Theo's fairly educated ears. "Get back to yer woman, Tom Brig, and don't go messin' wi' my customers." She stood over him, sleeves rolled up revealing massive forearms, a tattered fringe of filthy petticoat showing beneath her stained apron. Then, with another curse, she turned and went back inside. The door closed and the alley was in darkness again.

Tom Brig half rose to his knees, then subsided into the kennel with a whimpered exhalation, letting his head fall onto a heap of rotting cabbages, his eyes closing, a stale, beery froth bubbling at his open mouth.

Theo grimaced, stepped over him, and pushed boldly at the closed door. It swung open, and she found herself on the threshold of a square room, foul sawdust on the floor, sea coal belching

243

noxious fumes from the hearth, mingling with the acrid, greasy stench of the tallow rushes and the fish-oil lamps swinging from the blackened rafters.

Her eyes were streaming from the smoke, and for a minute she could see nothing. Then a voice exclaimed, "Well, lookee 'ere, then, Long Meg. Get an eyeful of what the river's dropped on us."

A sea of eyes swiveled toward her. Bloodshot eyes with yellow whites. Grinning mouths revealed blackened stumps, and the reek of unwashed bodies and stale breath enclosed her like a miasma. Then she saw Sylvester, up by the bar counter, a mug in his hand.

He stared at her for a minute, wondering if he'd had enough gin and water to create this image. The crimson velvet hood of her cloak was thrown back, revealing the blue-black hair in startling contrast. Her eyes were dark and intense in the glowing brown face, her lips parted as if on the verge of an eager message.

As he struggled to make sense of this extraordinary visitation, Theo pushed her way through the room toward him, ignoring the hands that grabbed at her cloak, the coarse voices that offered a variery of lewd suggestions for her entertainment.

"Sylvester, there's something I have to tell you." She reached him, smiling, putting her hand on his arm. "I don't believe anymore you've hurt me at all, and I think I've just been —"

Sylvester found his voice. "I must be going insane. What in the devil's name are you doing here?"

"I followed you," she said. "What's that you're drinking?" She picked up the tankard and sniffed its contents. "Is it blue ruin? It smells horrible, but I suppose it's what people drink in places like this."

She turned to look around her with a curious eye, feeling secure now that Sylvester was beside her. "Why would you come to a place like this, Stoneridge?"

Sylvester debated whether to wring her neck on the spot or wait until he could enjoy the exercise at his leisure. "How dare you follow me?" he said finally, aware of how inadequately the words expressed his feelings.

"I wanted to tell you I've realized that actually I don't mind

244

anymore that you tricked me into marrying you," she explained earnestly, her eyes huge and dark in the smoky dimness, her hand still on his arm.

"Well, I'm delighted to hear it," he responded with feeble sarcasm. "Such vital information couldn't have waited, of course, for a more suitable place and time."

"No, it couldn't," Theo declared. She took a sip from his tankard. "Ugh! It's disgusting."

He snatched the tankard from her and smacked her hand away sharply. It relieved his feelings a little, but not nearly enough.

"I can't deal with you here, but by God, I'm going to enjoy getting you home," he said grimly, flinging a shilling on the stained planking of the counter. "You've managed to ruin my own plans, endanger yourself —"

"Not so," Theo denied as he caught her wrist and pulled her behind him toward the door. "I can handle trouble, as you know perfectly well."

"Well, I'll tell you this much, my girl. The trouble I'm about to administer, you won't be able to handle," he asserted, pushing her through the door.

"What plans have I ruined?" Theo demanded, tripping over an uneven cobble and grabbing at his arm. "Oh, you have to pay my hackney. I didn't bring any money."

Sylvester cast his eyes and a prayer for patience heavenward and dug into his pocket for his purse.

"Did you see that man in the corner of the taproom?" Theo persisted. "He didn't look as if he belonged in a place like that either. . . . I mean either like you or me. What were you doing there, Stoneridge?"

Sylvester stopped at Theo's hackney with an arrested expression. "What man?"

"I'll show you if you come back inside," she said. "He was all muffled up, but his muffler was of good wool, and he wore top boots. And his cloak had a silk lining."

Sylvester stared at her in the darkness. "How did you see all that?"

"I'm very observant," she said. "So's Rosie. Even with her poor eyesight, not much passes her by."

245

"You goin' to pay me, guv, or jest stand there gabbin' all night?" The jarvey leaned down from his box. "Two shillin'."

"From Curzon Street! That's daylight robbery."

"But he did have to follow you," Theo pointed out. "He had to drive so that he could keep you in sight all the time."

"A formidable task. Clearly, I stand in his debt," Sylvester muttered with heavy irony. He handed over the two shillings.

"Shall we go back inside and I'll show you the man?"

"No." He bundled her over to the other hackney. "Jarvey, just pull to the far corner and stay there. I'll tell you when to move on." He followed Theo into the vehicle and sat forward, holding the leather curtain aside, his eyes fixed on the door to the Fisherman's Rest as the hackney pulled into the deep shadows thrown by a steeply pitched overhanging roof at the corner of the lane.

"Who is the man?"

"If I knew that, I wouldn't be here."

"Aren't you going to tell me anything else?"

"No. And if it's all the punishment you receive for this insane interference, you can count yourself lucky."

Theo contemplated his profile and decided she didn't have too much to worry about. There was a telltale curve to the chiseled mouth and a note in his voice that belied his words.

She sat back since there wasn't room for both of them to look out the window and contemplated the puzzle that had brought them to this insalubrious spot.

Suddenly it came to her. "Those men this afternoon! Someone set them on you, and they told you he would be here."

Theo was too sharp for her own good. He said nothing immediately, however, but kept his eye on the door.

His patience was rewarded. A tall man slipped outside, pausing in the lane to adjust the woolen muffler around his mouth. A flash of white silk showed as his cloak swung when he turned sideways, looking up and down the narrow alley.

Sylvester could see nothing of his face, but he knew who it was. There was something about the way the man held himself, about the set of his shouldets. Sylvester had been at school with Neil Gerard. He'd known him since they were terrified ten-year-

246

olds hiding from their bullying elders.

"Sweet Jesus," he murmured, pulling his head back into the carriage. Neil would have seen him in the tavern. But he didn't know that Sylvester had recognized him. Gerard would have seen only the diversion Theo had provided. Presumably, he'd been waiting for his hired assailants to make their report. When they hadn't appeared, and their intended victim had come in their stead, he would have guessed what had happened.

But he wouldn't know for sure that Gilbraith had seen him. Theo had done double service with her outrageous impulse. Provided distraction as well as the means for identification.

"Who was it?" Theo demanded in a low voice as he banged on the ceiling to give the jarvey the order to move off.

"I don't know," he lied. Theo's entanglement in this puzzle ended here and now. She was far too impulsive and unpredictable. She reminded him of an unstable Catherine wheel, liable at any moment to spin off its pin onto some darting, whirling course of its own. After this evening's exploit there was no knowing what she'd do if he opened the door even a fraction.

"But you must have some idea who would want to injure you," she persisted.

"Come here." He dragged her across the space that divided them and settled her on his knee. "Now, tell me again what it was that brought you hotfoot on my heels."

"But why would someone want to hurt you?" She tried again, pushing herself away from his chest. "You can't just stop discussing it as if it never happened."

"Oh, I believe I can do that," he said coolly. "Just as I can become extremely unpleasant on the subject of my wife's sticking her overinquisitive nose with unpardonable recklessness into my very private business. Now, do you wish to discuss that, or would you prefer to tell me what inspired this piece of foolishness?"

Theo sat in chagrined silence for a minute, and Sylvester, smiling, drew her head to his shoulder and slipped his hand beneath her cloak to find the soft swell of her breasts. "Come, gypsy," he said, softly cajoling now. "You came a long way to say something to me. I'd like to hear it again when I can concentrate."

Theo bit her lip in frustration. But she did want him to concentrate on what she had to say, and clearly he wasn't going to be prodded into confiding in her. She'd just have to go about discovering the truth in some other way.

"I wanted to tell you that I don't seem to mind anymore that you tricked me into marrying you," she said, sitting up on his knee and cupping his face in her hands. "Life with you is much more exciting than it ever was without you." She bent to kiss his face, her tongue flickering over his lips, dipping into the cleft of his chin, licking upward over his nose, flickering across his eyelids.

"And that's all that counts?" he murmured. "Excitement?" His teasing tone masked a sweet joy.

"It covers a multitude of delightful things," Theo responded, her tongue tracing the plane of his cheek and around to his ear. He shuddered with pleasure as the hot tip flicked, probed, licked the sensitive whorls, and her teeth nibbled on his earlobe.

"Who was the man? You did recognize him?" She couldn't resist one last try with the simple approach.

He kept his response light. "Blackmail, Theo."

"You should know. You're a fairly impressive exponent of the art yourself." Her tongue was a burning dart, and her loins moved sinuously over his so that his flesh sprang to life.

She slid a hand down to cup his arousal through the constraint of his britches, to press the erect flesh against her palm. "Of course, I had intended to suggest that we go back to Stoneridge, since I find London *very* boring. But now that we're in the middle of this adventure, I can see that it could become quite exciting."

"Theo, I am not involving you in my affairs just to satisfy your ennui," Sylvester declared, removing her hand abruptly. "Sit over there." He took her waist and deposited her on the opposite bench.

"But I am involved."

"You are not! And if you ever endanger yourself as you did tonight, I can safely promise that you will regret it."

The simple statement somehow carried more force than a more explicit threat. Theo nibbled a thumbnail in contemplative silence for a minute. She hadn't felt in the least endangered, but Sylvester wasn't in the mood to hear that.

She said cheerfully, "Well, since I don't wish to quarrel with you tonight, perhaps we can go back to what we were doing before?"

Crossing the narrow space, she sat on his knee again. "Now, where was I?"

"About here, I believe," he said, taking her hand.

"Ah, yes, now I remember. . . ."

Several hours later Sylvester lay in the darkness of his bedchamber, Theo's deep breathing filling the quiet, rustling across his chest, his fingers tangled in the fragrant cloud of her hair. Despite his relief that she'd at last decided that the why of this marriage no longer mattered when set beside the fact, he knew it disposed of only one of his problems. Theo's acceptance would do neither of them much good if Neil Gerard succeeded in inflicting the damage he seemed so set on.

But what could possibly drive Neil Gerard to attempt murder? What could Sylvester, his friend from their earliest schooldays, have done to drive a man to such desperate straits? Neil was a coward, inclined to panic, but Sylvester had understood his physical fears and had never condemned him for them. Indeed, he'd stood by him and stood up for him through some of the worst schoolboy hells. Neil had not returned the favor, though. At the court-martial he'd done everything but directly accuse his old friend and comrade of cowardice.

And he turned his back on him afterward.

The old serpents of hurt and self-disgust coiled in his belly, and their venom ran in his veins. Neil had made it clear that Sylvester Gilbraith had forfeited all claims to friendship and loyalty.

And now he was trying to kill him! His mind snapped clear of the pointless misery of the past. Why would a man who'd destroyed the reputation and career of another then decide to go one further?

Vimiera had to be behind this. There was nothing else that connected the two of them in antagonism.

What was Neil afraid of now? Was he trying to prevent something from happening? Sylvester must hold the key to some secret.

It was the only explanation. Some secret that would ruin Gerard.

He tried to force his mind back to those moments on that Portuguese plain. It had been sunset, and they'd been holding their position since dawn against continuous enemy forays. The river had been behind them, and his small company formed a lonely outpost protecting the bridge for the main body of the army, expecting to cross at some point in the night.

He knew all that. It was documented in the records at Horseguards. Captain Gerard was to come up with reinforcements. They had only to hold out until dusk.

Sylvester closed his eyes, trying to recreate those hours. A hawk circled in his internal vision, a dark shape against the dazzling blue expanse of the sky. How had he been feeling? Apprehensive . . . frightened even? Probably. Only fools were unafraid of battle and death. A young private, little more than a lad, had been wounded in the morning and had lain throughout the heat of the day, alternately whimpering and screaming, calling for his mother. He could hear his voice now, coming at him across the mists of memory. He could see the face of Sergeant Henley, hear his voice reciting the drill, exhorting the men to greater speed as they fired and reloaded at the undulating blue line of Frenchmen appearing over the small line of hills facing their position.

They'd beaten them off. How many times during that interminable day had they driven that line back beyond the hills? It would have been so easy to have withdrawn over the bridge, and yet not once had it occurred to him to do so. They would be reinforced at nightfall, and the bridge would be secured.

And then what had happened? The line was coming up at them again, the sun dipping into the hills behind the advancing French so it was hard for his men to see as they fired into the red glow.

And then what happened? It was as if his mind retained that single picture, a brightly colored picture surrounded by blackness. And a certain something hovered on the periphery of that picture, but it refused to take a tangible, recognizable form.

It was no good. He always got this far and no farther. There was only one other memory of hideous clarity — an isolated picture that had no physical context. He saw the face of the Frenchman standing over him, the bayonet poised. He saw the twisted light of a fanatic in the man's eyes and the flash as the bayonet descended. He thought he'd put his hands up to cover his eyes before the white light had burst in his head. And he remembered nothing else, except confused moments of delirium, punctuated by Henry's voice, until the brain fever left him months later in that stinking jail in Toulouse.

Sylvester eased himself out of bed. Theo murmured and rolled onto her stomach, her arms reaching across the bed as she searched for him in her sleep.

He poured himself a glass of water and stood at the window, watching the imperceptible lightening in the east.

But why, if Neil wanted him out of the way, hadn't he simply condemned him at the court-martial? It would have been so easy when Sylvester had nothing to say on his own behalf. Gerard could have said that Gilbraith had surrendered prematurely. That he himself had arrived exactly on time. And the verdict would have been cowardice in the face of the enemy and a firing squad.

But he hadn't said that. He'd taken the risk that Gilbraith would go free. And therefore that his secret, whatever it was, might somehow come out. And now he was trying somewhat clumsily to get rid of him. Presumably because he'd reappeared on the public scene. Licking his wounds and buried in shame in the wilderness, Sylvester would have seemed a minimal threat. But he'd come back to life, and the old scandal inevitably reared its head.

Even as a boy, Neil had reacted in blind panic to threatening situations. And it seemed he was doing it again. But was there more to this panic than the fear that Sylvester would come upon his secret? *Why* hadn't he condemned him at the court-martial? There'd been another witness, his sergeant. What had he said?

Sylvester shook his head impatiently. He could see the man's face; he was an ugly specimen of mankind. But he couldn't remember what he'd said. His testimony was pure formality, anyway.

"What are you doing?"

Theo's drowsy voice shattered his intense reverie. He swung

251

round to the bed. She was sitting up, blinking sleepily, the sheet tangled around her waist, her breasts lifting gently on the narrow rib cage with each breath.

"Watching the dawn," he said. "Go back to sleep."

Theo continued to sit there, however, regarding him gravely. What had he been thinking as he stood there gazing into the gray darkness? He *did* know the man's identity, she was certain of it. There had been something forbidding, chilling in his face as he turned to answer her. It had disappeared now, but she'd seen it. She wouldn't want to be in the shoes of whoever inspired that look.

She threw aside the covers and padded across the carpet toward him, black hair swirling around her creamy nakedness. "Is it dawn, already?"

"Almost." The bare skin of her arm brushed his own, making him startlingly aware of his own nakedness. Tense, he waited for more questions, but she merely leaned against him, her hair flowing over his shoulder, one hand lightly tracing the scar running down his rib cage and round the narrow waist.

"When did you get this?"

"Oh, some skirmish about ten years ago."

Theo nodded and looked up at him, into his face, where she saw the lingering pain behind the cool gray eyes. Her husband bore more scars than those visible on his body, and if she was ever going to understand him, she had to understand those scars too.

"Come on, back to bed," Sylvester said with sudden briskness. Catching her up, he carried her back to bed and dropped her on the feather mattress. He leaned over and smoothed her hair from her brow, smiling slightly. "What an intrepid, ramshackle gypsy I have for a wife."

"And you'd prefer another kind?" She couldn't prevent the flicker of anxiety in her eyes, but Sylvester shook his head.

"No, I've told you before we suit very well, you and I." He climbed in beside her, slipping an arm beneath her, rolling her into his embrace. "But there'd better be no more of these impetuous excursions, my love, however gratifying the reason for them."

252

Theo made no answer but lay quietly against him, relaxing into the warmth of his body. There was no point in further discussion. Prohibition or not, she'd have to conduct her own investigation. Maybe Edward would go with her to the Fisherman's Rest, and they could ask their own questions.

As the October sun rose over the Thames, Neil Gerard paced the small bare room in his anonymous lodgings, wondering what had gone wrong the previous afternoon. His men hadn't appeared for payment at the Fisherman's Rest, but Sylvester Gilbraith had come in their stead.

How he'd managed to overpower three armed thugs was a mystery when his only companions were a gaggle of young women, a child, and a one-armed cripple. Neil had only seen them from a distance, but it looked as if Gilbraith were escorting a schoolroom party. That notwithstanding, he'd overpowered his assailants and managed to learn about the rendezvous.

Neil's only comfort was the certainty that Gilbraith hadn't seen him, huddled in his shadowy corner behind a rickety wooden pillar. Gilbraith had been in the place just long enough to order a drink before the girl had arrived, and in the excitement and disturbance of that arrival, he certainly hadn't had a chance either to look around the room or to ask questions.

What a startling creature she was with that scarlet cloak and midnight-dark hair. Young, though. Very young for Sylvester Gilbraith. But her arrival had certainly annoyed and surprised the earl. Despite her confident smiles and the proprietary hand on his sleeve, he'd removed her in very short order.

She was presumably the earl's mistress. A woman not too unfamiliar with taverns like the Fisherman's Rest. Of course, Stoneridge had just married the Belmont chit. Probably he needed a little meat in his diet. A marriage of interest could make a thin meal, and there must have been an ulterior motive for that connection. Something to do with the entail. It was a common enough arrangement.

However, speculating about Gilbraith's marriage and extramarital connections wasn't throwing any light onto what had gone wrong at Astley's. Whatever it was had brought Gilbraith a dangerously close step toward Neil Gerard. It was time to change his tactics.

He glanced round the bare room with its few sticks of furniture and thin curtains. Wind gusted through the ill-fitting panes of the grimy window, and the small fire in the grate spurted.

He'd hoped to leave this miserable lodging with his problem solved and return to his elegant house on Half Moon Street and the life of the carefree bachelor, no longer obliged to pay his weekly visits to Spitalfields to hand over his blackmail.

A scrupulously cautious man, Neil Gerard had ensured that no one knew he was in London while he plotted the downfall of the Earl of Stoneridge. At these rooms on Ludgate Hill he was an anonymous lodger who paid his rent without fuss, and at the Fisherman's Rest he was an anonymous customer who had business other than drinking. As long as he conducted his business in these places, there was little chance he would accidentally run up against someone from his real life. But now his cover had been destroyed, and there was no point suffering this wretched discomfort any longer.

There was a scratch at the door, and a scrawny maidservant came in, her nose pink from the cold, a scuttle of coals in her hand.

"Make up the fire, sir?"

He nodded and stood watching her as she bent to the task, her skinny hips pressing against the rough linen of her skirt. The image of the girl in the Fisherman's Rest flashed through his mind. There was no comparison between that vibrant image and this work-roughened, scrawny creature, but he hadn't had a woman in several weeks, and his present failure-induced annoyance required soothing.

He moved to the dresser, selected a small coin from a pile, and tossed it to the floor beside the kneeling girl.

She looked up, her eyes widening. "Fer me, sir?"

"Are you clean?" He unfastened the tie of his dressing gown.

A flash of fright crossed her eyes, but she nodded dumbly, picking up the coin as she rose to her feet, wiping her hands on her apron.

"If you please, sir —"

"Well?" he said when she seemed unable to go on.

"I ain't never done it before." She dropped her eyes to the floor, twisting her hands in her apron.

Neil raised his eyes heavenward. It was an old trick. Virgins had a higher price, and he knew of several in the houses in Covent Garden who'd had their virginity restored at least half a dozen times. This girl was just trying to improve her own price.

"What kind of a gull d'you think me?" he said. When she still stood staring at the floor, he said impatiently, "If you're willing, get on the bed, girl. If you're not, get out of here."

The girl took a hesitant step to the bed, then lay down, closing her eyes tightly.

Neil threw off his robe and clambered over her. She shuddered as he pushed up her apron and petticoat. She was wearing no undergarments. It took him no more than a minute to realize she'd been telling the truth about her virginity. It increased his pleasure significantly, and when he'd finished with her, he took another coin from the dresser and tossed it to her as she limped from the room, weeping softly.

Considering that he'd been more than generous, he went back to bed, feeling sufficiently relaxed to return to sleep.

Later in the day he would leave this miserable place and resume the life of Captain Neil Gerard of Half Moon Street. An eligible bachelor of good though untitled family, with a respectable fortune and a starred army career.

He'd approach the problem of Sylvester Gilbraith from another angle. With the hand of friendship.

Chapter Twenty

"The Honorable Mrs. Lacey and Mr. Jonathan Lacey, Lady Theo," Foster announced the next morning from the drawing-room door.

"There, Clarry, I told you they would call," Theo said. "Show them up, Foster."

"Oh, this is so embarrassing," Clarissa said, dropping the skein of wool she was holding for Emily to roll. "Can you imagine what Mama would say if she knew what you'd done?"

"She'd say it was vulgar," Theo replied cheerfully. "But she's not going to know, is she?"

"Not unless Rosie lets something slip," Emily observed, bending to pick up the dropped wool.

Theo was on her feet, turned toward the door when Foster opened it and announced their guests.

"Mrs. Lacey, how good of you to call." She crossed the room, her hand outstretched. "And Mr. Lacey. I'm so happy to see you. Such a silly mistake of mine at the Pantheon, but I trust we can turn it to good purpose and become friends."

A strangled sound came from behind her, and Emily swiftly moved in front of the stricken Clarissa.

"Allow me to present my sisters," Theo said with complete composure. "Lady Emily Belmont."

Emily was as composed as her sister as she greeted the visitors, and by the time the courtesies had been exchanged, Clarissa was sufficiently mistress of herself to rise and be introduced.

Jonathan Lacey bowed over her hand. He *was* a very beautiful young man, Theo reflected, golden and willowy, but lacking steel. For her own tastes she preferred a man with steel to him — which was fortunate, since that was what the fates had given her.

But a Sylvester Gilbraith wouldn't do for Clarissa. She was glowing at the young man, who in his turn was gazing at her as if he'd never seen a woman before.

"You'll take tea, ma'am?" She pulled the bellrope and ushered her visitor to a seat on the sofa beside her. "Have you been in town long?"

The Honorable Mrs. Lacey launched into a long discourse on her recent widowhood, on the excellent Honorable John Lacey, a clergyman and the younger son of Lord Lacey, who'd wished most fervently that his only child would follow him to Balliol and into the ministry. But it seemed that Jonathan had other talents. Artistic talents. He was a very fine painter, and people had shown a great interest in his portraits.

"Indeed," murmured Theo, pouring tea.

Emily took over the conversation with an aptitude for small talk that her sister lacked. "Herefordshire is a very pretty county, I've heard, Mrs. Lacey."

The Honorable Mrs. Lacey began to expatiate on all the glories of the Herefordshire countryside, while lamenting the need to be in London, but it was necessary if dear Jonathan was to move in the circles where he might acquire commissions for his portraits.

Theo glanced across at Clarissa and Jonathan Lacey. They were sitting decorously apart on the chaise longue, but talking earnestly.

Stoneridge should commission a portrait of Clarissa, Theo decided. And then realized that that would look most peculiar. He'd have to commission one of herself, and then Clarissa could keep her company during the sittings. . . . Sittings! The very word filled her with horror. Hours and hours of sitting still while Clarry and her knight courted. No, sisterly love could only go so far. There had to be another way.

The sound of running feet came from the corridor outside the drawing room, and the door burst open to admit a breathless Rosie. "Theo, there is a book on spiders I most particularly wish to purchase in Hatchard's. But I have no pin money left, so could you lend me three shillings, please? Then Flossie and I can buy it immediately."

"Why do you need to buy it immediately?"

"Because it's the only copy, and someone else might snap it up."

"A book on spiders? 1 hadn't realized it was such a popular subject."

"Oh, Theo, please!"

"Rosie, where are your manners?" Emily chided, beckoning the child. "These are Theo's guests. Mrs. Lacey and Mr. Jonathan Lacey."

"How do you do?" Rosie said, offering a creditable bow. And then she frowned, and her sisters saw enlightened memory flash across her face. "Oh, aren't you —"

"Excuse me a minute, Mrs. Lacey." Theo rose swiftly. "I must find Rosie her three shillings." Before the child could say anything else, Theo had hustled her outside. "You mustn't say anything about the Pantheon, Rosie. Do you understand?"

"I wasn't going to. I was just going to ask if he was Clarry's knight."

"Well, he is, so you won't need to ask again."

"Why the whispered conference?" Sylvester appeared on the top stair from the hall.

"Oh, just family business," Theo said. "Could you find Rosie three shillings for Hatchard's, Sylvester? I have visitors."

"I'll pay you back, Stoneridge," Rosie said. "As soon as I have next month's pin money, only I find myself a little short this month."

"Oh, I believe an IOU will be satisfactory," Sylvester said solemnly. "What's the book?"

The question elicited a minute description of the book in question, to which her brother-in-law listened with every appearance of interest. He produced the required sum from his pocket, and Rosie, calling vociferous thanks, hurtled down the stairs to the hall, where her maid was waiting for her.

"Who are the visitors?" Sylvester turned back to Theo.

"Ah," she said, with a smug smile. "My friends from the Pantheon. It's a most lucky coincidence that Clarissa and Emily happen to be here too this afternoon. I think you should meet the Honorable Mrs. Lacey and cast a kind eye upon Mr. Jonathan. Maybe you could put him up for your clubs . . . or advise him on his coats. You know, the sort of things that men do for each other."

Even as she said it, she realized her mistake. If Sylvester was not accepted in those circles himself, he could hardly help Jonathan. "Well, maybe that would be a dreadful nuisance," she said hastily. "But at least come and meet them so it looks as if you approve of their being here."

Sylvester had read her mind as clearly as if she'd spoken aloud. He didn't know whether her swift retraction was harder to bear than the reason behind it.

Theo's eyes were on him, and he knew the grimness of his thoughts was in his face. He struggled with himself for a minute, then said with an assumption of lightheartedness, "You are a matchmaking hussy."

Relief flickered across her countenance, and she said in mock protest, "But it's for Clarry. It's family. Don't Gilbraiths ever put themselves out for family?"

Not often, Sylvester was obliged to admit. The Belmont clan, however, shared a unique closeness.

"Be a Belmont for once," Theo urged. "Clarry's knight is a portrait painter, and he's going to need introductions if he's to get commissions. We could take him up."

"Dear God!" Sylvester's eyebrows disappeared into his scalp at the ramifications of this, and some of the strain left his eyes. "You want me to be a patron of the arts?"

"Well, only of one little art," she said, slipping her arm into his. "Do come, please."

"Oh, very well."

He followed her into the drawing room, where he listened patiently to the chatter of the Honorable Mrs. Lacey. Jonathan Lacey, he discovered, had not the slightest interest in Corinthian pursuits. He did enjoy riding but considered hunting a savage sport. He had no opinion on the various merits of Stultz versus Weston and considered the clubs of St. James's to be quite above his touch.

Certainly, young Mr. Lacey was no coxcomb, Sylvester thought. But he did seem somewhat distanced from reality.

Clarissa smiled and nodded, hanging on to Mr. Lacey's every soft word, and Sylvester caught himself wondering what it must feel like to have a woman so uncritically admiring of one. He glanced across the room at Theo. He could see the effort it was costing her to conceal her boredom. She winked at him, and he decided he'd rather have a good fight than adoration any day.

But he didn't want her pity either. Pity or contempt, which would be worse? At the moment he seemed to have the former, and it made him want to scream. Never once, since that ghastly "At Home," had she suggested he accompany her to any social function, and she tiptoed around discussions of such events as if she were walking on eggshells. He knew he couldn't tolerate it much longer. But if he was on the right track, then this evening he was going to begin his attempt to unravel the knot.

Neil Gerard had returned to Half Moon Street. Whether he still chose to lurk in the slums of dockland on occasion remained to be seen. But he was back in the London inhabited by the ton. Sylvester had seen him that morning from a distance, sauntering down Piccadilly on his way to St. James's. At some point this evening he was bound to go to one of his clubs. Sylvester would spend his own evening visiting White's, Watier's, and Brooks's until Neil made an appearance. After his experience at Lady Belmont's, he could guess how he would be received by the members of his clubs, but he hadn't been blackballed or forced to resign, so he had every right to be there, and he would simply endure the embarrassment. If Neil cut him again, then he would leave, wait for him outside, and force a meeting.

He became aware of Theo's eyes on him and realized his distraction must have become obvious. He turned to Jonathan Lacey with a polite inquiry as to the kind of backgrounds he preferred for his portraits.

"You must call upon us, Mrs. Lacey," Emily was saying. "I know my mother would be delighted to receive you."

"Oh, you're too kind, Lady Emily. I don't go about much these days but should be most honored to meet Lady Belmont." She smiled fondly at Jonathan and rose to her feet. "We really must be going, Lady Stoneridge."

"Emily, I thought you and Clarissa promised Mama you would be home by four o'clock," Theo improvised. "Perhaps Mr. Lacey could escort you, since you're leaving together."

Sylvester pursed his lips in a soundless whistle at this Machiavellian maneuver. Emily and Clarissa moved smoothly into action, picking up their sister's cue without a false step. In five minutes Mr. Lacey, with a Belmont sister on each arm, was walking to Brook Street, and his mama was driving home in her landaulet.

"That was very satisfactory," Theo said when the front door closed on their visitors. "He seems to be every bit as smitten with Clarry as she is with him. How very extraordinary it is. They seem to be made for each other."

"Romantic twaddle," Sylvester said, taking snuff. "And I have never witnessed such barefaced scheming, gypsy. You ought to be ashamed of yourself."

"Nonsense," she responded. "I shall do everything I can to promote the match if it will make Clarry happy. The most important thing will be to get Jonathan some commissions. I don't think he has a private fortune, and Clarry's dowry won't be enough for them both to live on, will it?"

Would a fourth of the Belmont estate have been better provision? Not in the hands of Jonathan Lacey, Sylvester decided, squashing a twinge of conscience. He looked sharply at Theo, but there was no challenge in her eyes.

"The capital will yield a decent income," he said. "Not riches, but not starvation in a garret either. It's invested in the Funds at the moment, and if it's treated wisely could grow quite satisfactorily."

"Well, we can always help them, if necessary," Theo said matter-of-factly.

Sylvester raised an eyebrow. "Aren't you rather rushing things?"

Theo shook her head. "Clarry's fallen in love with him."

"Girls of her age fall in love all the time."

"But Clarry's always known that she'd recognize the right man when she met him," Theo said. "Just as she's always known she'd never settle for second best. She was perfectly prepared to die an old maid if her knight didn't appear."

Sylvester shook his head but said only, "Well, I'm sure you know your sister best." He stroked his chin for a second, then said with an air of resolution, "There's something I need to discuss with you."

"Oh?" Theo went very still, her blood seeming to slow in

her veins. Was he finally going to take her into his confidence?

Sylvester drew a sheet of paper from his inside pocket and tapped it against his palm. "This has just arrived . . . it's . . . it's a letter from my mother."

"Oh," Theo said blankly.

"She and my sister are coming to town for a few days. My mother wishes to consult her physician on Harley Street."

"Oh," Theo said again. "Where are they stay— oh, no," she said in dawning horror. "No, Sylvester, not here."

"My dear, I cannot deny my mother and sister the shelter of my own roof," he said.

"Oh, they'll be much more comfortable at Grillon's," Theo protested eagerly, clasping her hands in an attitude of prayer, her eyes wide with entreaty. "Just think, they can moan and complain about everything to their hearts' content, and no one will be offended —"

"No, Theo." He was half laughing at this assumption of prayerful supplication. "You know they have to come here."

"Oh, no . . . no . . . no . . . no . . . no!" Theo leaped onto the sofa and began an agitated dance of despairing protest. "Your sister will complain of the draughts and the maids, and your mother will pinch at me all the time. . . . Oh, *please* Sylvester, tell them they can't come." A high jump set the sofa springs complaining.

"Ridiculous creature, you're breaking the furniture. Get off!" Laughing now, knowing her display to be at least half-playful, he grabbed her by the waist and swung her into the air, holding her off the ground for a minute while she kicked in futile protest. "You may give Mary as many set-downs as you please, but you will be civil to my mother."

"But she won't be civil to *me!*" Theo wailed.

"That will be my affair." He smiled up at her disgruntled expression as he still held her above him, then set her on her feet again.

Theo sighed. "When are they coming?"

"She doesn't say."

"Hell and the devil! She'll arrive unexpectedly and nothing will be ready for her and —"

"Don't make unnecessary difficulties. Everything can be made ready in expectation, can't it?"

"I suppose so," she conceded, wrinkling her nose in disgust. "That's all I needed to improve the shining hour."

"It'll only be for a few days," he said, going to the door. "She hates London."

"That's some comfort, I suppose."

Sylvester laughed at her disconsolate expression. "I'll be late home tonight, but then so will you, if you're going to Almack's."

"I'll wait up for you," Theo said.

"And vice versa," he responded with a smile.

Theo stared in frowning silence as the door closed behind him. Then, with sudden determination, she ran up to her room for her pelisse, hat, and gloves. Five minutes later she was walking briskly to Albemarle Street, an attendant footman plodding stolidly in her wake.

Edward was just leaving his lodgings when Theo arrived. "Oh, good, I've caught you," she said without preamble. "I need to talk with you for a few minutes."

Edward had an appointment at Manton's Gallery, but it didn't occur to him to turn Theo away. "Come on in," he said amenably, ushering her through the front door and into his sitting room.

The footman stationed himself at the foot of the steps leading to the front door.

"So what can I do for you, Theo?"

"I need you to accompany me to a tavern on Dock Street." Theo came straight to the point.

"Now what are you up to?" Edward bent to warm his hand at the fire.

Theo explained the events of the previous evening. "And Stoneridge refuses to tell me anything," she finished. "I'm convinced he recognized the man in the tavern, so he knows who's behind these 'accidents,' and he won't let me help. So I'm going to have to find out for myself."

For once Edward was uncooperative. "If Stoneridge says it's not your business, then you can't make it so, Theo."

Her mouth took its familiar stubborn turn. "I have made it so." She paused and then with visible effort broached the most difficult subject. "You saw what happened at Mama's reception the other afternoon. He won't say anything about that, either. I can't ask him about it because . . ." She paused again, chewing her lip. "Because it . . . it must be something that he's ashamed of. There must be something that happened to him that he can't talk about. . . . It pains him deeply, I know."

She took a turn around the room, her stride impatient and agitated. "But I'm beginning to think that and the accidents have to be connected. It's too much of a coincidence otherwise, don't you think?"

She turned back to Edward. He was looking uncomfortable. Stricken almost, as he had done during Sylvester's humiliation in her mother's salon.

"What is it?" she demanded.

Edward shook his head. "It's just something I heard in the Peninsula. I don't believe a word of it, but I imagine it explains what happened at your mother's."

"Tell me." She came close to him, her eyes fixed on his face.

"I wasn't going to say anything, because there can't be anything to it. Anyone who knows Stoneridge has to realize that. I gather the Peer took his side at the —" He stopped. Court-martial was such a grim concept, even when it was part of due process: when a naval captain lost his ship, or an army commander lost the regimental colors.

"Cut line, Edward." Theo's expression was taut, and he could read anger in her eyes.

"Perhaps you should ask him yourself?" he suggested awkwardly. "I've only heard it third- or fourth-hand. I don't want to speak out of turn."

"Goddammit, Edward. If you've known something about this all along and haven't told me, I take it very ill in you," she declared furiously. "Now *tell* me!"

Edward sighed. He was in too deep to back away now, and he could understand Theo's anger, but it still felt like spreading gossip.

Succinctly, he told her what he'd heard. Theo listened in incredulous silence.

"Stoneridge a coward!" she exclaimed when he'd fallen into

264

an unhappy silence. "That's impossible. Oh, he has any number of difficult characteristics, but I'd stake my life on his courage. Wouldn't you?"

"Certainly," Edward agreed. "And he was acquitted, as I said. But Colonel Beamish said it was still murky. Damn murky, he kept saying. A man of few words is Colonel Beamish."

"But Sylvester was wounded — severely wounded." Theo struggled to fit what she knew of her husband into this history.

"A French bayonet to the head," Edward said. "But *after* he surrendered, according to Beamish."

"I don't believe a word of it." Theo began to pace the room again, her skirt swishing around her ankles with her impetuous stride. "I'm certain all these 'accidents' are connected to this, Edward. We must go to the Fisherman's Rest immediately."

"No," Edward said. "We're dining with your mother and then going to Almack's."

"Oh, fiddlesticks! This is so much more important."

"Theo, I am not going to poke and pry into Stoneridge's affairs," Edward stated flatly.

Theo stared at him. "What's happened to you, Edward? This is an adventure. We've always had adventures together."

"I'm not much use in an adventure now, Theo."

"Oh, you do talk such nonsense." But she flung her arms around his neck and hugged him. "You can shoot with one hand, can't you?"

"Not as well as with two. Anyway, Theo, that's beside the point. If Stoneridge wanted you to know, he'd have told you himself. And if he wanted your help getting to the bottom of it, he'd have asked for it."

"He just doesn't know he wants it," she said stubbornly. "He's dreadfully reserved, and he simply won't confide in me." It occurred to her that there'd been a time when she hadn't been able to share her own pain with Sylvester. But now she knew that she could. When had that changed?

Edward looked uncomfortable. He didn't like these glimpses into the intimacy of his friend's marriage. But he didn't think Theo would see it in that way. She was direct and candid to an almost embarrassing degree.

265

"So you won't come with me?" Theo said after a minute.

"It's a bad idea, Theo." His voice was cajoling, pleading almost. "Stoneridge can look after his own concerns. You don't know what stones you'll turn up if you go barging into something that you know nothing about."

"Very well." She shrugged in acceptance. She knew she could probably persuade him if she pushed it, but it would make him miserable. However, she didn't accept his reasoning, only that she must do this alone. "I'd better get home, if I'm to be in Brook Street for dinner."

Edward regarded her, doubt in his eyes. "I'm sorry if you feel I've let you down, Theo."

She shook her head. "I don't think that. Still, I think the army's made you stuffy." Her smile teased him, taking any sting from the words.

"I think it's maturity and experience," he retorted. "And it's not so much being stuffy as behaving responsibly, Theo. We don't know what we'd be looking for, and what the hell do you think we'd do with whatever it is if we found it?"

"That would rather depend on what it was," she said. "But we won't talk of it again."

Edward saw her out and went on to Manton's, still uncertain. He was not convinced Theo had dropped her planned excursion to the Fisherman's Rest, and if she was going to insist on going, then he'd have to accompany her. She certainly couldn't go alone to the kind of place she'd described. If he knew about her plans and let her go into danger alone, Stoneridge would be entitled to call him out. Or more likely take a horsewhip to him. A man couldn't in honor bound meet a one-armed cripple on the dueling field.

The dismal reflection did nothing to improve his frame of mind later as he dressed for dinner at Brook Street. But neither would it ever have occurred to him to tell Stoneridge of his wife's intentions. A man didn't rat on his friend.

Chapter Twenty-one

Sylvester saw Neil Gerard as soon as he entered White's. The captain was playing faro and seemingly absorbed in his cards. Excitement prickled along Sylvester's spine. The excitement of a huntsman scenting his quarry.

He stood for a minute in the doorway, watching the scene, then casually sauntered into the room. A group seated around a port decanter on a table fell silent as he passed; then the conversation picked up again. Heads were turned. He knew his face to be bloodless, his eyes to be veiled, all emotion wiped clean from his countenance as he strolled across to the faro table.

Neil Gerard felt Sylvester's arrival, and his fingers trembled slightly as he took up his cards. There was an almost imperceptible hush in the room, a sense of suspended animation as the Earl of Stoneridge reached Neil Gerard's table and paused beside his chair.

Neil looked up from his cards and nodded pleasantly. "Stoneridge, how d'ye do." A collective breath was released around the faro table, and now people were looking openly at the scene. Gerard held out his hand. Sylvester took it in a firm clasp. The hand of a man who was trying to kill him.

"Well, I thank you, Gerard." He laid the faintest emphasis on the word "well," and his eyes were hooded, hiding the raging speculation. For some reason Neil was not going to cut him again.

Gerard indicated his cards. "Care to take a hand?"

"Delighted, if there's no objection." Pointedly, the earl glanced around the table at Gerard's fellow players. The Duke of Carterton held the bank. It was almost amusing to see how faces were rearranged to adapt to the idea of Sylvester Gilbraith back in Society's fold.

"Take a chair, Stoneridge," the duke boomed, and a little rustle of relaxation ran around the table. Lord Belton moved his chair sideways, gesturing to the space beside him. "Porter, bring another chair for Lord Stoneridge."

A dainty gilt chair appeared instantly, and Sylvester sat down, nodding to his neighbor. "I trust all's well, Belton. It's been a while."

"Yes . . . yes, so it has," his lordship mumbled.

"Lady Belton quite well?"

"Oh, yes, in the pink . . . in the pink," his lordship declared, taking up his claret glass. "Try a glass of this, Stoneridge. An excellent wine." He gestured to the porter again, and a glass of claret appeared at the earl's elbow.

He smiled his thanks and picked up the cards the duke dealt him. So Neil was prepared to behave as if the court-martial had never happened. Such an attitude from the man who'd started the scandal in the first place would oblige others to follow suit and would put a stop to any further speculation. But why would he reverse himself in this way?

A man who could forget ties that went back more than twenty years was capable of anything, Stoneridge thought with a surge of bitterness. Ties and obligations. Neil Gerard owed him for countless acts of friendship during those years, and he chose to repay them by destroying his reputation and threatening his life.

They played for half an hour; then Gerard cast in his cards and rose from the table. "Care to join me in a glass, Sylvester?"

"By all means." Sylvester excused himself from his fellow players and followed Gerard to a secluded table in the window embrasure. His expression was bland, his eyes as cool as ever, but he was as much on his guard as he would be if he were manning a picket at the front line on the eve of battle.

"Congratulations on your marriage, Stoneridge." Neil filled two glasses from the decanter on the table. "Is Lady Stoneridge also in town?"

Whom did he think he'd seen in the Fisherman's Rest? Sylvester wondered as he said, "Yes, indeed, she is. Her mother and sisters are here, also."

"Not all under your roof, I trust," Neil said with a laugh. "A man can't call his soul his own with a monstrous regiment of women at his table."

Sylvester smiled faintly at this sally. "Lady Belmont has her own establishment on Brook Street."

"I shall do myself the honor of calling upon Lady Stoneridge,"

Neil said. "I assume she'll be attending the Subscription Ball at Almack's this evening."

"Yes, with her mother and sisters." Sylvester sipped claret, leaning back in his chair, legs crossed, his eyes resting placidly on his companion across the table.

"I thought I'd drop in myself," Neil said. "Show m' face, you know. I've only just come to town."

"I thought I hadn't seen you," Sylvester said deliberately. Did he imagine the twitch of Neil's eyelid? But his companion was continuing in the same hearty tone.

"You must dine with me, Sylvester. It's been a long time since we dined together."

"At least three years," Sylvester agreed without expression.

"Good . . . good. Shall we say Thursday?" Neil's flat brown eyes shifted, although his mouth smiled.

"I should be honored."

"Good. Half Moon Street at eight, shall we say? And a few hands of whist after. You were always a formidable opponent at the whist table."

"You exaggerate," Sylvester said, with the same placid smile.

"You're not thinking of dropping in at the Assembly Rooms yourself tonight?"

"I hadn't been," Sylvester responded.

"It's a trifle insipid, of course," Neil agreed. "But one must be seen, mustn't one?" He laughed, but his eyes shifted again. "I don't suppose you'd care to accompany me?"

If he entered Almack's at the height of a Subscription Ball in the company of Neil Gerard, his rehabilitation would be complete. Just what in the devil's name was the man up to? But if he didn't play along, he'd never discover.

"Why not?" he said casually. "I'll have to go home and change." He gestured to Neil's satin knee britches, striped stockings, and white waistcoat.

"Then I'll meet you here later and we can stroll across together."

Sylvester nodded his agreement and took his leave after another five minutes of desultory chat. As he left the salon, a few hands were raised in greeting. He responded with a bow, but his cool smile couldn't disguise the ironical glitter in his eye. Two old friends had publicly made up their quarrel; how very satisfying for the audience.

But the game was now in the open, and he had an enemy he could see. And an enemy he knew he could defeat. His heart lifted on a surge of jubilation. He knew Neil Gerard's weaknesses as if they were his own. He'd known them from childhood. And within those weaknesses lay the answer to Vimiera.

The two of them arrived at Almack's Assembly Rooms just five minutes before the doors were closed at eleven o'clock.

They strolled up the stairs and entered the ballroom. Lady Sefton was the first of the patronesses to see them and came gliding over. "Lord Stoneridge, your wife has made quite an impression on us all," she declared, raising her lorgnette and subjected him to a piercing scrutiny. "Quite an unusual young woman, we find. Captain Gerard. You've just come to town."

Both men bowed since neither of her Ladyship's statements required a response.

Sylvester's eyes searched for his wife. She was waltzing with a gentleman of middle height, his appearance distinguished by his silver eyebrows and the matching silver flashes at his temples. There was an indefinable aura of authority about him, but he and Theo seemed to be engaged in a most earnest conversation, enlivened by glimpses of Theo's mischievous smile and the enthusiastic glow in her eyes.

She was wearing a simple gown of bronze silk over a half slip of cream lace, a costume that, despite her own lack of interest in her wardrobe, was in the first style of elegance. But they had Lady Belmont to thank for that, he thought with a half smile. The Stoneridge topaz necklace was clasped at her throat, delicate matching studs glimmered in her ears, and her hair was drawn into a heavy knot at her nape, with artful ringlets drifting over her ears.

It was an old-fashioned hairstyle, but it was the perfect foil for her gamine face and those great pansy-blue eyes. And when he took the pins out later, that raven's-wing cascade would serve as the most erotic nightgown.

"You must make me known to Lady Stoneridge," Neil said

casually, putting an abrupt stop to Sylvester's unruly train of thought. "Oh, there's Garsington, signaling to us. I've been meaning to ask him what he fancies at Harringay next week. You know how reliable he is when it comes to form."

Sylvester allowed himself to be ushered across the room to where the viscount and his cronies stood gathered. Their reaction to the sight of him with Gerard was the same as the men's at White's. Surprise followed by confusion followed by hasty rearrangement of expression into one of casually friendly greeting.

Theo broke off in the middle of her conversation with Nathaniel, Lord Praed, and almost stopped in the middle of the dance floor.

"Is something the matter, Lady Stoneridge?" Lord Praed, never much of a dancer, nearly tripped over her suddenly slowed feet.

"Oh, no . . . no, I do beg your pardon. Did I trip you up? It's just that my husband's arrived."

"A matter for astonishment, clearly." He raised a silver eyebrow.

Theo looked self-conscious and said awkwardly, "Well, yes it is. He doesn't care for such occasions, you should understand."

"Oh, I do," Lord Praed said immediately. "Both understand and sympathize. I detest them myself."

Theo looked up at him. "How very ungallant of you, sir. And there was I thinking I was keeping you tolerably amused."

Lord Praed laughed. "Ma'am, I can safely say I have never had such an entertaining discussion on the subject of fertilizers with anyone."

Theo chuckled, but it was clear she was distracted, and after another turn his lordship suggested he escort her to her husband.

"Yes, if you don't mind," Theo said with betraying eagerness. What could have brought Sylvester here? And what had happened? He was perfectly at his ease in a group of men talking and laughing as if they'd known each other intimately for years. Had they never heard of the scandal of Vimiera? Was it possible?

Sylvester excused himself as he saw Theo and her partner leave the floor. He moved round the room to where Elinor sat talking with a tall titian-haired woman in a startling gown of black velvet.

"Lady Belmont, I give you good evening." He bowed and

271

she smiled, but he could detect the curiosity behind the serene exterior. Elinor couldn't fail to notice how his reception differed this evening from that he'd received in her drawing room. However, she'd said nothing then, and he couldn't imagine she'd comment now.

"Stoneridge, what a pleasant surprise. Are you acquainted with Lady Praed?"

"Not as well as I would wish," he said, raising her hand to his lips. "I see my wife was dancing with your husband."

"Gabrielle," Lady Praed chuckled. "Nathaniel detests dancing, but he and Lady Stoneridge seem to share the same enthusiasm for marl. Your wife was describing a marl pit recently discovered on Stoneridge land, and he swept her onto the floor, where they could discuss its various merits as a fertilizer without interruption."

Sylvester laughed, but before he could respond, Theo and Lord Praed reached them.

"Allow me to return your wife, Stoneridge," Nathaniel said. "Your arrival for some reason eclipsed my own poor attempts to entertain her."

"Oh, for shame, sir," Theo said, flushing slightly. "You should know you're a farmer after my own heart. A man of great sense."

"You do me too much honor, Lady Stoneridge," Lord Praed said solemnly. He raised her hand to his lips. "I'll do myself the honor of calling upon you, if I may. I'd like to show you the pamphlet I was talking about."

He offered his arm to his wife. "Gabrielle, I believe you said you wished to visit the supper room." They made their farewells and strolled away arm in arm.

"I need some dry bread," Gabrielle said as they entered the supper room.

"What?" Nathaniel looked at her, startled. And then his expression changed. "Dry bread? Gabrielle, you're not . . . ?"

"It's the only time I crave dry bread," she said with a tranquil smile.

"Oh, lord," he muttered.

"I wonder if it'll be twins again," Gabrielle mused, examining the offerings on the long table with a critical frown.

"Knowing you, there'll be three of them," Nathaniel said, offering her a basket of rolls. "You always improve on your performances, my love."

Gabrielle laughed, breaking off a piece of cast. "Six children in the house?"

"A daunting prospect for a man who didn't think he wanted *one*." Nathaniel shook his head, but his mouth curved in a smug little smile. "Come, I find I want you at home immediately." He put his arm around her shoulders, directing her toward the door.

Gabrielle made no demur. When her husband's eyes burned in that fashion, she wasn't about to argue.

Theo watched them leave, frowning slightly. "I don't think I offended Lord Praed. You're not vexed, are you, Mama?"

"It would be a lost cause, dear," Elinor said. "Have you seen Clarissa?"

"She was dancing with Lord Littleton, the last I saw. But she's not going to be happy coming to Almack's if we can't manage to acquire vouchers for Jonathan Lacey. Couldn't you ask Lady Jersey?"

"He seems a perfectly pleasant young man," Elinor said. "If somewhat vague on occasion. But I should wish to meet his mother. What's your opinion, Stoneridge?"

"Since I've been informed that Clarissa has found the love of her life, ma'am, I daren't offer one."

"That may be true," Elinor said matter-of-factly. "But I shan't give my blessing until I've met his mother."

Theo's frown deepened, and she turned to the puzzle uppermost in her mind. "We weren't expecting you, Sylvester."

"No, but I thought I'd drop in and see how you were doing," he said smoothly, reading the riot of questions in her eyes. "It's not so unusual for a husband to do such a thing."

"No," she said, her frustration clear in face and voice.

"Sylvester, may I beg the honor of an introduction to Lady Stoneridge?"

Neil Gerard glided up to them, his question breaking into the baffling whirligig of her thoughts.

Sylvester's eyes were hooded, although his mouth smiled as

he made the introductions. "My dear, allow me to introduce you to a very old friend of mine. We've just met up again after some considerable separation."

Theo found herself looking into a thin-featured face, sharply aquiline nose, flat brown eyes, smooth brown hair; tall, athletic figure. There was something oddly familiar about him, and she took an instant dislike to Neil Gerard, although she tried to conceal it as she smiled and shook hands.

Neil bowed over her hand, amusement and surprise warring in his mind. So that vibrant creature who'd marched into the Fisherman's Rest hadn't been Sylvester's mistress? It had been the Belmont chit.

No, he amended. This was no chit. Young, certainly, but no flummery about her. No simpering miss, this. He remembered how he'd been struck by the brazen sensuality of the woman who'd smiled and touched the Earl of Stoneridge, and taken a disgusted sip from his drink, and had her hand slapped for her pains.

"I'm delighted to make your acquaintance, Captain Gerard," Theo was saying. "Were you in the army with my husband?" She examined him covertly, looking for a reaction. Did this man know of Vimiera?

"We were also at school together, Lady Stoneridge," he said, answering the question by default, and giving Theo no clues in the process. "We've stood shoulder to shoulder in many a ticklish situation, isn't that so, Sylvester?" He turned with a hearty laugh toward the earl, who merely inclined his head, his eyes unreadable.

There was a moment's pause, but before Sylvester's silence could become noticeable, Neil continued with another hearty chuckle. "Ah, yes, Lady Stoneridge, your husband and I have known each other since we were grimy lads of ten."

"Grimy?" Theo raised her eyebrows, casting her husband an arch glance as she played along with the banter. "I find it hard to imagine Stoneridge as anything but immaculate."

"But, then, when I was ten, my dear, you were hardly in a position to know me," Sylvester said.

He could feel Gerard's interest in Theo like a pulsing heat.

He must have recognized her from the Fisherman's Rest, but there was a quality to his interest that went beyond the merely curious. There was a hunger to it; the man was aroused by Sylvester's wife.

On the thought Sylvester briskly tucked Theo's arm in his. "Forgive us, Gerard. But my wife expressed a wish to be escorted home without delay."

Neil Gerard took his leave, promising to call upon the countess at her earliest convenience.

"No, I didn't," said Theo.

"No, but I wish to take you home," her husband said. "Indulge me in this."

Theo glanced up at him. The strong mouth curved in a smile of pure masculine intent, his eyes glittered with sensual promise, and she knew that he was going to ensure she asked no questions of him tonight.

Chapter Twenty-two

"Is Lady Theo in, Foster?"

"I'm afraid not, Lady Emily." The butler held the door as Emily and Edward walked past him into the hall.

"Then we'll wait," Emily said. "We're probably a little early."

"Her ladyship was expecting you?" Foster sounded doubtful.

"Yes, we're engaged to call upon Mrs. Lacey. Lieutenant Fairfax is going to escort us."

"Did she say what time she'd be back?" Edward asked, tossing his hat onto the pier table.

"No, sir. Will you wait in the library?"

"Yes, and bring some tea, please," Emily said. Foster might be officially employed by the Earl of Stoneridge, but the Belmont girls continued to treat him as their own personal butler, just as they treated Belmont House and Stoneridge Manor as their own.

Foster bowed. "Claret for Lieutenant Fairfax, perhaps?"

Edward smiled. "Thank you, Foster. Did Lady Theo say where she was going?"

"No, sir." Foster backed out of the library and went off to fetch the required refreshments.

"Don't you think that's a little strange?" Edward said, going over to the window looking out onto the street. It was a sunny afternoon, and a small girl was bowling an iron hoop along the pavement under the eye of a nursemaid.

"Not to tell Foster where she was going?" Emily frowned. "Not necessarily. Theo's always going off on her own business."

"This isn't Lulworth, Emily. Theo doesn't have business to do here." He remained at the window but turned back to the room as Foster came in with the tea tray and the claret decanter. "Did she go on foot, Foster? Or in the barouche?"

"On foot, I believe, sir." Foster poured a glass of claret.

"With her maid, or with a footman?" He took the glass with a smile of thanks, reasoning that if Theo was going for some serious exercise, she'd take the footman.

Foster frowned. "I don't believe anyone accompanied her, sir."

Edward whistled, an uneasy sense of foreboding building as he turned back to look out the window, hoping to see Theo hurrying up the street. "Stoneridge won't be pleased to hear that."

"What won't I be pleased to hear?" Sylvester inquired from the doorway. His many-caped driving coat was dusty, a handful of whip points were thrust into the top button hole, his long driving whip was curled in his gloved hand.

"Oh, there's just a conspicuous absence of Theo," Emily informed him blithely. She wasn't about to tell Stoneridge that her sister was roaming the streets of London unaccompanied.

The earl turned to his butler, raising an eyebrow. "Since when, Foster?"

"I couldn't rightly say, my lord." The butler had been covering for his young mistress since she was a small girl and slipped easily into the accustomed role, without questioning why he should be doing so on this occasion.

"An hour? Two?"

"Perhaps half an hour, my lord."

"Is there something strange about that?"

"We were engaged to drive out together," Emily said. "Theo doesn't usually forget engagements."

"I see." He shrugged. "Well, I'm certain she'll be back soon. What do you think of that claret, Edward?"

"Excellent, sir." Edward's mind was whirling as foreboding became conviction. He knew exactly what had driven their engagement from Theo's mind. He knew where she had gone, unaccompanied and presumably in a hired hackney.

He put his glass on the table. "Emily, I must ask you to excuse me. I . . . I've suddenly recollected a most urgent appointment, with . . . with my tailor." Under Emily's astonished gaze he pushed past the butler and almost ran from the house.

"Now what in the world is going on?" Stoneridge demanded of his butler and sister-in-law, both of whom were looking confused.

"I couldn't say, sir." Foster bowed and left the library.

Emily regarded her brother-in-law somewhat nervously, but she could think of nothing to say. She had the feeling she should improvise some reasonable explanation for Edward's odd depar-

277

ture, but she wasn't a quick thinker at the best of times, and under Stoneridge's penetrating gray gaze she was completely tongue-tied.

"Tell me something, Emily," Stoneridge said, deceptively casual. "Does Edward often recollect appointments in that fashion?"

"Occasionally," Emily mumbled.

"Mmm." He stroked his chin, frowning. "But would I be right in thinking that those occasions generally have something to do with Theo?"

Emily's quick flush was answer enough, although she tried to think of some disclaimer.

"So just what did he suddenly guess my wife was up to?"

Emily shook her head. "I don't know."

"But you'd agree with me that he'd suddenly had a flash of insight?"

"Possibly. They . . . they're very close. They always have been." She was beginning to feel like one of Rosie's pinned butterflies and thought bitterly of her fiancé and her sister, who'd abandoned her to this seemingly gentle but nerve-racking interrogation. She didn't even know what she wasn't supposed to say.

Sylvester strolled across to the window, where Edward had been standing a minute earlier. Maybe the position would bring him the same inspiration. Lady Belmont's barouche stood at the door, the coachman dozing on the box, his docile carriage horses standing quietly in the sunshine.

"May I ask where you were going with Theo?"

"To call upon Mrs. Lacey," Emily said, happy to answer this unproblematic question. "Edward was going to invite Jonathan to accompany him to Tattersall's tomorrow. He's intending to purchase another riding horse and thought that Jonathan might meet some useful people."

Another instance of Edward evincing family solidarity, Sylvester reflected. And presumably he'd just gone hotfoot to Theo's assistance?

Prickles of unease ran up his spine. Why would Theo need assistance?

And then it came to him, crystalline in its clarity. Could she have taken Edward into her confidence about the visit to the Fisherman's Rest?

What did he mean, *could* she? Of course she would have done so. About that and all her private speculations — whatever they might be. Not for one minute did he believe that just because he'd refused to discuss his own plans, Theo had ceased to speculate. She'd yielded to his silence easily . . . too damn easily. He could see the obstinate set of her mouth, the lift of her pointed chin that always meant: You may believe what you wish, but I have my own ideas.

Theo had returned to the Fisherman's Rest.

He'd told her as clearly as he knew how that he would not tolerate another such reckless excursion, and she'd taken not a blind bit of notice of him. But it was his own fault. How the hell had he ever been fool enough to trust that Theo would obey orders?

The strength of his fury astounded him. By disobeying his direct injunction and interfering in his private affairs, she had recklessly put herself in grave jeopardy. Without a moment's reflection she had plunged alone into the rat-infested sewer that was Dock Street, where the desperate face of poverty informed the brutalized souls of its inhabitants. They would kill her for her kid gloves and toss her body into the Thames without a qualm.

And as if that weren't enough, she was wading hip deep into the quicksand of Vimiera and right into the path of a dangerously desperate man.

"Emily, permit me to escort you to your carriage," he said abruptly, turning toward her.

Emily quailed before the blazing countenance. The scar that she thought she'd become so used to she barely noticed it anymore stood out, a livid white line. The cool eyes were now liquid fire, and his mouth was a taut line.

"There's no need," she said. "Foster will escort me."

He ignored her words. *"Come."*

Emily rose immediately. What had Theo done to cause this terrifying transformation? On the whole, these days Emily was quite at ease with her brother-in-law, but at the moment she thought he was the most frightening man she'd ever met . . . even more so than her grandfather in one of his rages.

She practically ran ahead of him out of the library and out of the house. His large hand under her elbow almost lifted her into the barouche so that she felt as fragile and vulnerable as a leaf in the wind. She'd seen him handle Theo in this way, lifting her in and out and on and off things with a brisk lack of ceremony that her sister never seemed to mind. But Emily wouldn't repeat the experience for all the tea in China. She sat back with relief as Stoneridge ordered her driver to move off and her brother-in-law's black countenance retreated.

Stoneridge turned back to the house, running up the steps, his clipped voice giving orders before he'd reached the hall. "Foster, have my curricle brought round again. But not the chestnuts, they've had a long run already."

"Yes, my lord." The butler kept his expression impassive before his employer's tightly reined anger, but like Emily his mind was filled with furious speculation.

Five minutes later Stoneridge was on his way to Dock Street, driving a team of roans, forcing from his mind the dreadful images of what might even now be happening on Dock Street as he drove at breakneck speed through the narrow streets, oblivious of the stares and curses from startled pedestrians as they leaped out of the way of the white-faced man with the livid scar on his forehead.

Neil Gerard stared at Jud O'Flannery's disfigured countenance. His ex-sergeant was grinning, revealing his one black tooth. "Cat got yer tongue, cap'n?" he inquired with mock solicitude.

"I don't know what the devil you're talking about." Neil tried to sound angry and contemptuous, but it came out more as a bluster, his fear slippery beneath the bold front, like ice under snow. He could feel the eyes on his back as Jud's customers drank their ale and regarded the scene at the bar counter with squint-eyed curiosity. His gaze fixed on the tavern keeper's massive fists, curled loosely on the counter. A pelt of dark hair covered the backs thickly and sprouted over the knuckles.

One blow from those fists would put a man under the table

with a broken jaw. The grip of those fingers would squeeze the life out of a man in a minute. And one flick of his eyes would bring the group of ruffians to their feet, moving across the tap room toward Neil Gerard.

"Well, I 'as me sources," Jud was saying in a musing tone, but his one green eye was sharp with a glint of sardonic humor. He knew Neil Gerard was scared. The man scared easily. No one knew that better than Sergeant O'Flannery.

"An' like I was sayin', these sources tell me that you've been patronizin' another tavern. Quite 'urt me feelins that did, cap'n, sir." He took a healthy swig of ale from his tankard. "You comes in 'ere, regular like, never takes a drink or says a civil word to an old comrade in arms, an' then I 'ear you goes into the Fisherman's Rest an' drinks and chats somethin' chronic in there. Better class of folk Long Meg 'as? That it, cap'n sir?"

Neil felt sweat break out on his forehead. He wanted to wipe it off, but to do so would draw attention to his fear. How much did Jud know?

"A man's entitled to drink where he pleases," he said, hearing how feeble it sounded. He plunged his hand into his pocket and took out his purse. "Here." He shook out the five golden guineas and turned to leave.

"Jest a minute, cap'n, sir." Jud's voice had hardened. Reluctantly, Neil turned back. "Well?"

"I wouldn't like t'think you've bin lookin' fer a way to stop this nice little arrangement we 'ave. Now, you wouldn't be doin' anythin' like that, would you, cap'n, sir?"

Suddenly, he leaned over the counter, so close Neil could smell the beer and the reek of decaying teeth on his breath. An arm shot out, grabbing the captain by the fine starched cravat that had taken him a full half hour to tie to his satisfaction.

"You wouldn't be doin' anythin' like that, would you?" Jud repeated in a fine mist of saliva. Neil tried to turn his head away from the menacing stare.

"I don't know what you're talking about," he said again.

Jud nodded his head slowly, his grip tightening on the cravat. "I think p'raps one of me friends could explain it better." He pushed his captive backward with a violent shove, and Neil went reeling into the arms of a grinning henchman, who picked him up as if he were a baby and threw him across the room. Neil crashed into a table. A mug of ale went flying, its contents spilling over his immaculate driving cape and dripping onto his buckskins.

"Eh, careless!" someone bellowed as he struggled to his knees. "Spillin' me drink like that." A man, red-faced with mock indignation, grabbed him by the cravat and hauled him to his feet. Holding him steady, he drove his fist into Gerard's jaw.

Neil saw stars, tasted blood, felt the ultimate humiliation as warm liquid trickled down his leg. Then he was released amid a burst of raucous laughter.

"Be seein' you next week, cap'n, sir," Jud called cheerily after him as he stumbled out the door into the crisp, sunny afternoon. The lad who was holding his horses stared in unabashed curiosity at the gentleman, whose right eye was rapidly swelling, blood trickling down his chin, staining his torn cravat. The reek of beer and urine wafted from him as he cursed the lad, knocking him aside as he stumbled up onto the driving seat of his curricle.

" 'Ere, what about me fee, guv?" the lad cried. "That's me pa in the Black Dog."

Neil threw a vile curse at him, but he had no desire to renew the acquaintance of anyone in the Black Dog. He dug a sixpence from his pocket and hurled it to the ground at the feet of the grinning lad, who scooped it up and dashed off down the street before anyone bigger and stronger decided to relieve him of his earnings.

Neil whipped up his horses, and they plunged forward in the narrow alley. The leader caught a hoof in an uneven cobble and almost went down to his knees. Gerard hauled back on the reins and tried to get a grip on himself. Physical violence terrified him. The simple threat of violence had reduced him to a gibbering wreck as a child and made him the perfect target for the bullies who stalked the halls of Westminster School. How he'd envied Sylvester Gilbraith, who, even as a ten-year-old new boy, had faced the tormentors with fists and tongue and refused to be intimidated. They'd beaten him often, but he'd always bounced back, and finally they'd left him alone. Not so Neil Gerard, who'd suffered hells during those years that he could barely endure remembering.

And it had just happened again. At the hands of a group of dockside ruffians, laughing at him and enjoying his terror even as they'd beaten him. And he'd have to go back next week and face the grinning Jud O'Flannery. Next week and the next week and the next week. An eternity of humiliation stretched ahead, because he could no longer look for hired assassins in this neighborhood.

He was passing the end of Dock Street, heading for Tower Hill. His eye darted down the street toward the Fisherman's Rest. Who had recognized him there as Jud's gentleman mark? Someone in that fetid hole had reported his negotiations to O'Flannery. The man he'd sent into Dorset had been angry when he'd refused to pay for failure and therefore to compensate him for the time and trouble he'd taken. The man had cursed him and threatened him with vengeance. But Neil had dismissed it as so much bluster.

A hackney was drawn up outside the Fisherman's Rest. A most unusual sight. He watched as a cloaked figure jumped lightly to the cobbles. A woman. Curiosity for a minute made him forget his throbbing jaw and the foul condition of his raiment. The woman was saying something to the jarvey, her head tilted as she looked up at the box. The hood of her cloak fell back, revealing blue-black hair.

Now, what in the name of all that was good was the Countess of Stoneridge doing at the Fisherman's Rest? *Alone!*

If Sylvester paid another visit, it wouldn't be surprising. He'd learned nothing from the first visit, and he was bound to try again. Not that he'd discover anything. Neil was never going to cross that threshold again, and no one could put a name to him, or even an accurate description.

But what was his wife doing here, alone? Looking for information for her husband? It was extraordinary. And he couldn't believe that Stoneridge had countenanced it. He'd made no attempt to hide his annoyance when she'd appeared before. And no reasonable man could blame him. Wives didn't follow their husbands to such places. And they most certainly didn't go to them alone.

283

An idea glimmered as he started his horses again. Lady Stoneridge might well be worth cultivating seriously. Supposing she could provide the route to her husband? She was obviously unconventional and indiscreet. How else would one characterize her presence at the Fisherman's Rest? Insanely impulsive? Recklessly courageous? Such a person could surely be led up the paths of fatal indiscretion with the right carrot. If he could find the right carrot.

He suddenly understood that he didn't have to remove Gilbraith, merely neutralize him. Blackmail was the way to end his own calvary at Jud's hands. If he was certain that Gilbraith would never open his mouth about Vimiera, even if he knew the truth, he could afford to tell Jud what he could do with his threat of exposure. Well, perhaps not that. The thought of such an encounter flooded him with a nauseating terror. But his visits to the Black Dog could cease without explanation.

He would disappear from London for a while in case Jud decided to pursue him, but he was fairly certain the ex-sergeant would quickly turn his attention to other pigeons worth plucking. And if Jud decided to go to Horseguards and tell his version of events at Vimiera, it would be considered no more than the ramblings of a disaffected old soldier with a grudge against his commander . . . so long as Gilbraith wasn't able to confirm the story with his own recollection of the truth.

He wiped blood from his split lip with the back of his gloved hand as he encouraged his horses to a smart trot. His panic was over. The cultivation and manipulation of an attractive but naive and clearly reckless young woman was a much pleasanter prospect than arranging accidents at the hands of hired dockside killers. And blackmail was a much cleaner tool than murder.

Theo, happily unaware of the witness of her arrival at the Fisherman's Rest, pushed open the door and stepped into the dim, reeking taproom. It was almost deserted at this time of day, although an old man sat nodding by the fire, puffing a clay pipe. A slatternly young woman, a baby at her breast, leaned against the counter.

"Twopence of gin, Long Meg."

"I'll see the color of yer money first," Long Meg rasped from somewhere in the darkness behind the counter.

" 'Ow about a bit o' credit?" the young woman whined. "Gin puts the babby to sleep."

Long Meg reared up out of the darkness, as big and crimson-faced as Theo remembered her, when she'd come after Tom Brig with a rolling pin.

"I told yer last time, no more —" She stopped, staring at Theo. "Well, well," she said slowly. "What 'ave we got 'ere, then? You want somethin', young miss?"

"I'd like to ask you some questions," Theo said, smiling in a friendly fashion as she picked her way through the sodden sawdust.

"An jest who would be askin' 'em?" the woman demanded, her eyes narrowed, mighty arms akimbo.

"My name's Pamela," Theo said, having prepared for this.

"You was in 'ere t'other night," Long Meg said suspiciously. "Wi' that gentleman cove. Jest what's the likes o' you got to do wi' the likes o' me?"

"I wanted to ask you about one of your customers."

Long Meg threw back her head and laughed, but it was not a pleasant sound. "We don't answer no questions around 'ere, missie. Me customers mind their own business an' I mind mine. We don't want no snoops around 'ere." She lifted the flap of the counter and came into the room. She seemed even larger in this small dim space than she had the other night, and Theo felt the first stirrings of alarm.

"I'm not snooping," she said, although it seemed as accurate a term as any for what she was doing. "I'll pay for any information —"

"Oh, will you, now?" The woman stepped closer until she was towering over Theo. "An' jest what've you got in that dainty little reticule, then?" She made a grab for Theo's reticule. Theo danced backward, snatching her arm away. Long Meg lunged forward, and Theo swung her reticule at her head as she brought one leg up and aimed a kick at the mountainous belly.

Long Meg roared, and two men suddenly appeared from the back regions. The slatternly young woman with the baby still leaned against the counter; her eyes, dulled with gin, followed the scene, and she moved aside in desultory fashion as the two men barged through the opening in the counter.

Theo knew she didn't stand a chance against three of them. Why hadn't she thought to bring a pistol? Why hadn't the possibility of robbery occurred to her? She jumped backward, hurling a bench between herself and the purposeful advance of her assailants. If she could get out into the street, she could make a dash for the hackney.

But the men were flanking her now, their eyes fixed on her as they moved sideways, and Long Meg kept on coming, a vicious expression on her face. Theo's kick had hurt her, but not enough to slow her down, only enough to enrage her.

Desperately, Theo grabbed up an ale pot on the table and threw it into the face of the man approaching on her left. The other one lunged at her, catching her arm. She jerked her arm upward, twisting her body and catching him on her hip, breaking his hold. But she knew she couldn't keep this up.

Then suddenly a shot exploded through the dark room.

"Get away from her."

"Edward." Theo turned in dazed relief. He stood in the doorway, a flintlock pistol in his one hand.

"Hurry," he said, and she realized that he couldn't reload and that it wouldn't take more than a second for her attackers to recover from their surprise and understand both that and the fact that her rescuer had only one arm.

She took the three paces to the door at a run as Edward stepped backward into the street. Long Meg and her two assistants rushed after them, and Theo spun and kicked the door closed in their faces.

"Run!" She grabbed Edward's arm and then stared wildly down the empty street. The hackney carriage had disappeared.

Edward swore as he struggled one-handed to reload his pistol. His own hackney had disappeared as completely as Theo's, and he guessed that the sound of the pistol shot had driven both jarveys away to a less volatile neighborhood.

The door of the Fisherman's Rest crashed open, and the two men leaped into the street, Long Meg on their heels.

286

Edward abandoned his attempts to reload and turned to run with Theo. Their pursuers bellowed as they came after them, and Theo realized grimly that they were calling for support. She stumbled, fell to one knee, and was up and running again in the same breath. The pounding of heavy booted feet behind her seemed to be in her blood, and she could almost feel the hot breath of their pursuers on her neck. Edward couldn't run as fast as she could, his body was unbalanced, and she hung on to his hand, desperately trying to keep him from tripping.

And then the curricle bowled around the corner from Smithfield. The galloping team drove straight past the fugitives and came to a plunging, rearing halt in front of their followers, who fell back in terror before the flailing hooves, the wildly rolling eyes of the four magnificent animals.

Theo and Edward gulped air into their tortured lungs, allowing the slow relief of salvation to seep through them. The Earl of Stoneridge said nothing to the three from the Fisherman's Rest, but he sat still as a graven image, the curricle and team blocking the street. His hands moved on the reins and the horses reared again. The two men and Long Meg retreated backward to the door of the tavern and disappeared behind it.

Only then did the earl bring his horses under control. The street was too narrow for him to turn his equipage. He cast a glance over his shoulder to where Edward and Theo stood, still gasping for breath.

"Get up," he said. "Both of you."

Theo gazed at her husband's face, and the realization crept inexorably over her that she was about to exchange the frying pan for the fire.

She stepped up to the curricle. "You mustn't blame Edward for —"

"I don't," he interrupted with icy calm. "Get up."

287

Chapter Twenty-three

The curricle wasn't built to accommodate three people, and Theo found herself sitting practically in Edward's lap once they'd scrambled up to the seat.

Sylvester said nothing and beyond moving sideways a couple of inches offered no assistance as they scrunched into place. Once sure that they were securely seated, he gave his horses the office to start. No one said anything until Dock Street was well behind them; then Edward cleared his throat and spoke with more than a hint of constraint.

"I beg your pardon, sir, for bungling it like that. I should have thought . . . remembered —"

"I don't hold you responsible for my wife's actions, Fairfax," Sylvester interrupted, his voice as hard as iron.

Edward fell silent, wrestling with his mortification. Once he would have been able to handle that situation; instead, he'd had to be rescued like a cocky schoolboy who'd tried to take on the school bully.

Theo touched his arm in sympathy, knowing exactly how he was feeling, but he glared at her, blaming her for his grief and embarrassment, for involving him in a situation where he was forced to acknowledge his limitations.

She glanced at her husband's profile. There was no reassurance there. His mouth and jaw looked as if they'd been carved in granite, and she knew his eyes would be spurting fire in the arctic-gray depths.

"Sylvester?" she began hesitantly.

"I presume you'd prefer not to hear what I have to say to you on the open street, so I suggest you hold your tongue."

Theo was silenced, and they drove without speaking another word through the City with its banking houses, past St. Paul's Cathedral, and along the Strand, where the landscape became more familiar, the streets broader, the private houses more imposing, the shop windows filled with the luxury items that would appeal to Fashionable London at the height of the Season.

Sylvester, no longer under the spur of fear, weaved his way

at a more leisurely pace through the streets, giving a reasonable berth to elegant landaus and heavy drays, and allowing the throng of foot traffic ample time to move out of his way. With Theo safe beside him he felt emptied of all emotion, as if skin and bone merely contained a vast, cold void.

"You'll have no objection if I put you down at Piccadilly, Fairfax?" The curt question came after such a long silence that both Edward and Theo jumped.

"No, of course not, sir. I'm much obliged," Edward said miserably.

Sylvester drew up at the corner of Piccadilly and St. James's, and Edward awkwardly descended to the pavement. He stood for a moment, trying to think of something to say; then Sylvester bade him a brusque good day and the curricle moved off.

Alone with her husband, Theo looked over her shoulder and raised a hand in forlorn farewell. She had the air of one in a tumbrel on her way to the guillotine, Edward thought, feeling sympathy despite his own distress. He'd rarely seen her apprehensive, ever, as a child on the occasions when she faced the wrath of her grandfather, but her anxiety on this occasion struck him as perfectly justifiable. He didn't think he'd ever seen anyone quite as intimidating as the Earl of Stoneridge that afternoon.

With Edward's departure the vast, cold void filled up again, and Sylvester's anger burned anew with a fierce flame. Theo had frightened him more than he'd ever been frightened before. When he'd rounded the corner of Dock Street and understood how a minute later would have been too late, the pure terror that he'd been holding down had ripped through him, turning his gut to water. When he thought of how only the most accidental of circumstances had alerted him to her dangerous exploit, he felt sick, his internal vision once again filled with images of her stripped body floating in the greasy black waters of the Thames.

He drove into the mews and alighted from the curricle, tossing the reins to the head groom before holding up an imperative hand to assist his wife.

Theo barely touched his fingers as she jumped to the ground. The scar stood out, a blue-tinged slash across his forehead, and she realized that she'd seen him angry before, but never quite like this. Foreboding swirled in her belly, lifted the fine hairs on the nape of her neck, turned her knees to jelly. She had never been frightened of anyone before. She hadn't even been afraid this afternoon; there hadn't been time. But at this moment, facing the consequences of what now struck her as a piece of foolhardy craziness, she was scared stiff.

She didn't know this man, who now governed her life, because he wouldn't let her know him. Oh, she knew his body, she knew what gave him pleasure. And she knew what would make him laugh and what would annoy him. All trivial pieces of present knowledge. But how could she truly know her husband if he kept his innermost thoughts from her, shielded her from his plans and decisions, and told her only the bare facts of his previous existence with none of the emotions and responses that would have shown her the man who had lived that life?

She couldn't begin to guess what was going to happen.

Sylvester moved her ahead of him with a hand in the small of her back, out of the mews and around to the street entrance of Belmont House.

Foster opened the door for them, but his greeting died on his lips as he took in the countess's white face and the earl's stark severity.

Sylvester's hand moved around her waist, sweeping her with him across the hall and toward the stairs, so fast now her feet skimmed the parquet. The marble staircase seemed to rise interminably in front of her. She was acutely conscious of his closeness, his breath rustling over the top of her head, the warmth of his body. But it was a menacing proximity. Always before just the sense of him close to her had sent jolts of arousal into her belly and ripples of anticipation over her skin. But the jolts and the ripples now arose from a dreadful suspense.

The long corridor stretched ahead as they reached the top of the stairs, and she was swept along to the double doors at the end. Sylvester leaned forward to fling open one door, and then they were inside her own apartment, surrounded by the familiar objects, the gracious furnishings, the cheerful glow and crackle of the fire. But she could find no reassurance there.

Sylvester banged the door at his back. Theo turned to face

him, and the tension on the gamine face, the strain in the midnight eyes, brought him a certain grim satisfaction — tiny recompense for his own gut-wrenching fear for her.

"How dare you do something so unutterably stupid and reckless!" he demanded.

Theo clasped her hands tightly. "I know it was stupid. I didn't think to take a pistol, I —"

"What!" he interrupted in disbelief. "Is that all you can say? You defy my orders, you meddle in my affairs, willfully expose yourself to danger, and all you can apologize for is forgetting to take a pistol!"

"Oh, don't you understand?" she cried. "What else could I do? You promised me a partnership. You . . . you *seduced* me with the promise of a partnership. I would never have married you if you hadn't promised that. Instead, you keep your *self* away from me. You won't permit me to know anything about you . . . anything important, that is." She flung away from him, tears of frustration blurring her vision.

"You dare to blame me for your defiance and your stupidity?" Furiously, he took a step toward her and then stopped, aware that his hands were shaking with his rage. He took a deep breath. "I'm too angry to deal with this now," he stated. "I can't trust myself in the same room with you!" He turned back to the door. "You'll stay in here until I come back."

"What?" Startled, she swung to face him again.

"I intend to know where you are — every step you take from now on," he declared savagely. "So you'll stay in this room until I've cooled off enough to be rational. And so help me, Theo, if you so much as stick your little toe outside this door, you'll regret it to your dying day."

Theo stared, dumbstruck, as he stormed out and the door crashed closed behind him. She felt sick and shivery. Angrily, she dashed the tears from her eyes with her forearm and went to the window. Sylvester appeared in the street below. He glanced up once at the house, but if he saw her in the window, he gave no indication. Then he turned and strode off down the street, slashing at the neat privet hedges with his cane.

Theo stepped back into the room. She filled a glass with water from the pitcher on the washstand and drank slowly, waiting for the nausea to recede and for her breathing to steady.

The fat really was in the fire now.

She kicked off her shoes and dropped into a deep armchair by the hearth, drawing her legs under her, gazing into the wreathing flames. The devil of it was that she'd been forced to reveal her own hand. Sylvester now knew that she wasn't prepared to accept his silences as royal commands, and knowing her husband, he was bound to take serious steps to prevent her continuing along her chosen path.

If she couldn't persuade him to take her into his confidence, it rather looked as if she was stymied.

She let her head fall back against the cushions and cursed under her breath. Sylvester was presumably stalking the streets of London devising some foolproof scheme to turn her into a model wife who never questioned her husband's decisions or asked awkward questions or, heaven forbid, took matters into her own hands. A nice, meek little wife who'd warm his slippers and order his favorite foods and hang her head in mute obedience to his every command.

Well, he wasn't going to find it easy. She turned her head and looked at the closed door of her bedroom. Maybe he *wasn't* going to find it easy, but, somehow, she didn't feel like defying his parting order.

The sound of commotion in the street below brought her out of her reverie, and she sprang up from her chair, going to the window. A post chaise had drawn up before the door, boxes and portmanteaus strapped to its roof. Its yellow painted wheels were coated with mud, and the side panels were thickly splattered. Obviously it had come quite a journey. Six outriders, with blunderbusses, sat their horses — a dangerous journey, presumably.

As Theo stared down, a postilion flung open the door and let down the footstep. Lady Gilbraith descended to the street, shaking down her skirts, adjusting her bonnet with a sharp jerk as if the garment had in some way offended. She took up her lorgnette and examined the facade of Belmont House just as Foster came hurrying down the front steps to greet her, and Mary alighted from the post chaise swathed for some extraordinary reason in a purple blanket and clutching a white handkerchief to her nose.

In horror Theo stared at the amount of baggage on the roof of the vehicle. How the hell long were they coming for?

She turned at a hasty rap at her door. "Beggin' your pardon, m'lady, but 'is lordship's ma . . . I mean, Lady Gilbraith 'as jest arrived," Dora announced, slightly breathless from her haste. "Mr. Foster sent me to tell you."

"Thank you, Dora." Theo turned to the mirror, hiding a slight smile. She had an interesting choice before her: to obey her husband's express commands or to greet his mother with all due courtesy and hospitality. She thought she would do the latter. Sylvester would be hard-pressed to find fault.

Her tousled reflection looked out at her from the mirror. An afternoon fighting and running for her life from a gang of dockland thieves didn't lend itself to a tidy appearance.

"Help me change my dress, Dora . . . the cream silk will do." She began to pull the pins from her hair, shaking it loose. "And I'll have to do my hair again, but be quick. I mustn't keep Lady Gilbraith waiting."

Ten minutes later she hurried down the stairs to the hall, where her dismayed eyes took in the mountain of luggage still being carried in by the footmen.

"Her ladyship and Miss Gilbraith are in the salon, Lady Theo," Foster informed her. "I ventured to suggest they might care for some tea, but her ladyship didn't believe we could make a pot to her satisfaction."

"Bring coffee instead. I seem to remember her ladyship prefers it," Theo said, giving him a conspiratorial wink, dropping her voice to a whisper. "How long are they going to stay?"

Foster's lips twitched. "I couldn't say, my lady. It's to be the Chinese room for Miss Gilbraith and the Garden suite for her ladyship?"

Theo nodded, braced her shoulders, and entered the salon. "My dear ma'am, welcome to Belmont House. I trust the journey was not too fatiguing?"

"It was tedious in the extreme," her mother-in-law declared, putting up her glass and subjecting Theo to a long and unnerving

293

scrutiny. "Hmm. You seem to have lost some of that brown tinge to your complexion . . . something of an improvement." She managed to convey surprise rather than approval. "Where's Stoneridge?"

Marching the streets in a fury. "He had to go out, ma'am. I'm certain if he'd known you were to arrive today, he would have made sure he was here to welcome you."

Theo turned to her sister-in-law, still huddled in her astonishing purple blanket, still clutching a white handkerchief to her scarlet nose. It clashed most interestingly with the blanket. "Mary, I trust you're well."

"Does she look well?" demanded her ladyship. "Sniveling and snuffling. It's to be hoped that fool Weston can do something for the gal. Not that I put much store in doctors . . . quacks the lot of 'em . . . and demmed expensive."

"If I could just have a mustard bath, Mama," Mary pleaded thickly. "I'm sure I'll be better directly."

"Coffee, ma'am." Foster entered the salon bearing a tray.

"Thank you," Theo said. "And, uh . . . uh, Miss Gilbraith would like a mustard bath, if it could be arranged." She turned back to the sufferer, inquiring solicitously, "Just for your feet, Mary, or would it be wiser to immerse your whole self?"

Mary spluttered, looking outraged at such a suggestion made in the hearing of a butler.

"I'll have a basin taken to the Chinese room, my lady," Foster said in repressive accents, shooting his young mistress a reproving look. "Your maid, Lady Gilbraith, has been directed to your apartments and awaits your pleasure."

Theo poured coffee and offered more milk as her mother-in-law declared the brew too strong for a liverish constitution. "Do you also consult Dr. Weston, ma'am?" she inquired sweetly, filling the cup to the brim with milk. "For your liver, perhaps?"

"My liver, gal, is my own concern," Lady Gilbraith announced. "I'm surprised your mother didn't teach you not to ask impertinent questions, but, then, the Belmonts always did lack finesse."

Theo felt her cheeks warm, and she bit down on her tongue until she had it under control. "Coffee, Mary?"

"I don't drink it," Mary said petulantly as if Theo should have been aware of that. "I should like to go to my room."

"By all means, I'll take you upstairs." Theo rose and moved to the door. She glanced toward the long windows looking out onto the street and saw the unmistakable figure of her husband striding toward the house. Her heart jumped into her throat, and she sent a swift prayer heavenward that he'd cooled off enough to react rationally to her presence downstairs.

The post chaise had been taken to the mews, so when Sylvester strode into the house, he had no notion of visitors. His expression was still grim, but the unruly edge to his fury had been blunted, and he was now well in control of himself. He was going to send Theo to Stoneridge first thing in the morning. It was a simple decision, one that would keep her out of the way while he dealt with Gerard and would, not incidentally, ensure she dug no deeper into his secrets.

Banishment would also make clear to his wife that he wouldn't tolerate her interference and her reckless impulses.

He entered the hall just as a footman was hefting the last of the portmanteaus onto his shoulders.

"Oh, Sylvester, you're back." Theo's clear tones came from the salon. "See, your mama and sister are come." She came into the hall, smiling. But her smile was tight and her eyes were dark with anxiety as they raked his face. "I have been making them welcome," she said softly, with a tiny apologetic shrug and a what-would-you-have-me-do quirk of her lips.

He accorded her a brief nod that told her little of his reaction to her disobedience and turned to greet his parent and sister, receiving a series of complaints and a great many sniffles from Mary for his pains.

"I am about to escort them to their chambers," Theo said. "Your sister wishes for a mustard bath, and I'm sure Lady Gilbraith would like to rest before dinner."

Sylvester inclined his head in acknowledgment, saying to his mother, "I'm afraid I'll have to leave you to dine alone with Theo this evening, ma'am. I have a previous engagement, and I cannot cry off."

Theo's indignantly indrawn breath almost made him smile. An evening alone with his mother and sister was a neat retribution; he couldn't have devised a more appropriate one if he'd tried.

He escorted them upstairs and then left them, saying he had to change his dress for his dinner engagement, but he'd see them in the morning. His eyes flicked across his wife's countenance as he said this, and she understood that that statement was to include her. She'd have to wait until the morning to hear whatever fate he'd devised for her.

Theo glared at his retreating back in mute dismay, then, gritting her teeth, turned back to her in-laws.

Henry recognized that his master was in no mood for conversation as he helped him change into evening dress. The earl was frowning, and his fingers were unusually clumsy with his cravat so that the pile of discarded squares mounted as he struggled with the intricate folds.

He couldn't send Theo away while his mother was there. He'd just have to hope that his mother and sister would keep her so occupied she wouldn't have time to go spinning off on her own frolics, and once the visitors had left, he'd pack her back to the country.

He left the house half an hour later, dwelling with a degree of satisfaction on the irksome evening Theo was going to spend, unaware that a messenger was already hotfoot to Brook Street with a desperate plea for support in the evening ahead.

The Belmonts, Edward Fairfax, and Jonathan Lacey arrived at Curzon Street within the hour to rescue a desperate Theo from perdition.

In his small, elegant house on Half Moon Street, Neil Gerard prepared to receive his guests. They were all members, past and present, of the Third Dragoons, and they were the only people who might continue to regard Sylvester Gilbraith askance. Neil hoped to overcome whatever lingering prejudice they might carry.

That done, Sylvester would surely have no need to dig into the past himself. It would be against his interests to exhume the rotting corpse of a scandal that everyone was prepared to leave buried. But as the ultimate insurance, Neil would plan a little excursion for the busy Lady Stoneridge. He knew Sylvester's pride. The man would be willing to sign anything, even a full confession to something he didn't remember, rather than have his wife's supposedly adulterous indiscretions exposed to Society. And that piece of paper would signal the end of Gerard's excruciating contract with Jud O'Flannery.

The door knocker sounded, and he heard his servant hurrying to open it. From the sound of voices, it appeared that several of his guests had arrived together.

"Good evenin', Neil." A bewhiskered captain entered, rubbing his hands. "Nippy out there tonight." His gaze fell on his host's countenance. "Good God, man, whatever happened to you? That's quite a shiner."

Neil touched his blackened eye, smiled thinly with his swollen lip. "Took a tumble from my horse," he explained. "Nasty brute, I've a mind to send him to the knacker's."

"Nothin' to be done with an ill-tempered nag, that's what I always say," the captain said cheerfully. "Now, see who I found on your doorstep." He indicated a florid gentleman with mild blue eyes, who had stepped into the room behind him. "Haven't seen old Barney here for months. Where've you been hiding, old chap?"

"In Spain with the Peer."

"Headquarters, eh?" The captain nodded and accepted a glass of wine from his host. "So what's goin' on?"

The other man didn't reply immediately. He glanced at the table set in the window alcove. "You expectin' quite a crowd, Neil?"

"Only five of us," Neil said, handing him a glass. "Yourselves, Peter Fortescue, and Sylvester Gilbraith."

"Stoneridge?" Barney raised an eyebrow. "I'd heard he was in town. Married, isn't he?"

"Quite recently. Soon after he inherited the title."

"Mm. Thought you had no time for him, after that nasty business at Vimiera."

Neil shrugged. "It's water under the bridge. No one really knows what happened. He was acquitted. It's hard to dismiss an old friend out of hand."

The other two nodded thoughtfully. "Well, I own I've always

297

thought of him as a decent fellow," the captain declared into his now empty glass. "I'm ready enough to give him the benefit of the doubt."

"Good." Neil smiled and refilled his glass just as the door knocker sounded again. He hoped it would be Fortescue, so that by the time Sylvester arrived, everyone would be in agreement as to how to greet him.

The stringy figure of Major Fortescue loomed in the door behind the servant. He was greeted warmly by his friends, a glass pressed into his hand, his questions as to his host's battered countenance answered.

"Gerard's expectin' Gilbraith," the captain said. "D'you remember that rum business about the colors?"

"Yes, and I never believed a word of it," Fortescue declared. "He was a damn fool to resign from the regiment. Made him look guilty."

"He was severely wounded," Neil reminded him.

"True, but he had no call to resign." The major took a deep draft of his wine.

Sylvester heard their voices as he stood in the hall, handing his cape and gloves to the servant. They were well-remembered voices from the past. Gerard hadn't told him who his fellow guests would be, but he'd set up a reunion of old comrades. What the devil was he playing at now? Was this to be some twisted exercise in mortification, despite his previous gestures of friendship?

Sylvester stiffened his shoulders as he prepared to enter the room.

"Lord Stoneridge, sir." The servant announced him.

"Ah, Sylvester, welcome." All smiles, Neil came across the room, hand extended. "Before you ask about my eye, I took a tumble from my horse. Now, you know everyone, of course."

"Of course. But it's been a long time," Sylvester said deliberately.

"Too long," Fortescue declared, grasping his hand in a warm clasp. "Why the hell did you resign in such a hurry, man?"

"A head wound is no light matter, Peter," Sylvester said. "It still plagues me."

His old friend examined him closely. He seemed to be hesitating, and Sylvester guessed he was about to bring up Vimiera, but his eyes were puzzled rather than hostile.

Before he could do so, however, Gerard spoke with brisk heartiness. "A glass of claret, Sylvester, and come to the fire." And the other two men moved forward with their own greeting, and the moment was past.

And it never came again. There was to be no opportunity to air the subject; it was as if it had never happened. For a moment Sylvester thought how easy it would be to settle for that. People were willing to forgive and forget . . . to give him the benefit of the doubt. He could resume a normal life. Except that he couldn't live with himself any longer; he could no longer live under the shadow of cowardice. And then, of course, there was the fact that Gerard had tried to kill him.

As the evening wore on, he watched Gerard and recognized with the eye of experience the man's fear, the edge of near panic in the flat eyes. How often during their boyhood had he seen it? He was filled with a depthless disgust for the man, a disgust far greater and more potent than simple anger, and realized that he'd always felt it to some extent, even in their schooldays when he'd tried to persuade the boy to stand up to the bullies.

And how had he acquired that black eye and split lip this time? Not in the corridors of Westminster School, certainly, but his face had come into contact with more than the hard ground.

As they sat around the card table, it was clear to everyone that Neil's game of whist was distracted, infuriating the captain, who was his partner. As the party broke up, Major Fortescue voiced the opinion of the group.

"You serve too fine a claret, m'boy, for a man who's not the world's best card player." He flung an arm around Gerard's shoulder. "Damn fine claret it was. Can't say I blame you for over-imbibing."

"Well, I can," the captain grumbled. "Lost me fifty pound clear, you have, Gerard. I should have let Barney have my place."

Sylvester wondered why he had been the only one to notice that Gerard drank little. Deliberately he hung back as the others left.

299

"Another glass, Sylvester?" Neil didn't sound too enthusiastic as he made the offer out of courtesy.

"Thank you." Sylvester sat down beside the fire, blandly ignoring the reluctant tone. "An excellent evening, Neil. I owe you a debt of gratitude."

Smiling, he accepted a refilled glass and calmly began the hunt. "Tell me, did you discuss Vimiera with our friends before I arrived?"

Neil's eyes shifted and then he smiled stiffly. "A word, perhaps. We're all agreed that the story's dead as the proverbial dodo. No point ruining good friendships over it. You'll not find it mentioned again by anyone."

"I do indeed stand in your debt," Sylvester said thoughtfully, his eyes hooded so that his companion couldn't see their sardonic glitter. "I know it's been a long time, but could you tell me again exactly what happened to you that afternoon?"

Gerard's lips thinned. He moved a hand through the air in a vaguely dismissive motion. "It'll do no one any good to go through it again, Sylvester."

"You were coming up in support. Did you see me surrender?"

Gerard closed his eyes as if the memory were too painful. "As I said at the court-martial, I wasn't with you when you surrendered, so I can have no opinion on the matter. The facts spoke for themselves."

"But you were coming up in support?"

"Yes. As it had been agreed at the battle plan."

"With a sizable force?" Sylvester probed slowly.

"A hundred and fifty men."

"Then why in the name of grace would I have surrendered?" Sylvester raised his head and fixed Neil Gerard with a piercing stare. "Goddammit, man. I was told they slaughtered half my men like pigs after they'd taken the colors. They had a damn good try at slaughtering me."

"I don't have the answer, Gilbraith." Neil stood up abruptly. "No one will ever know the truth, so why don't you just let sleeping dogs lie?"

Sylvester rose to his feet also and said deliberately, "I can't do that, Neil. I can't live with the possibility that I *might* have

done something so dastardly. I have to find out what happened."
He watched the other man's face closely and saw the panic flare, a naked flame, in Gerard's flat brown eyes.

He set his glass on the table, and the click of glass on mahogany sounded in the silence like the clash of cymbals. He shrugged with an assumption of carelessness.

"Ah, well, I must take my leave. I trust I haven't outstayed my welcome, but it's good to spend an evening like the old days," he said cheerfully, strolling into the hall. "I'll just have to trust that my memory of that half hour, or however long it was, returns." He took his hat and cape from the servant.

"Thank you again, Gerard, for a most pleasant evening." His smile was friendly, his eyes devoid of all expression as he shook his host's hand. Then he frowned. "What was the name of your sergeant? The one who testified at the court-martial. Savage-looking piece of work, but a useful man to have beside one in a fight, I'd imagine."

Gerard shook his head. "I don't recall his name."

"Pity. I might have tracked him down. Well, good night again."

He walked rapidly down the two steps of the narrow house onto the pavement, turned, and raised a hand in farewell. Gerard's face was thrown into relief by the lamplit hall behind him. His expression was one of pure terror, and the fingers of his right hand worried at his black and swollen eye. Then the door closed and the light was gone.

Jud O'Flannery had been the monosyllabic sergeant. Sylvester could see his face with that eye patch and the great scarlet cicatrix slashing his cheek as clearly as if it were yesterday.

And the passing reference to the man had brought that look of terror to Gerard's battered, cowardly face.

Sylvester stood for a minute on the pavement, looking thoughtfully toward the flickering gas jets lighting Piccadilly at the far end of the street, before he turned to walk in the opposite direction to Curzon Street.

Neil Gerard flung on his coat and left the house by the back alley. He strode to Jermyn Street, to a house where he was well-known, where his tastes were as well-known and readily catered to. The little girl they brought him, dressed in a spotted pinafore, her hair in pigtails, trembled convincingly and wept and screamed most satisfactorily at the appropriate moments. But her eyes were sharp and knowing even through the pain he inflicted with a savage need to make someone pay for his terror.

Chapter Twenty-four

It was after midnight when Foster let the Earl of Stoneridge into the house, and Sylvester was surprised to find his household still busy, the main salons still brightly lit.

"What's to do, Foster?" He sidestepped a servant hurrying from the dining room with a tray of dirty dishes. His mother and sister kept early hours, and the household should have been abed long since.

"Oh, quite a party we've had, sir." Foster beamed, taking his cape and cane. "Quite like old times it was, my lord, to have the family all around the dinner table, and Mr. Edward, too, and Lady Clarry's beau."

He closed the front door, observing judiciously, "That young Mr. Lacey seems a nice gentleman. He and Lady Clarry will be making a match of it before Christmas, you mark my words."

He turned back to the earl, his beam fading as he took in his lordship's expression, a mixture of chagrin and acute exasperation. "Am I to understand Lady Belmont and the girls were here to dinner?" Sylvester asked slowly. "With my mother and sister?"

"Oh, yes, indeed, sir. But Lady Gilbraith and Miss Gilbraith retired early, before tea. I understand her ladyship does not approve of lottery tickets and such trivial amusements." Foster's voice was now expressionless, his face impassive, except for his eyes, where Sylvester swore he could detect a glimmer of unholy amusement.

"The family do tend to become a little noisy, of course, when playing such games," Foster continued blandly. "Many's the time I've heard Lady Belmont beg them to quieten down, but never too seriously. . . . Will I lock up now, my lord?"

"Yes, I'm going to bed," the earl said curtly, striding to the stairs.

"Oh, by the by, my lord. Miss Gilbraith had to be moved from the Chinese room," Foster intoned. "She found the dragons on the wallpaper made her bilious. Good night, my lord."

Sylvester's lip quivered despite his annoyance, but he managed to keep his amusement from his voice as he bade the butler good night.

He strode upstairs in a seething muddle of acute frustration and reluctant amusement. Instead of suffering a boring and thoroughly disagreeable evening, Theo had obviously had a wonderful time with her favorite people, contriving to exclude his mother and sister into the bargain. He was getting very tired of being outmaneuvered by that ramshackle gypsy.

And then he thought of Mary and the dragons, and a reluctant little chuckle escaped him. Bilious, indeed! He could imagine how his in-laws would have enjoyed it. Even Elinor would have had her quiet smile.

A thin gold line of candlelight showed under Theo's door as he went past to his own room. Presumably, she was relishing the success of her ploy. He marched into his room, letting the door bang shut behind him, hoping it had made her jump . . . hoping she might even be a little apprehensive, knowing he was back.

Henry never waited up for him, and his own room was lit by the banked fire in the grate and a single lamp, turned down low on the dresser. Yawning, he undressed and was about to climb into bed when he heard a chair scraping across the wooden floor in the room next door.

Theo was still awake. He shrugged into his dressing gown and softly opened his door onto the corridor, where candlelight now flickered from the wall sconces and there was the deep hush of a sleeping house. He glanced down and saw the light still below Theo's door.

He lifted the latch and pushed open the door. Theo was standing at the dresser, her back to him, a glass in her hand. She saw him in the mirror and spun around, placing the glass beside a small brown bottle on the dresser.

"Sylvester!"

"Why aren't you asleep?" he asked, coming into the room.

"I wasn't feeling very sleepy." She pushed her tumbled hair away from her face.

"Too stimulating an evening, perhaps," he observed dryly.

A slight guilty flush tipped her cheekbones. "I thought your

304

mother might enjoy the company."

"Fustian!" he declared.

Theo's flush deepened. She regarded him in silence for a minute, then said with an air of resolution, "I am truly sorry about this afternoon, Sylvester. It was stupid and reckless and anything else you want to call it."

He strode across to her, catching her chin, saying roughly, "What you mean is that forgetting to take your pistol was all of those things. Isn't that what you mean, Theo?

"Isn't that what you mean?" he repeated when she didn't immediately respond.

"I suppose so," she confessed. "I do believe everything would have been fine if I'd thought it through. Only I didn't."

"No, you didn't, and nearly got both yourself and Edward killed." His fingers tightened on her jaw. "Well, it's not going to happen again, Theo. As soon as my mother leaves, you're going back to Stoneridge."

"Alone?" Startled indignation flared in the purple eyes.

"Alone," he confirmed. "I have some unfinished business here. When it's done, I'll come myself."

"Oh, so that's it!" She jerked her head sideways, away from his hold. "You're afraid I might dip my toes in your unfinished business! You don't understand. You just don't understand! I want to be a part of what's troubling you. I want to help you. People who care for people want to help them. But you don't understand that because you don't understand what it is to care for someone." Her voice thickened on an angry sob as she flung away from him.

"What do you mean, I don't care?" Sylvester said, taken aback. "Of course I do."

She was standing in front of the fire, and the shape of her body was outlined beneath the almost transparent lawn of her nightgown. He could see the pale swell of her breasts and the darker shadow of her nipples. His body stirred, sprang to life.

"Come here," he said softly, reaching for her hands, drawing her against him. "Let me show you how much I care."

"No!" Theo said fiercely, trying to push him away. "Don't touch me! I don't want you to touch me, Stoneridge. In fact,

I don't think I want you to touch me ever again!"

"Now, that's a silly thing to say." And she knew that it was.

He caught her wrists in one hand, clipping them behind her back, pressing her body against his, his other hand tilting her chin so that she had to look up at him. Her eyes were a battlefield of confusion, need, and anger.

She jerked her head aside as he bent to kiss her.

His mouth bumped into her ear, which struck him as good a place as any other. His tongue darted, a hot, moist lance, and Theo struggled in his hold, but he laughed and tightened his grip as his tongue explored the intricate whorls of the dainty shell lying flat against the side of her head.

"I adore your ears," he murmured, his breath a warm and tickling rustle. Theo tried to pull her head free of his grasp, struggling to resist the irresistible. He knew how sensitive her ears were, how after a very few moments she would yield to the tormenting, arousing stimulation that would spread from the spot where his tongue danced right down to her toes.

His teeth nibbled her earlobe, and she bucked and jerked in his hold, every sinuous wriggle increasing his determination to transform her resistance to passion. She was too slender and light to have much muscle power, and he knew her strength lay in the way she could use her body. Swiftly, he adjusted his hold so that he held her sideways across his thighs. She was now unbalanced and could get no leverage. He swung a leg over hers, imprisoning her legs just in case she was contemplating one of her devastating high kicks, and then, confident that he had her firmly secured, he smiled down into her furious, flushed face.

"That's better. Now, are you going to let me get on with giving us both pleasure, or shall we wrestle some more?"

There was something different about him, she thought. Something carefree and impulsive, as if he'd shed some restraints. Desire danced in his eyes, and she could smell brandy sweetness on his breath as he laughed down at her.

"You're foxed," she accused, forgetting her predicament for the moment. It was hard to imagine Sylvester allowing cognac to erode the tight control he kept over himself and his life . . . and his private concerns, she remembered with a fresh surge of anger.

He shook his head. "Not in the least, my love." He lifted her into his arms. "My dear little gypsy, don't look as if you're going to the gallows." He laid her on the bed and she gazed up at him, her eyes huge and unreadable, her hair a black mantel flowing over the billowing folds of her white nightgown.

He put a knee on the bed beside her and lightly traced the curve of her cheek with his fingertip. Theo didn't move. He ran his thumb over her mouth, expecting her tongue to dart forth in her usual response, flickering against the pad of his thumb. But she continued to lie motionless beneath the caress, although her eyes had darkened and he could read their sensual glow. The glow deepened as he slid his hand down the column of her throat, and his fingers tiptoed into the neck of her nightgown, dancing over the swell of her breast, circling her nipple without touching.

The glow deepened but she didn't move, just lay gazing up at him. There was challenge in her eyes, something he wasn't used to seeing in the bedroom.

He stood up, shrugging out of his dressing gown, letting it fall to the floor before kneeling on the bed again. Theo's eyes darted involuntarily down his body, and he suppressed a smile. He placed a hand on her ankle and smoothed upward over her shin, cupping her rounded kneecap. Pausing, he watched her face. She gazed at the ceiling, but her mouth was soft, a delicate pink blossoming on her cheek.

She wasn't capable of hiding her responses, he thought, allowing his hand to continue its upward journey. Her body tensed, her skin rippled as his fingertips crept into the heated cleft and flickered momentarily against the tight bud of her sex.

He withdrew his hand, and Theo drew a swift breath of surprise and what he hoped was disappointment. Catching up the hem of her nightgown, he began to fold it backward with deliberate care, smoothing each fold before beginning the next, baring her body inch by inch.

Theo fought her unruly responses as the cool air laved her skin. And then this slow exposure paused for what seemed an eternity at the top of her thighs, and she found she was holding

307

her breath. It took every ounce of self-control to keep from moving, from murmuring her impatience, from putting her hands on his chest, lifting her head to touch her tongue to his nipples as he knelt above her. But still she resisted the temptation.

"Stubborn little gypsy," Sylvester murmured, half smiling, feeling her struggle as if it were his own. He took another fold in the fine lawn of her nightgown and then another, until the material lay in a flat roll at her waist. He bent to kiss her bare belly, drawing his tongue over the smooth skin in a damp, heated stroke that set her muscles jumping with a life of their own. But still she kept silent and made no voluntary move.

"Perhaps I should try another approach," he mused, as if talking to himself, and promptly flipped her onto her stomach.

Theo was taken aback. She'd been expecting that moist and tantalizing exploration to continue its downward progression. But now he was rolling up the back of her nightgown as he'd done with the front, baring her body inch by inch until he reached the small of her back. She felt his breath warm on her skin as his tongue darted into the dimpled indentations above the flare of her buttocks. His hand slid between her thighs as he kissed his way over the damask rounds, his fingers probing, stroking, flickering, opening. And finally Theo moaned and her body lifted to his caress, tightening around the thumb that was within her and the delicate teasing fingers at the core of her sensitivity.

Sylvester knelt beside her, his free hand sliding up and under the nightgown, pressing against her spine, working up the bony column to the nape of her neck, and she stretched and arched catlike as the firm pressure released little knots of tension along her back.

He swept the black river of her hair aside and bent to kiss her neck, nibbling and nuzzling, inhaling the sweet fragrance of her skin and hair. There was something wonderfully innocent about the back of her neck, something milky and soft about its scent. Even when she drove him to distraction with her stubborn impulses or her blunt statements, he had only to think of this delicate, soft-skinned column for his anger to lose its sting.

"Draw your knees up," he whispered, running his hand down again, stroking over her bottom while his other hand continued its work between her thighs.

Theo obeyed the soft command, her face buried in the coverlet. He moved behind her, his flat palms spreading her thighs. The intimacy of his caressing fingers deepened, and she could no longer control her soft, whimpering moans of pleasure, and when she felt his flesh glide within her, she reached behind her blindly, to touch the rock-hard thighs that drove him on this joy-bringing, joy-taking voyage.

At her touch Sylvester knew he'd won. He moved within her until the little ripples of the satin sheath that held him began to gather momentum. Then he withdrew and, before Theo could react, turned her onto her back.

"Now," he said, "I want to see your face, my partner in pleasure."

He drew her legs up onto his shoulder and plunged to her core, his hands sliding over the backs of her thighs, and gripping the firm flesh of her backside.

Theo cried out as the changed position deepened the sensation of his flesh in hers, and she reached up to touch his chest, his nipples, to stroke down the concave belly, to slide between his thighs and upward on a deeply intimate journey that drew a low groan of delight from her lover.

He smiled down at her, and there was no triumph in the smile. Theo's tongue touched her lips, her eyes aglow, her skin flushed, and he knew that for the moment she'd forgotten everything that had brought them to this glorious plane.

She began to move, urgent and insistent, and he held himself still. "Wait a little, gypsy."

Theo shook her head, and there was a glimmer of mischief in her eyes. With one devastating wriggle of her exploring finger she broke his last reserve of control, and his body seemed to explode as her own convulsed around him and she no longer knew where his skin began and hers ended. His flesh was integral to her own body and his joy was hers.

"You wicked witch," he gasped when the wave receded and he could draw breath. "I was taking my time."

"You can't expect to have everything your own way." There was a tart edge to the mischievous rejoinder despite her

309

languorous tone.

Sylvester grinned. "I gave up expecting that many months ago, my dear girl . . . but neither, I'll have you know, can you."

He fell onto the bed beside her, pushing an arm under her body, brushing a damp lock of hair away from the alabaster curve of her cheek. Theo lay still, her head on his shoulder, her eyes closed, wrestling with the idea of defeat. But it wasn't over yet. She still had a few days, until his mother and sister left. Perhaps she'd better try to make her in-laws a little more welcome.

"Why the face?" Sylvester asked languidly at her unconscious grimace.

"I'm thirsty," she improvised.

Sylvester sat up and swung himself to the floor. "Will water do you?"

"Yes, thank you."

She watched him through half-closed eyes as he crossed to the water jug on the washstand. "Where's the glass?"

"On the dresser."

He picked up the glass she'd been drinking from when he came in and filled it with water. He drank himself before refilling the glass and bringing it across to her. "What's in that bottle?" He handed her the water.

"Oh," Theo said, taking a drink. "Well, it's something I should have mentioned earlier."

"Why do I have the feeling I'm not going to enjoy this?" Sylvester mused, picking up the brown bottle and holding it to the light.

"It's a potion that will prevent conception," she said. "I got it from a herbalist in Lulworth."

"*What.*" Sylvester stared at her, trying to understand what she'd said. Women didn't make those choices, they weren't theirs to make. He turned the bottle over in his hands, gazing at her in stunned disbelief. "Are you telling me you've been taking this since our marriage."

"Yes," Theo said. "Didn't you wonder why I hadn't conceived?"

"It did cross my mind," he said grimly. "Dear God in heaven, Theo! Why didn't you discuss this with me?"

"Well, at the beginning you said you wanted to set up your nursery without delay, and I didn't feel ready, and I thought if you refused to listen to me —"

"I'm not a brute, Theo," he interrupted. "I wouldn't force you to carry my child."

"Well, I didn't know that then." She plaited the sheet with restless fingers. "From what I understand about these matters, men don't expect their wives to have an opinion, let alone a way of enforcing that opinion. But I did."

Sylvester ran a hand through his disheveled locks, struggling with a mélange of disbelief, resentment, and hurt. Of course, he'd expected her to do as other women did in these matters and simply accept the realities of the marriage bed.

"Why don't you want to bear my children?" he asked finally.

His wounded feelings were clear in his voice and his eyes as they rested gravely on her face, and Theo chewed her bottom lip, trying to think of how to assuage his hurt.

"It isn't that I don't want to," she said. "I just don't want to *now*. It's what Dame Merriweather said: It's best to look after the loving before you start breeding." She offered a tentative smile.

Sylvester looked down at the bottle he still held. "Do you have any idea what's in this? Have you the slightest idea what damage this kind of stuff can do you? It may well have prevented pregnancy, but what other effects was it having?"

"Dame Merriweather wouldn't give me anything that would harm me," she said with conviction.

"A country herbalist! What the devil does she know?" He put the bottle down and came over to the bed. "Listen, these medicines can do incalculable harm, I've heard horror stories aplenty." Not, however, among the kind of women Theo spent her time with. He kept the wry thought to himself.

Theo frowned. It was true the potion played havoc with her monthly cycle. "So what do you suggest?"

"There's a perfectly simple precaution I can take that involves no dangerous substances," he said, bending to extinguish the bedside candle. "So we'll leave it up to me from now on." Sliding a hand beneath her, he lifted her body so that he could pull

311

down the coverlet. "Get in."

Theo wriggled between the sheets, sliding over to make room for him. "Just until I'm ready," she said.

"Yes," he agreed with a mock sigh. "Until then."

"Perhaps we could try your method now." Her hand moved seductively over his body as he came in beside her. "I'd really like to see how it works. . . ."

312

Chapter Twenty-five

Theo awoke to bright sunshine. Sleepily, she hitched herself on her elbows to look at the clock. It was almost ten. How could she ever have slept so late? But then she remembered. She lay back on the pillows, her hands drifting over her naked form, reminding her skin of the touches that had brought so much pleasure during those joyous hours before dawn.

She turned her head and frowned at the empty space beside her. When had Sylvester left her? Presumably he'd woken long ago; he rarely slept after the sun came up. She closed her eyes again, running her hand over the sheet where he'd lain, over the pillow that still bore the indentation of his head.

He claimed to care for her, yet he demanded that she keep her distance from him in all but passion. What kind of love was that? But, then, perhaps no one had ever loved him, so he didn't know how to express such an emotion.

She thought of Lavinia Gilbraith, mean-spirited, carping witch that she was. It was impossible to imagine her loving anyone, even her son.

She would just have to teach her husband herself . . . by example.

On that energetic determination Theo sprang from bed, guiltily thinking of her mother-in-law, who was presumably waiting for her hostess's attention. She hoped the cabbage roses in the pink bedroom hadn't upset Mary's delicate digestion. After pulling on her dressing gown she reached for the bellpull to ring for Dora.

She heard Henry's voice in Sylvester's room next door. It was pitched very low. Then she heard a sound that sent chills down her spine, and her hand dropped from the bellpull. It was an inarticulate, animallike moan of pain, interspersed with the dreadful sounds of helpless dry retching.

She crept to the wall and pressed her ear against it. What was happening? Was Sylvester ill? The dreadful moan came again, a sound that chilled her blood, it was so filled with despairing endurance.

313

Sylvester had that headache again. That other part of his past — his precious privacy — that was forbidden to her.

She went out into the corridor and tried to lift the latch on Sylvester's door. The door was locked. In the name of goodness, she thought with a surge of exasperation, how could he expect to spend a lifetime with her, to grow old with her, all the while keeping the most vulnerable parts of himself secret from her? And most particularly this hideous curse?

Back in her own room, she stood thinking for a minute, then went to the window. There was a narrow iron balcony, little more than a foothold outside. Its twin was outside Sylvester's room, a large sideways footstep away. Curzon Street was two floors below. A barouche bowled down it at a fast clip as she leaned out. She craned her neck and saw a scrap of curtain at Sylvester's window flutter in the wind. The long window was cracked open.

Without conscious decision she ran to the armoire, pulled out her riding habit with the divided skirt, and dressed rapidly. She braided her hair, slipped a pair of light, soft-soled slippers on her feet, and returned to the window.

Heights had never bothered her. For years she and Edward had clambered over the cliff face at Lulworth Cove searching out gull rookeries without once considering the crashing surf and jagged rocks beneath them. But a busy London street below was unnerving in a way surf and rocks had never been.

Theo turned her back on the street, faced the wall, and threw her leg over the low ornate railing, feeling for the brick ledge that ran between the two balconies. Her foot found it, and she straddled the railing, taking a deep, steadying breath. She'd have to bring her other foot over, and for a minute she'd be standing on this narrow ledge that would accommodate only her toes. But her hand could reach the other balcony. She stretched her arm, and her fingers closed over the iron. She would have a firm grip on both balconies while her feet were in no-man's-land. Once she'd got her left foot onto Sylvester's balcony, she'd be home and dry.

It was pure craziness. It was exhilarating. More than anything, though, it was necessary. Sylvester needed her. She had opened herself to him. He must open himself to her.

With a swift prayer to the gods, who certainly owed her something, Theo swung her other foot to the ledge and for a terrifying second was poised above the street, her toes clinging to the ledge, her hands, white-knuckled, gripping the balcony on either side. Her heart thudded in her throat as she gingerly raised her left foot. Now she was held by five toes and ten fingers. She swung her left leg sideways, over the rail behind her left hand, and as the cold metal touched her calf she heaved a sigh of relief. The rest was easy.

A minute later she was standing foursquare on Sylvester's balcony, easing open the window.

Soft-footed, she stepped into the darkened bedchamber that, despite the slightly opened window, felt as stifling as a greenhouse.

"Who's there!" Henry spun from the curtained bed, his eyes glowing in the dimness, his outraged whisper hissing in the quiet.

"It's me," Theo said calmly, crossing the room. She had very little to do with Henry — none of the household did. It was accepted that he had a special relationship with the earl, one that Theo decided was more intimate in essentials than her own. But that was going to change.

"My lady!" His outrage was superseded only by his astonishment as he gazed at the window behind her, the curtain fluttering in the breeze.

"What is it, Henry?" Sylvester's voice was a cracked thread, like the voice of a very old man. It put Theo in mind of her grandfather in his last days.

"It's all right, m'lord, don't go fretting now," Henry said, laying a hand on Theo's arm. "You must leave here at once, my lady. His lordship can't have visitors."

"I'm not a visitor, Henry." She shook his hand off her arm, and her eyes flashed in the darkness, her voice frigid in contrast. "I am his lordship's wife."

"My lady, I must insist!" He renewed his hold on her arm.

"Take your hand away, or I might break your wrist," Theo said with the same soft, cold ferocity. She raised her free hand, the edge of her rigid palm hovering like a steel blade above the

315

wrist of the manservant's gripping hand.

The dreadful dry retching came from the tented bed, and a groan that filled Theo with a horrified pity, but she maintained her menacing stance, and after a second Henry's hand dropped from her arm.

"Thank you," she said, brushing her sleeve pointedly. "You may remain if you wish, but I will be responsible for nursing Lord Stoneridge, as is my duty."

Henry stood openmouthed as she walked quickly to the bed, gently drawing aside the curtain at the head.

Sylvester's face was a pale shadow on the pillows, gray and waxen, his right eyelid so swollen that it was almost closed. Lines of pain etched his brow and ran down his nose to his mouth, as deep as the furrows of a plowshare.

His hand moved, shuffling to the bedside table where the bowl and a glass of water stood. She took the glass and gently slipped an arm beneath his neck, holding the glass to his lips.

"Theo?" he croaked. "What the hell are you doing here?"

"Hush," she said. "Henry's right, you mustn't become agitated."

"But how in the devil's name did you get in here?"

"I flew through the window," she said, bending to lay her lips on his forehead. "I wish I could take it away."

His mouth twisted in what might have been a gruesome travesty of a smile, but whatever he'd been about to say was lost as he groaned and reached for the bowl.

Henry jumped forward, but Theo forestalled him, holding the bowl until Sylvester fell back on the pillows, racked with renewed torment.

Theo wiped his mouth, gently bathed his face, and laid a lavender-soaked cloth on his forehead, ignoring the hovering Henry.

"Theo, go away," Sylvester murmured after a minute. "I appreciate what you're trying to do, but I don't want you . . . don't want you here, seeing me —"

"Hush," she interrupted with quiet force. "You're my husband, and I *will* be a part of your suffering. There's nothing you can do about it anyway."

Whether through weakness or acceptance, he ceased to object

and lay still and silent, wrestling with his agony.

Theo moved away from the bed and whispered to the still outraged Henry, "I have to go down and see Lady Gilbraith, but I'll be back directly. You're to leave the door unlocked." There was such crisp authority in her eyes and the set of her jaw, such an edge to her soft voice, that Henry bowed and moved to open the door for her.

Theo sped downstairs. She could hear her mother-in-law's irritable voice from the hall.

"I cannot think how a household can be run in this fashion. It's past midmorning, and there's no sign of either Stoneridge or his wife."

"I do beg your pardon, ma'am," Theo said, jumping down the last two steps. "Sylvester is ill."

"Ill? What on earth do you mean, ill? He's never had a day's illness in his life. And what kind of a slugabed are you, girl, to appear to your household at this late hour?"

Theo ignored this latter complaint. "Sylvester has a war wound that afflicts him with severe headaches," she said with an attempt at patience. "I'm afraid I must leave you to your own devices today, I'm needed at his bedside. Please feel free to order things as you wish, and, of course, if you'd like to take the air, or pay some calls, then the barouche is at your disposal. Now, if you'll excuse me —"

"Goodness me, gal. If the man has a headache, it's ten to one he dipped deep in the cognac last night. He should take a powder and sleep it off. There's no need for you to dance attendance on him, and I wish you to accompany me on some errands. Mary's too busy sniffling and moaning to leave her bed."

"My apologies, ma'am, but I must beg you to excuse me. Foster will attend to everything for you."

Lady Gilbraith's complexion turned a curious mottled salmon color, and she began to huff, but Theo didn't wait for the head of steam to burst forth. She turned and ran back upstairs.

Henry looked up from the bedside as she came quietly in, but he moved aside when she came over.

Throughout that interminable day, and half the next night, she sat beside the bed, offering what little relief she could, con-

317

cealing her horror at the hideous pain that turned a powerful, self-determining man into an inarticulate, groaning husk barely capable of raising his head from the pillow.

Henry, initially tight-lipped, changed his attitude as the hours went by, and she didn't flag, didn't shrink, from performing whatever service was necessary, and didn't hesitate to ask his advice. He found himself telling her of how he'd found the major in the prison transport, barely alive, his head wrapped in foul, blood-soaked bandages. He described the hellhole where they'd languished without medical attention or supplies for the best part of a twelvemonth.

Theo listened, and a few more pieces of the puzzle that was her husband fell into place.

"Were you at Vimiera with his lordship?" she whispered when they'd drawn away from the bed and were eating supper over by the open window, so the smell of food wouldn't increase his misery.

Henry shook his head. "No, ma'am. But his lordship talked of it during his illness."

"What did he say?" Theo tried to hide her intense curiosity.

"Oh, he was out of his head mostly, ma'am. It was all disjointed, like. Couldn't make hide nor hair of it, mostly. Besides, he couldn't remember what happened before that damned Froggie bayoneted him."

"Oh." Theo was disappointed. She returned to her vigil beside the bed.

"We'll give him the laudanum now, my lady?" Henry spoke softly behind her. "It's been all of fifteen minutes since he last vomited, and maybe he'll keep it down long enough to fall asleep."

"Will that be the end of it?" she asked anxiously, watching as he measured a few drops into the class of water. Sylvester seemed barely conscious, although his swollen eyelids jumped and twitched.

"Please God," the manservant said. "Here, my lord." He slid a strong arm around his neck and lifted him, holding the glass to his lips.

Sylvester swallowed the opiate without opening his eyes. He seemed no longer aware of either of his attendants and lay

318

still on the pillows.

Henry stepped back, drawing the curtains around the bed again. "You'd best get some rest yourself, my lady. I'll sleep on the truckle bed in here."

Theo was dead tired; last night had been a very short one, but she looked doubtfully at the shrouded bed, listening as Sylvester's breathing deepened.

"He'll sleep now, my lady," Henry said insistently.

"Yes," she said. "Did he have these attacks when he was a prisoner, or did they come on afrerward?"

"No, he had them even worse in France," Henry told her, his face screwing into an expression of loathing. "Damned French wouldn't give him anything, not even a drop of laudanum. And he'd be screaming . . . screaming that name all the time."

"What name?"

Henry shook his head. "I can't rightly remember, ma'am." He bent to pull the truckle bed from beneath the poster bed. "Gerald, I think it was. Miles . . . Niles . . . Gerald. Miles Gerald or some such."

Miles, or Niles, Gerald. Theo shrugged and turned to the door. "Good night, Henry. Call me if I can be of help."

"Good night, my lady."

Theo went into her own bedroom and closed the door quietly behind her. She was almost too tired to undress but somehow managed to drag her clothes off and fall into bed, sliding into a dreamless sleep almost immediately.

She awoke very early the next morning and, still half-asleep, slipped from her room and quietly put her head around Sylvester's door. She heard only the deep, stertorous breathing from behind the curtains, interspersed with low rumbling snores from the truckle bed. The sound of his sleeping filled her with sweet relief. What must it be like to live every day with the knowledge that that hideous, degrading agony could — no, would — sweep over you without warning, and there was no cure, no promise of a future without such a curse?

Back in her own room she rang for Dora and, when the maid appeared, asked her to bring up hot water for a bath. She bathed and dressed in leisurely fashion, sipping chocolate and nibbling

319

sweet biscuits, contemplating her next move. She must go to Brook Street and enlist her mother's help in the entertainment of Lady Gilbraith. If she could shuffle off some of those responsibilities, she'd have more time to tackle the mystery surrounding her husband. Maybe Edward could find out if anyone who had been at Vimiera with Sylvester was in London. It would be a place to start . . . although not as promising as the Fisherman's Rest.

It was still very early, and when she went downstairs, Foster answered her inquiry by informing her that neither Lady Gilbraith nor Miss Gilbraith had yet rung for their maids. That gave her a couple of hours before they'd be up and about and demanding attention, Theo reasoned. "Have my curricle brought around, Foster, I'm driving myself to Brook Street."

While she waited, she went into the library and wrote a note to Sylvester, then ran back upstairs. In her own room she adjusted her hat in the mirror, arranging the silver plume on her shoulder, then, picking up her gloves and riding whip, she tiptoed out to Sylvester's door and opened it softly. The curtains were still drawn around the bed, but Henry was now moving around in the dim light, setting the room to rights.

"Is he still asleep, Henry?"

"Aye, m'lady." He came to the door.

"Give him this when he awakens, please." She handed him the folded paper.

The manservant took it with a respectful nod.

"Yes, m'lady."

It was a beautiful morning, and her spirits rose as she stepped up into her curricle. Something had happened during the long hours she'd spent by Sylvester's bedside, impotently sharing his suffering, wishing she could take it from him. Theo was *in* love with her husband. At least, that was the only explanation she could come up with to explain this joy she felt at the prospect of seeing him well again, with his dry smile and his strong, elegant hands and his cool gray eyes. Her blood sang and her heart danced. She knew she'd come to care for him many weeks ago, but she'd not expected this quicksilver pleasure at the very thought of him. Everything in the crisp and beautiful morning seemed especially magical. The deep russet tones of the leaves on the trees lining the streets, the tang of smoke from a bonfire, a trio of rosy-cheeked children playing ball in a square garden.

She bowled around the corner onto Berkeley Square, enjoying the neat fashion in which she caught the thong of her whip, sending it up the stick with an elegant turn of her wrist. Sylvester would have approved.

Neil Gerard was strolling across the square when Lady Stoneridge's curricle came into view. His heart jumped. Sylvester's wife was alone but for her groom. It had been two days since he'd seen her outside the Fisherman's Rest. He'd called at Curzon Street the previous day, hoping to begin the cultivation of his quarry, but the butler had said her ladyship wasn't receiving. However, this was a perfect opportunity to bait his hook.

Theo was still congratulating herself on her whip play when she became aware of a waving figure on the pavement. She drew rein immediately, recognizing Neil Gerard.

Miles Gerald.

An accidental juxtaposition? Perhaps not. A surge of excitement lifted the hairs on the nape of her neck.

"Good morning, sir." She smiled down. "You're abroad early, Captain Gerard."

"I might say the same of you, Lady Stoneridge." He approached the curricle, resting one hand on the footstep, smiling up at her in the weak sunlight. "I don't wish to be impertinent, but you took that corner in capital fashion. You're a most accomplished whip."

"Why, thank you, sir. I don't consider that in the least an impertinent compliment. I'm going to Brook Street. May I take you up if you're going in my direction?" Theo had no clear plan of campaign, but she trusted inspiration would come to her once she had the man captive in the carriage. His face looked rather as if it had recently come into contact with a hard object.

"You do me too much honor, Lady Stoneridge." He climbed aboard the curricle. "Brook Street is on my way."

Theo flicked the reins and the horses walked on. "Were you at Vimiera with Stoneridge?" she asked casually. "I can't remember if you said so the other evening at Almack's."

Neil's thoughts and conjectures raced through his brain. What did she know? What did she want to know? This was the woman who'd been in the Fisherman's Rest — not once but twice. "We were, but not in the same engagement."

"I see. Then it seems you were lucky, sir. In view of what happened to my husband." She smiled sweetly, slowing her horses as they crossed Grosvenor Street.

"That was an old scandal, best forgotten, ma'am," he said.

"What scandal?" She turned to him with a look of complete innocence. "Do you mean the court-martial? I understood it was routine in such cases. My husband was exonerated, was he not?" She turned her eyes back to the road, and he didn't see the intense speculation racing in their blue depths.

"Of course," he replied smoothly. "As you say, it was a purely routine matter. But it caused some unpleasantness for your husband."

"Yes, so I understand." She glanced up at him. "Were you in the vicinity of the engagement, sir?" It was a shot in the dark, but if Gerard's name had haunted Sylvester's delirium, then there must be a reason.

The cold brown eyes shifted, and something fearful flared beneath the flat surface. "Uh, no, ma'am. My company was engaged elsewhere," he said after an imperceptible pause.

You lie, sir. The blood began to speed through her veins, and her pulses raced with this sudden and absolute conviction. The man was lying, and for some reason he was afraid.

"I understand your sister, Lady Emily, is betrothed to Lieutenant Fairfax," Gerard said abruptly. "He also served heroically in the Peninsula."

"Yes, indeed," Theo responded, willing to change the subject for the moment. She had enough to think about. "The wedding date is set for June."

They reached the intersection with Brook Street, and she drew rein behind a carter's dray that was making a delivery in Three Kings Yard.

"I will set you down here, Captain Gerard, if this suits you." She smiled pleasantly, extending her gloved hand in farewell.

"Thank you, Lady Stoneridge." He shook hands and jumped

lightly to the pavement. "I hope I may return the courtesy. Would you do me the honor of driving with me tomorrow?" His smile was as inviting as he knew how to make it. "I'd dearly like to see you handle my chestnuts."

A triumphant rush of excitement swept through Theo. The man was playing into her hands. "I should be delighted, sir," she responded with a warm smile, and drew back into the stream of traffic.

Could it have been Neil Gerard in the Fisherman's Rest?

But of course it must have been. It explained that strange inkling she'd had that the man was familiar. It explained almost everything. The puzzle pieces tumbled in her head and formed the picture. Gerard was behind the attacks on Sylvester, and Sylvester knew it. And it was all to do with Vimiera. But what and how?

She drew rein outside her mother's house and jumped down, handing the reins to her groom. "Stable them in the mews here, Billy. I shan't be needing them for several hours."

"Right y'are, Lady Theo." The groom led the horses away, and Theo ran up the steps to the house.

What had happened at Vimiera? Sylvester couldn't remember, but whatever it was, it concerned Neil Gerard. And Gerard would provide the answer . . . somehow. She was driving with him tomorrow, a golden opportunity if she could think how to use it.

The door opened under her brisk knock. "Morning, Dennis." She greeted the butler with an ebullient smile. "Is Lady Belmont up and about yet?"

"Her ladyship and the young ladies are in the breakfast parlor, Lady Stoneridge."

"Don't announce me." She tossed her whip onto a chair and bounded down the corridor at the rear of the hall, stripping off her gloves as she went. "Good morning, everyone." She flung open the door to the small parlor at the back of the house, looking out on a square walled garden.

"Theo!" Lady Belmont looked up in surprise. "You're abroad early."

Theo bent to kiss her mother. "Yes. The witches are still abed,

323

so I took the opportunity to escape. . . . No, don't scold," she said, seeing her mother's disapproval. "I only say it in private, not to their faces. I am starving," she continued almost without a breath. "I left before breakfast."

"I came to Curzon Street yesterday, but Foster said you were with Stoneridge and I couldn't see you," Rosie stated, sounding a trifle aggrieved, a piece of toast halfway to her mouth.

"Yes, Sylvester was indisposed," Theo said. "He gets these hideous headaches, Mama. He had one at Stoneridge, if you remember."

"Poor man," Elinor said compassionately. "I've heard of such curses. He's better now, I trust."

"He was sleeping peacefully when I left." She sat down at the table. "Emily and Clarissa, I need you to come on an errand with me. May we take the barouche, Mama? I drove myself here, but the curricle isn't comfortable for three."

"What errand?" Emily inquired, passing her sister the coffeepot.

"It's a secret," Theo said, pouring coffee. "But I need you both to come for moral support."

"Theo, what mischief are you planning?" Elinor demanded, recognizing the aura of energy and purpose surrounding her daughter, whose eyes and skin were aglow.

"No mischief," Theo said with an innocent smile, helping herself to a slice of ham and buttering a roll.

"Lieutenant Fairfax, my lady," the butler intoned before Elinor could respond to this insouciant reassurance.

"I trust I'm not intruding, Lady Belmont." Edward came in on the announcement, his eyes immediately searching out his betrothed. "I know it's early, but —"

"You couldn't keep away," Rosie finished for him matter-of-factly. "I don't know why you don't live here, Edward. I'm sure it's more comfortable than your lodgings, and it would save you a deal of traveling time."

"*Rosie!*" protested Emily. "You make it sound as if Edward isn't welcome."

"Oh, but of course he is," Rosie said placidly, taking another piece of toast. "It was only an observation. Clarry's knight is

324

the same. He's practically moved in, too."

"That's enough, child," Elinor rebuked her. "Sit down, Edward. You know we're always pleased to see you."

Edward sat down next to Theo, observing with a grin, "You managed to escape the tabbies."

"Edward, for shame!" Elinor protested. "Such an example for Rosie!"

"Oh, I don't mind," Rosie said. "Did the dragons really make Mary go green? Clarry said she was quite pea-colored when she came downstairs."

"That's enough. I don't want to hear another word about the Gilbraiths," Elinor said in a tone that they all knew meant business.

"Very well, Mama," Theo said with a placating smile. "But will you invite her to go visiting with you or something . . . just to relieve me of a little of the burden?"

Elinor's expression so clearly indicated how little she relished such a prospect that her daughters burst into peals of laughter, and accusations of "hypocrite" flew around the table. Elinor shook her head ruefully. "I suppose we should all take a turn."

Edward took the cup of coffee Emily poured him. "Well, I hope you'll excuse me this morning. I was hoping to persuade Emily to drive with me in the park after breakfast."

"Oh, it'll have to be later," Theo said. "Emily and Clarry are coming on an errand with me."

"Oh, well, I'll accompany you, then."

Theo chuckled. "I don't think you want to do that, Edward. You'll be most uncomfortable." She turned to her mother. "We may have the barouche, mayn't we?"

Elinor sighed. "I suppose so, if you promise you're not up to some mischief."

"Mama, I am a married woman," Theo declared loftily. "How could you possibly think such a thing?"

"Very easily," Elinor said wryly.

"Well, I have to be back by eleven o'clock, because Jonathan is coming to finish his portrait," Clarissa said. "He's going to hang it in the hall of his mother's house, and she's going to give a soiree so that people may see it. Once they realize how talented he is, he's bound to get a host of commissions."

"I haven't seen it yet," Theo said. "Do you like it?"

Clarissa blushed. "He won't let me see it, not until it's finished."

"Well, if I were you, I'd just take the cloth off and have a peek when he's not here," Rosie declared.

"That's cheating," Clarissa exclaimed.

"I don't see why. It's a picture of you, not anyone else, so it sort of belongs to you. At least that's what I think."

"You have the same unorthodox attitude to conventional rules as your sister," Edward said pointedly.

Theo glanced at him. They'd had no chance to talk in private about the disastrous events at the Fisherman's Rest. He seemed to have forgiven her for involving him, but she knew he was curious to know what had transpired between herself and Stoneridge. She would tell him later, when she explained about the other scheme percolating in her mind. She'd need his involvement there too, but his role wouldn't require physical intervention. Once she'd explained her suspicions and her plan to him, she was convinced he would give her his wholehearted support, as he'd always done.

She leaned across and pecked him on the cheek. "Don't be stuffy."

"Someone needs to be where you're concerned," Edward said, burying his nose in his coffee cup to hide his reluctant grin.

Theo, perfectly satisfied with this response, pushed back her chair. "If Clarry has to be back in two hours, and I have to be back to look after my mama-in-law, we'd better get moving. I've no idea how long this is going to take."

A renewed chorus of *What?* rose round the table, but she just grinned mischievously and went into the hall to give order for the barouche to be brought around.

Fifteen minutes later the three of them were on their way to a discreet establishment on Bond Street.

Chapter Twenty-six

Sylvester awoke while his wife was spearing bacon in the Belmont breakfast parlor. He lay for a few minutes savoring his bodily ease and the miraculous absence of pain. His mind still retained the ghastly memories of his agony, and the memories made the present sense of well-being even more precious.

"My lord." Henry, alert to the slightest hint of movement from the bed, drew back the bed curtains, an anxious smile on his lips.

"Good morning, Henry. What's the time?"

"Past nine o'clock, sir."

"Good God!" His mind flew to Theo. He saw her face, hovering over him, her smile, those pansy-blue eyes filled with compassion and something even deeper than that. It was that something that had soothed him, had stopped his protests at her presence during his torture. He could feel her hand on his brow, cool and soft.

He sat up on his pillows. "I'm not mistaken in believing that Lady Stoneridge was in here?"

"No, my lord."

"Why the devil did you let her in?"

Henry cleared his throat. "I didn't, sir. She came through the window."

"*What?*" He remembered she'd told him she'd flown through the window, but it had meant nothing to him at the time.

He swung out of bed and strode to the window, flinging it wide onto the noisy bustle of London town waking for business. He stepped out onto the balcony, looked across at Theo's, then looked down into the street. His scalp crawled as he imagined that perilous crossing.

The woman was incorrigible. Utterly, totally incorrigible. He returned inside, shivering at the chill wind blowing through his nightshirt. "Bath, Henry."

"Right away, my lord. And breakfast." Henry hurried to the door, then paused. "Oh, her ladyship asked me to give you this as soon as you awoke." He hastened back to the secretaire and handed the earl the folded paper.

"Thank you." Just what was she up to now? Sylvester ran a hand over his unshaven chin with a grimace. "Hurry with that hot water, man."

Henry left, and the earl opened the sheet. Theo's distinctive script jumped off the page at him:

Dearest Sylvester,
Henry assured me that you'll be quite well when you awake,
or I wouldn't have left. I will be in Brook Street when you're
able to come and find me. Your mama is still asleep, so I feel
sure she won't need me for a couple of hours.
Love, Theo.

Two large impetuous-looking kisses followed the signature. He folded the letter again and placed it in a drawer in his secretaire, a slight smile curving his mouth. She had never called him "dearest" before. The whole tone of the note was different from her usual undecorative communications, and he knew Theo was incapable of dissembling her feelings. They spilled from her with the purity of the bubbling source of a mountain stream. He saw her eyes again as they'd been during those dreadful hours, and a spurt of joy shot into his veins.

Henry came in with a breakfast tray, followed by two footmen bearing a hip bath and jugs of hot water. Sylvester's nose twitched at the aroma of coffee, and he sat down hungrily to break his long fast while his bath was filled.

Theo was still going to have to go back to Stoneridge, he decided. Just until he'd sorted out Neil Gerard. Then, with the past securely behind him and no shameful revelations to fear, he would go to her and they would break new ground with this marriage.

That settled, he enjoyed a leisurely bath and shave and dressed in buckskins and top boots. Henry eased a coat of olive superfine over the powetful shoulders and handed him gloves and his hat.

Filled with the euphoric well-being that he knew as well as the hell that preceded it, Sylvester strolled down the stairs. There seemed to be no sign of his mother or his sister, he thought with guilty relief. With luck he'd be out of the house before

328

they put in an appearance.

"Have my horse brought round, Foster."

"Yes, my lord."

"With all dispatch," he added, casting an involuntary glance over his shoulder at the stairs.

Foster bowed, that glimmer of unholy amusement in his eye again. "Certainly, my lord. And what should I tell her ladyship when she comes down?"

"Uh . . . uh . . . oh, that Lady Stoneridge and I had some very important business to conduct, but that we'll join them for nuncheon," Sylvester said.

"Quite so, my lord."

"So what do you think?" Theo made a slow turn in front of Edward.

Edward stared at this extraordinary vision. "It's shocking," he said slowly.

"Yes, isn't it?" Clarry agreed. "I couldn't believe it. Emily and I just sat there like dummies while Monsieur Charles snipped away and it all fell all over the floor, yards and yards of it."

"Oh, you exaggerate," Theo said. "There wasn't that much."

"There was," Emily said. "You've never cut it, not even an inch."

"Well, I have now," Theo declared with undeniable truth. "I know it's a shock, Edward, but do you like it?" She stood on tiptoe to peer at her reflection in the mirror above the mantelpiece.

"It's very sophisticated," Edward pronounced after a minute. "And you don't look at all like yourself."

"But is that a good thing or a bad thing?" Theo demanded impatiently. "*I* like it. What do you think, Jonathan?"

Clarissa's beloved looked up from his easel, cast an abstracted eye in Theo's direction, and announced, "Clarissa must never do such a thing."

Theo raised her eyebrows, wondering if that was an answer to her question. If it was, it wasn't particularly encouraging, although judging from Clarissa's delicate flush, she had found the proscription thoroughly pleasing.

"Theo, Stoneridge has just ridden up," Emily said from the window, where she'd been gazing down onto the street.

"Ah," her sister said, coming to stand beside her at the window. Sylvester swung off Zeus, tossing the reins to an urchin who'd run up to him as soon as he'd drawn rein.

"This is going to be interesting," Theo murmured, her heart jumping with pleasure as she looked down at him, anticipating the feel of him beside her. Sylvester stood for a minute on the pavement, tapping his whip into the palm of one hand, before he strode rapidly up the steps to the front door.

Theo turned to face the parlor door, a tiny smile on her lips.

The door opened and Sylvester entered the room. Whatever he'd been about to say died at birth. He stared in disbelief at his wife. "What the *devil* have you done, Theo?" he demanded, once he got his breath back.

"Do you like it?" She tilted her head on one side, imps of mischief dancing in her eyes that seemed even larger than usual.

"Come here!"

"Do you like it?" she repeated.

"I said *come here!*"

Everyone but Theo jumped, and Clarissa flinched at this bellowed command. Theo obeyed with some alacrity.

He caught her chin, turning it from side to side to examine her profile. Then he turned her round and examined the back view. "I ought to wring your scrawny little neck," he declared finally.

"But you like my neck," she said with an air of injured innocence, turning back to face him. "Don't you think it's a sophisticated cut?"

"Yes," he said reluctantly. "But I've lost my gypsy." Theo was transformed. The raven's-wing hair now clustered in soft curls around the small head, glossy ringlets falling over her ears and wisping over her forehead. It gave an elfin look to the gamine features and accentuated the size and depth of her eyes in the most startling way.

"Oh, *Theo.*" Elinor's shocked voice came suddenly from the open door behind them.

"My sentiments exactly, ma'am," Stoneridge said dryly. "Why

330

would you do such a thing, Theo?"

"I've been meaning to for days," she said. "It is my hair, Sylvester. Mine to do with as I please."

"Did you sell it?" asked Rosie, who'd come in with Elinor.

"Sell it?" Theo looked down at the child in surprise. "Good heavens, no. What do you mean?"

"I read in the *Gazette* how you can get a lot of money by selling your hair," Rosie informed her. "Particularly if it's unusual, like yours is . . . or was," she added bluntly. "They make wigs out of it for people who don't have enough of their own."

"I've never heard of such a thing," Theo said. She shrugged. "Well, I left mine on Monsieur Charles's floor."

"Then I expect he sold it himself," Rosie said. "And he'll get all the profit. I suppose you didn't think about it because you have plenty of money. I always seem to find myself short," she said in doleful afterthought.

"On which subject, Stoneridge . . ." She turned to her brother-in-law with an air of resolution. "I still owe you that three shillings for the spider book. Would you mind if I paid it in installments? I could pay one shilling this month."

Sylvester blinked, for a moment confused. Then he remembered. "It was a gift, Rosie."

"Oh, no," she said solemnly. "I most particularly remember that it was a loan. You said my IOU would be satisfactory."

Sylvester looked distinctly embarrassed at the implication that he would take three shillings from a little girl. He felt as he had done that summer afternoon when he'd eaten her apple tartlets. "My child, I was only funning. Of course it was a gift."

Rosie considered this, then said, "Well, thank you very much, Stoneridge. I didn't quite understand that at the time." She wandered out of the room.

"Not much else you could say, really?" Theo murmured to Sylvester. "She rather put you on the spot."

"Are you saying she brought up the subject in that fashion deliberately?"

"It's hard to tell with Rosie." Theo chuckled. "But she does like to have things explained exactly, and since you didn't say it was a gift, I'm sure she genuinely assumed it was a loan."

331

"Well, it wasn't," he said, aggrieved, and wondered how long it would take him to get the hang of these complicated Belmonts. Every time he thought he was almost there, one or the other of them did or said something unfathomable.

"Do you really dislike my hair, Mama?" Theo had turned to her mother, and there was genuine anxiety in the question.

"No, I believe it suits you," Elinor said slowly. "We'll get used to it. In a day or two I'm sure we'll forget what it used to be like."

Sylvester doubted that he would. That blue-black river had been the focus of some of his most richly sensual pleasures. But Elinor was right — it *did* suit Theo.

"Clarissa, please don't move your head," Jonathan said suddenly from his corner, where he stood with his back to the wall, jealously guarding the canvas on the easel.

Clarissa murmured an apology and tried to sit still. "Couldn't I see it, Jonathan?"

"Yes, let us see it," Emily begged. "We're all dying of curiosity, and we've been so good and haven't so much as peeked when you're not here."

"An artist always keeps his canvases private until they're finished," Jonathan said, frowning. "It's customary."

"Oh, break custom, just this once." Theo crossed the room. "We know it must be wonderful. Do let us see?"

The young man flushed and laid down his brush and palette, saying hesitantly, "Well, if you really wish to —"

"We do." Theo smiled encouragingly. "Won't you turn it around?"

With an air of resolution Jonathan turned the easel to face the room. There was a moment of silence.

"Why, that's charming, Mr. Lacey," Elinor said faintly.

Sylvester felt Theo quivering with suppressed laughter and clasped the back of her neck firmly. His own countenance was severely schooled to an appropriate gravity.

Clarissa examined the portrait. "It's . . . it's very pretty, Jonathan. Does it really look like me?"

"Of course," Theo said stoutly, responding to the cue given by the warm, hard fingers on her neck. "It looks just like you

332

would look if you were a nymph in a Roman pavilion. Jonathan has the curve of your mouth exactly right, and the color of your hair."

"But why would you paint her in those funny pieces of material floating all over the place when she's wearing a perfectly pretty gown?" asked Rosie, who'd returned as vaguely as she'd left. "And if you're painting her in the parlor, why is she sitting by that fountain?"

"It's the artistic vision, Rosie," Clarissa said in vigorous championship of her knight. "Artists paint what they see."

"Well, you must have very strange eyes, Mr. Lacey," Rosie observed, taking an apple from a fruit bowl on the table and scrunching into it. "Even worse than mine."

"Don't comment on things you don't understand," Emily said, coming to the support of her sister and the now beleaguered-looking artist. "It's very beautiful, Jonathan, and I know you'll have a host of commissions when people see it. What do you think, Stoneridge?"

"Undoubtedly," the earl agreed smoothly, increasing the pressure of his fingers as Theo quivered again. "It's a most accomplished piece of work, Mr. Lacey. Don't you agree, Edward?"

"Oh, uh, certainly," Edward said hastily, trying very hard not to look at Theo.

"Why, thank you." Jonathan looked gratified at these endorsements from those who surely knew better than an impertinent child.

"Oh, I forgot to say that Dennis says nuncheon is ready. There are cheese tarts," Rosie announced through a mouthful of apple.

"Oh, good," Theo said. "I haven't had cheese tarts in ages."

"I hate to disappoint you," Sylvester said. "But we have some obligations at Curzon Street."

"Oh, yes, for a glorious minute I'd forgotten," Theo said with a groan. "We must go, Mama."

"Of course, dear," Elinor said promptly. "Do you accompany us to the Vanbrughs' rout party tonight. I'm certain Lady Gilbraith and Mary would be most welcome to join us."

Theo looked up at her husband. Sylvester smiled. "It's a long-standing engagement, my love, of course you must go. I'm certain

333

my mother won't wish to accompany you; she doesn't go about in Society much these days, and Mary is clearly in no fit condition to be gallivanting. I'm sure they'll both be glad of a quiet evening."

"Or you could entertain them?" Theo suggested.

"Unfortunately, I'm engaged elsewhere," he responded without the blink of an eye.

Theo grinned. "How surprising." She turned to Edward. "Edward, you could come for me. You wouldn't mind, would you?" She smiled at him, and he had little difficulty reading the imperative message in her eyes. Theo wanted more than his escort. Instinct told him to make some excuse, but the habits of long friendship and the knowledge that someone needed to know what she was up to had him agreeing.

"I'll come for you at nine."

Theo nodded her thanks, and Sylvester ushered her out of the house. Instructing Billy to walk Zeus back to Curzon Street, he handed Theo into her curricle and took the reins himself.

Only then did Theo give in to her laughter. "Of all the absurd fantasies," she declared. "Jonathan's made Clarry look like some simpering dryad on a chocolate box. It's the most ghastly piece of stylized pretension. He'll never make a living out of portrait painting, so we'll have to do something for them."

"Oh, I wouldn't be so sure about that," Sylvester said. "Those romantic backgrounds and classical allusions are becoming very fashionable. It wouldn't surprise me if young Mr. Lacey didn't find himself all the rage in a month or two."

"You're not serious?" Theo stared at him in mock horror. "People will *pay* for that rubbish?"

"Most certainly. I wonder how he'd choose to depict you," he mused with a wicked gleam in his eye. "Some wood sprite, I'd lay odds. All dark curls and mystery, with a hart or some such pretty woodland creature in the background."

"Over my dead body," Theo exclaimed, revolted. "I was toying with the idea of suggesting you commission a portrait of me, just to start him off, you understand, but not even for Clarry would I let him come within a mile of me with a paintbrush."

"Has he proposed to Clarissa, yet?"

"No, but he's spoken most sensibly to Mama," Theo said in accents remarkably like those of the Honorable Mrs. Lacey. "He explained how he didn't feel able to make a formal offer for Clarry until he'd sold one painting. Then he'd feel his career was really taking off." She pulled a face. "But that's never going to happen, so Clarry will have to do the proposing herself."

"Somehow I don't see Clarissa taking such a thing into her own hands," Sylvester said. "Rosie, perhaps. You, certainly. But Emily and Clarissa . . . ?" He shook his head. "Definitely not."

"Now, that's where you're mistaken," Theo asserted. "Clarry's found her knight, and it'll be snowing in hell before she lets him slip away from her."

Sylvester contemplated this in the light of what he knew of the Belmonts and was forced to conclude that, unlikely though it seemed, Theo was probably right.

They turned onto Curzon Street, and Sylvester was suddenly silent. Theo glanced at his face. His mouth was grave, his eyes cool and serious.

She waited uneasily, but Sylvester didn't say anything until he drew rein outside the house.

"Look up at the house, Theo."

Startled, she looked at the redbrick double-fronted facade of the elegant mansion. It looked no different from always.

"Look *up*," he emphasized. "There are two balconied windows up there."

Theo raised her eyes and looked at her unorthodox route to her husband's bedside. From the ground it looked utterly terrifying, even more so than when she'd been negotiating it. She cast him a rueful grimace.

"Do you have any ideas as to what we should do about you?" he inquired with mild curiosity. "I confess I've run out of inspiration."

"It looks a lot worse from down here," she said. "But I needed to get to you. I didn't really think about anything. I just needed to come to you, and so I did."

"Yes, you did." Sylvester agreed with this simple truth. Suddenly there was a warm light in the gray eyes bent upon her upturned countenance. "So you did, gypsy." He placed his hand against the curve of her cheek. "And you brought me much comfort."

Theo didn't answer, but she nestled her cheek into his cupped palm.

"That said," he continued, flicking the tip of her nose with his forefinger, "I can't help feeling I'd be failing you and neglecting my marital duty if I didn't express some legitimate husbandly wrath."

"No," Theo agreed. "Shall we agree that you have done so, and I've taken it to heart?"

"Incorrigible," he said, sighing. "Utterly incorrigible."

They must have been seen from the house, because the bootboy came running down the steps. "Shall I take the curricle to the mews, m'lord?"

Sylvester regarded the lad, who didn't look more than ten, with a surprised frown. "Can you manage them?"

"Oh, yes, m'lord. I can, can't I, Lady Theo?"

"Yes, you need have no fear, Sylvester. Timmy's dad's the head groom at the vicarage in Lulworth, but his mother wanted him to be an inside servant, so he's languishing among the boots instead of with the horses. Which is where he'd rather be, isn't that so, Timmy?" She smiled at the lad as she jumped to the pavement.

"Oh, yes, ma'am," Timmy said with a heartfelt sigh. "But it'd break me mam's heart. Leastways, that's what me dad says."

"Of course, she wouldn't need to know what you do in London," Theo said thoughtfully. "What do you think, sir?"

"I think young Timmy should take himself to the stables and ask Don to put him to work," Sylvester pronounced, resigned to a role of simple reinforcement when it came to Theo's household decisions and dispositions.

"But what of Mr. Foster, sir?" The lad's eyes grew wide with the prospect of a dream fulfilled.

"I'm sure he can find another bootboy." He ushered Theo up the steps as Timmy, crowing with delight, led the horses away.

"A messenger brought you a letter, Lady Theo." Foster's jaw dropped at her ladyship's altered appearance.

"Oh, thank you, Foster." Theo smiled at him as she took the wafer-sealed paper.

"You'll forgive the personal comment, but . . ." Foster indicated her coiffure. "Most pleasing, Lady Theo."

"Thank you, Foster." She patted his arm. "You always do know the right thing to say."

His elderly face flushed with pleasure. "Get along with you, now, Lady Theo. . . . Oh, Lady Gilbraith and Miss Gilbraith have gone to the physician on Harley Street. They took the barouche."

"Oh, that's wonderful." Theo's jubilant eyes flew to her husband's face. "I mean, I'm sure the physician will be able to help Miss Gilbraith's sniffles and her ladyship's liver . . . or whatever is troubling her." Her voice faded as she was about to find herself in realms of gross indelicacy.

"In that case we'll take nuncheon abovestairs in the little parlor," Stoneridge said into the moment of silence.

"Certainly, my lord. I'll see to it at once." Foster took himself off to the back regions with his usual stately tread.

"What if they return while we're . . . otherwise occupied?" Theo looked over her shoulder at Sylvester, her eyes now mischievous. Nuncheon in the little parlor could mean only one thing.

"Get upstairs," he ordered, pushing her ahead of him with a hand on her bottom. "Who's the letter from?"

"I don't know yet. I'll open it later." She skipped up the stairs, wondering if the message was from Neil Gerard. The handwriting was definitely masculine and unfamiliar. She hoped it was confirmation of their arrangement to drive tomorrow. If so, Sylvester mustn't know about it.

"I'll join you in a minute," Sylvester said, turning aside to his own chamber.

Theo hesitated, her hand on her own doorknob. "You're not still going to insist I go back to Stoneridge, are you?"

He regarded her thoughtfully for a minute before saying, "Can you give me your word of honor that you'll go nowhere and do nothing without my knowledge?"

Sylvester waited, then said quietly, "You have your answer, Theo." He stretched out a hand and tugged one of the ringlets clustering around her ears. "Don't look so disconsolate, love. You've been complaining about the boredom in London ever since we got here. I'll join you shortly, I promise."

She still had a few days to prove her point. She shrugged, and with relief he took her silence as acceptance.

He ran his fingers upward through the curls, flicking them around her face, saying teasingly, "I'm beginning to get used to this. In fact, it's quite an appealing little gypsy, one way or another." Catching her chin, he kissed her. "Why don't you go and put on a wrapper . . . make life easy for me for once?"

Playfully she nibbled his bottom lip. "But surely one appreciates what's hard-won much more than what comes easily."

"I wouldn't know," he said. "So far nothing's come easily where you're concerned, so I have no basis for comparison."

"Unjust!" Her tongue darted into the corner of his mouth.

He put her from him and turned back to his door. "Five minutes, and I'll expect to find you prepared to smooth my path."

Theo grinned and whisked herself into her own bedroom, imagining how best to fulfill such a demand. Unbuttoning her jacket with one hand, she broke the wafer on the letter and unfolded the sheet. It was from Gerard, who would do himself the honor of calling upon her at ten the following morning, in the hopes that she would drive with him to Hampton Court if the weather was clement. Until then he was her obedient servant.

Theo refolded the letter and slipped it into a pigeonhole in her secretaire. Gerard couldn't have chosen a better venue for her purposes.

Throwing off the rest of her clothes, she slipped into a filmy wrapper of apple-green muslin edged with lace. Sitting before her dresser mirror, she brushed her hair, enjoying the novelty of her bared neck and the lightness of her head. Her sisters had given her a small vial of perfume on her wedding morning. She rarely used it because she was always in such a hurry to get dressed that such niceties tended to be forgotten, but now seemed like an appropriate occasion. Sylvester wanted her dressed for seduction, so that was what he should have.

She put a few drops behind her ears, at her throat, and on her wrists. Then, with a little smile, she applied the delicate fragrance behind her knees and on the inside of her thighs. Where else did Sylvester like to play? Her navel, the dimpled hollows in the small of her back, the high, arched insteps of her long, narrow feet.

Deciding she must smell like a whorehouse, she cast one last glance at her reflection before leaving the room and speeding barefoot down the corridor to the small parlor overlooking the rear garden, where they spent time when they wished to be private from the household.

Sylvester was already there, pouring wine into two glasses. "No cheese tarts, I'm afraid," he said as she came in. "But there's —" The words died on his lips. Slowly, he set the glasses back on the table, his eyes narrowed as he examined her.

Dark curls clouded around her face, softening her features in a way the plain, uncompromising plaits had never done; her cheeks were aglow, her eyes banked fires at midnight; the wrapper clung to every sinuous line of her body, the narrow girdle accentuating her waist and the slight flare of her hips. London and winter weather had done away with the tanned complexion, leaving her skin the color and texture of clotted cream.

"I really have lost my gypsy," he murmured. "But just look what I have in her place."

"What?" she said, stepping toward him.

"A most beautiful woman," he replied simply. "A wayward and unruly wife, but a most beautiful woman."

"Oh, don't scold," Theo protested, coming into his arms.

"It was a statement of fact, not a scolding," he said, smiling, running his hands down her body, feeling the warmth of her skin beneath the delicate material, the ripple of muscle in her back as she reached against him.

"Take it off, Theo." There was a husky rasp to his voice, and he took a step backward from her.

Her eyes fixed on his face, she unfastened the robe and let it slip to the floor.

His eyes ran slowly down her body, devouring every inch of skin, the firm, jutting breasts, the dark nipples, growing hard and erect under his scrutiny, the flat belly, the cluster of dark curls at the apex of her long creamy thighs. Then he made a little circular motion with his forefinger, and she turned obediently. He gazed at the straight, narrow back, the pointed shoulder blades, the curve of her buttocks, the backs of her thighs, and the softness behind her knees.

He knew every inch of her body, and yet each time it was as if it were uncharted territory.

"Let's eat," he said into the silence, where lust quivered so thick one could almost touch it.

"Eat?" Theo spun round, astonishment and a touch of indignation in her eyes. "Now?"

"Now." He handed her a glass of wine, his own eyes filled with sensual amusement. "No," he said when she bent to pick up the discarded wrapper. "Stay just as you are. I want to enjoy you with my eyes for a while."

"I'm to eat naked?"

"Just so." He pulled out a chair for her. "You'll not be cold by the fire." He bent to kiss the nape of her neck as she sat down, and Theo shuddered with pleasure and anticipation.

This was something they had never done before. It felt most peculiar to sit naked in the room while he was fully clothed. Peculiar but most arousing. The fire lapped against her right thigh, and the embroidered seat of the chair was slightly scratchy under her bottom and thighs. She gave a little experimental wriggle.

Sylvester sipped his wine, watching her. "Open your thighs a little," he instructed softly.

Theo's eyes widened and her tongue touched her lips. She shifted again on the seat and bit her lip suddenly. "How can I eat?"

"You'll manage." He took another sip of wine and deliberately carved a slice from the breast of a cold chicken, placing it on her plate. "Pickled mushrooms?"

Theo nodded silently and he passed her the dish. She took a spoonful, her breasts brushing against the edge of the table as she leaned forward. Her nipples burned, and she sat back with a little gasp. "I can't do this, Sylvester."

"Yes, you can." He began to eat, watching her as he did so. "Tell me what you feel."

340

Theo took a mouthful of chicken, then gave up. This game had chased away all vestige of ordinary appetite. She leaned back in her chair, her breasts lifting on her rib cage. "Everything?" Her voice was low, her eyes a swirling riot of arousal.

"Everything."

Chapter Twenty-seven

"So you see, Edward, it won't be at all dangerous for either of us." Theo sat back in the swaying darkness of the carriage, bearing them to the Vanbrughs' rout party that evening.

Edward shook his head. "You are suggesting that you'll lead Neil Gerard into the maze at Hampton Court and get him to talk at gun point about Vimiera, while I hide behind a goddamned box hedge listening, so if he says anything incriminating, there'll be a witness? Theo, you have windmills in your head."

"It'll work," she said stubbornly. "He was at Vimiera, and he's behind these attacks on Sylvester. Now we just have to find out what really happened. Then we can tell Sylvester what we've discovered, and he can do what he wants with it. If it's enough to reopen the court-martial, then he can clear his name once and for all."

"But just why hasn't Stoneridge hit upon such a brilliant plan himself, if, as you're so certain, he knows that Neil Gerard is the man who's been trying to kill him?" Edward inquired with naked sarcasm.

"I don't know," Theo said as stubbornly as before. "I don't know because he won't tell me anything. But this *will* work — only there has to be an objective witness."

Edward sighed. "You're playing with fire, Theo. As badly as you were on Dock Street. And if Stoneridge sends you to live with his mother, I wouldn't blame him," he declared unequivocally.

"Oh, you're so infuriatingly priggish these days." Theo sat forward urgently, laying her hand on his satin-clad knee. "Nothing could be simpler. He wishes to drive to Hampton Court, and it's a perfect place. You be waiting on Curzon Street and simply follow us. Gerard will never notice a curricle behind him. And he won't notice anyone following in the general press of people at Hampton Court. My wanting to go into the maze will be the most natural thing in the world. There's no way he could harm me in such a place, and anyway, I'll be the one with the pistol."

342

"And what makes you think he won't be armed himself?"

Theo detected the beginning of a waver in her friend's opposition. "Why would he be? Besides, I don't think he's too clever."

"What makes you think that?" Edward asked glumly.

"If he had been, he'd have succeeded in killing Sylvester by now. He strikes me as thoroughly clumsy."

Edward couldn't find any argument to this terse rejoinder. However, he felt obliged to point out that even the not so bright and clumsy could be extremely dangerous. In fact, possibly more so, since they could be unpredictable.

"Yes, but we won't be in the least danger," Theo said impatiently. "How could we be, in such a circumstance?"

The carriage arrived at their destination, and Edward took advantage of the opportunity to delay his response. "I'll tell you at the end of the evening," he said, jumping down and reaching up his hand to help her alight. "But if you mention it again before we're in the carriage on the way home, I won't entertain the idea. Is that understood?"

"Yes, Edward," Theo said meekly, laying her hand on his arm, wondering why the men in her life had become such high sticklers.

Link boys were running up and down the street directing the press of carriages, and lights blazed from the open door at the head of a red carpet rolled over the pavement.

"Oh, dear," Theo said, "I do so hate these parties."

But Edward didn't seem to hear. He was trying to catch the eye of a tall gentleman in naval uniform some yards ahead of them under the awning as they proceeded to the entrance.

"Who is it?" Theo asked curiously, standing on tiptoe.

"I'm certain it's Hugo Lattimer," Edward said. "He was first lieutenant on the ship that brought me from Spain. Without his aid I'm sure I would have died. He gave me his cabin and slung his own hammock in the gun room. He was the soul of kindness, always ready to talk when I was really hipped, and his man Samuel nursed me as if I were a baby."

"Then I owe him my thanks," Theo declared. Cupping her hands around her mouth, she called, "Lieutenant Lattimer, sir?"

The tall young man turned, piercing green eyes raking the startled throng. Theo, blushing as she realized the attention she'd drawn to herself, waggled her fingers at him.

"Theo! How could you?" Edward exclaimed in a fierce whisper, but the naval officer had stepped aside from the column and was waiting for them to reach him.

"Fairfax," he said warmly, extending his hand. "It's good to see you looking so well, man."

"Oh, I'm doing well enough, Lattimer. May I introduce the Countess of Stoneridge. Theo, this is Lieutenant . . . oh, no I beg your pardon, *Captain* Lattimer. I didn't notice the epaulets, Hugo. Congratulations."

"I do beg your pardon for shouting in that indecorous way, sir," Theo said. "But I was so infected with Edward's enthusiasm that I became carried away. He was saying how good you were to him on the voyage, and since he is my very best friend, I couldn't wait to meet you and thank you."

"Your very best friend?" drawled a pleasant, slightly husky voice. "Fairfax is indeed a lucky man."

"Well, there is my husband, of course," Theo said cheerfully. "But we are friends in a rather different fashion, you should understand, sir."

"Oh, I believe I do." The naval officer's slightly startled eyes shot toward Edward.

"Theo and I have known each other since nursery days, Hugo," he said.

"That would explain it," Hugo Lattimer said. "Are you recently arrived in London, ma'am?"

"It seems we've been here forever," Theo said, finding something very comfortable about this man. It wasn't just that Edward spoke highly of him, although that would have been enough, but there was a humorous spark in his eyes and a twist to his mouth, and when he laughed, as he did now, it was a rich, merry sound. He would be about twenty-five, she decided, a couple of years older than Edward.

"That tedious, eh?"

"Precisely, sir." Laughing with him, Theo entered the house and moved to the stairs to greet Lady Georgiana Vanbrugh.

She'd hoped to spend some more time with Edward's savior, hoped even for a dance, but to her disappointment Hugo Lattimer disappeared as soon as they'd reached the ballroom. She glimpsed him once or twice throughout the evening, standing against the wall, a glass in his hand, and his expression had lost the cheerful spontaneity that had so appealed to her. In fact, he looked morose, and there were shadows in the green eyes.

She thought of approaching him herself, but there was now something strangely forbidding about him, as if he were constructing a thicket around himself.

"Captain Lattimer doesn't seem to be enjoying himself," she observed to Edward when they'd met up with Elinor and her sisters and were sitting in the supper room.

"I've never yet met a naval officer who's content when he's waiting for a new command," Edward said. "They exist on half pay and haunt the Admiralty, and twiddle their thumbs the rest of the time."

"Mmm." Theo didn't sound convinced.

"He drinks a great deal," Edward said somewhat reluctantly. "Not while he's sailing, but as soon as he's in port. I was with him at Southampton, when we landed. There's something that troubles him. He calls them painted devils."

"Oh," Theo said. "Invite him to join us, Edward."

"I don't think that's wise, Theo," Elinor said, glancing at her older daughters. "If the gentleman chooses to keep himself to himself, then we should respect that."

Her mother meant that she didn't want any inebriated visitors at her table, Theo knew, but she said no more.

As they were leaving, however, Hugo Lattimer came over to them. There was brandy sweetness on his breath and just the faintest fog in his eyes, but his voice was perfectly steady, and he was entirely coherent as he told Edward that he had a new command, a frigate on the stocks at Portsmouth. He was going down to see to her fitting in the morning, so it was farewell to Society for what he hoped was a very long spell.

He took his leave of the Countess of Stoneridge with the same easy humor of before, declined a ride in their carriage, and walked off into the night.

"You'll see Theo home, Edward," Elinor said, stepping into her own carriage.

"There's no need," Theo said. "Tom Coachman can convey me home perfectly safely. I'm sure Edward would prefer to see Emily home. There's room for him in your carriage if you all squeeze up."

Elinor looked doubtful but, since neither of her elder daughters or their swains offered any objection, decided it would have to be.

"Edward can see me to my carriage, however," Theo said. He had an answer to give her.

Edward handed her into the town chaise with the Stoneridge arms emblazoned on the panels.

"Well?" When he didn't immediately respond, she said blandly, "I'll have to go without you if you won't come."

"And I'll tell Stoneridge what you're up to," he fired back.

"You don't seriously expect me to believe that, do you?"

Edward sighed. It was, of course, inconceivable he should do such a thing. "Very well," he said with obvious reluctance. "I'll wait at the corner of Curzon Street in the morning."

"Bless you. I knew you hadn't changed that much." Theo kissed him soundly. Edward closed the door, and the coachman set his horses in motion.

While his wife was busily plotting at the Vanbrughs' rout party, the Earl of Stoneridge was at White's, playing faro at the same table as Neil Gerard. The bottles of burgundy circulated as the groom porters intoned the odds at the hazard tables, and voices rose and fell in various degrees of inebriation as the evening moved into the early hours.

Neil was playing with a degree of flamboyance, but like the earl's, his glass was always full but rarely enriched by the circulating bottles.

The earl was talking to Gerard about his imprisonment in Toulouse. His plan was a simple one, but what he knew of Neil Gerard made it certain to succeed. The man had no strength of character or will, and he was already panicked. Sylvester was going to drive him to the breaking point. He was going to corner him and goad him until he spilled his guts to whoever happened to be around.

Sylvester's tone made light of his prison experience, as the rules of masculine society dictated, and he gave the appearance of a man chatting with an old friend about something they both understood. Now and again he would muse aloud about what could have happened before he surrendered. His tone was low enough to be heard only by Neil Gerard, but it was also clear to the captain that he wasn't unduly bothered by the subject's being aired in public.

Once or twice a curious look was cast in their direction when a word or two was overheard, and Sylvester would immediately include the man in his conversation, which again he made sound as if it were perfectly innocuous.

It became clear to Gerard that this was not the man at the court-martial — a man confused and shamed by an implicit accusation against which he had no defense. And Gerard began to feel like the hunted. Only by reminding himself of his plan could he keep the panicky flutters from obscuring cool thought.

Sylvester finally rose from the table, several hundred guineas ahead of himself. "A better night next time," he commiserated with Gerard, who had been scrawling IOUs to the bank for the last half hour.

"Oh, I'll come about yet," Neil said, remaining in his seat. "The night is young."

"So it is," Sylvester said. "For some." He smiled, and Neil had a sudden vivid picture of Lady Stoneridge as she'd been in the Fisherman's Rest, vibrant, bubbling with sensuality. And as she'd been that morning, laughing white teeth, sparkling eyes, red lips. And how she'd be in the morning, when they drove to Hampton Court.

"Of course, marriage offers inducements for an early night," he said.

"Oh, Stoneridge is still a bridegroom," a man bellowed jocularly from the far side of the table. "Won't last, dear fellow. I assure you."

"I can't argue with experience," Sylvester said with a mock bow. "Nevertheless, I bid you good night, gentlemen." He strolled off, and Neil Gerard settled down to his cards with a sigh of relief. Now he'd be able to concentrate.

347

"Oh, by the by, Gerard." Sylvester was back again, smiling. Neil looked up at him. The light of a chandelier fell on the earl's face, illuminating the scar, and the gray eyes held a strange glitter. His mouth smiled, but it was a smile that sent chills along Neil Gerard's spine. "Jud O'Flannery — that was your sergeant's name, wasn't it?"

Neil could feel the color draining from his cheeks, and he imagined he could feel the blood pooling in his feet. The room spun, and black spots danced in front of his eyes. If Gilbraith found O'Flannery, he would pay whatever the blackmailer demanded for the testimony that would clear his name. He was now wealthy enough to pay a lump sum that would exceed several years of accumulated blackmail payments. Jud would jump at it.

"Perhaps you don't recall," Sylvester was saying, his voice coming from a great distance. "I'm certain it was that. It's a puzzle to know where to find him, though. Somewhere in the East End, I should think, wouldn't you?"

Neil shook his head. Even as he tried to answer with suitable carelessness, he knew his unspoken reaction had given him away. "Perhaps. I wouldn't know. He was a nasty piece of work. They probably hanged him ages ago. Either that or he's rotting in the prison hulks at Greenwich."

"Probably," agreed Sylvester casually. With a wave of farewell, he walked off.

Panic weaved a red mist around Neil Gerard. He couldn't wait. There was no time for a subtle cultivation of the lady. He would have her in his phaeton tomorrow morning; it would have to be then. He pushed back his chair abruptly, casting in his cards.

"Forgive me. I've remembered another engagement. You have my IOUs, Belton?"

Lord Belton nodded with a grunt, gathering up the papers and stuffing them into his waistcoat pocket.

Neil Gerard left White's. He had little time and a lot to do.

Sylvester strolled home, well satisfied with the evening's work. Gerard was about to break. He was like an overripe plum — one prick at the right point, and he'd split asunder.

The threat of violence would do it, of course. Gerard was a coward. He could still see him blubbering and cowering in the halls of Westminster School, begging on his knees to be left alone as the grinning circle of bullies surrounded the perfect victim of a regime of terror.

He would do anything to avoid pain. But Sylvester needed witnesses to any coerced statement, and he couldn't see himself threatening to beat Gerard to a pulp in front of the objective spectators who would be the only credible witnesses on Horseguards.

So it was a simple question of coming up with the right pressure to effect the break, and the right set of circumstances in which to engineer it.

Light shone from beneath Theo's door as he passed along the corridor. Marriage did offer inducement for abandoning the card table at a relatively early hour. Smiling, he opened the door.

Chapter Twenty-eight

Theo was still deeply asleep when Sylvester awoke in the morning. A dark ringlet tickled his nose, and he brushed it aside, propping himself on an elbow to look down on her sleeping face. She seemed peaceful enough now, but there'd been a wildness to her in the night, a fervid, almost febrile, quality to her sensual excitement. He hadn't found it cause for complaint at the time — far from it; but thinking about it now, he felt a faint flicker of unease. Was she plotting something?

Not that she'd tell him if he asked. He'd just have to try to second guess her. At the moment, innocently asleep, she presented him with no problems. Smiling, he brushed his lips over her forehead before sliding out of bed, careful not to wake her, pulling the sheet up over her bared shoulder.

Softly, he left the room in the gray light of dawn. He'd engaged to drive his mother and sister to Brook Street after breakfast; Elinor had nobly offered to accompany them on a visit to the Elgin Marbles. Later he intended to continue his goading of Neil. He could smell blood now; if only he could get the man to fall apart in one of their clubs.

Theo awoke when Sylvester was breakfasting dutifully with his mother and sister. She'd dined with them the preceding evening before going to the Vanbrughs', so felt quite justified in breakfasting in peace abovestairs. She was dressed when they left the house at nine-thirty to drive to Brook Street and watched them leave from her bedroom window, Mary swathed in a heavy pelisse, Lady Gilbraith tapping her foot impatiently on the pavement as the footman took an instant too long to open the door to the barouche.

Sylvester climbed in behind his mother and sat beside her, his expression stoic as he inclined his head to listen to what looked to the watcher above to be some considerable diatribe.

It couldn't have been a more convenient absence, Theo reflected. He'd be well out of the way when Neil Gerard came to collect her.

Critically, she examined her image in the mirror. Gerard hadn't seen her new haircut, and she had every intention of making the most of the surprise.

She wasn't planning seduction, but with cold-blooded certainty Theo knew that the more alluring she could look, the more likely she would be able to slide beneath his guard. A chip straw hat with dark-blue velvet ribbons allowed the glossy ringlets full play as they dangled over her ears and wisped on her forehead; her driving dress of blue velvet matched the ribbons; kid half boots offered a nice touch to a neat ankle. York tan gloves and fur muff completed a picture that her mother and Madame Hortense, the milliner, had gone to a deal of trouble to put together, without much help from the Countess of Stoneridge, the countess was obliged to admit. However, examining her reflection, she decided that maybe she would pay a little more attention to such details in future. They were very useful when one needed to call upon them.

She tripped lightly down the stairs, offered Foster a sunny smile, and said she would await Captain Gerard in the library. She didn't have long to wait, however, before the butler announced the gentleman in the flat tones that Theo knew denoted disapproval. Foster did not like the idea of the countess's going out with a strange man. While he wouldn't bat an eyelid at her unescorted excursions around Stoneridge and Lulworth, driving out alone with a strange gentleman through the hazardous streets of London town was another thing altogether.

"What should I tell his lordship, should he inquire your whereabouts, Lady Theo?" he asked ponderously, holding open the front door.

"Why, that I have gone for a drive with Captain Gerard," Theo said with an innocent smile. She intended to come back from this drive with her present for Sylvester, so it wouldn't matter if he knew who she was with once they were on their way. "The captain will return me safely. Won't you, sir?" The innocent smile turned arch.

"But of course, ma'am. I'm aware of how precious is my charge." He bowed, his flat brown eyes skimming over her countenance.

Theo felt a tiny prickle of unease, quickly dismissed. The toad didn't know she suspected anything. But why was he interested in cultivating her? The wife of his enemy.

And why hadn't she thought of that before? But it was too late now. She'd been so busy pursuing her own plans, she hadn't stopped to wonder why Neil Gerard should have played so neatly into her hands.

Anyway, it didn't matter. She had her pistol and Edward was following her.

Smiling, she laid her hand on Gerard's arm and allowed him to hand her into his phaeton, resisting the urge to look behind her to see if Edward's curricle was waiting at the corner.

Edward waited until the phaeton was halfway up the street, then set off in pursuit. The streets were busy, and it was easy to keep a reasonable distance behind his quarry without drawing attention to himself. They proceeded along Piccadilly and into the Strand. Edward assumed Gerard would turn down New Bridge Street and cross the river at Blackfriars, but instead he headed up Ludgate Hill.

Odd, Edward thought. Presumably he intended to cross the river at Southwark. It was eccentric, but perhaps he wished to show Theo some site or point of interest.

A brewer's dray lumbered into the road ahead of Edward's curricle, its four shires with braided manes planting their massive iron-shod hooves on the steeply rising road with noisy deliberation. Edward cursed. He still wasn't comfortable maneuvering his horses in a confined space one-handed. He was learning to hold the reins in his teeth while he directed with a flick of his whip, but it was tricky at best, and not something to be tried in a crowded thoroughfare when anything might spook one of his animals.

He was forced to hold back until the road widened a little and he was able to pull out and pass as they crossed Old Bailey. Only then did he see that the phaeton had disappeared. The dome of St. Paul's Cathedral crowned the top of the hill up ahead, and there was no sign of Neil Gerard and his phaeton.

Edward's heart began to thump with uneasy premonition. Could they have turned down toward the river, retracing their steps to Blackfriar's Bridge? Theo had disappeared in the company of a man intent on murdering her husband. He swore as the bitter taste of his own futility washed through him anew. If he'd been able to pass the dray, he wouldn't have lost them. Why had he allowed Theo to coerce him into this? He'd known it was a mistake. He knew his limitations, but he just didn't want to accept them.

He glanced to his left into the dark shadows of a narrow court, and his heart jumped into his throat. The phaeton was drawn up before a door at the rear of the court. Instinctively, Edward drove past the entrance to the court, pulling into the side of the road a few yards up the hill.

"Hey, lad!" He beckoned an errand boy carrying a basket of loaves on his head. "Hold my horses for a couple of minutes. There's sixpence in it."

"But me loaves'll go cold, guv," the lad objected. "Master'll 'ave me 'ide if 'e gets complaints."

"Two minutes, and a shilling," Edward said brusquely, clambering down.

The lad deposited his fragrantly steaming basket on the pavement and gingerly took the reins. "Don't 'old with 'osses," he muttered. "They won't bite me, will they, guv?"

"No. Just stand still with them," Edward threw over his shoulder as he ran back to the entrance to the court. Standing in the shadows, he stared into the gloomy, noisome three-sided space created by the backs of tall, narrow houses. The kennel running down the middle of the court overlowed with garbage, and the mired cobbles were thick with filthy straw.

The phaeton still stood at the door. Gerard and a massive man in a leather apron stood on the steps of the carriage, looking down into the interior.

Where the devil was Theo? Edward's heart was beating so hard, he could hear the blood roaring in his ears. The big man bent and hoisted something into his arms. Edward felt sick as he stared helplessly at the scene, recognizing the unresisting bundle the man threw over his shoulders.

What had they done to her? Why hadn't she used her pistol? He took a hasty step into the court and tripped over a bundle of sacking that cursed vilely. Looking down, he saw a pair of hollow, burning eyes glaring at him, filled with a malevolence that sent chills down his spine. A clawlike hand in fingerless mittens clutched a stone jar.

"Gi' us a shillin', guv." Edward stepped back as the fetid stench of stale gin exuded from a toothless cavern. The claw reached out and seized his ankle. Edward kicked out, fighting a moment of panic as he felt himself unbalanced, with only one free leg and one arm. If he went down to these slimy cobbles, he'd have the devil's own job to get to his feet again, and he couldn't afford to draw the attention of Neil Gerard or his henchman.

The fingers slipped from him, and with another foul curse, the shape huddled into its sacking again, lifting the stone jar to its mouth.

The man carrying Theo had disappeared through the now open door, and Gerard was following. Edward turned and ran back to his curricle. The lad greeted him with a grin of relief, took his shilling, touched his cap, heaved his basket of bread onto his head again, and went off whistling.

Edward sat for a moment fighting with himself. His blood ran hot with rage, urging him to burst into that house and wrest Theo from her captors. But he knew he was no match for one man, let alone Gerard and that massive ruffian, even if Theo were conscious and able to help. He had to get help.

He turned the curricle with a skill born of desperation and drove as fast as he would have done with two good arms along Fleet Street and the Strand. He had no idea where he would find Stoneridge, and beneath this urgent need lurked the terror of what they were doing to Theo at the moment. What if they moved her while he was away? If they got back to that house in Hall Court and found it deserted? The thought of the vast maze of London streets hammered in his fevered brain. She could vanish into that maw without a trace.

He made a tight turn onto Haymarket, shaving the varnish of a landau and hearing the indignant bellow of the coachman and the squeals of the vehicle's female occupants. His horses tossed their heads, sensing that the hand on the reins wasn't really steady enough for this pace, and he forced himself to pull back on the reins a little. And then he saw Jonathan Lacey on the other side of the street, strolling casually in the sunshine.

Edward hailed him but without immediate result. He drew rein and bellowed again in an agony of urgency. He couldn't drive across the stream of oncoming traffic. Jonathan would have to come to him. But still Clarissa's swain continued to stroll on, his head presumably full of idyllic settings for his sugary portraits, Edward thought viciously. Standing up, he yelled with the full force of his lungs. The other man stopped, looking around him in puzzlement.

"Jonathan!" Edward's voice was hoarse as he waved frantically, finally catching the artist's eye.

Jonathan waved back with an amiable smile and looked for a minute as if, greeting made, he were about to continue his walk. Edward beckoned furiously, and finally Jonathan got the message. He stood on the pavement looking both ways, waiting an eternity for an ambling tilbury to pass, before he crossed.

"Good morning, Fairfax." He greeted Edward, looking somewhat puzzled at the imperative summons.

"I need you to find Stoneridge and give him a message," Edward said without preamble. "Immediately, Jonathan."

"Find Stoneridge?" The young man blinked. "But where would I find him?"

"I don't know." Edward struggled to hang on to his patience. "If he's not at Curzon Street and Foster doesn't know, try his clubs, or Mantons, or Gentleman Jackson's. Someone will know where he is."

"He was at Brook Street earlier," Jonathan said vaguely. "But he left before I did."

"Then that's not much help, is it? Now, listen, when you find him, tell him to meet me at Hall Court, off Ludgate Hill. Tell him it's of the utmost urgency and he must come prepared."

"Prepared for what?" Jonathan blinked again.

"He'll know what I mean," Edward said. "Now, don't delay. Can you remember the address?"

"Hall Court, off Ludgate Hill," Jonathan said promptly. "But this is most inconvenient, Edward. I have an engagement with a lady from whom I have every expectation of securing a commission."

355

Edward's mouth tightened, and the other man quailed at the look that sprang into the usually benign eyes. "If you're intending to marry Clarissa, Lacey, you'll have to learn the cardinal Belmont rule — we help each other before we help ourselves," he declared with ice-tipped clarity. "Now, *find Stoneridge!*"

Without waiting to see how Jonathan responded to this ferocious command, he backed his horses into an alley and turned back the way he'd come, driving his horses through the crowds as heedlessly as before.

Jonathan lifted the curly brim of his tall beaver hat and scratched his head. Then he shrugged and set off toward Mayfair. St. James's was as good a place as any to begin his search.

He drew a blank at Brooks's and Watier's, but the footman at White's acknowledged that Lord Stoneridge might be on the premises. He left Jonathan kicking his heels in the hall and sailed up the gilded staircase to the coffee room.

Stoneridge looked up from his conversation with Major Fortescue as the footman coughed at his elbow. "Well?"

"There's a young gentleman inquiring after you, my lord. Should I deny you?"

"That rather depends on the identity of the young gentleman." Sylvester raised an eyebrow.

The footman extended the silver tray with a card. "Now what the devil does young Lacey want with me?" Sylvester said, frowning. "You'd better send him up."

Jonathan appeared in the doorway a minute later. He stood looking round with every appearance of fascination, then flushed slightly as several gentlemen raised eye glasses and stared fixedly at the inquisitive intruder in this exclusive salon. He made his way hastily across the room, tripping over a small spindle-legged table in his embarrassment, righting it swiftly, only to catch his toe in the fringe of a Turkey carpet.

"It is something of an obstacle course, I agree," Stoneridge observed. "Pray sit down, Mr. Lacey, before the obstacles get the better of you."

"Your pardon, Lord Stoneridge." Jonathan mopped his brow with a large checkered handkerchief. "But I have been looking all over for you."

The first faint prickles of unease crept over Sylvester's scalp. "I'm flattered," he said calmly.

"Fairfax sent me with a message. A matter of the utmost urgency. I'm not at all sure what it could mean."

The prickles ran rampant up and down his spine. "It's to be hoped *I* shall. Pray continue."

"He wishes you to meet him at Hall Court, off Ludgate Hill — I believe that's correct. Oh, and he said to come prepared. He said you would know what that meant."

"Indeed, I do." Sylvester rose, no sign on his face of his inner turmoil. "Obliged to you, Lacey." He nodded briefly. "You'll pardon me, Peter."

"Of course. Anything I can do?"

But the offer was made to the earl's back as he strode from the salon.

What the *hell* trouble was Theo in now? He couldn't begin to imagine, and speculation was terrifyingly futile. His unease that morning had obviously been justified.

Concentrating only on immediate plans, he strode back to Curzon Street, where he thrust a pair of dueling pistols into his belt, dropped a small silver-mounted pistol into his pocket, tucked his sword stick under his arm, and slipped a wicked stiletto-bladed knife into his boot. Edward had said to come prepared.

He would make faster time on horseback, and within ten minutes he was galloping Zeus toward the Strand.

Theo swam upward through a murky pond where weeds snatched at moments of lucidity and waves kept tumbling her back into the dark world below. But slowly, her mind cleared and her eyes opened. Her head was pounding as if half a dozen hammers were at work, and gingerly she turned sideways on the pillow, feeling at the back of her head for the source of the hammers. Her fingers encountered a lump the size of a gull's egg.

She was feeling sick and giddy, and her eyes could make no sense of her surroundings. Something heavy was round her right ankle, and experimentally she moved her leg. There was a heavy clunking sound, and whatever it was rasped painfully

357

against her ankle bone.

The dark waters of the pond closed over her again, but this time she fought back, dragging herself upward into the light. It was a dim light, but the fog was clearing from her mind despite the continued pounding in her head.

Someone, and it hadn't been Neil Gerard, had hit her on the back of the head. They'd been driving up Ludgate Hill. She'd said that it seemed a strange route to take when they should be crossing Blackfriar's Bridge. Gerard had smiled and said he had something of interest to show her.

Then they'd turned aside into that reeking, gloomy court. And like the dumb fool she was, she still hadn't grasped what was happening. She'd sat there like a gaby a minute too long before going for her pistol, and someone had hit her from behind.

Without much hope she felt in her pocket. No pistol. Sylvester was right, Theo thought disgustedly. She was a naive, impetuous baby who needed all the protection and surveillance a caring and watchful husband could give her. If she ever got out of this situation in one piece, she'd lock herself in her room and give him the key!

Struggling up onto one elbow, she surveyed her surroundings. It was a small room lit only by a grimy skylight. She was lying on a narrow cot, on a straw palliase covered with rough striped ticking. Apart from this there was a table and chair, and a small coal fire burning in the hearth.

There was a chain around her ankle. Her right leg was shackled to the bed. Sitting up properly, Theo stared in disbelief; then she reached down, ignoring the pounding in her head, and lifted the chain. It was heavy, but it seemed long enough to allow her to get off the cot. Carefully, she stood up; her head swam, and cold perspiration broke out on her forehead as a wave of nausea washed over her. She sat down again and waited for the moment to pass.

Then, with renewed effort, she stood up and took a step toward the table in the middle of the room. The chain had sufficient play to enable her to get that far. There was a carafe of water on the table, and she drank thirstily. The cold liquid helped to clear her mind even further, and she continued her investigation of her prison.

She dragged the chain to the door. There were heavy bolts at the top and bottom on the inside — useful should she decide to lock herself in. Again without much hope, she raised the latch. It came up sweetly, and the door swung open onto a narrow passage. Her heart lifted and she stepped forward, only to discover she was at the limit of her chain, and the links bit into her ankle bone.

Theo pulled the door closed again and returned to the bed. Her foot kicked something as she sat down. At least Gerard or his assistant had provided her with a chamber pot. But what did they want with her?

There came the sound of footsteps in the passage outside, and instantly she lay down again, closing her eyes. It might be useful to pretend she was still unconscious, at least until she had a better sense of what was intended.

Gerard came into the room, closing the door behind him. He trod softly to the cot and stood looking down at the white-faced, unconscious figure. He laid a hand on her brow and was relieved to find her skin warm. Dan didn't know his own strength, and Neil had been afraid the blow had been unnecessarily hard. He needed the Countess of Stoneridge alive and well when it came to negotiating with her husband.

He allowed his gaze to roam over the still body. The soft rise and fall of her breasts, the way her skirt clung to her flat belly. The hem was rucked up, showing the curve of her ankle and calf. He bent and pushed it up a little farther, remembering the vibrant sensuality that had so struck him when he'd first laid eyes on her. His hand slid up her silken-clad leg beneath her skirt and petticoat. A madness seemed to have entered him. There was something incredibly exciting about having this immobile, unaware body at his disposal. His fingers insinuated themselves into the leg of her drawers, creeping upward over the warm skin.

And then there was a loud banging at the door. With a muttered curse he jerked his hand away and straightened.

" 'Ow is she?" Dan's huge head appeared around the door. "Awake yet?"

"Not as yet." Gerard moved casually away from the cot. "Send that girl of yours to me. To the front room."

"Fancy a bit, do ya?" Dan chuckled and his red eyes leered. "Well, you do good by 'er, an' I've no objections. I'll listen out fer yon missie fer a spell."

Gerard said nothing but drew his arm sharply aside as he passed so that he wouldn't brush against the man. Dan's sneering chuckle followed him as he went to the front room that he'd once occupied, to await the scrawny maidservant he'd used there before to ease his hunger pangs.

Chapter Twenty-nine

Theo opened her eyes, once she was sure she was alone. She was shuddering from head to toe, her skin where he'd touched her crawling as if it were alive with slugs leaving their sticky trail. The sense of violation was so powerful, she wanted to retch. She'd been too shocked and too disoriented to resist, and by the time she'd recovered from her shock, it had stopped. But he wouldn't do it again.

She got up and rinsed out her mouth, then dipped her finger into the water and scrubbed at her flesh where his fingers had been. Her head still ached, but it was an almost irrelevant discomfort now. She had to get out of there.

Had Edward seen what had happened? He'd not have been able to do anything single-handed, but perhaps he'd gone for help. But whether he had or not, she must still help herself.

When Gerard returned, he would find her wide awake and composed, and if he attempted to touch her again, he'd get more than he bargained for.

Presumably, he had the key to the chain somewhere on his person.

Then she knew what she had to do. He wouldn't find her wide awake and composed. He would find her just as he'd left her. With her skirt hiked up, her body defenseless and inviting. And when he approached and bent over her, she'd be ready for him.

Sylvester rode up Ludgate Hill, looking for Hall Court. He saw Edward's curricle first, drawn to the side of the thoroughfare and in the hands of an urchin who stood holding the reins, idly picking his teeth.

Edward was standing in the shadows at the entrance to Hall Court, his eyes fixed to the door through which Theo had been carried.

"Thank God Jonathan found you," he breathed as Sylvester dismounted beside him. "I believe she's still in there. Gerard's phaeton is still there, at least."

"Gerard? What's Theo doing with that sewer rat?"

Edward, looking wretched, said, "She thought he might have the truth about Vimiera."

Sylvester whitened. "You?"

Edward nodded in acute discomfort. "I hadn't intended to, sir. It was gossip I heard in the Peninsula, and of course I didn't believe it, but somehow Theo . . ." He shrugged. "After Lady Belmont's reception she guessed something and, well, she wormed the story out of me. She didn't believe it anymore than I did."

So the secret he'd been so desperately trying to keep had been no secret at all. Fairfax had known all along and never given him the slightest indication. And Theo had known for days, and it hadn't mattered one iota to her. She simply hadn't believed it. He should have known, of course. He just hadn't trusted enough.

A joy of such piercing intensity almost took his breath away; then he said briskly, "So tell me how she got herself into this mess."

He listened to Edward's tale in growing incredulity and then wondered why he was incredulous. It had Theo's mark all over it. She'd asked the right people the right questions and drawn her own correct conclusions, then simply plunged headlong into a situation that he already had well under control.

"What am I going to do?" he demanded, almost a cry of despair, when Edward fell silent. "Just what the devil am I going to do?"

Edward stared at him, clearly wondering if he was in the grip of temporary insanity. "Why, we must go in and rescue her."

"Yes . . . yes," Sylvester said impatiently. "That's the least of my problems. I mean, what in God's good grace am I to do about Theo?"

"Oh." Edward nodded his comprehension. "Well, people who know Theo well, sir, tend to do what she thinks best. Rather in the manner of Mohammed and the mountain, if you follow me."

"Oh, I follow you, Edward," he said. "And just look what letting her do what she thinks best leads to."

Edward shook his head and said tentatively, "As to that, sir, I think you're mistaken, if you'll forgive my saying so. Theo

362

wanted to prove to you that she's capable of helping you and that she deserves your confidence. If you had taken her into your confidence, she wouldn't have gone off on her own like this. She would have expected you to involve her, and she would have followed your lead."

Sylvester glared into the shadows of the court, wrestling with what he recognized as the truth. If he'd trusted in her responses from the beginning, they would all have been spared a mountain of grief and trouble. It was time to throw in the towel. If he didn't involve Theo, she would involve herself; she would find out whatever she wanted to discover, and it seemed as if he couldn't do a damn thing about it. God knows, he'd given it his best shot.

She wanted a damn partnership, and it looked as if he'd acquired a partner whether he wanted one or not.

A tiny smile touched his eyes. Of all the possible repositories of his confidences, he couldn't think of any more honest and reliable than his forthright gypsy. And at least, if he was directing operations, she wouldn't shoot off on lethal tangents with only half the facts.

"How shall we get in, sir?" Edward's urgent voice brought him back to the reality of Ludgate Hill, where behind them ordinary life continued in the busy thoroughfare, and in front of them lay the dank court and a world of shadows.

"Knock on the door, of course," Sylvester said calmly. "Do you prefer a sword stick or a pistol?"

"Sword stick," Edward said promptly. "I find I can fence one-handed with little difficulty, and I won't have to worry about reloading."

"Right." Sylvester handed him the stick and drew the two dueling pistols from his belt. "I've a knife and pocket pistol as well, so I think we're armed to the teeth, my friend."

His tone was light, but it didn't conceal the murderous fury in his eyes. He didn't believe Gerard intended serious harm to Theo; it would benefit him nothing. But he had hurt her already, if Edward was right, and he was going to pay in blood.

"I'll knock first. You keep behind me so they don't see you," he said in a low voice as they approached the door. "When I step forward, jump in behind me."

Upstairs, in the room with the skylight, Theo was lying very still on the cot, breathing evenly and deeply, waiting for the moment when Gerard would come back. The door had opened once in the five or ten minutes since he'd been gone, and she'd felt someone's eyes on her, but whoever it was hadn't come close. How long would it take Gerard to finish with the girl in the front room? Not long, she thought. The exchange with the other man had given the impression that he was after a swift, un-ceremonious satisfaction of an immediate need.

Her muscles surged with energy now; her mind, despite the continued pounding of her head, was crystal clear; and it was very hard to feign unconsciousness. She went over the moves in her head. Which ones she used would depend on Gerard's position when he came close enough.

Then the door opened. She felt her eyelids flutter and forced herself into total immobility, although her muscles ached with the effort.

Gerard approached the bed. She was lying exactly as he'd left her, the hem of her skirt pushed up above her knee, high enough to show the frilled leg of her drawers. Five minutes with the scrawny maidservant had slaked his immediate hunger, but ex-citement still stirred at the image of the Countess of Stoneridge, chained to the bed, available.

What kind of woman was it who went for a drive to Hampton Court bearing a pistol? The same woman, of course, who ventured alone into the twilight world of London's dockland. Had she suspected him in some way?

Not that it mattered now. He had her exactly as he wanted her, and he was going to keep her here for two days, after which her reputation would be ruined if he chose to make it so. If Stoneridge chose to make it so, he corrected himself with a sat-isfied smile. If the lady's husband refused to toe the line — an unthinkable possibility.

But while he had her here, why shouldn't he enjoy her anyway — make the scandal a true one? His tongue darted, moistening his lips. Stoneridge wouldn't be able to retaliate, not when Gerard held his written confession of cowardice over his head. But the

Countess of Stoneridge wouldn't tell her husband what had occurred anyway. No woman, even one as foolhardy as this one, would voluntarily admit to her husband that she'd had carnal knowledge of another man, even if it was coerced. It would give any man a disgust of his wife.

He stood at the foot of the cot, looking up her body.

Come closer. For pity's sake come closer. The chant went round and around in Theo's head. If she weren't hampered by the chain, she could use her legs, but she daren't risk missing the only chance she would have.

She shifted slightly on the rough ticking, moving one leg restlessly so that her thighs were slightly parted.

She heard Gerard's breathing grow heavier. Then she sensed the warmth of his flesh. It was as if every pore and cell of her skin was acutely sensitized. She could feel rather than see the shadow of his body behind her closed eyelids. *Wait. Wait.*

Then she knew he was close enough. Her fingers went for his eyes as she lunged forward in one smooth movement. Gerard screamed, falling back on the bed, fingers blindly worrying at his eyes, and Theo swung her body up and over him bringing the slack of the chain across his throat as she maneuvered herself onto her feet at the foot of the bed.

The sounds of violent banging filled the narrow house. Feet thudded. Gerard lay half-strangled by the weight of the chain across his Adam's apple, one hand still covering his eyes that miraculously remained in their sockets.

Theo was breathing heavily, her face damp with perspiration, but exhilaration surged through her veins. She listened to the commotion and guessed it was Edward. Not alone, of course. Which meant Stoneridge, who would discover that she'd rescued herself. Or at least partially. Whether that would count in her favor remained to be seen. Her grand scheme lay in ruins, bungled by her own incompetence and impulsiveness. Stoneridge was entitled to take what reprisals he chose.

"Give me the key," she demanded, jerking her leg so the chain tightened.

Gerard gasped, choked, scrabbled wildly at his coat, trying to find the inside pocket. A pistol shot cracked from downstairs and someone cried out, a shrill, high-pitched screech.

"Hurry," she said coldly, contempt mingling with the icy rage in her eyes. "Or I'll begin to take a little walk around this pretty chamber. I certainly owe you some grief . . . although I doubt you're worth the effort."

His fingers closed over the key and he dragged it forth, waving it at her.

"Thank you." Theo took the key, then reflected that when her husband found her, she was going to need all the help she could get, and she presented a very arresting picture with her captor held by the chain in this way, immobilized for whatever Sylvester might decide to do with him. "Perhaps I won't use it just yet." She folded her arms and faced the door as it burst open.

Sylvester took in the scene in one swift glance. Sweet relief seeped through his pores. Whatever they'd done to Theo, she was none the worse for wear. A glint of laughter appeared in his gray eyes as Theo put her head on one side in her habitual unspoken challenge, although he could detect a slightly apprehensive question mark in her gaze.

"Well, well, my dear," he drawled. "It seems you had no need of knights errant after all."

"I haven't exactly managed to get out of the house," Theo pointed out, anxious he shouldn't feel his efforts were unappreciated. Matters were tricky enough as it was.

"No, but perhaps you haven't had sufficient time," he said smoothly. "I can't imagine another reason."

Edward's chortle turned into a violent coughing fit.

"How did he hurt you?" Sylvester asked, and there was no amused drawl in his voice now.

Theo gingerly touched the back of her head. "Somebody hit me . . . but it wasn't that slimy piece of flotsam."

Sylvester nodded. "I'll still add it to the account. Secure the door, would you, Edward? I have some business to conclude, and I would hate to be interrupted."

He snapped his fingers for the key to the chain, and Theo handed it over. She wasn't at all sure how to read her husband in this mood. There was something infinitely dangerous about him, but she didn't feel threatened herself. Wisdom, however, dictated a course of passive compliance for the next minutes.

Edward bolted the door and stood with his back to it, the sword stick held lightly in his hand. There was blood on its tip, Theo noticed absently as the key turned in the shackle and her ankle was released.

Sylvester took the freed end of the chain and jerked it. "Time for a little chat, Gerard," he observed pleasantly. "Edward, would you take note of everything that is said in this room?"

"That was my plan," Theo said, forgetting her resolution of a minute ago in this opportunity to salvage something of her grand design. "It's a good one, I believe."

"I'll deal with you later, gypsy. If you wish to minimize what's coming your way, you'll hold your tongue."

That was rather more along expected lines, but Sylvester never called her gypsy when he was truly displeased. Thoughtfully, Theo went to stand beside Edward, who grinned at her, his eyes glowing with jubilation. "I haven't lost my touch," he whispered against her ear, indicating the bloody sword stick.

"You were always a superb fencer," she said, smiling, kissing his cheek by way of congratulation. "Did you kill him?"

Edward shook his head. "No, merely pinked him, but it certainly stopped him in his tracks. He was wielding an ugly-looking cudgel."

"Let us return to Vimiera, Gerard," Sylvester was saying. He wrapped the chain round his wrist and moved behind the bed. "There's something I believe you want to tell me."

There was silence from the bed. "Come, now," Sylvester said softly. "You're not going to make this any harder on yourself than you must. I know you too well, Gerard. What was it?" The chain jerked again.

Gerard's voice rasped from the cot. "You were outnumbered."

"As we'd been all day." All expression left Sylvester's voice now, and he seemed no longer aware of either of his listeners. He was standing in a dank, ill-lit chamber off Ludgate Hill, but in memory he was back on a scorched plain, looking into the Portuguese sunset and the ever-advancing line of the enemy.

The line of French was coming up at them. His men were

firing into the sunset. Sergeant Henley's face hung in his internal vision. He was saying something urgently. Telling him something he'd been expecting. *They had two rounds of ammunition left.* They could maybe beat off this attack, but after that they would be helpless.

Where the hell was Gerard? He was looking across the flat plain ringed by hills. A slice of blue sea peeped between two of the lower hills. Behind him was the bridge that he had to hold. Gerard would bring his reinforcements over that bridge.

Sylvester stared at the gibbering, craven wretch on the bed, but he barely saw him. His mind was racing across the red-tinged barren landscape of a Portuguese plain. Memories crowded in now — faces, snatches of conversation, the frustration and helplessness as he faced the prospect of losing now, after a long day of battling the odds, buoyed by the certainty of support hurrying to their aid. Now they were going to be defeated, and the lives of the boys lying on the scratchy earth round him had been expended in vain.

The void of amnesia was filling rapidly, like an empty bucket in a rainstorm. The face of the young ensign who'd been acting lookout in the topmost branches of a spindly tree appeared before him. The lad's eyes were wild, and he was out of breath after his mad dash from his post. He could barely speak as he brought forth his unbelievable message: Redcoats had appeared on the high ground beyond the bridge. He'd seen the sunlight flash off a glass as someone had surveyed the battleground before them. Then they'd disappeared.

Sylvester had been unable to grasp this message. He'd made the lad repeat himself. He'd told him that heat and fear had addled his brain, ruined his eyesight. But the ensign had stuck to his story.

They'd been abandoned. Captain Gerard's reinforcements were not coming. *Why?* And even as he'd been wrestling with this, the young ensign at his side had fallen, a musket ball through his throat, and the horde of French were racing across the plain screaming their war cry: *Vive l'Empereur.* And he'd ordered his men to lay down their now useless arms. Only the ensign and Sergeant Henley knew that the reinforcements were not coming.

And the sergeant had died under a French bayonet.

And at the court-martial Neil Gerard had said that he was coming up in support, but for some reason, a reason lost in the mists of amnesia, Major Gilbraith had surrendered his colors by the time the reinforcements had arrived. The captain's force had chased the French across the plain but hadn't been able to overtake them.

The bright light of memory flooded Sylvester's brain, and he felt as if some massive weight had been lifted from his spirit. Neil presumably assumed that Sylvester knew nothing of his retreat. It was only the sharp eyes of an ensign and an unlucky ray of sun that had given him away. All he'd had to do at the court-martial was insist he'd been following the orders they'd all received, and Major Gilbraith, with no living witnesses to his decision and convicted by his own actions even if his motive remained a mystery, couldn't gainsay him. But why had he then tried to kill him?

"Yes," he said, his voice startling in the dreadful silence that had fallen in the room. "Yes, we were outnumbered and you turned your back on us."

"We saw you. There was nothing we could do. Behind the hill facing you, there were three more regiments of French." Gerard was babbling now. "I had only a hundred and fifty men. We'd be slaughtered with the rest of you if we came up in support. Damn it, Sylvester, headquarters didn't know what they were asking."

"Yes, they did," Sylvester stated flatly. "If you'd come up, we could have held the bridge for the two hours necessary before the main army arrived. We were running out of ammunition, Gerard." His voice now was as deadly as a rapier thrust. "It was all that kept us from continuing."

"No. You're fooling yourself." Gerard's voice rose to a pitch of desperate conviction. "We'd all have been slaughtered. You were on the plain, you couldn't see what I saw from the hill."

"So you cut and ran," Sylvester said. "And we were destroyed and the colors were lost, and the bridge was lost. Quite a record of achievement one way and another. But tell me" — his voice became almost confidential — "just why did you need to kill

369

me? You'd ruined me, forced my resignation from the regiment. Why try to deliver the coup de grâce?"

Fear blossomed anew in Gerard's flat brown eyes. "My sergeant," he mumbled.

"Ah . . . ," Sylvester said slowly. "O'Flannery, wasn't it? Was he blackmailing you, Gerard?"

There was no answer from the bed, and Sylvester's face twisted in an expression of revulsion. He spun suddenly to face Edward, and his eyes were living coals beneath the blue-tinged scar. "Did you hear all that, Fairfax?"

"Yes, sir. Every word." Edward almost stood to attention, and Theo shrank back against the door, suddenly wishing to make herself invisible. Whatever was going on now in this room among the three of them was outside her own experience. It dealt with a world whose perils and rules she knew nothing about.

Sylvester nodded. He released the chain, and as Gerard struggled up on the bed, he took off his coat. Very deliberately, he began to roll up his sleeves. "Take Theo downstairs and wait for me in the curricle, Fairfax. I have some unfinished business that I believe I am going to enjoy."

Gerard's face was the color of whey as he sat massaging his throat, watching mesmerized as the powerful forearms were revealed, watching as Stoneridge flexed his hands, pulled at his fingers to loosen the joints.

Theo knew she couldn't let this happen, whether she understood the ramifications of the issue or not. She had no sympathy for the despicable Gerard, her skin still crawled at the memory of his touch, but she knew that if Sylvester yielded to his murderous need for vengeance, something dreadful and irretrievable would happen. And it would live with him forever.

She moved forward, laying a hand on her husband's arm.

He turned his pale anger onto her, and she flinched from it, but she said, "Sylvester, I know what you're feeling. I know you feel it's owed you, but you have what you came for. You'll kill him. He's no match for you — look at him. He's a louse; no, Rosie would say that's disparaging lice. He's despicable and a coward, but he's not worth your vengeance. What satisfaction will you get from pounding such a creature to a pulp?"

370

Slowly, Sylvester came back to the room on Ludgate Hill. He looked into Theo's impassioned eyes and heard her wisdom. He had been at the brink of control, and he knew that once his bare fist had smashed into the brittle bones and thin skin of the coward that was Neil Gerard, he would have lost himself in an orgy of blood vengeance for that eternity of confused shame and hideous self-doubt.

"Please," Theo said, softly now, reaching up to touch his cheek. "It's over, love. Let it go. I'm here, I'll help you."

He allowed himself to slide into the deep-blue pools of her eyes, to receive the balm of her words. He saw in her eyes what he'd seen when she'd been at his bedside during his agony, and slowly, the long anger slid from him. He clasped her wrist as she continued to stroke his cheek.

"Yes," he said with a twisted smile. "You're here, gypsy. And you're going to help me whatever I do or say."

"You married a Belmont," Theo responded, with a smile of her own now as she heard his changed tone and saw the light in his eye. "It goes with the territory. Like it or not."

He caught her chin, fixing her gaze with his own. "I find I like it." Bending his head, he brushed her lips with his own in a kiss as delicate as the flutter of a butterfly's wings. "And we have much to talk about, madam wife."

Theo simply nodded.

Edward said somewhat hesitantly, "Perhaps you should take the curricle, and if you'll trust your horse to me, sir, I'll ride him back to Curzon Street and pick up the curricle there."

"That sounds like a good plan," Sylvester said coolly. He picked up his coat, glancing at the cot where Gerard still cowered. "I suggest you take an extended trip abroad. I shan't press for a new court-martial, but it won't be necessary once Lieutenant Fairfax has reported your confession at Horseguards."

He put on his coat and for a moment toyed reflectively with one of the dueling pistols. "I'd challenge you, but a man doesn't match his honor against a coward. Come, Theo." He swept her ahead of him out of the dingy chamber and down the stairs. A scared face peeped out at them from a door in the lightless lower hall. A door that Theo noticed had a bullet hole in it.

She thought of the blood on Edward's sword and wondered how many people in this malodorous hole were licking wounds. No one hindered their departure at all events.

Sylvester tossed Theo up into the curricle and sprang up after her. "Edward, we'll see you later." He leaned down, holding out his hand. "A man couldn't wish for a sounder ally."

"What about me?" Theo demanded with a touch of indignation. "I'm a *very* sound ally."

"That is a matter for further discussion," her husband said, failing lamentably to hide a broad grin. "Stand away from their heads, lad."

The urchin jumped back, catching the half sovereign as it flew through the air toward him, and the horses plunged forward.

"I'm as sound an ally as Edward," Theo insisted, prepared to capitalize on circumstances, now that things had turned out so favorably. "My plan took an unexpected turn, I grant you, but the result was the same. You have your confession and an objective witness."

"True," Sylvester agreed, adding pointedly, "How's your head?"

"A bit achy," she confessed. "All right, so it didn't turn out right, but I couldn't think of anything else to do."

"No," he said. "In the circumstances, I can quite see that."

"I love you," Theo said, just in case he was still missing the point.

"Yes, I know," Sylvester responded quietly. "And I've loved you since I first laid eyes on you. You've tried my patience almost beyond bearing on many occasions, sweetheart, but never my love." He looked down at her, the stern lines of his face softened, the once cool eyes aglow. "Never in my wildest dreams, or do I mean my craziest nightmares, did I imagine falling hopelessly in love with a passionate, wayward, managing, and unruly gypsy. But that's what happened."

Theo smiled, thinking of her grandfather. Whatever had really been behind the conditions of his will, he wouldn't have intended to hurt her in any way. Had he perhaps heard something of this Gilbraith . . . something that made her believe he would make his granddaughter happy? He was such a devious old man, it wouldn't surprise her to discover that he'd set out to learn about his heir from the moment of Kit Belmont's death. But whatever the truth, the outcome would have pleased him as it pleased everyone else — and brought his granddaughter such sweet joy.

She moved her thigh so that it pressed hard against her husband's and allowed her head to drop onto his shoulder, a deep peace filling her, as if she'd been relieved of the most enormous weight.

They drew up in front of the house, and Sylvester jumped down as young Timmy came running to take the horses. Sylvester lifted Theo down and carried her up the steps and into the house.

"Is everything all right, my lord?" Foster asked in concern. Theo, despite her bravado, was looking rather wan.

"It will be," Sylvester said. "Tell Dora to bring a cold compress and arnica up to Lady Theo's bedroom."

Foster's air of concern deepened. "Yes, right away, my lord. Lady Emily, Lady Clarissa and Lady Rosie are awaiting your return in the library."

"Oh, well, bring it to the library in that case." Sylvester turned aside with his burden.

"Whatever's happened?" Emily jumped up as they came in. "Theo, you're as white as a ghost."

"Oh, it's nothing," Theo said hastily. "I . . . I . . . uh . . . I tripped on the pavement and fell in front of an oncoming carriage, but Sylvester managed to pull me back in time."

Her husband made no comment, and only Rosie noticed the raised eyebrow and the slight twitch of his lips as he settled Theo on a sofa.

A footman came in with the required items and set them on a low table beside the sofa. They all waited in silence until he'd bowed himself out. Sylvester was aware of an air of suppressed excitement in the room as he moved behind Theo and delicately parted her hair at the base of her skull, feeling for the lump.

Theo was aware of it too. "What is it?" she demanded of her sisters. Clarissa in particular was bubbling with exuberance.

"Oh, Theo, Jonathan has a splendid commission to paint Lord Decatur's daughter, so he's asked Mama for my hand and she

373

said yes," Clarissa declared, her voice a passionate throb, her hands clasped tightly to her bosom.

Theo smiled warmly, trying not to wince at Sylvester's probing fingers. "That's wonderful, love."

"Yes, but it's not exactly a surprise," Rosie put in, peering myopically at a plate of shortbread on the table in front of her. "Clarry's behaving as if there was ever any doubt." She selected a piece and bit into it.

"Well, we came to tell you that," Emily said swiftly before her sister could respond to this dampener. "But also we wished to ask Stoneridge something." She gave him a shy smile as he looked up intently from his first aid. "We're going to have a double wedding —"

"What a lovely idea," Theo interrupted. "You'll be married from Stoneridge, of course."

"But of course," Sylvester agreed.

Emily flushed slightly. "That would be wonderful, but it wasn't what we wanted to ask exactly. We wondered if you would be willing to give us both away, Stoneridge?"

"No one else feels right," Clarissa said. "Uncle Horace . . . or Cousin Cecil . . . they're not family in the same way."

A slow smile spread over Sylvester's face as he wrung out a cloth in cold water and gently applied it to Theo's bump. "I should be deeply honored."

"Will you give me away too?" Rosie piped up, brushing sugar dust off her lips. "When the time comes."

"No, I think I'll hang on to you," Sylvester responded dryly, gently smoothing arnica over the bruising. "Save some poor soul from a ghastly fate."

Emily and Clarissa chuckled, and Rosie, unbothered by the teasing, responded matter-of-factly, "Well, I don't particularly expect to marry anyway. I'd have to find someone who's particularly interested in snails and beetles and things. I don't think many men like that kind of thing."

"Oh, the right kind of men turn up in the most unexpected places," Theo said carelessly, reaching up to grasp Sylvester's wrist. "And from the most unexpected families."

"Even Gilbraiths," he said with a smile.

374

"You're no Gilbraith," Theo stated. "You must have been a changeling."

"Theo, my dear, whatever's happened to you? Foster said you're hurt." Elinor entered the room with a most unusual haste, her customary composure vanished.

"She fell in front of a passing carriage," Rosie informed her mother. "At least that's what Theo said. Stoneridge didn't say anything."

Elinor glanced sharply at her son-in-law as she bent to examine Theo's injury. His expression was wry, but he offered no further explanation.

"I don't believe it's serious, ma'am. The skin isn't broken."

"No," she said, scrutinizing the bruising. "But you must have a headache, dear."

"Like the pounding of Thor's hammer, I should imagine," Sylvester said. "She should be in bed. You'll excuse us, I'm sure, if I see to it."

"Yes, of course. I'll suggest to Lady Gilbraith that she and Mary might join us for nuncheon in Brook Street. They've just gone upstairs to take off their hats." Elinor was unable to help herself from sounding a little weary. She'd already spent an interminable morning with them.

Sylvester shook his head as he scooped Theo off the sofa. "There's no need to put yourself out further, ma'am. If my mother is unable to amuse herself for the afternoon, then I'm afraid she must go to the devil."

Elinor struggled with herself for a second, then laughed. "An unfilial sentiment, Sylvester, but I can't help but agree with it. Come, girls. Theo needs to rest."

"I'm sure I don't really," Theo protested from her husband's arms as they went into the hall.

"There's resting and resting," Sylvester said blandly, mounting the stairs.

"But what about my sore head?"

"I wasn't intending to focus my attentions on your head."

"Ah," Theo said, shifting in his hold so she could put her arms around his neck. "That's all right, then."

F Feather
Feather, Jane
Valentine

$24.00